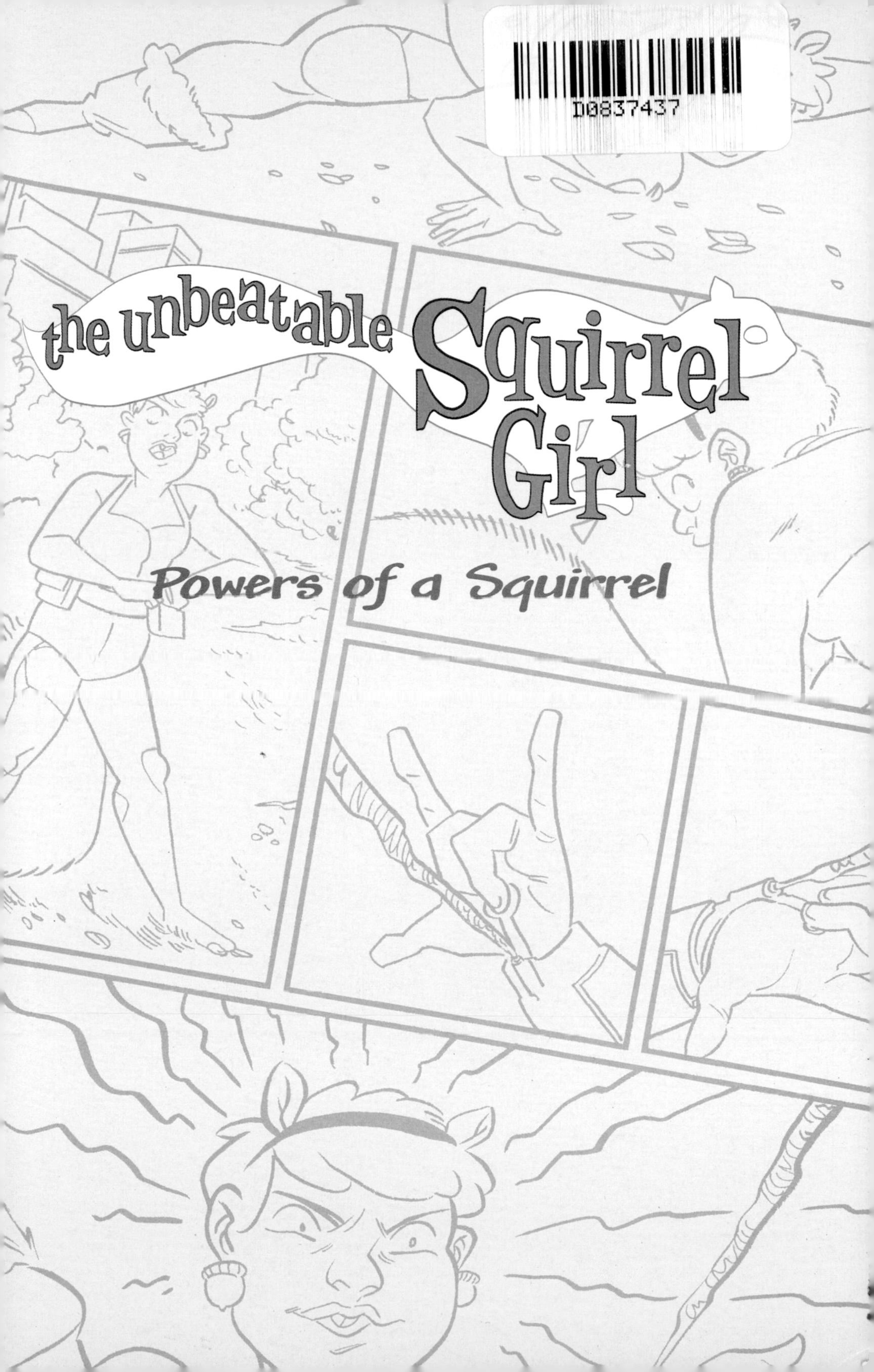

the unbeatable Squirrel Girl

Powers of a Squirrel

Contents

THE UNBEATABLE SQUIRREL GIRL: POWERS OF A SQUIRREL. Contains material originally published in magazine form as THE UNBEATABLE SQUIRREL GIRL (2015 A) #1-8. First printing 2019. ISBN 978-1-302-92045-6. Published by MARVEL WORLDWIDE, INC., a subsidiary of MARVEL ENTERTAINMENT, LLC. OFFICE OF PUBLICATION: 135 West 50th Street, New York, NY 10020. © 2019 MARVEL No similarity between any of the names, characters, persons, and/or institutions in this magazine with those of any living or dead person or institution is intended, and any such similarity which may exist is purely coincidental. **Printed in Canada.** DAN BUCKLEY, President, Marvel Entertainment; JOHN NEE, Publisher; JOE QUESADA, Chief Creative Officer; TOM BREVOORT, SVP of Publishing; DAVID BOGART, Associate Publisher & SVP of Talent Affairs; DAVID GABRIEL, VP of Print & Digital Publishing; JEFF YOUNGQUIST, VP of Production & Special Projects; DAN CARR, Executive Director of Publishing Technology; ALEX MORALES, Director of Publishing Operations; DAN EDINGTON, Managing Editor; SUSAN CRESPI, Production Manager; STAN LEE, Chairman Emeritus. For information regarding advertising in Marvel Comics or on Marvel.com, please contact Vit DeBellis, Custom Solutions & Integrated Advertising Manager, at vdebellis@marvel.com. For Marvel subscription inquiries, please call 888-511-5480. **Manufactured between 10/25/2019 and 11/26/2019 by SOLISCO PRINTERS, SCOTT, QC, CANADA.**

10 9 8 7 6 5 4 3 2 1

the unbeatable Squirrel Girl

Powers of a Squirrel

WRITER
RYAN NORTH

ARTIST
ERICA HENDERSON

TRADING CARD ART
**MARIS WICKS (#1), KYLE STARKS (#3),
CHRIS GIARRUSSO (#4) & ELOISE NARRINGTON (#5-6)**

COLOR ARTIST
RICO RENZI

LETTERER
VC$ CLAYTON COWLES

COVER ART
ERICA HENDERSON

ASSISTANT EDITORS
JON MOISAN & JAKE THOMAS

EDITOR
WIL MOSS

EXECUTIVE EDITOR
TOM BREVOORT

SPECIAL THANKS TO CASSIE HART KELLY & LISSA PATTILLO

SQUIRREL GIRL CREATED BY WILL MURRAY & STEVE DITKO

collection editor JENNIFER GRÜNWALD
assistant editor CAITLIN O'CONNELL • associate managing editor KATERI WOODY
editor, special projects MARK D. BEAZLEY • vp production & special projects JEFF YOUNGQUIST

director, licensed publishing SVEN LARSEN • svp print, sales & marketing DAVID GABRIEL
editor in chief C.B. CEBULSKI • chief creative officer JOE QUESADA
president DAN BUCKLEY • executive producer ALAN FINE

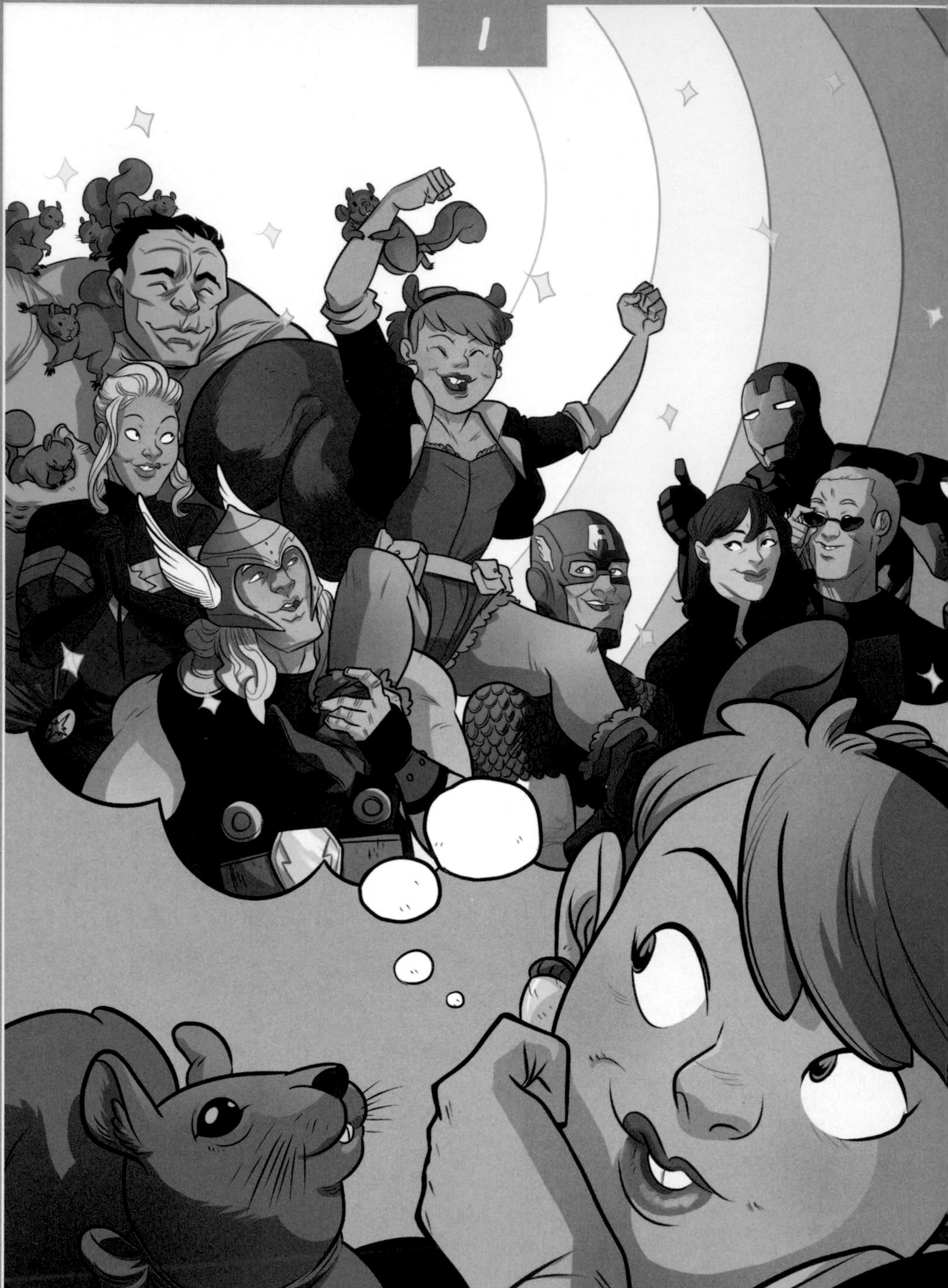
1

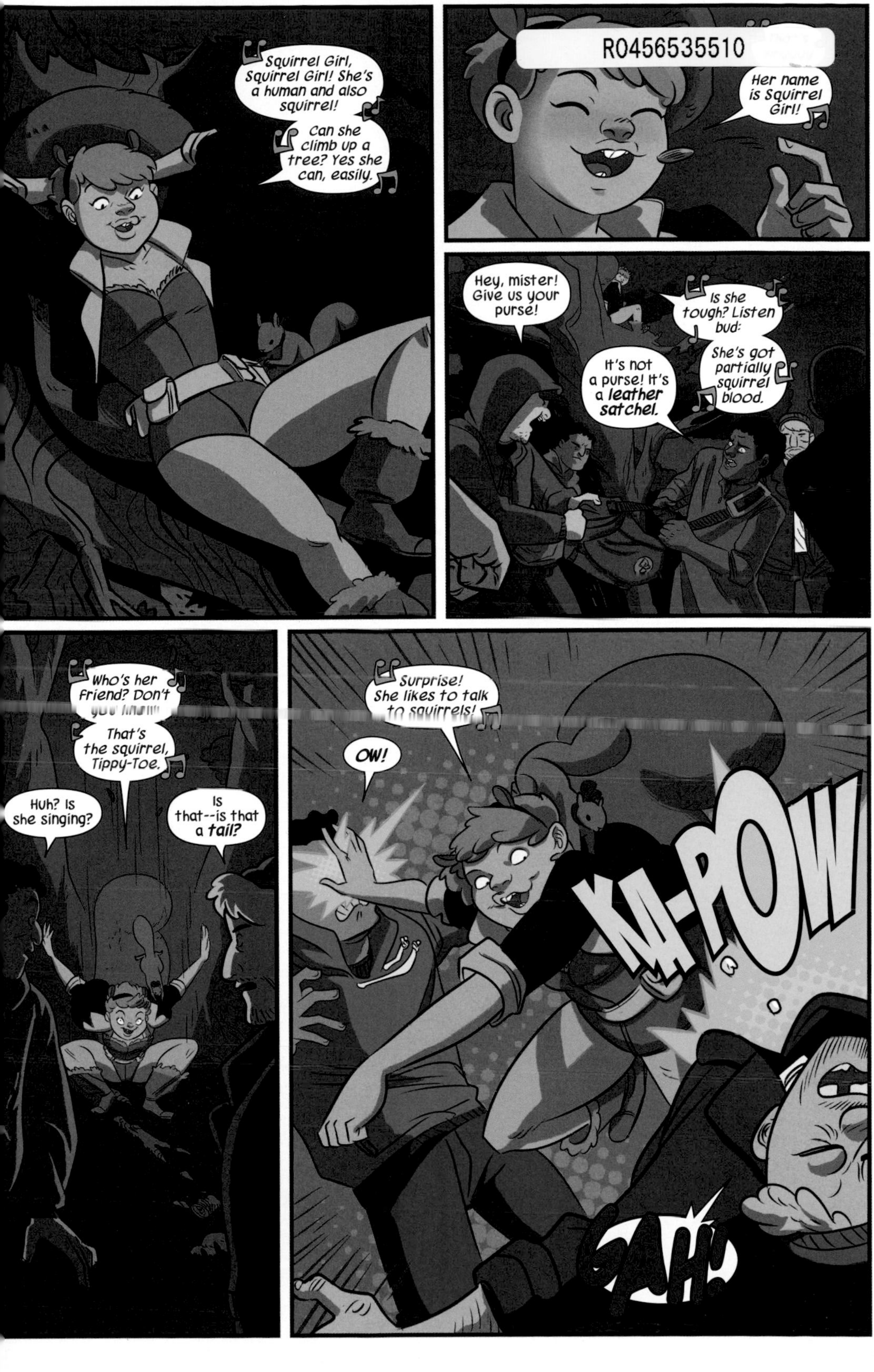

Squirrel Girl, Squirrel Girl! She's a human and also squirrel!
Can she climb up a tree? Yes she can, easily.
Her name is Squirrel Girl!
Hey, mister! Give us your purse!
It's not a purse! It's a **leather satchel.**
Is she tough? Listen bud:
She's got partially squirrel blood.
Who's her friend? Don't
That's the squirrel, Tippy-Toe.
Huh? Is she singing?
Is that--is that a *tail?*
Surprise! She likes to talk to squirrels!
OW!
KA-POW
GAH!

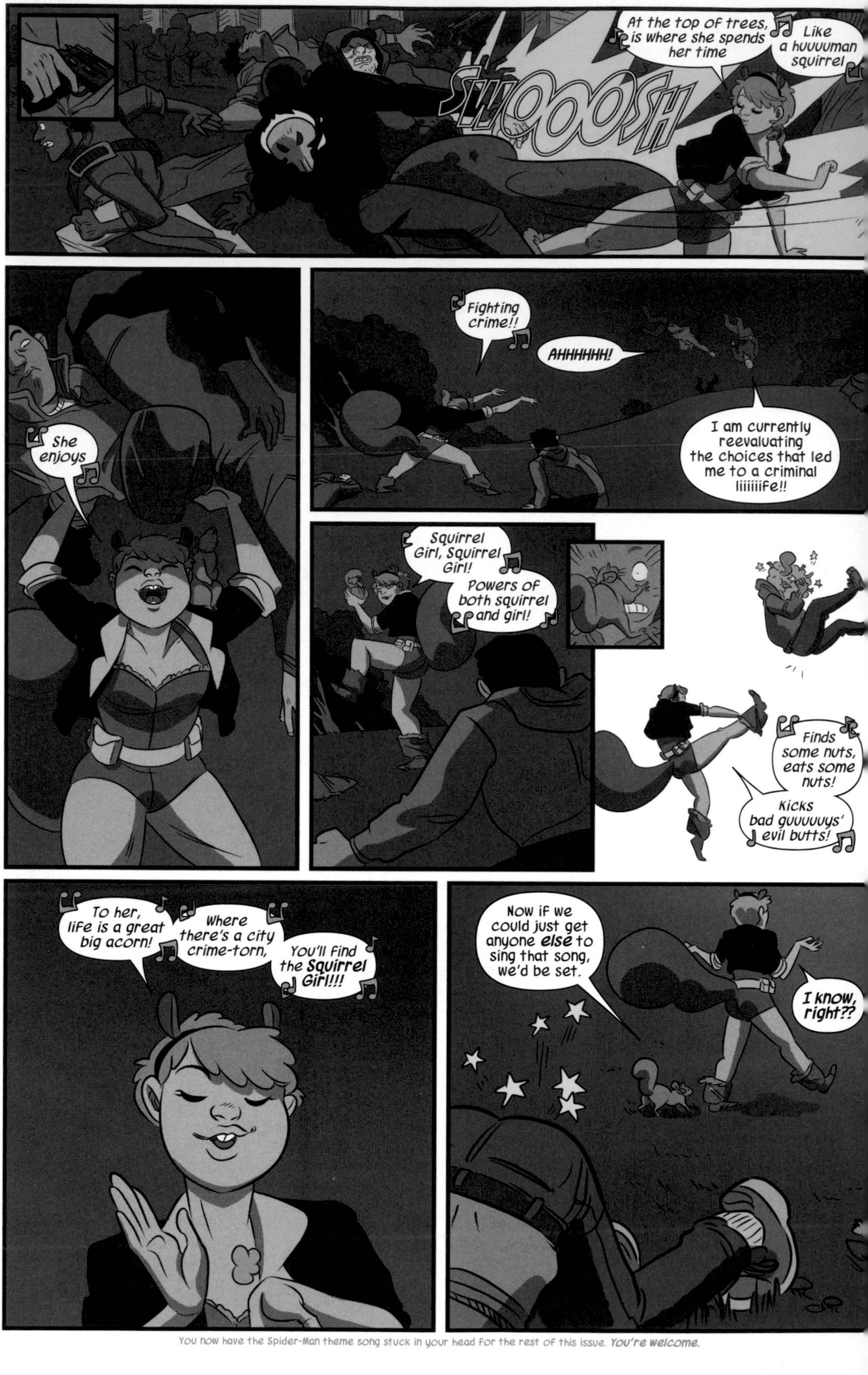
At the top of trees, is where she spends her time
Like a huuuuman squirrel
SWOOOSH
She enjoys
Fighting crime!!
AHHHHHH!
I am currently reevaluating the choices that led me to a criminal liiiiiife!!
Squirrel Girl, Squirrel Girl!
Powers of both squirrel and girl!
Finds some nuts, eats some nuts!
Kicks bad guuuuuys' evil butts!
To her, life is a great big acorn!
Where there's a city crime-torn,
You'll find the Squirrel Girl!!!
Now if we could just get anyone else to sing that song, we'd be set.
I know, right??

You now have the Spider-Man theme song stuck in your head for the rest of this issue. *You're welcome.*

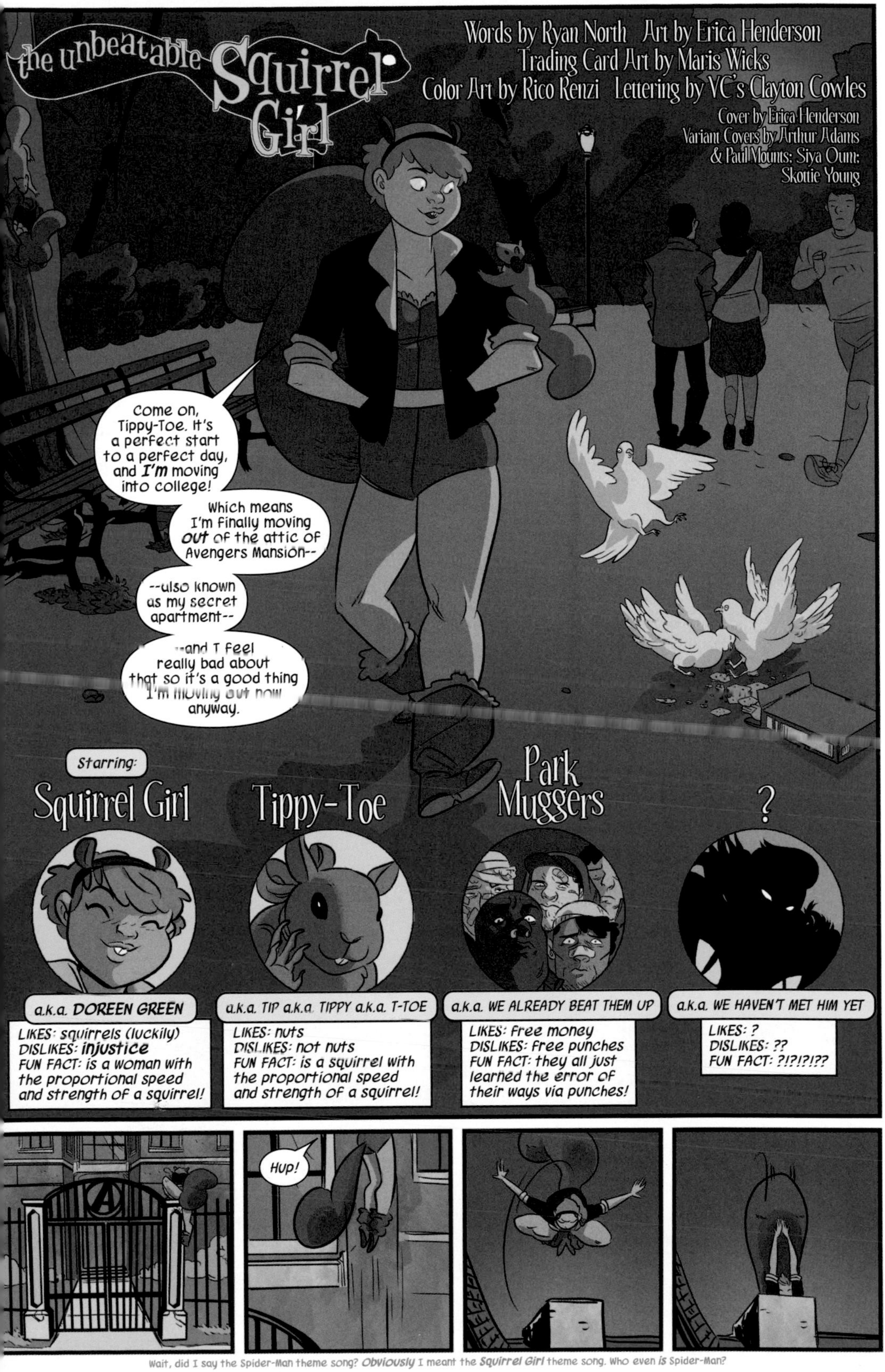
the unbeatable Squirrel Girl
Words by Ryan North Art by Erica Henderson
Trading Card Art by Maris Wicks
Color Art by Rico Renzi Lettering by VC's Clayton Cowles
Cover by Erica Henderson
Variant Covers by Arthur Adams & Paul Mounts; Siya Oum; Skottie Young
Come on, Tippy-Toe. It's a perfect start to a perfect day, and I'M moving into college!
Which means I'm finally moving OUT of the attic of Avengers Mansion--
--also known as my secret apartment--
--and I feel really bad about that so it's a good thing I'm moving out now anyway.
Starring:
Squirrel Girl
a.k.a. DOREEN GREEN
LIKES: squirrels (luckily)
DISLIKES: injustice
FUN FACT: is a woman with the proportional speed and strength of a squirrel!
Tippy-Toe
a.k.a. TIP a.k.a. TIPPY a.k.a. T-TOE
LIKES: nuts
DISLIKES: not nuts
FUN FACT: is a squirrel with the proportional speed and strength of a squirrel!
Park Muggers
a.k.a. WE ALREADY BEAT THEM UP
LIKES: Free money
DISLIKES: Free punches
FUN FACT: they all just learned the error of their ways via punches!
?
a.k.a. WE HAVEN'T MET HIM YET
LIKES: ?
DISLIKES: ??
FUN FACT: ?!?!?!??
Hup!

Wait, did I say the Spider-Man theme song? *Obviously* I meant the *Squirrel Girl* theme song. Who even *is* Spider-Man?

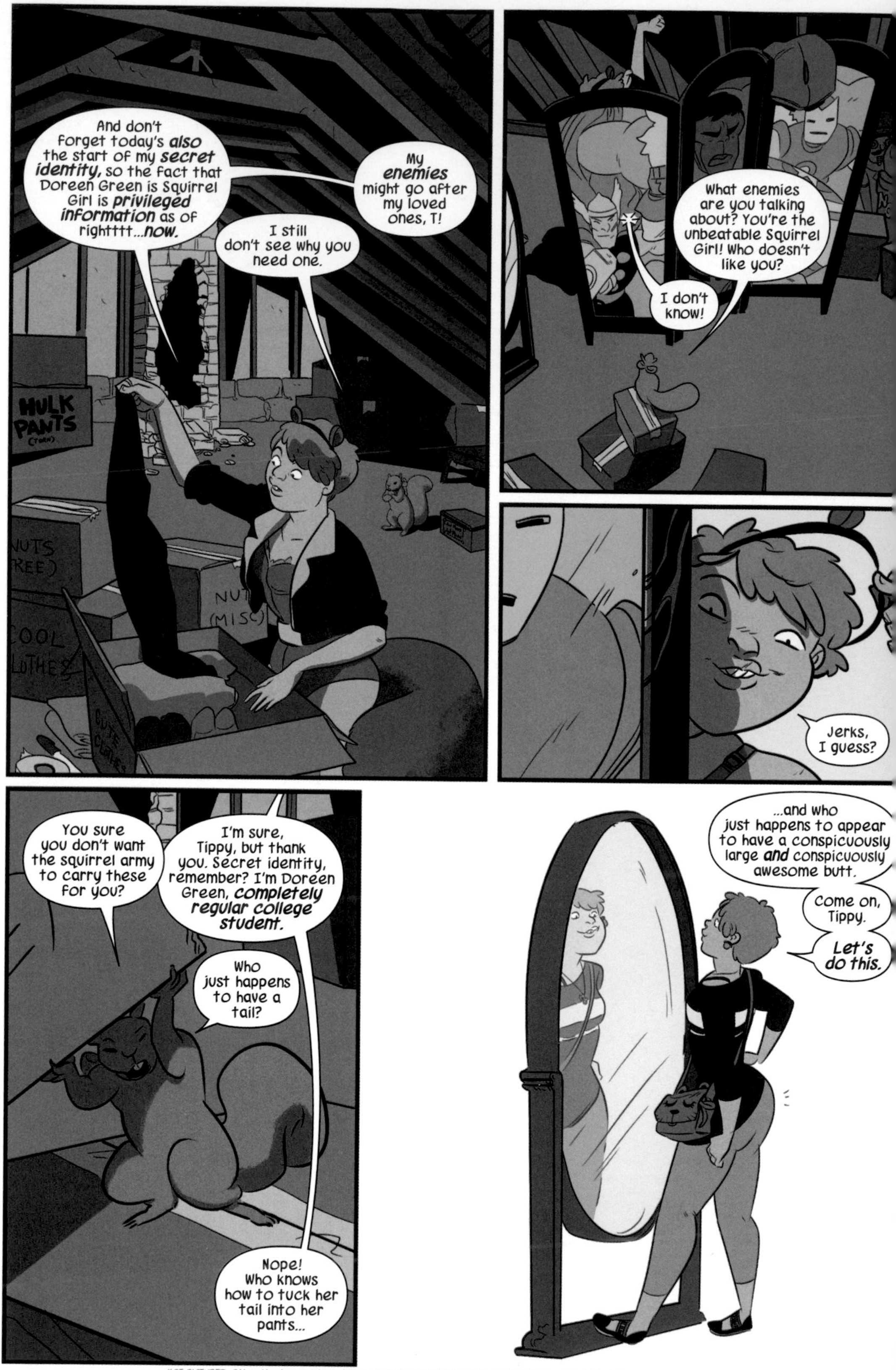
And don't forget today's **also** the start of my **secret identity,** so the fact that Doreen Green is Squirrel Girl is **privileged information** as of righttttt...**now.**
My **enemies** might go after my loved ones, T!
I still don't see why you need one.
HULK PANTS
What enemies are you talking about? You're the unbeatable Squirrel Girl! Who doesn't like you?
I don't know!
Jerks, I guess?
You sure you don't want the squirrel army to carry these for you?
I'm sure, Tippy, but thank you. Secret identity, remember? I'm Doreen Green, **completely regular college student.**
Who just happens to have a tail?
Nope! Who knows how to tuck her tail into her pants...
...and who just happens to appear to have a conspicuously large **and** conspicuously awesome butt.
Come on, Tippy.
Let's do this.

NOT PICTURED: Other tiny boxes labelled "Ant-Man's Tiny Vans," "Ant-Man's Aunt's Flans," and "Ant-Man's Rejected Costumes (Off-Brand)"

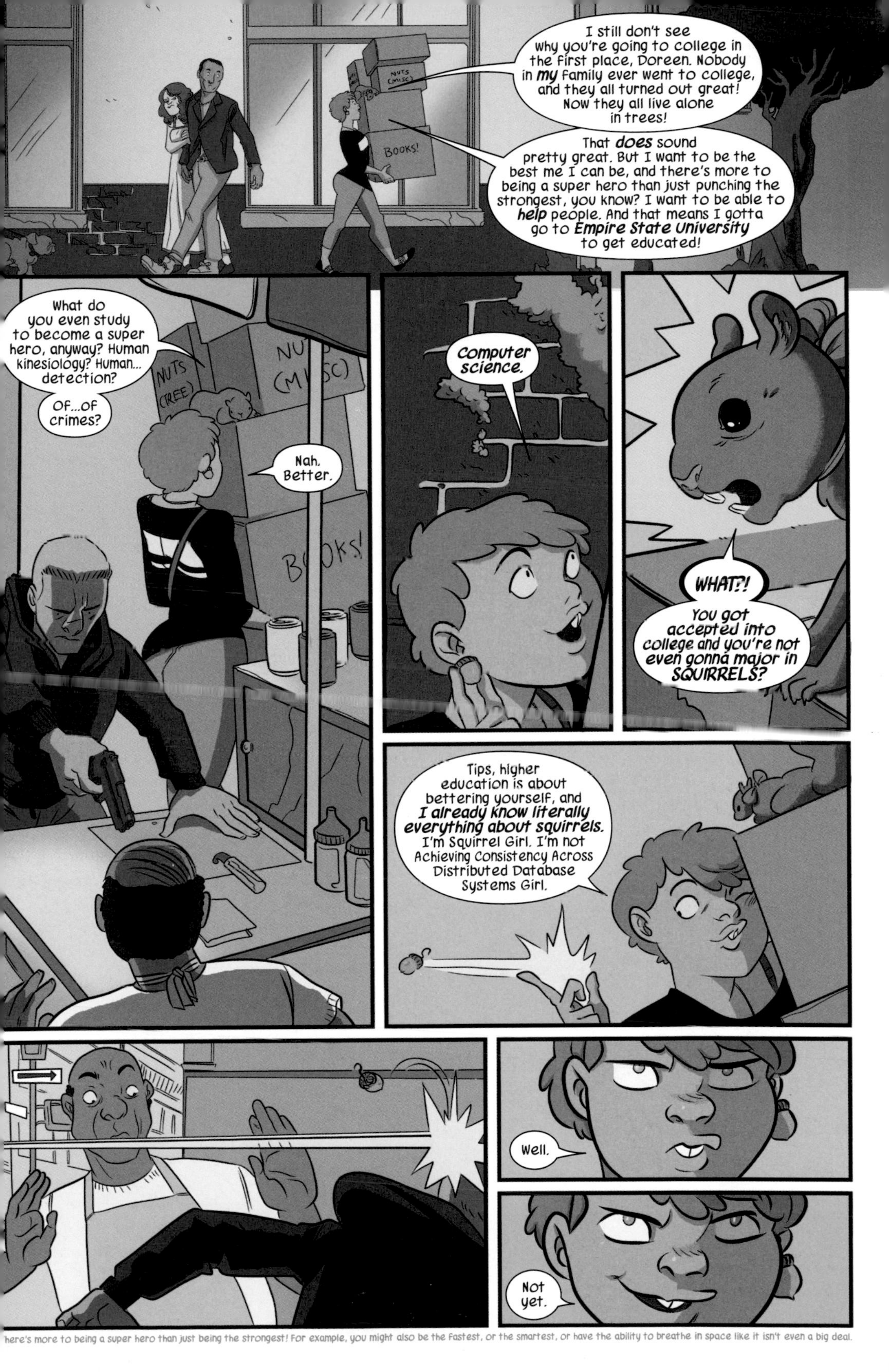
I still don't see why you're going to college in the first place, Doreen. Nobody in *my* family ever went to college, and they all turned out great! Now they all live alone in trees!
That *does* sound pretty great. But I want to be the best me I can be, and there's more to being a super hero than just punching the strongest, you know? I want to be able to *help* people. And that means I gotta go to **Empire State University** to get educated!
What do you even study to become a super hero, anyway? Human kinesiology? Human... detection?
Of...of crimes?
Nah. Better.
Computer science.
WHAT?!
You got accepted into college and you're not even gonna major in SQUIRRELS?
Tips, higher education is about bettering yourself, and *I already know literally everything about squirrels.* I'm Squirrel Girl. I'm not Achieving Consistency Across Distributed Database Systems Girl.
Well.
Not yet.

here's more to being a super hero than just being the strongest! For example, you might also be the fastest, or the smartest, or have the ability to breathe in space like it isn't even a big deal.

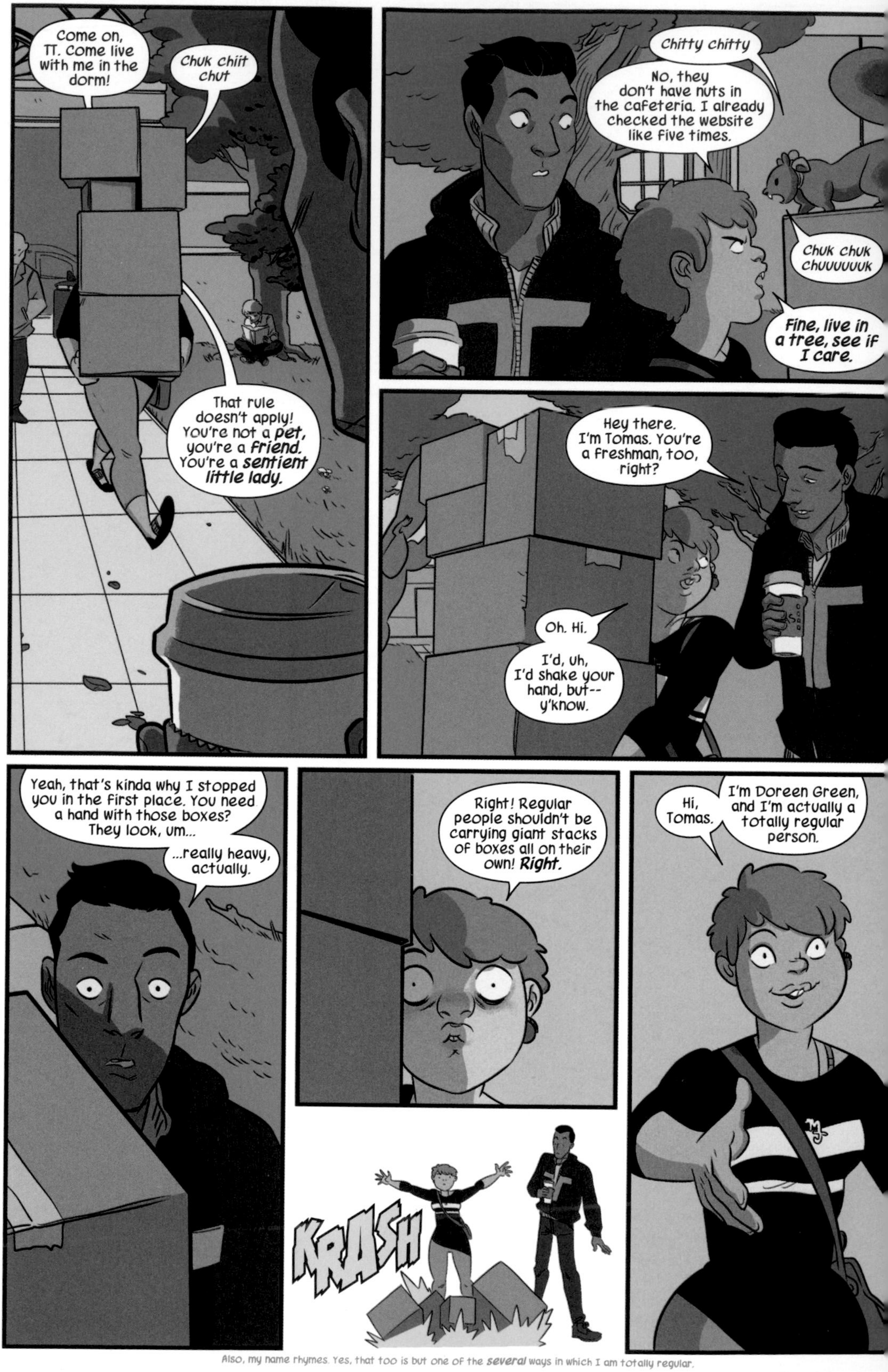
Come on, TT. Come live with me in the dorm!
Chuk chiit chut
That rule doesn't apply! You're not a *pet*, you're a *friend*. You're a *sentient little lady.*
Chitty chitty
No, they don't have nuts in the cafeteria. I already checked the website like five times.
Chuk chuk chuuuuuuk
Fine, live in a tree, see if I care.
Hey there. I'm Tomas. You're a freshman, too, right?
Oh. Hi.
I'd, uh, I'd shake your hand, but-- y'know.
Yeah, that's kinda why I stopped you in the first place. You need a hand with those boxes? They look, um...
...really heavy, actually.
Right! Regular people shouldn't be carrying giant stacks of boxes all on their own! *Right.*
Hi, Tomas.
I'm Doreen Green, and I'm actually a totally regular person.
KRASH

Also, my name rhymes. Yes, that too is but one of the *several* ways in which I am totally regular.

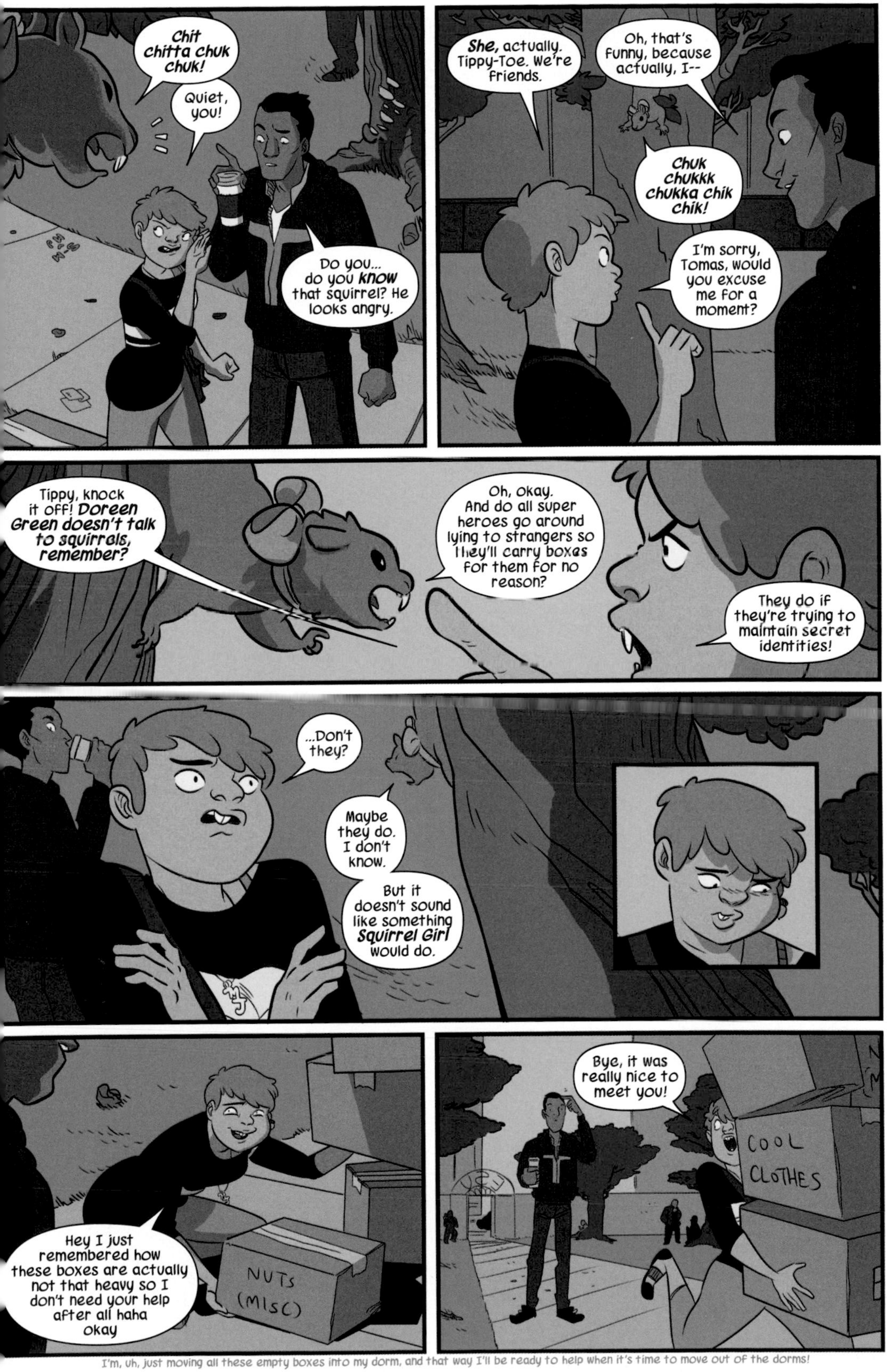

Chit chitta chuk chuk!
Quiet, you!
Do you... do you know that squirrel? He looks angry.
She, actually. Tippy-Toe. We're friends.
Oh, that's funny, because actually, I--
Chuk chukkk chukka chik chik!
I'm sorry, Tomas, would you excuse me for a moment?
Tippy, knock it off! Doreen Green doesn't talk to squirrels, remember?
Oh, okay. And do all super heroes go around lying to strangers so they'll carry boxes for them for no reason?
They do if they're trying to maintain secret identities!
...Don't they?
Maybe they do. I don't know.
But it doesn't sound like something Squirrel Girl would do.
Hey I just remembered how these boxes are actually not that heavy so I don't need your help after all haha okay
NUTS (MISC)
Bye, it was really nice to meet you!
COOL CLOTHES

I'm, uh, just moving all these empty boxes into my dorm, and that way I'll be ready to help when it's time to move out of the dorms!

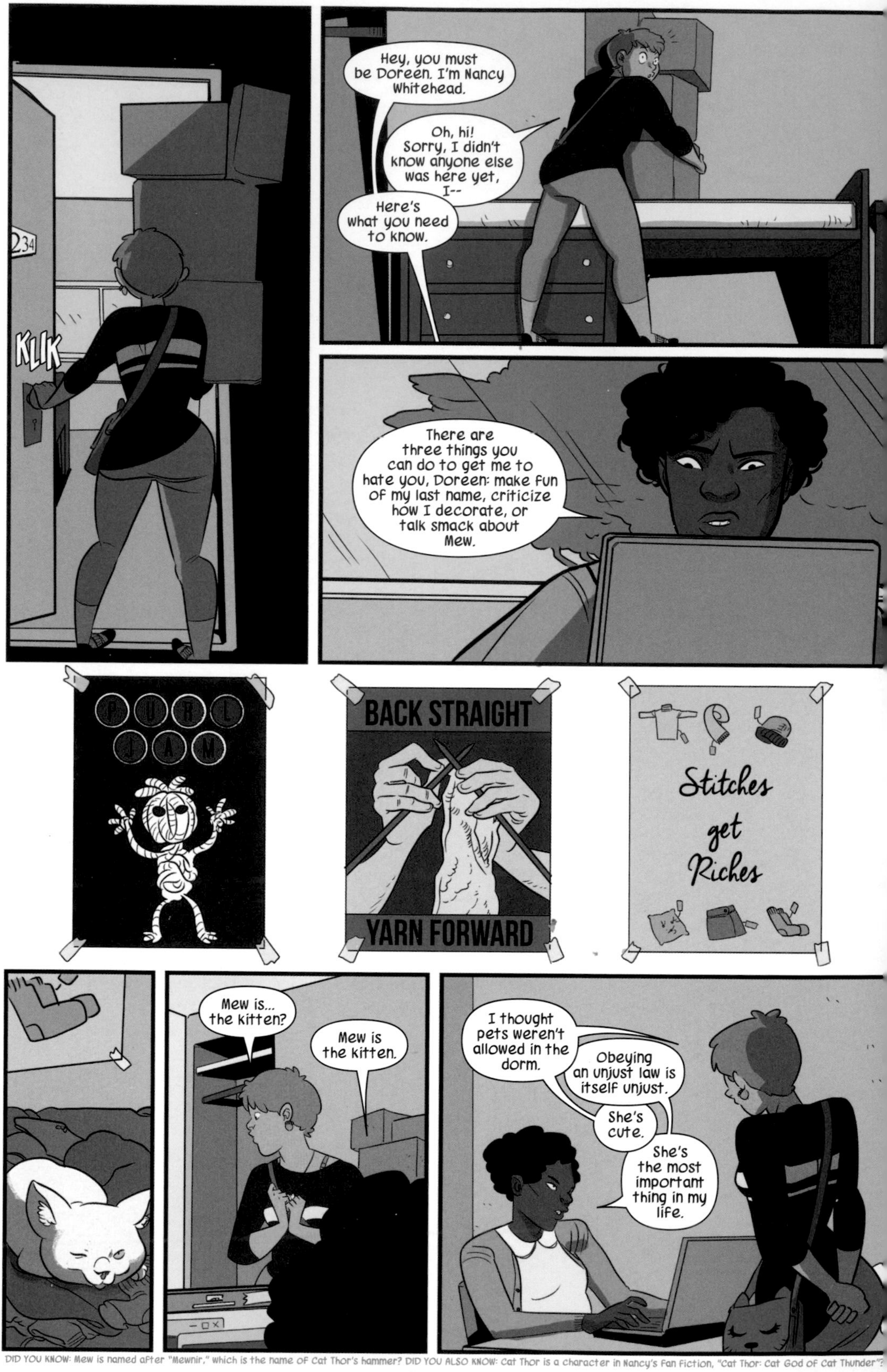
KLIK
234
Hey, you must be Doreen. I'm Nancy Whitehead.
Oh, hi! Sorry, I didn't know anyone else was here yet, I--
Here's what you need to know.
There are three things you can do to get me to hate you, Doreen: make fun of my last name, criticize how I decorate, or talk smack about Mew.
PURL JAM
BACK STRAIGHT
YARN FORWARD
Stitches get Riches
Mew is... the kitten?
Mew is the kitten.
I thought pets weren't allowed in the dorm.
Obeying an unjust law is itself unjust.
She's cute.
She's the most important thing in my life.

DID YOU KNOW: Mew is named after "Mewnir," which is the name of Cat Thor's hammer? DID YOU ALSO KNOW: Cat Thor is a character in Nancy's Fan Fiction, "Cat Thor: Cat God of Cat Thunder"?

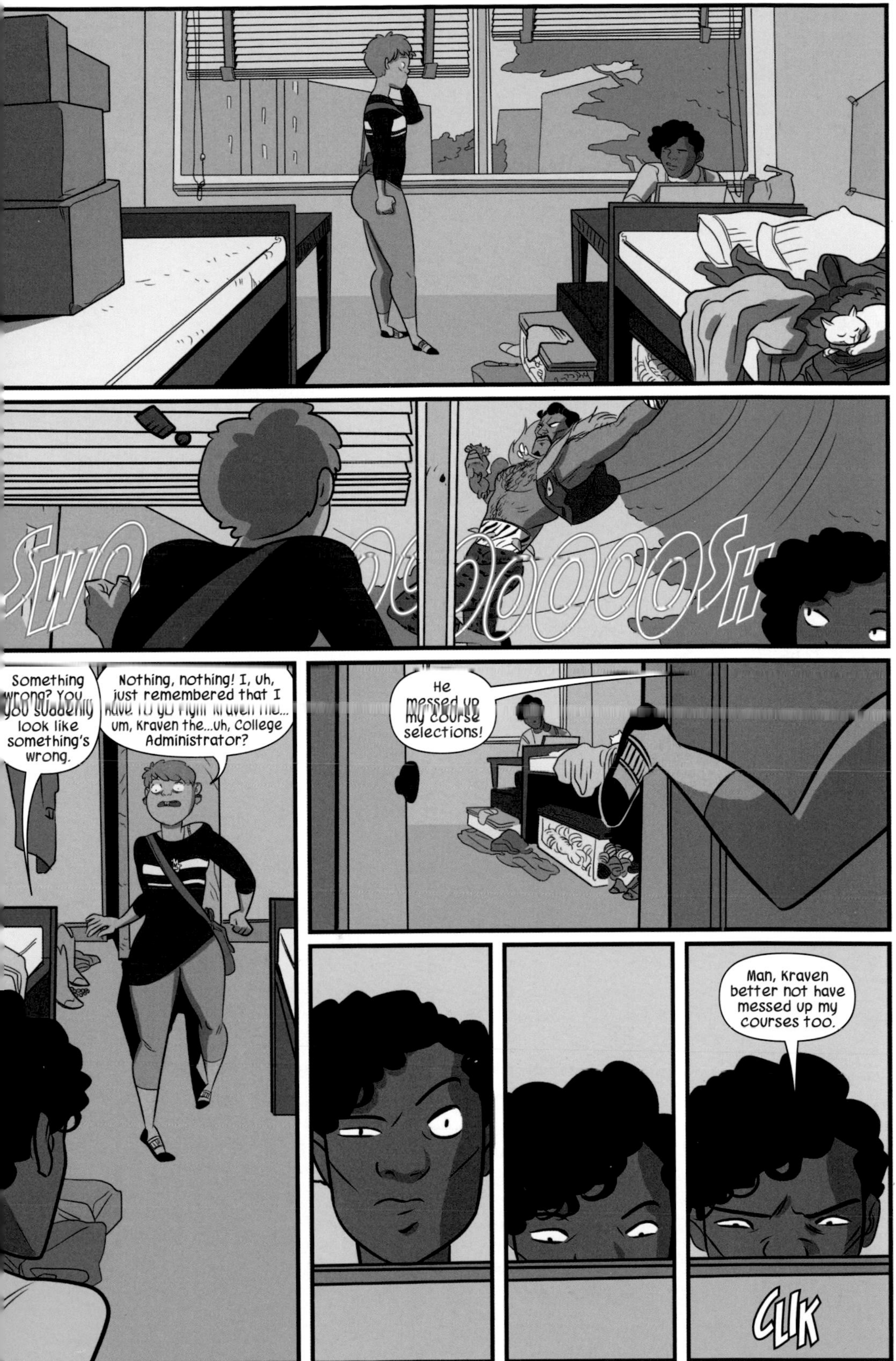
SWOOOOOOOSH
Something wrong? You... you suddenly look like something's wrong.
Nothing, nothing! I, uh, just remembered that I have to go fight Kraven the... um, Kraven the...uh, College Administrator?
He messed up my course selections!
Man, Kraven better not have messed up my courses too.
CLIK

DID YOU KNOW: college administrator was the job Kraven the Hunter was training for before he took a chance weekend safari getaway? Yes! It's almost possibly a fact!

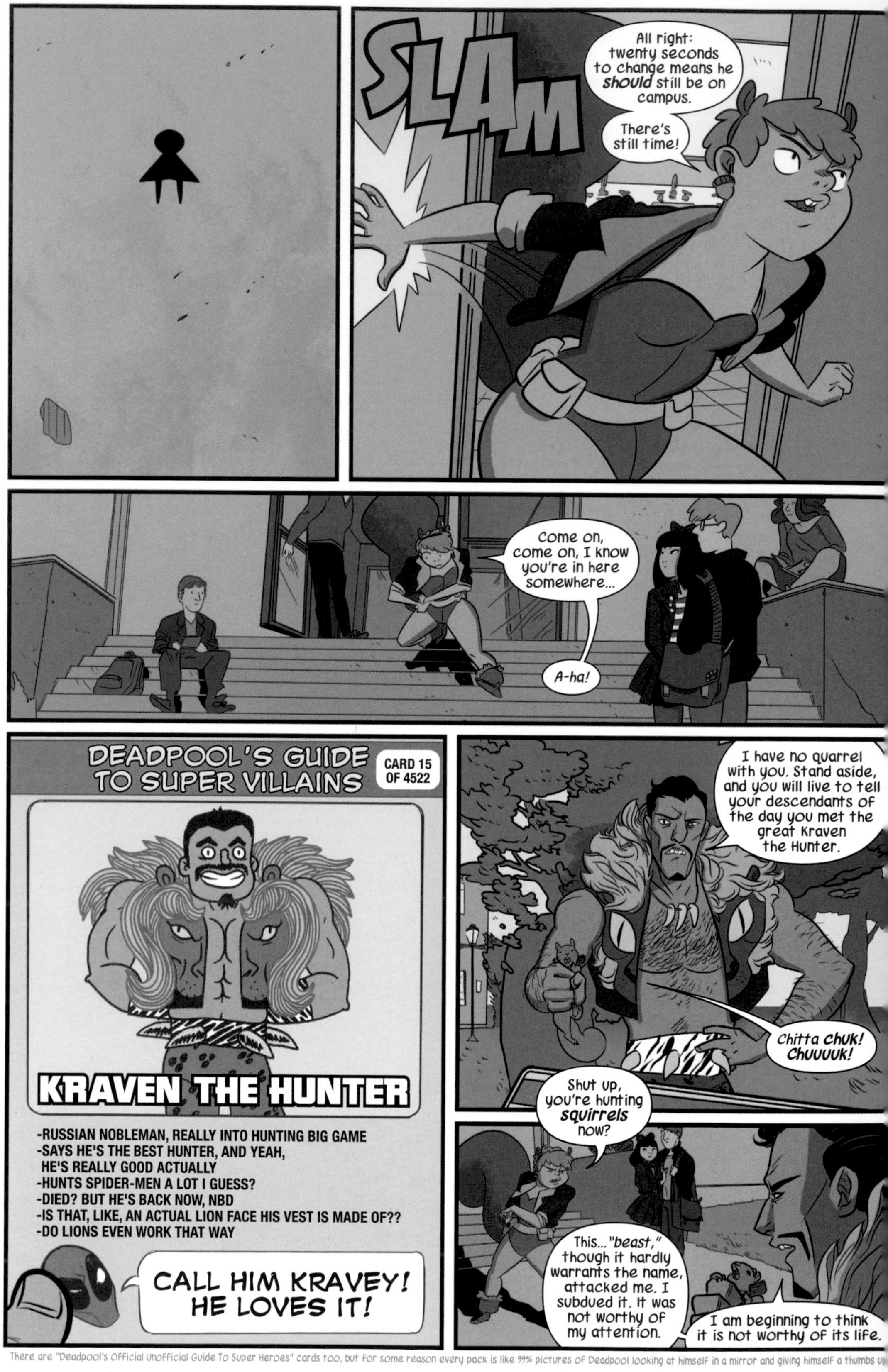

SLAM
All right: twenty seconds to change means he *should* still be on campus.
There's still time!
Come on, come on, I know you're in here somewhere...
A-ha!
DEADPOOL'S GUIDE TO SUPER VILLAINS
CARD 15 OF 4522
KRAVEN THE HUNTER
-RUSSIAN NOBLEMAN, REALLY INTO HUNTING BIG GAME
-SAYS HE'S THE BEST HUNTER, AND YEAH, HE'S REALLY GOOD ACTUALLY
-HUNTS SPIDER-MEN A LOT I GUESS?
-DIED? BUT HE'S BACK NOW, NBD
-IS THAT, LIKE, AN ACTUAL LION FACE HIS VEST IS MADE OF??
-DO LIONS EVEN WORK THAT WAY
CALL HIM KRAVEY! HE LOVES IT!
I have no quarrel with you. Stand aside, and you will live to tell your descendants of the day you met the great Kraven the Hunter.
Chitta *CHUK!* *CHUUUUK!*
Shut up, you're hunting *squirrels* now?
This... "*beast*," though it hardly warrants the name, attacked me. I subdued it. It was not worthy of my attention.
I am beginning to think it is not worthy of its life.

There are "Deadpool's Official Unofficial Guide To Super Heroes" cards too, but for some reason every pack is like 99% pictures of Deadpool looking at himself in a mirror and giving himself a thumbs up

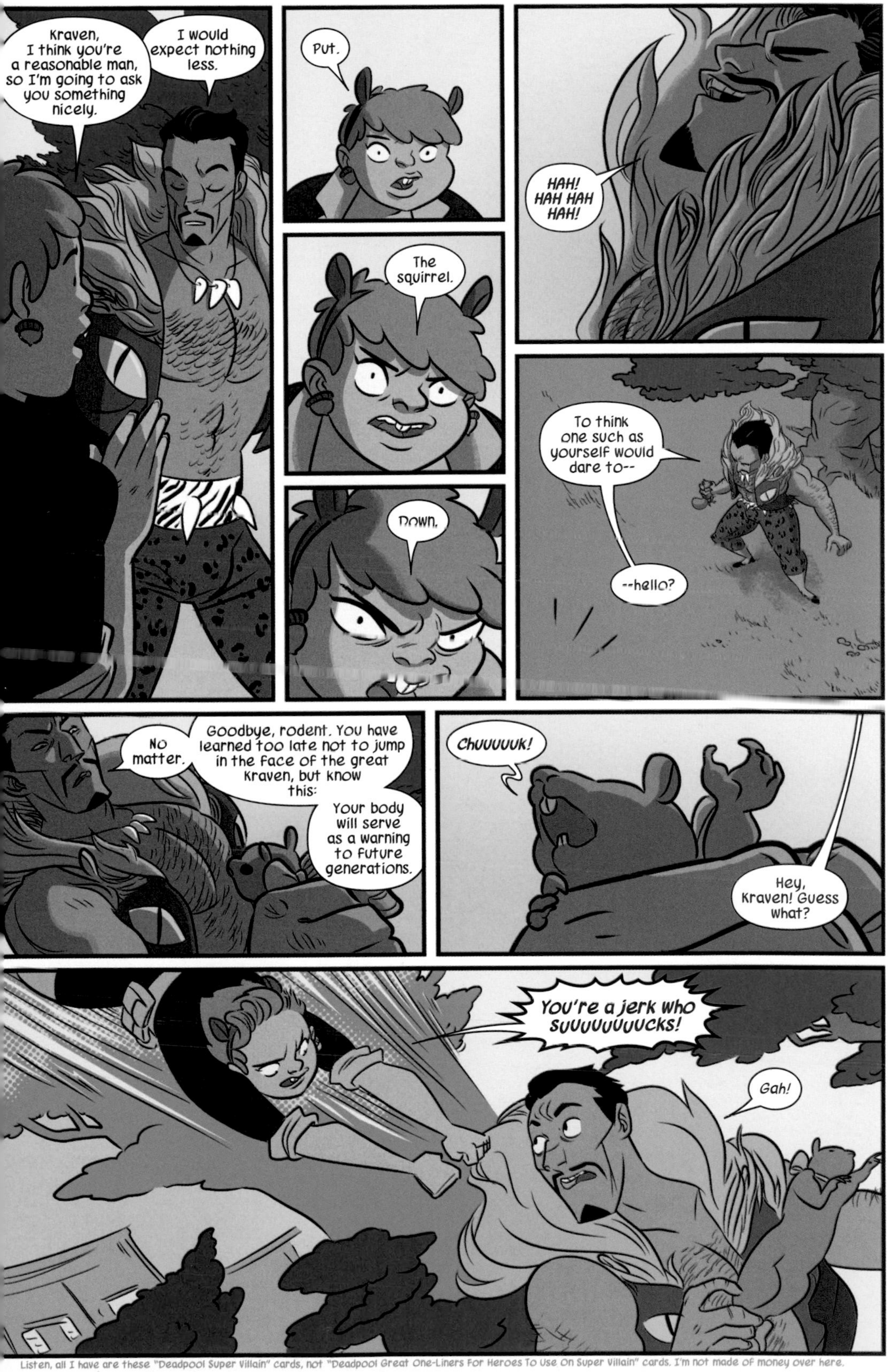

Kraven, I think you're a reasonable man, so I'm going to ask you something nicely.
I would expect nothing less.
Put.
The squirrel.
Down.
HAH! HAH HAH HAH!
To think one such as yourself would dare to--
--hello?
No matter.
Goodbye, rodent. You have learned too late not to jump in the face of the great Kraven, but know this:
Your body will serve as a warning to future generations.
Chuuuuuk!
Hey, Kraven! Guess what?
You're a jerk who suuuuuuuucks!
Gah!

Listen, all I have are these "Deadpool Super Villain" cards, not "Deadpool Great One-Liners For Heroes To Use On Super Villain" cards. I'm not made of money over here.

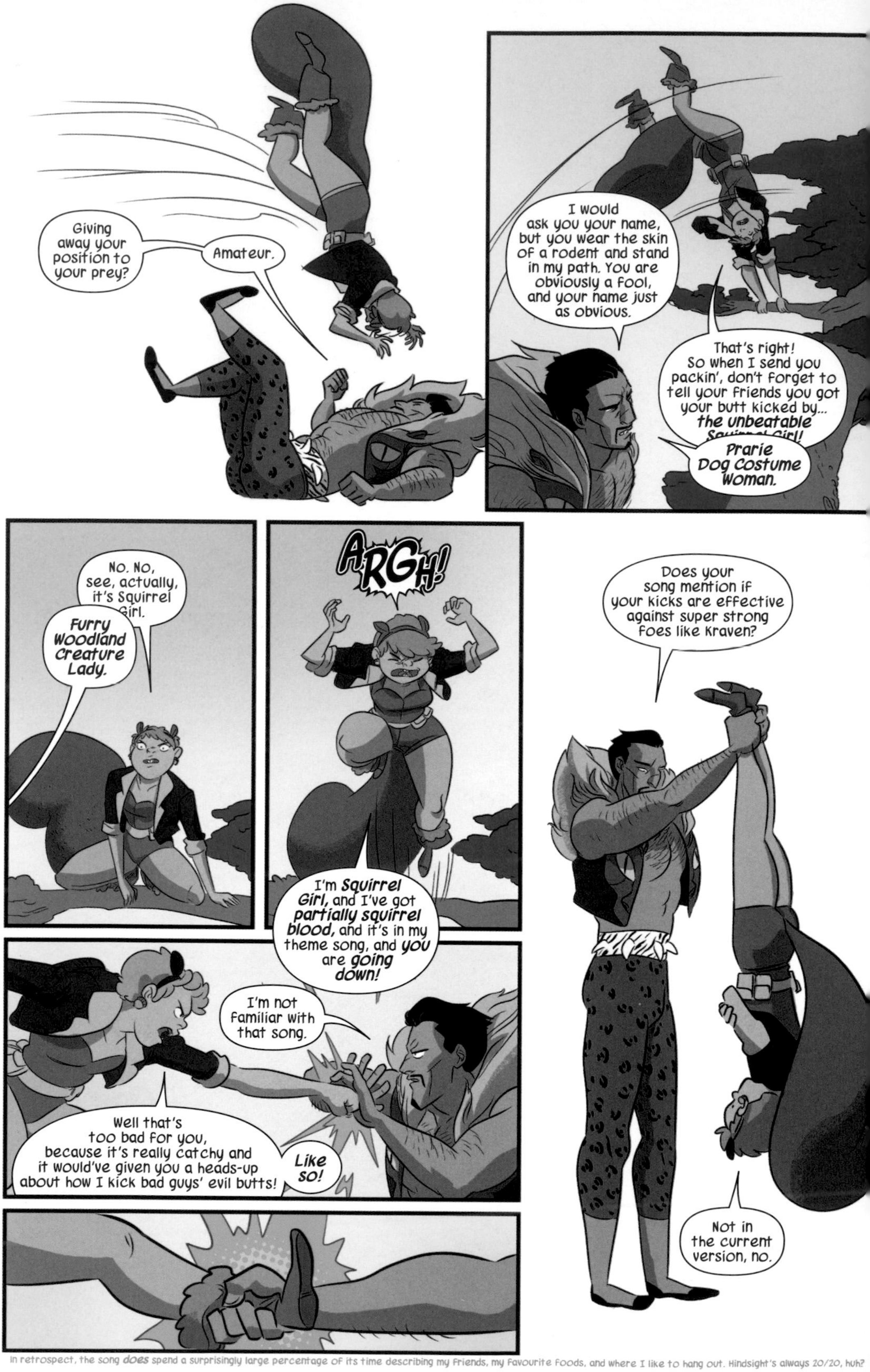

Giving away your position to your prey?
Amateur.
I would ask you your name, but you wear the skin of a rodent and stand in my path. You are obviously a fool, and your name just as obvious.
That's right! So when I send you packin', don't forget to tell your friends you got your butt kicked by... the unbeatable
Prarie Dog Costume Woman.
No. No, see, actually, it's Squirrel Girl.
Furry Woodland Creature Lady.
ARGH!
I'm Squirrel Girl, and I've got partially squirrel blood, and it's in my theme song, and you are going down!
I'm not familiar with that song.
Well that's too bad for you, because it's really catchy and it would've given you a heads-up about how I kick bad guys' evil butts!
Like so!
Does your song mention if your kicks are effective against super strong foes like Kraven?
Not in the current version, no.

In retrospect, the song *does* spend a surprisingly large percentage of its time describing my friends, my favourite foods, and where I like to hang out. Hindsight's always 20/20, huh?

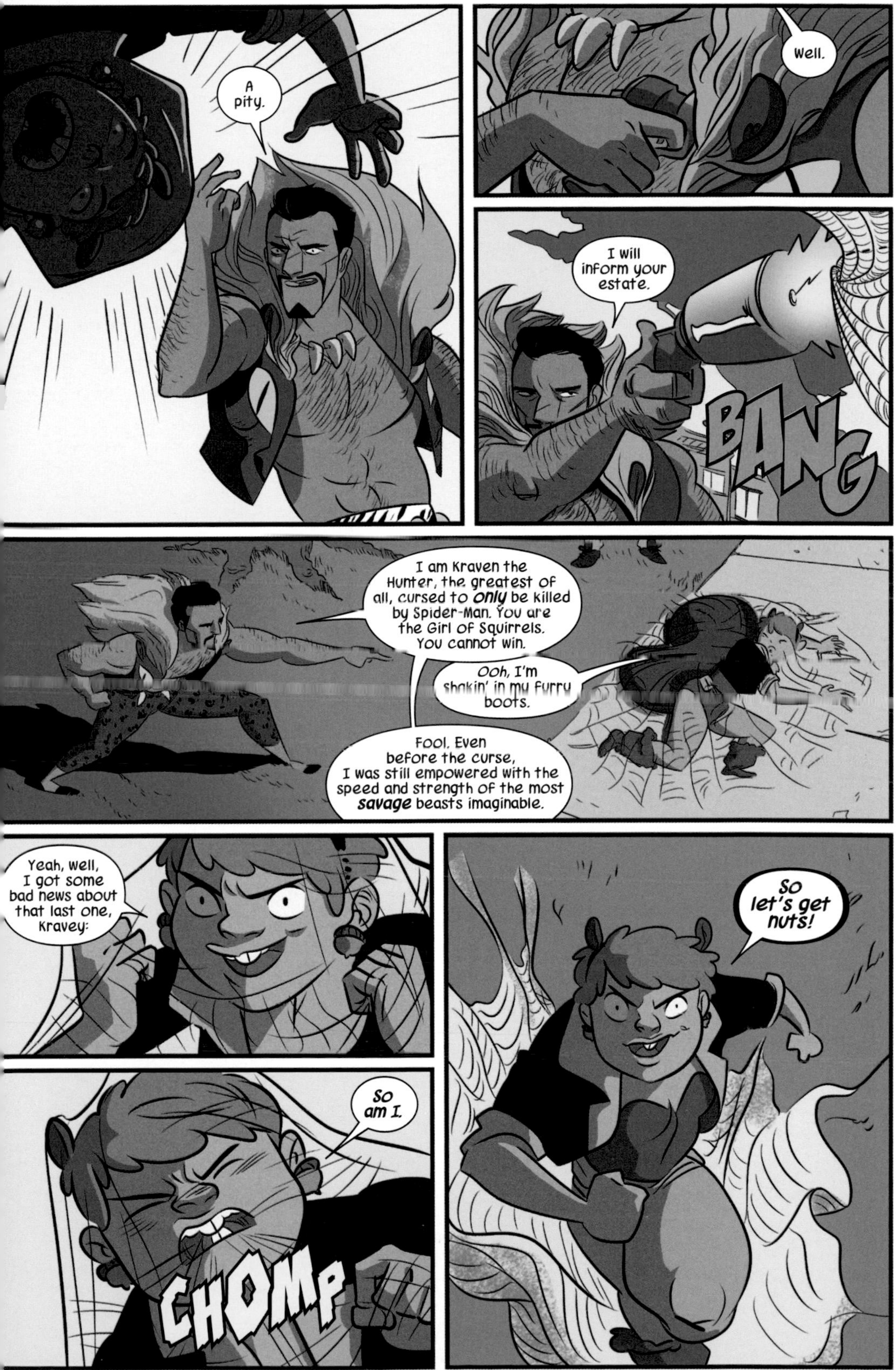
A pity.
Well.
I will inform your estate.
BANG
I am Kraven the Hunter, the greatest of all, cursed to only be killed by Spider-Man. You are the Girl of Squirrels. You cannot win.
Ooh, I'm shakin' in my furry boots.
Fool. Even before the curse, I was still empowered with the speed and strength of the most savage beasts imaginable.
Yeah, well, I got some bad news about that last one, Kravey:
So am I.
CHOMP
So let's get nuts!

ngratulations to "LET'S GET NUTS" for beating out runners-up "LET'S GET CRAZY" and "LET'S BECOME ECCENTRIC" in the What Should Squirrel Girl Say When Biting Her Way Out Of A Net Competition, 2015

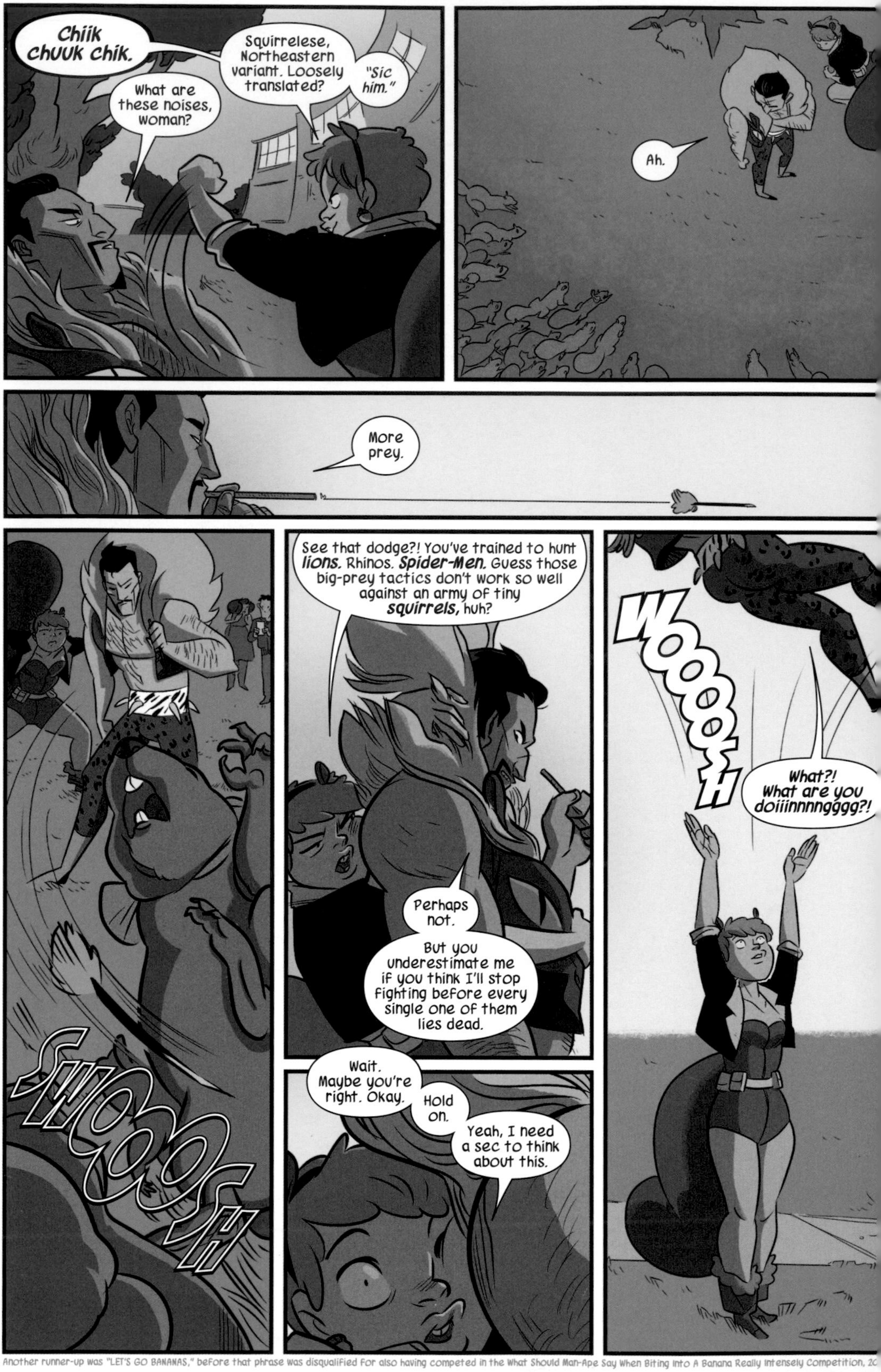
Chiik chuuk chik.
What are these noises, woman?
Squirrelese, Northeastern variant. Loosely translated?
"Sic him."
Ah.
More prey.
See that dodge?! You've trained to hunt lions. Rhinos. Spider-Men. Guess those big-prey tactics don't work so well against an army of tiny squirrels, huh?
Perhaps not.
But you underestimate me if you think I'll stop fighting before every single one of them lies dead.
SHOOOSH
Wait. Maybe you're right. Okay.
Hold on.
Yeah, I need a sec to think about this.
WOOOOSH
What?! What are you doiiinnnngggg?!

Another runner-up was "LET'S GO BANANAS," before that phrase was disqualified for also having competed in the What Should Man-Ape Say When Biting Into A Banana Really Intensely Competition, 20

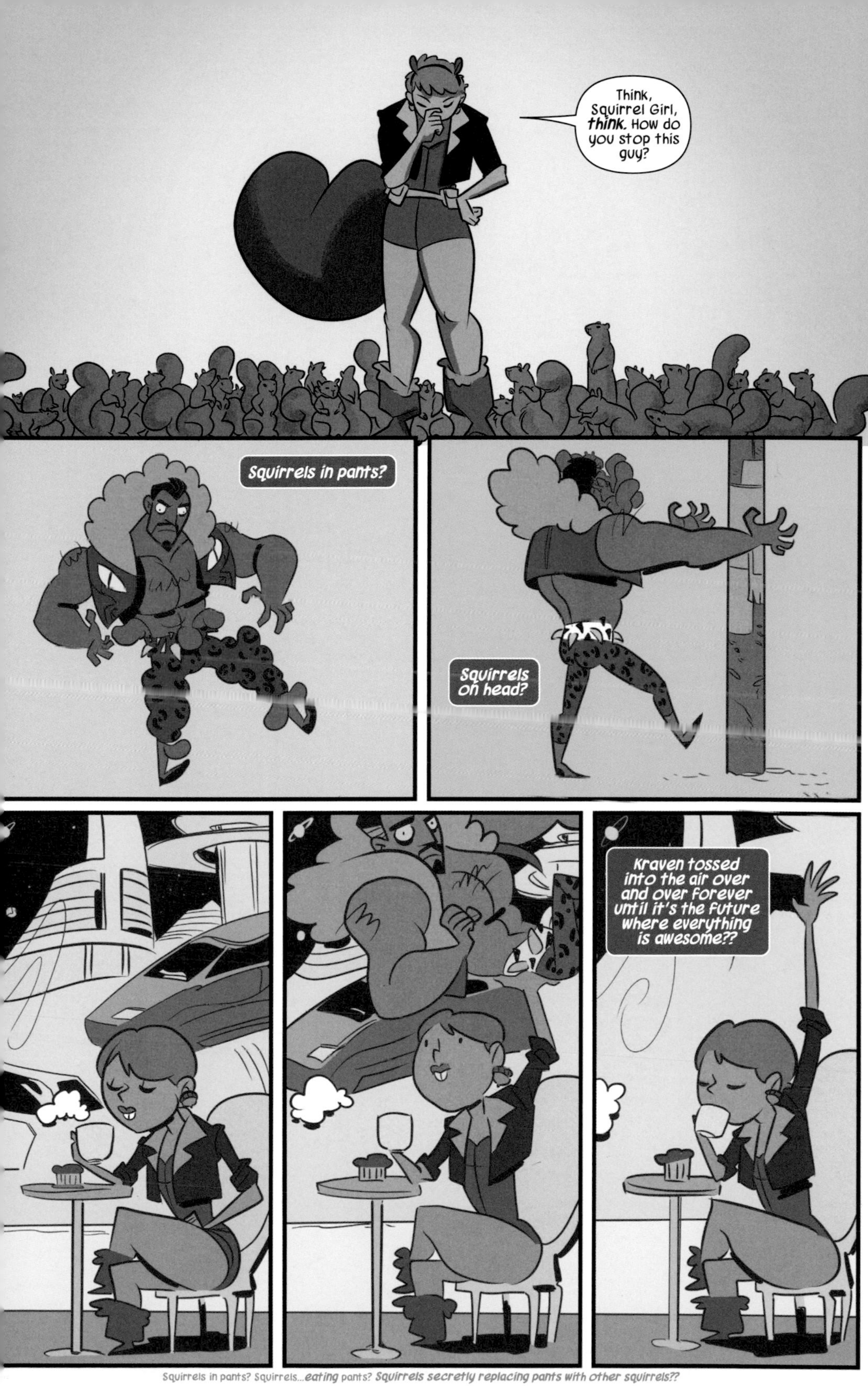
Think, Squirrel Girl, *think.* How do you stop this guy?
Squirrels in pants?
Squirrels on head?
Kraven tossed into the air over and over forever until it's the future where everything is awesome??

Squirrels in pants? Squirrels...*eating* pants? *Squirrels secretly replacing pants with other squirrels??*

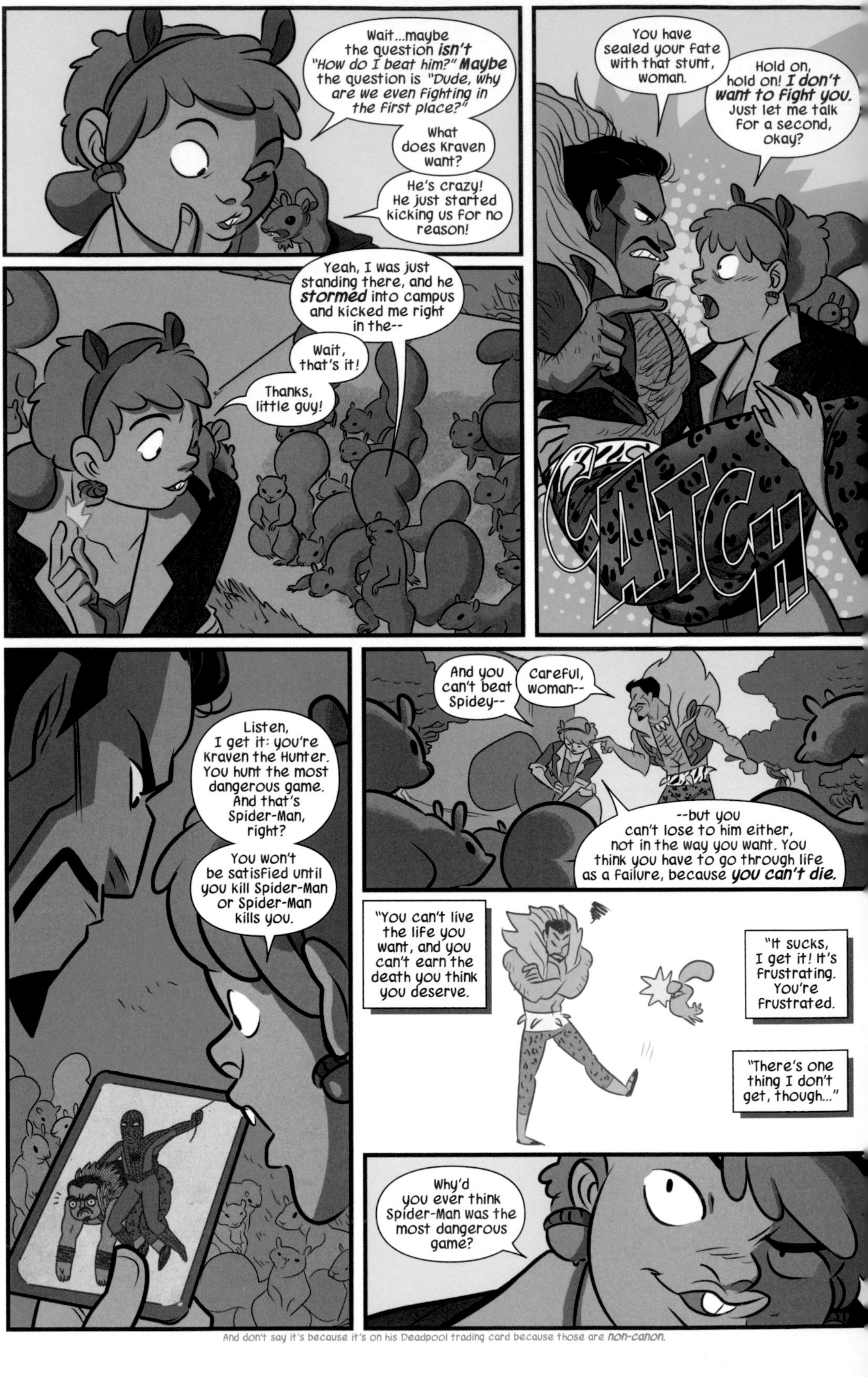
Wait...maybe the question isn't "How do I beat him?" Maybe the question is "Dude, why are we even fighting in the first place?"
What does Kraven want?
He's crazy! He just started kicking us for no reason!
You have sealed your fate with that stunt, woman.
Hold on, hold on! I don't want to fight you. Just let me talk for a second, okay?
Yeah, I was just standing there, and he stormed into campus and kicked me right in the--
Wait, that's it!
Thanks, little guy!
CATCH
Listen, I get it: you're Kraven the Hunter. You hunt the most dangerous game. And that's Spider-Man, right?
You won't be satisfied until you kill Spider-Man or Spider-Man kills you.
And you can't beat Spidey--
Careful, woman--
--but you can't lose to him either, not in the way you want. You think you have to go through life as a failure, because you can't die.
"You can't live the life you want, and you can't earn the death you think you deserve.
"It sucks, I get it! It's frustrating. You're frustrated.
"There's one thing I don't get, though..."
Why'd you ever think Spider-Man was the most dangerous game?

And don't say it's because it's on his Deadpool trading card because those are *non-canon*.

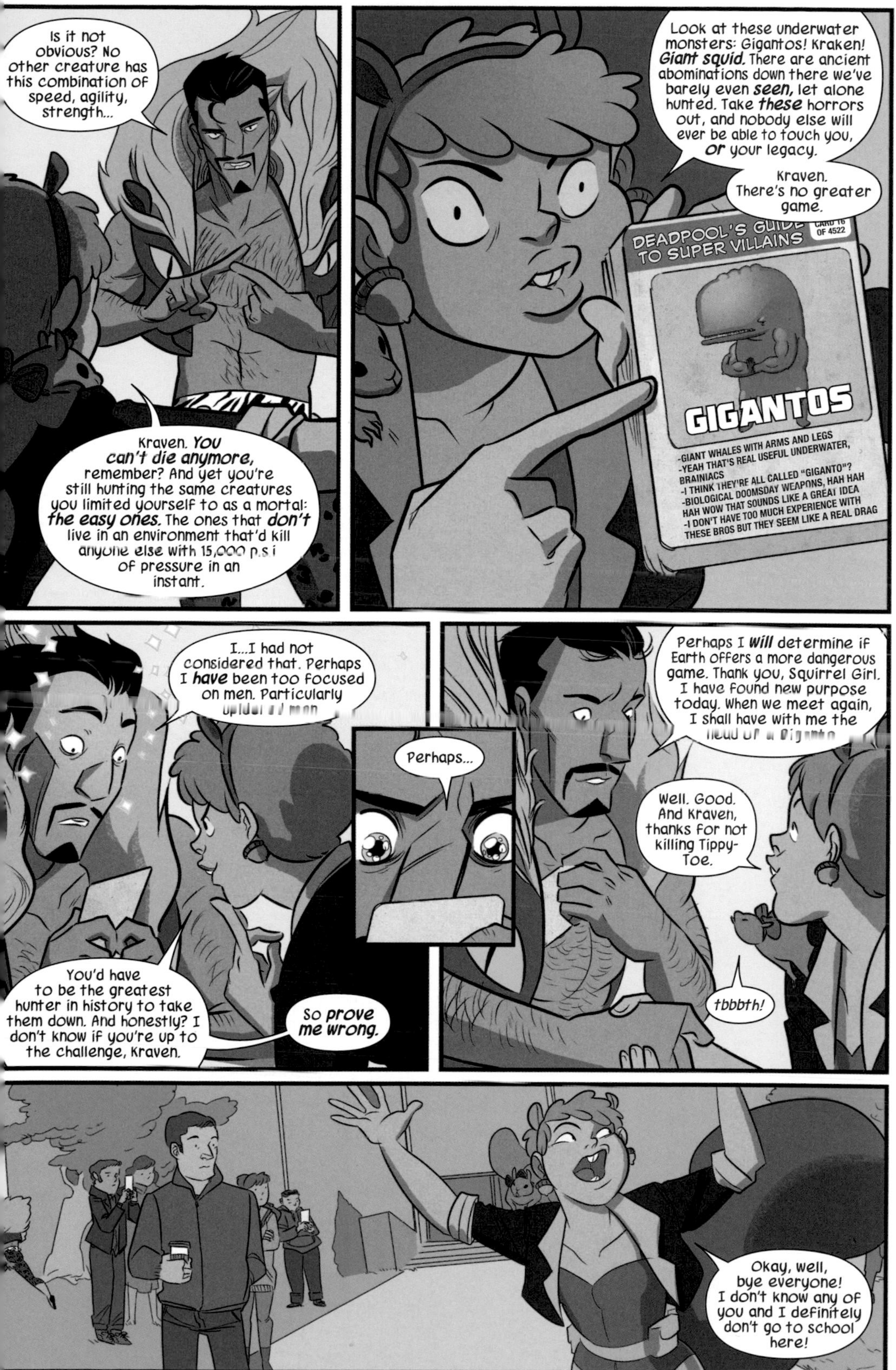

Is it not obvious? No other creature has this combination of speed, agility, strength...
Kraven. You can't die anymore, remember? And yet you're still hunting the same creatures you limited yourself to as a mortal: the easy ones. The ones that don't live in an environment that'd kill anyone else with 15,000 p.s.i of pressure in an instant.
Look at these underwater monsters: Gigantos! Kraken! Giant squid. There are ancient abominations down there we've barely even seen, let alone hunted. Take these horrors out, and nobody else will ever be able to touch you, or your legacy.
Kraven. There's no greater game.
DEADPOOL'S GUIDE TO SUPER VILLAINS
CARD 16 OF 4522
GIGANTOS
-GIANT WHALES WITH ARMS AND LEGS
-YEAH THAT'S REAL USEFUL UNDERWATER, BRAINIACS
-I THINK THEY'RE ALL CALLED "GIGANTO"?
-BIOLOGICAL DOOMSDAY WEAPONS, HAH HAH HAH WOW THAT SOUNDS LIKE A GREAT IDEA
-I DON'T HAVE TOO MUCH EXPERIENCE WITH THESE BROS BUT THEY SEEM LIKE A REAL DRAG
I...I had not considered that. Perhaps I have been too focused on men. Particularly
You'd have to be the greatest hunter in history to take them down. And honestly? I don't know if you're up to the challenge, Kraven.
So prove me wrong.
Perhaps...
Perhaps I will determine if Earth offers a more dangerous game. Thank you, Squirrel Girl. I have found new purpose today. When we meet again, I shall have with me the
Well. Good. And Kraven, thanks for not killing Tippy-Toe.
tbbbth!
Okay, well, bye everyone! I don't know any of you and I definitely don't go to school here!

If you *think* there's someone who goes here and who looks like me then my only comment on that matter is *"Okay wow she sounds hot!"*

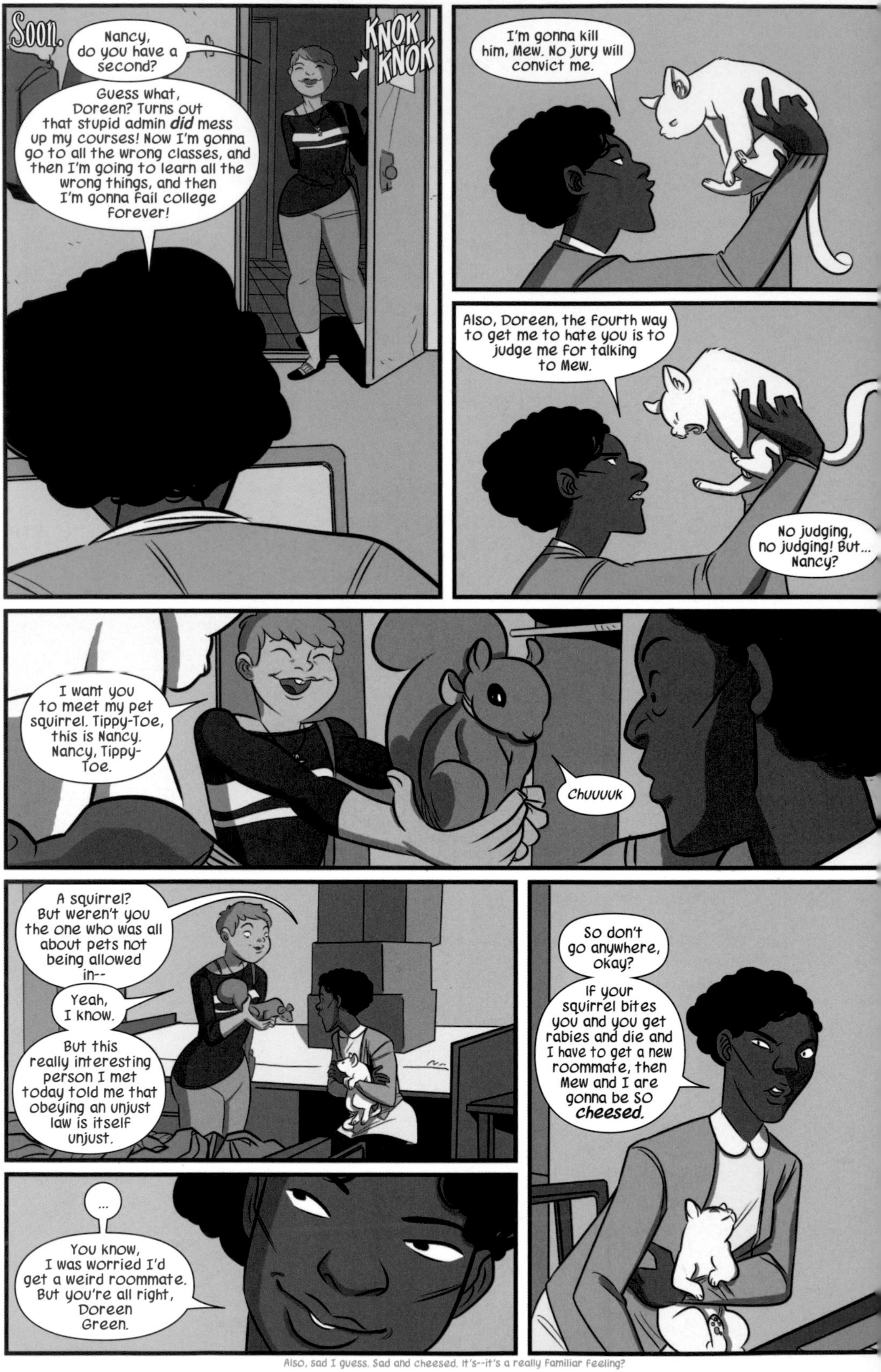
Soon.
Nancy, do you have a second?
KNOK KNOK
Guess what, Doreen? Turns out that stupid admin *did* mess up my courses! Now I'm gonna go to all the wrong classes, and then I'm going to learn all the wrong things, and then I'm gonna fail college forever!
I'm gonna kill him, Mew. No jury will convict me.
Also, Doreen, the fourth way to get me to hate you is to judge me for talking to Mew.
No judging, no judging! But... Nancy?
I want you to meet my pet squirrel. Tippy-Toe, this is Nancy. Nancy, Tippy-Toe.
Chuuuuk
A squirrel? But weren't you the one who was all about pets not being allowed in--
Yeah, I know.
But this really interesting person I met today told me that obeying an unjust law is itself unjust.
So don't go anywhere, okay?
If your squirrel bites you and you get rabies and die and I have to get a new roommate, then Mew and I are gonna be SO *cheesed.*
...
You know, I was worried I'd get a weird roommate. But you're all right, Doreen Green.

Also, sad I guess. Sad and cheesed. It's--it's a really familiar feeling?

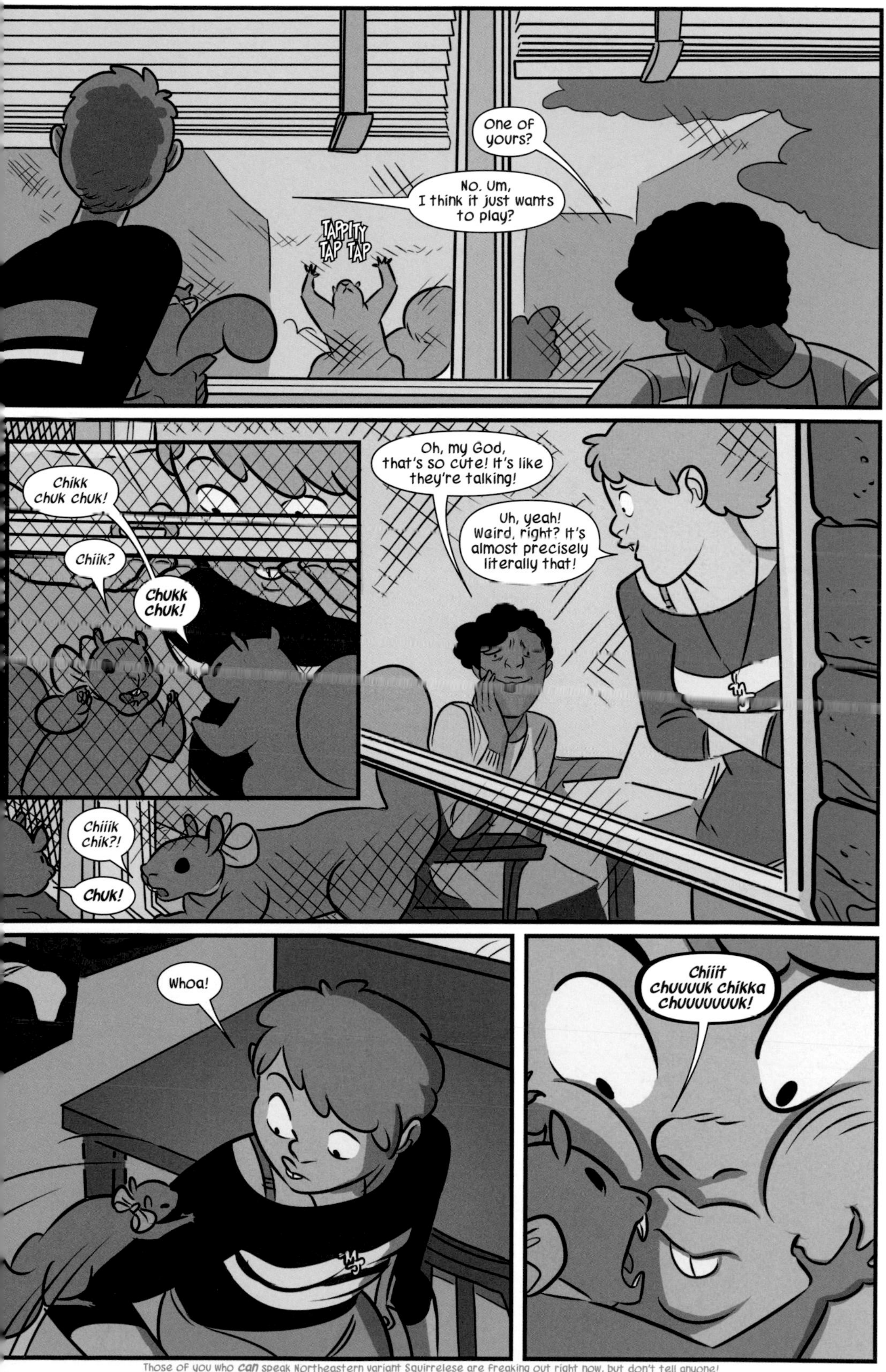
One of yours?
No. Um, I think it just wants to play?
TAPPITY TAP TAP
Oh, my God, that's so cute! It's like they're talking!
Uh, yeah! Weird, right? It's almost precisely literally that!
Chikk chuk chuk!
Chiik?
Chukk chuk!
Chiiik chik?!
CHUK!
Whoa!
Chiiit chuuuuk chikka chuuuuuuuk!

Those of you who *can* speak Northeastern variant Squirrelese are freaking out right now, but don't tell anyone!
Keep it a surprise for the rest of us who have to read the next page to find out what the deal is, okay?

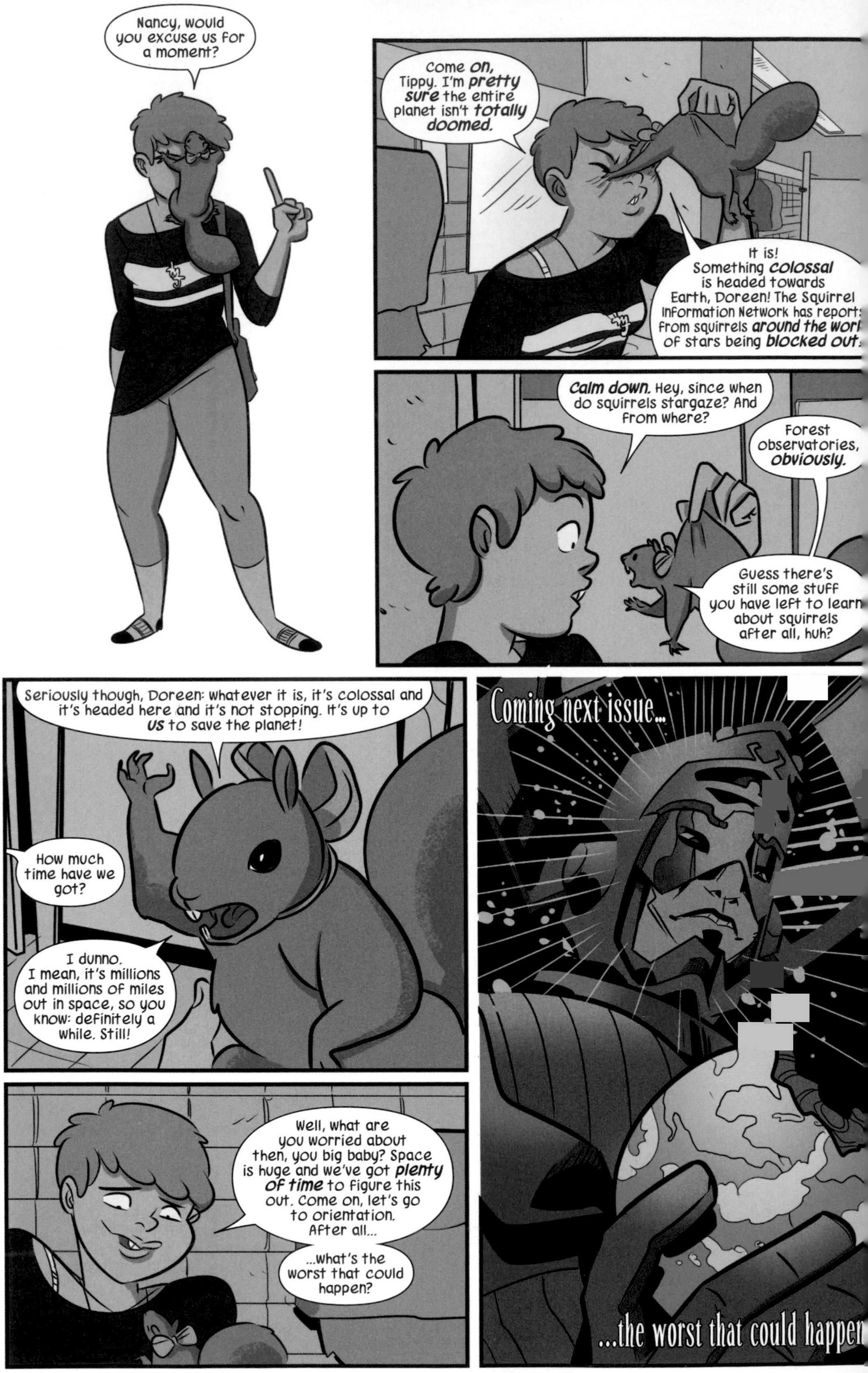
Nancy, would you excuse us for a moment?
Come on, Tippy. I'm pretty sure the entire planet isn't totally doomed.
It is! Something colossal is headed towards Earth, Doreen! The Squirrel Information Network has reports from squirrels around the world of stars being blocked out!
Calm down. Hey, since when do squirrels stargaze? And from where?
Forest observatories, obviously.
Guess there's still some stuff you have left to learn about squirrels after all, huh?
Seriously though, Doreen: whatever it is, it's colossal and it's headed here and it's not stopping. It's up to US to save the planet!
How much time have we got?
I dunno. I mean, it's millions and millions of miles out in space, so you know: definitely a while. Still!
Well, what are you worried about then, you big baby? Space is huge and we've got plenty of time to figure this out. Come on, let's go to orientation. After all...
...what's the worst that could happen?
Coming next issue...
...the worst that could happen

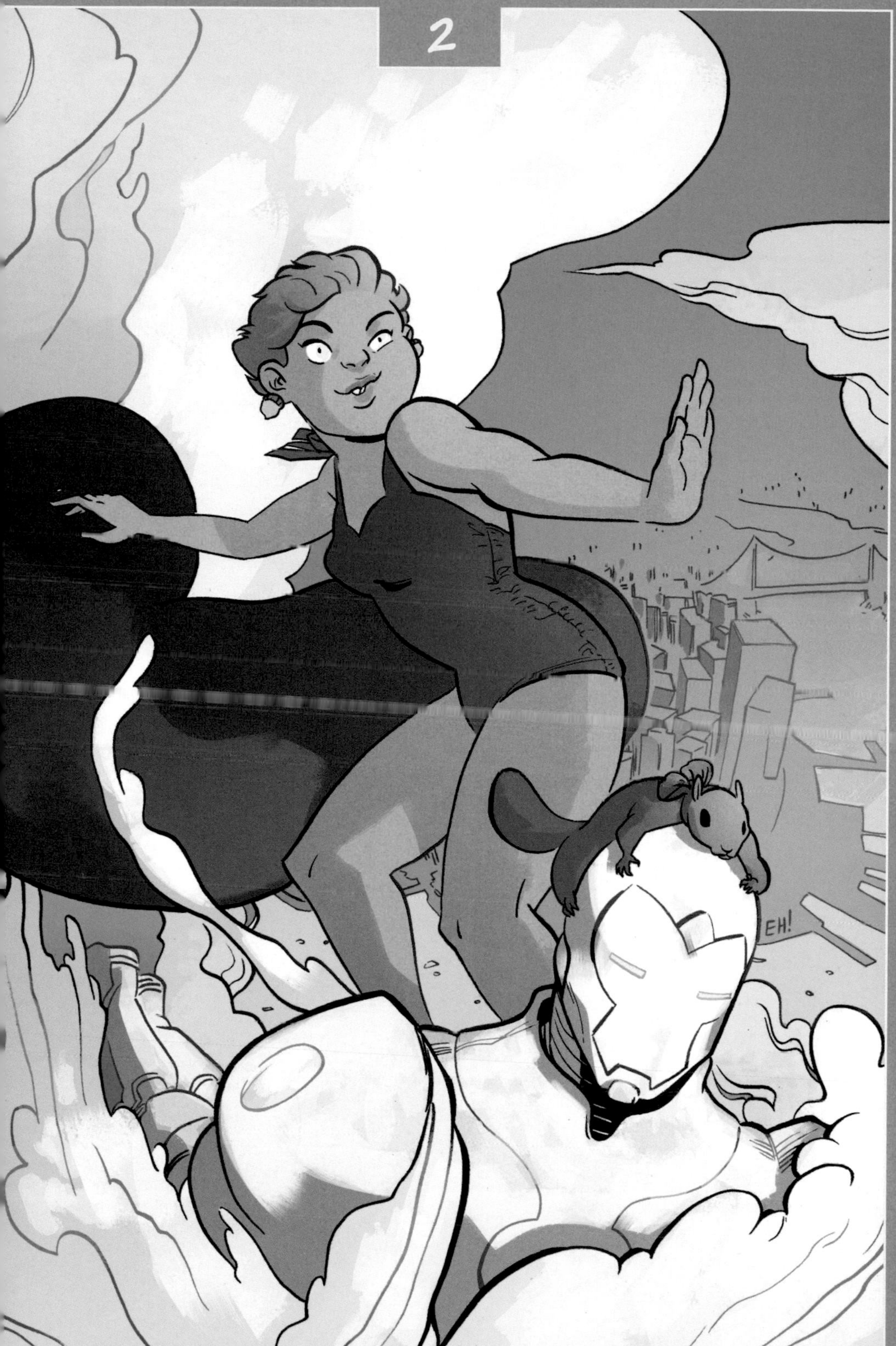
2
EH!

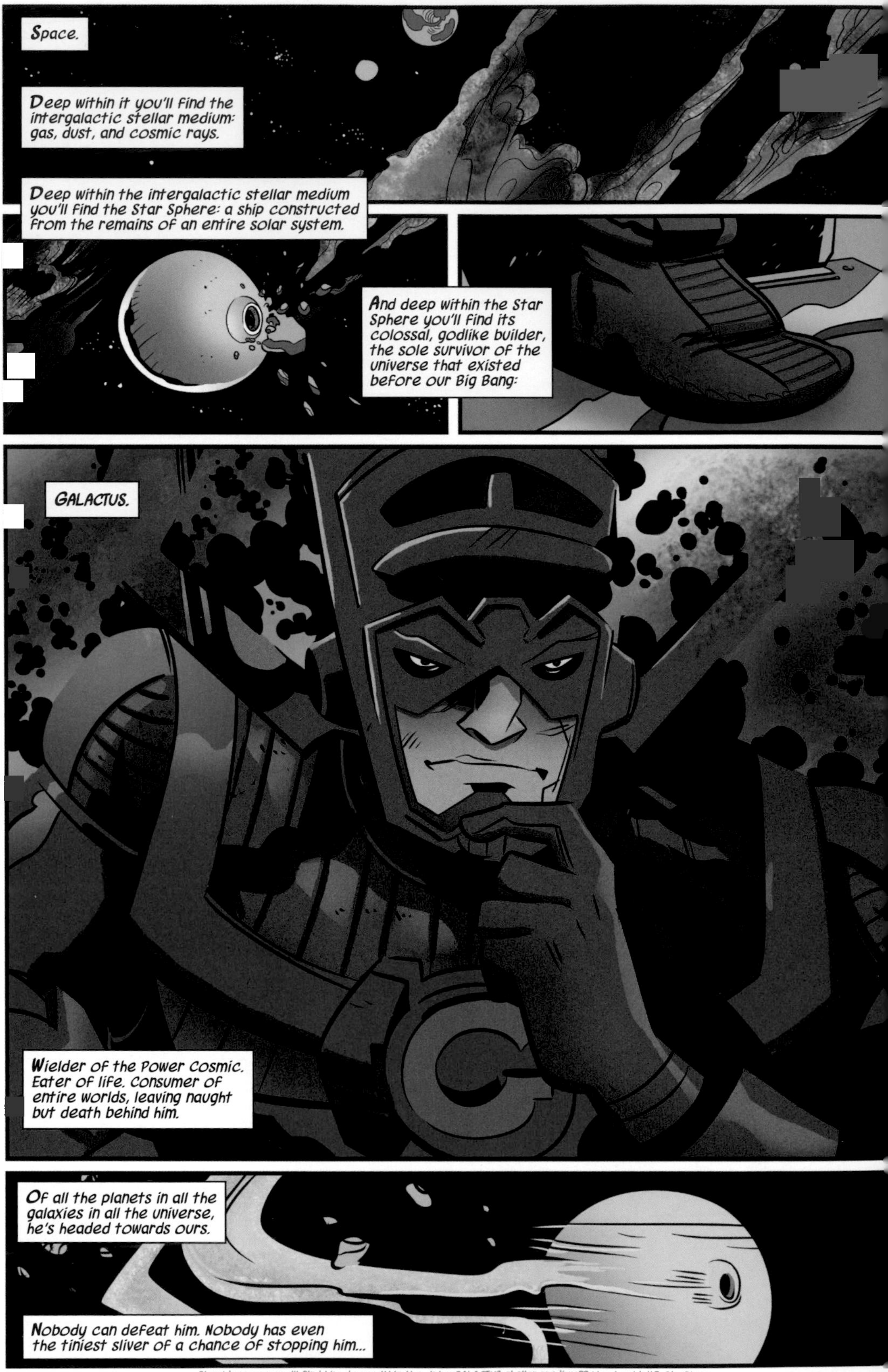
Space.
Deep within it you'll find the intergalactic stellar medium: gas, dust, and cosmic rays.
Deep within the intergalactic stellar medium you'll find the Star Sphere: a ship constructed from the remains of an entire solar system.
And deep within the Star Sphere you'll find its colossal, godlike builder, the sole survivor of the universe that existed before our Big Bang:
GALACTUS.
Wielder of the Power Cosmic. Eater of life. Consumer of entire worlds, leaving naught but death behind him.
Of all the planets in all the galaxies in all the universe, he's headed towards ours.
Nobody can defeat him. Nobody has even the tiniest sliver of a chance of stopping him...

Should we say you'll find him deep within the...interGALACTUS stellar medium?? We shouldn't? Oh. Okay.

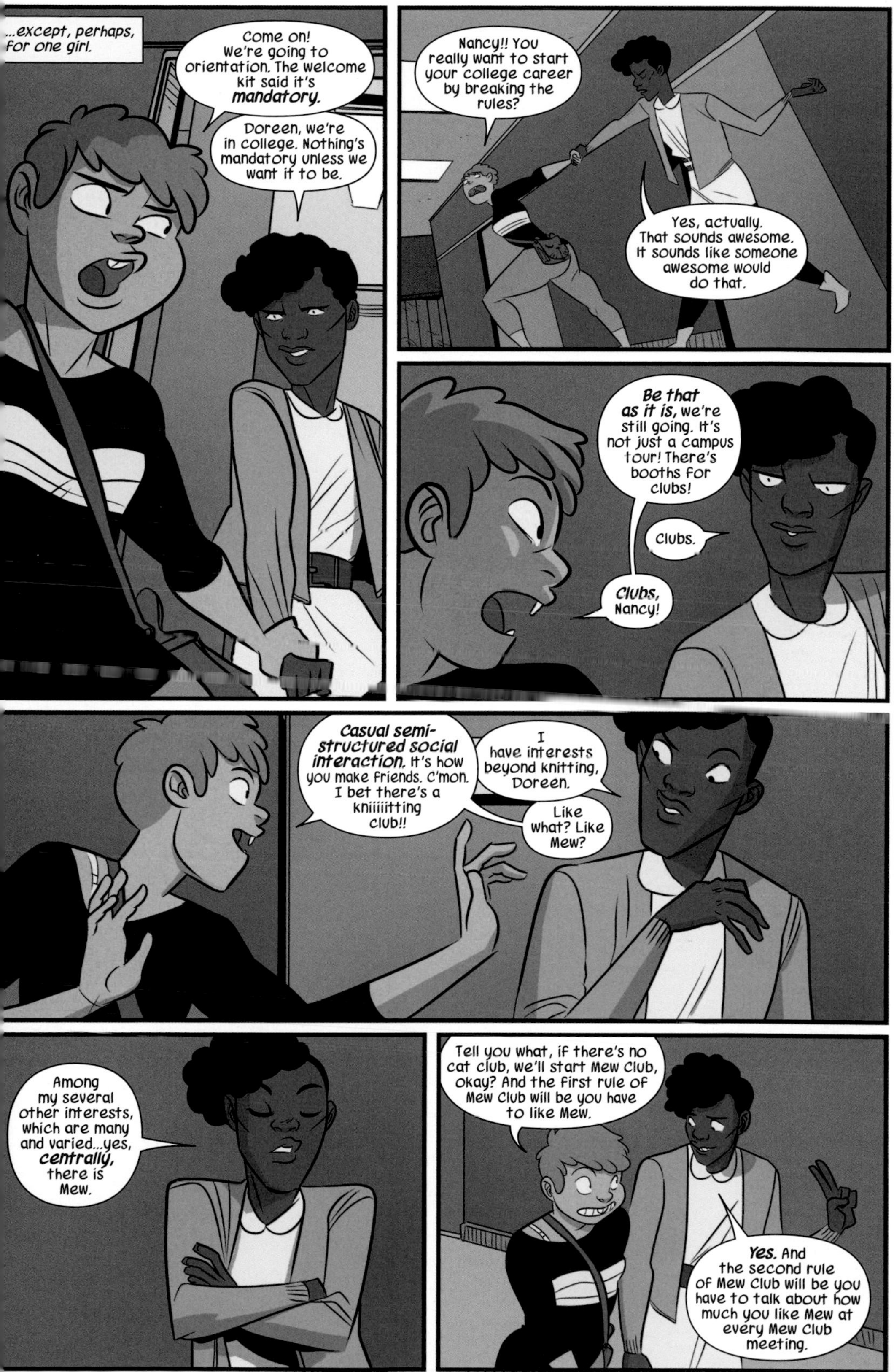
...except, perhaps, for one girl.
Come on! We're going to orientation. The welcome kit said it's *mandatory.*
Doreen, we're in college. Nothing's mandatory unless we want it to be.
Nancy!! You really want to start your college career by breaking the rules?
Yes, actually. That sounds awesome. It sounds like someone awesome would do that.
Be that as it is, we're still going. It's not just a campus tour! There's booths for clubs!
Clubs.
Clubs, Nancy!
Casual semi-structured social interaction. It's how you make friends. C'mon. I bet there's a kniiiiitting club!!
I have interests beyond knitting, Doreen.
Like what? Like Mew?
Among my several other interests, which are many and varied...yes, *centrally,* there is Mew.
Tell you what, if there's no cat club, we'll start Mew Club, okay? And the first rule of Mew Club will be you have to like Mew.
Yes. And the second rule of Mew Club will be you have to talk about how much you like Mew at every Mew Club meeting.

The next five rules of Mew Club are to tell everyone about Mew Club; we need members really badly

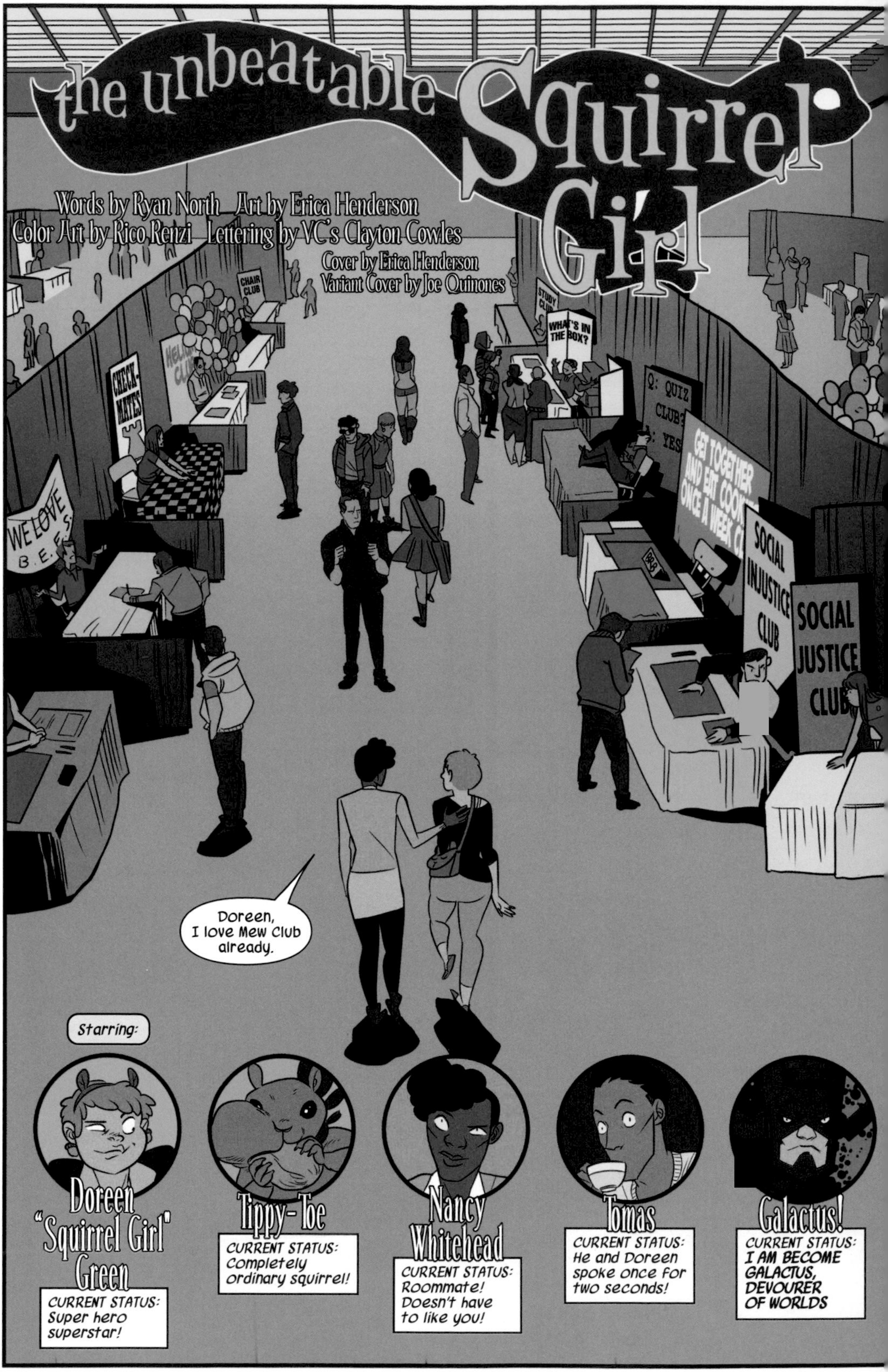
the unbeatable Squirrel Girl
Words by Ryan North Art by Erica Henderson
Color Art by Rico Renzi Lettering by VC's Clayton Cowles
Cover by Erica Henderson
Variant Cover by Joe Quinones
CHAIR CLUB
STUDY CLUB
WHAT'S IN THE BOX?
CHECK-MATES
Q: QUIZ CLUB? A: YES
GET TOGETHER AND EAT COOKIES ONCE A WEEK CL
WE LOVE B.E.E.S.
SOCIAL INJUSTICE CLUB
SOCIAL JUSTICE CLUB
BRB
Doreen, I love Mew Club already.
Starring:
Doreen "Squirrel Girl" Green
CURRENT STATUS: Super hero superstar!
Tippy-Toe
CURRENT STATUS: Completely ordinary squirrel!
Nancy Whitehead
CURRENT STATUS: Roommate! Doesn't have to like you!
Tomas
CURRENT STATUS: He and Doreen spoke once for two seconds!
Galactus!
CURRENT STATUS: I AM BECOME GALACTUS, DEVOURER OF WORLDS

Not pictured: Way Too Lazy To Set Up A Booth Club

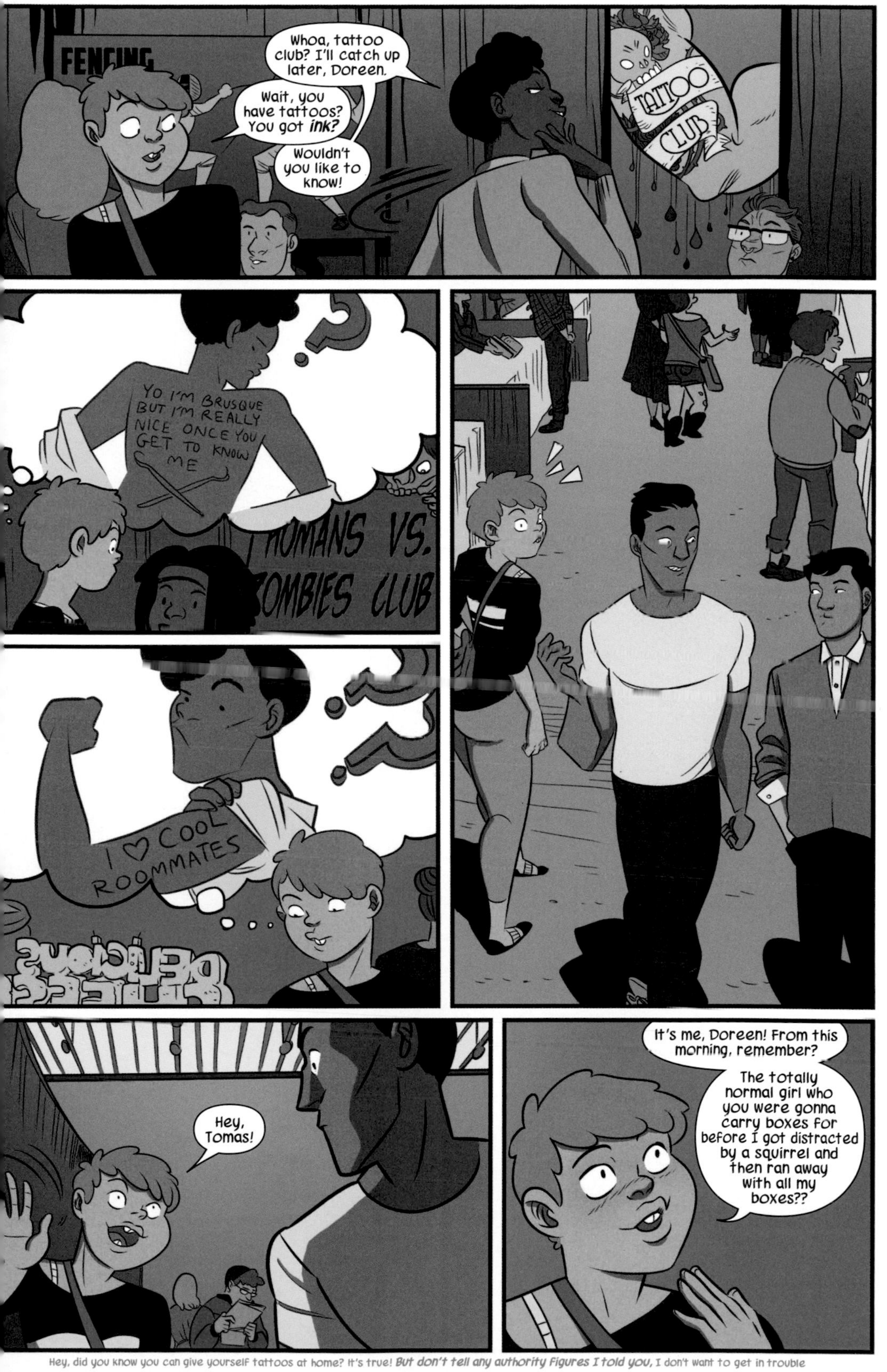
FENCING
Whoa, tattoo club? I'll catch up later, Doreen.
Wait, you have tattoos? You got *ink?*
Wouldn't you like to know!
TATTOO CLUB
YO I'M BRUSQUE BUT I'M REALLY NICE ONCE YOU GET TO KNOW ME
HUMANS VS. ZOMBIES CLUB
I ♡ COOL ROOMMATES
Hey, Tomas!
It's me, Doreen! From this morning, remember?
The totally normal girl who you were gonna carry boxes for before I got distracted by a squirrel and then ran away with all my boxes??

Hey, did you know you can give yourself tattoos at home? It's true! ***But don't tell any authority figures I told you,*** I don't want to get in trouble

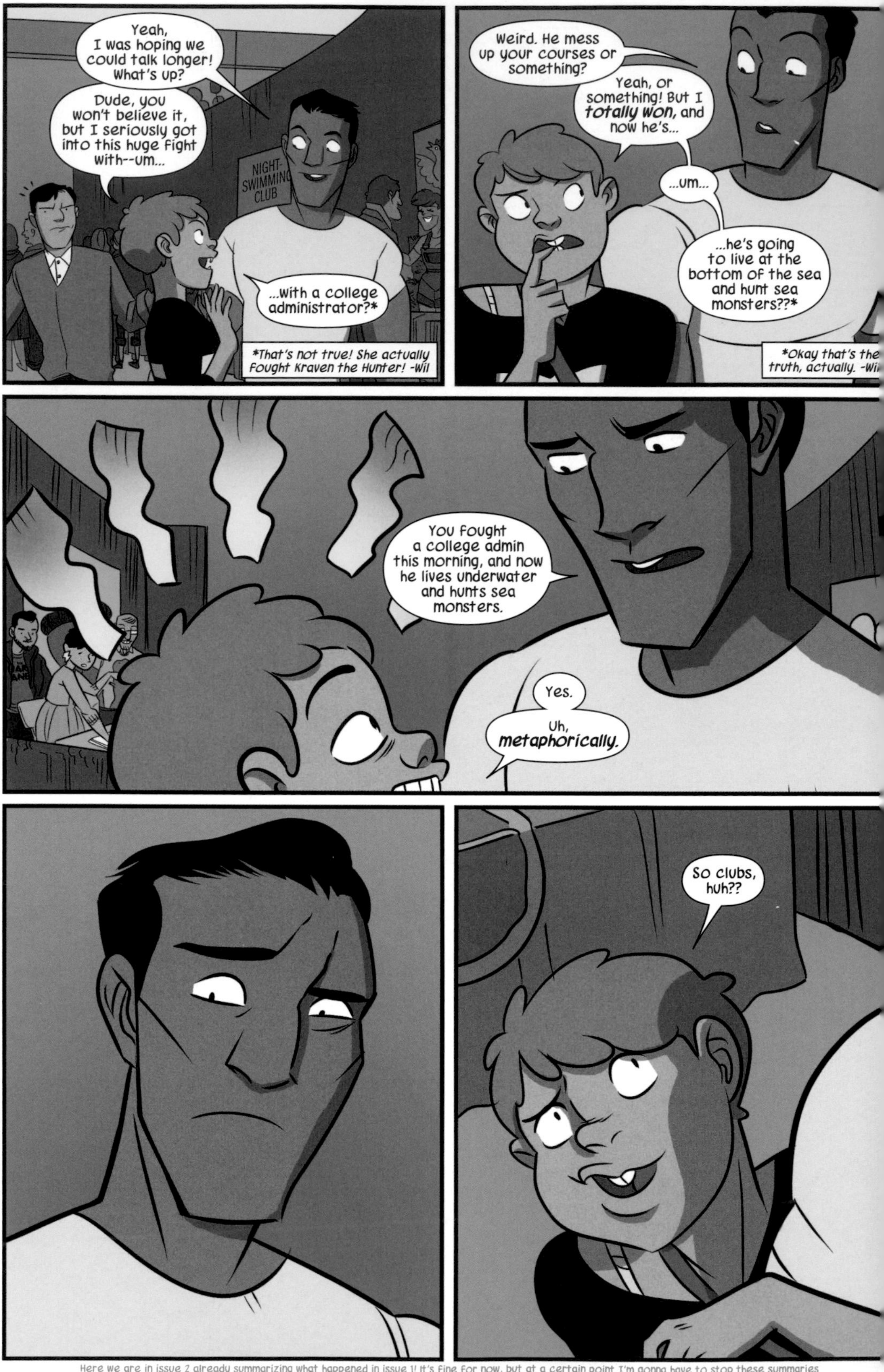
Yeah, I was hoping we could talk longer! What's up?
Dude, you won't believe it, but I seriously got into this huge fight with--um...
NIGHT-SWIMMING CLUB
...with a college administrator?*
*That's not true! She actually fought Kraven the Hunter! -Wil
Weird. He mess up your courses or something?
Yeah, or something! But I totally won, and now he's...
...um...
...he's going to live at the bottom of the sea and hunt sea monsters??*
*Okay that's the truth, actually. -Wi
You fought a college admin this morning, and now he lives underwater and hunts sea monsters.
Yes.
Uh, metaphorically.
So clubs, huh??

Here we are in issue 2 already summarizing what happened in issue 1! It's fine for now, but at a certain point I'm gonna have to stop these summaries and you'll just have to buy the comics to find out what happened, okay??

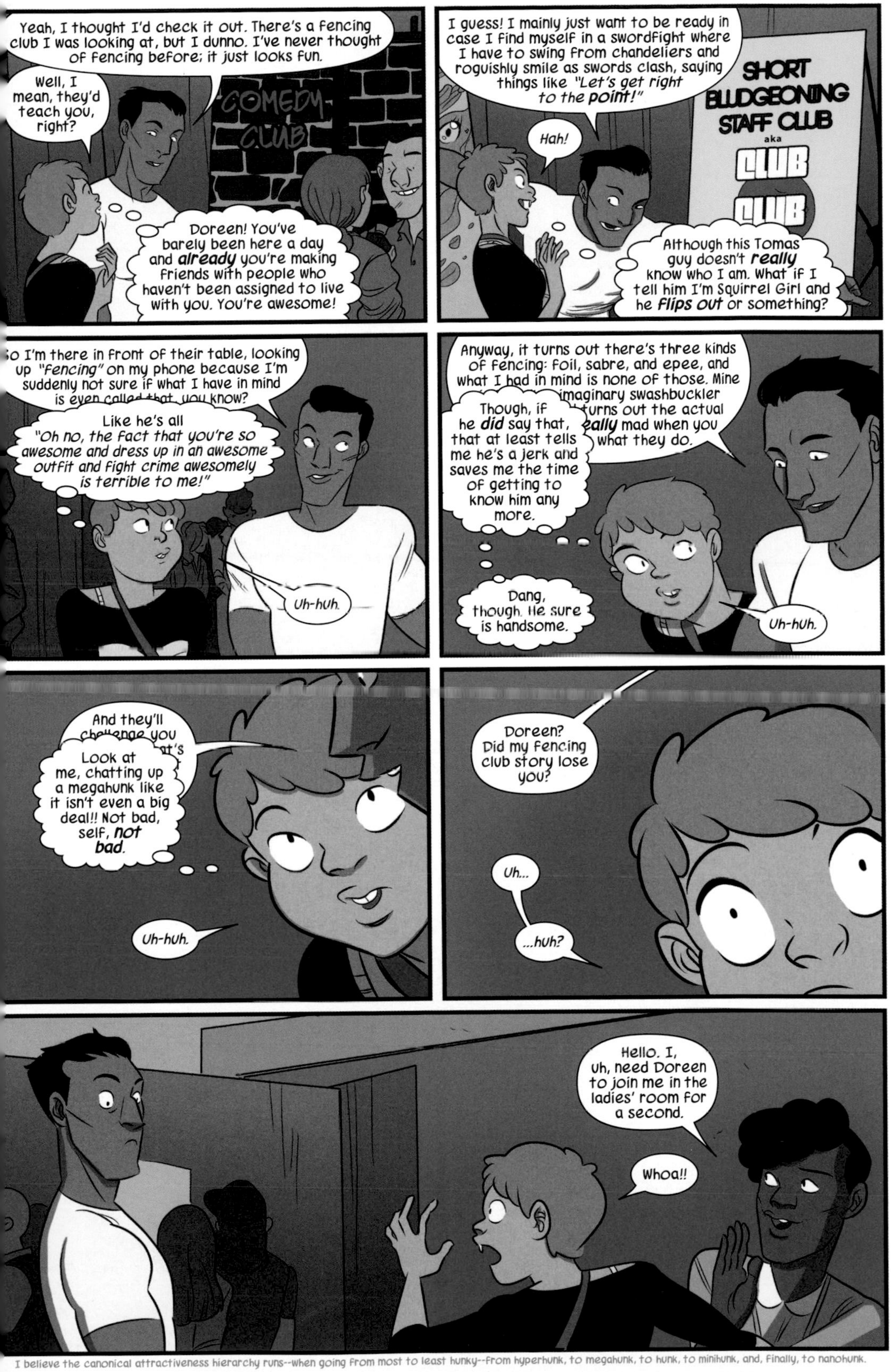
Yeah, I thought I'd check it out. There's a fencing club I was looking at, but I dunno. I've never thought of fencing before; it just looks fun.
Well, I mean, they'd teach you, right?
COMEDY CLUB
Doreen! You've barely been here a day and *already* you're making friends with people who haven't been assigned to live with you. You're awesome!
I guess! I mainly just want to be ready in case I find myself in a swordfight where I have to swing from chandeliers and roguishly smile as swords clash, saying things like *"Let's get right to the point!"*
SHORT BLUDGEONING STAFF CLUB aka CLUB CLUB
Hah!
Although this Tomas guy doesn't *really* know who I am. What if I tell him I'm Squirrel Girl and he *flips out* or something?
So I'm there in front of their table, looking up *"fencing"* on my phone because I'm suddenly not sure if what I have in mind is even called that, you know?
Like he's all *"Oh no, the fact that you're so awesome and dress up in an awesome outfit and fight crime awesomely is terrible to me!"*
Uh-huh.
Anyway, it turns out there's three kinds of fencing: foil, sabre, and epee, and what I had in mind is none of those. Mine
imaginary swashbuckler
turns out the actual
eally mad when you
what they do.
Though, if he *did* say that, that at least tells me he's a jerk and saves me the time of getting to know him any more.
Dang, though. He sure is handsome.
Uh-huh.
And they'll
Look at me, chatting up a megahunk like it isn't even a big deal!! Not bad, self, ***not bad***.
Uh-huh.
Doreen? Did my fencing club story lose you?
Uh...
...huh?
Hello. I, uh, need Doreen to join me in the ladies' room for a second.
Whoa!!

I believe the canonical attractiveness hierarchy runs--when going from most to least hunky--from hyperhunk, to megahunk, to hunk, to minihunk, and, finally, to nanohunk.

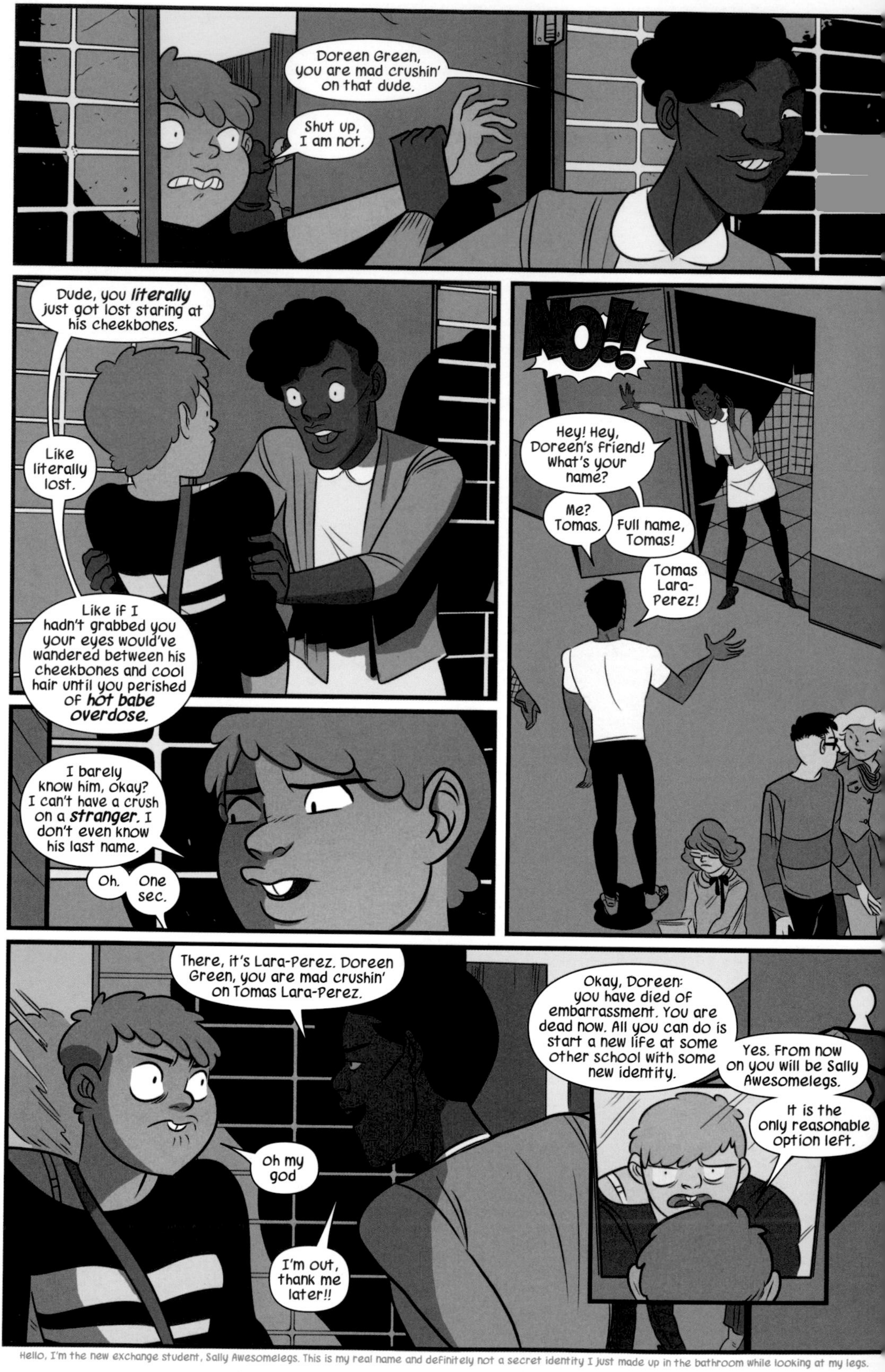
Doreen Green, you are mad crushin' on that dude.
Shut up, I am not.
Dude, you *literally* just got lost staring at his cheekbones.
Like literally lost.
Like if I hadn't grabbed you your eyes would've wandered between his cheekbones and cool hair until you perished of ***hot babe overdose.***
NO!!
Hey! Hey, Doreen's friend! What's your name?
Me? Tomas.
Full name, Tomas!
Tomas Lara-Perez!
I barely know him, okay? I can't have a crush on a ***stranger.*** I don't even know his last name.
Oh.
One sec.
There, it's Lara-Perez. Doreen Green, you are mad crushin' on Tomas Lara-Perez.
Oh my god
I'm out, thank me later!!
Okay, Doreen: you have died of embarrassment. You are dead now. All you can do is start a new life at some other school with some new identity.
Yes. From now on you will be Sally Awesomelegs.
It is the only reasonable option left.

Hello, I'm the new exchange student, Sally Awesomelegs. This is my real name and definitely not a secret identity I just made up in the bathroom while looking at my legs.

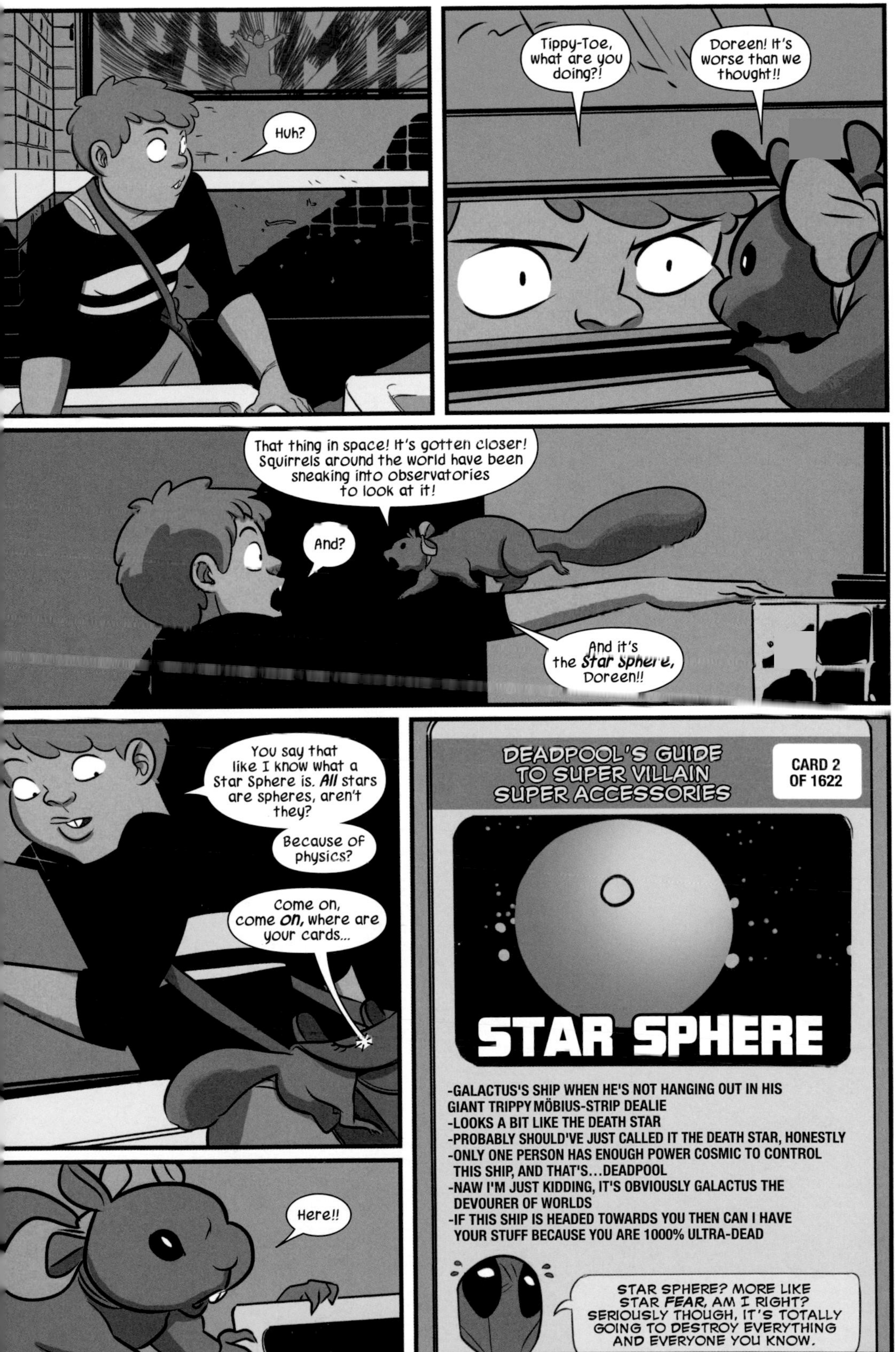
Huh?
Tippy-Toe, what are you doing?!
Doreen! It's worse than we thought!!
That thing in space! It's gotten closer! Squirrels around the world have been sneaking into observatories to look at it!
And?
And it's the Star Sphere, Doreen!!
You say that like I know what a Star Sphere is. All stars are spheres, aren't they?
Because of physics?
Come on, come on, where are your cards...
Here!!
DEADPOOL'S GUIDE TO SUPER VILLAIN SUPER ACCESSORIES
CARD 2 OF 1622
STAR SPHERE
-GALACTUS'S SHIP WHEN HE'S NOT HANGING OUT IN HIS GIANT TRIPPY MÖBIUS-STRIP DEALIE
-LOOKS A BIT LIKE THE DEATH STAR
-PROBABLY SHOULD'VE JUST CALLED IT THE DEATH STAR, HONESTLY
-ONLY ONE PERSON HAS ENOUGH POWER COSMIC TO CONTROL THIS SHIP, AND THAT'S...DEADPOOL
-NAW I'M JUST KIDDING, IT'S OBVIOUSLY GALACTUS THE DEVOURER OF WORLDS
-IF THIS SHIP IS HEADED TOWARDS YOU THEN CAN I HAVE YOUR STUFF BECAUSE YOU ARE 1000% ULTRA-DEAD
STAR SPHERE? MORE LIKE STAR FEAR, AM I RIGHT? SERIOUSLY THOUGH, IT'S TOTALLY GOING TO DESTROY EVERYTHING AND EVERYONE YOU KNOW.

Yes, Tippy-Toe did absolutely start this page imagining that window would dramatically smash around her as she leapt through it.

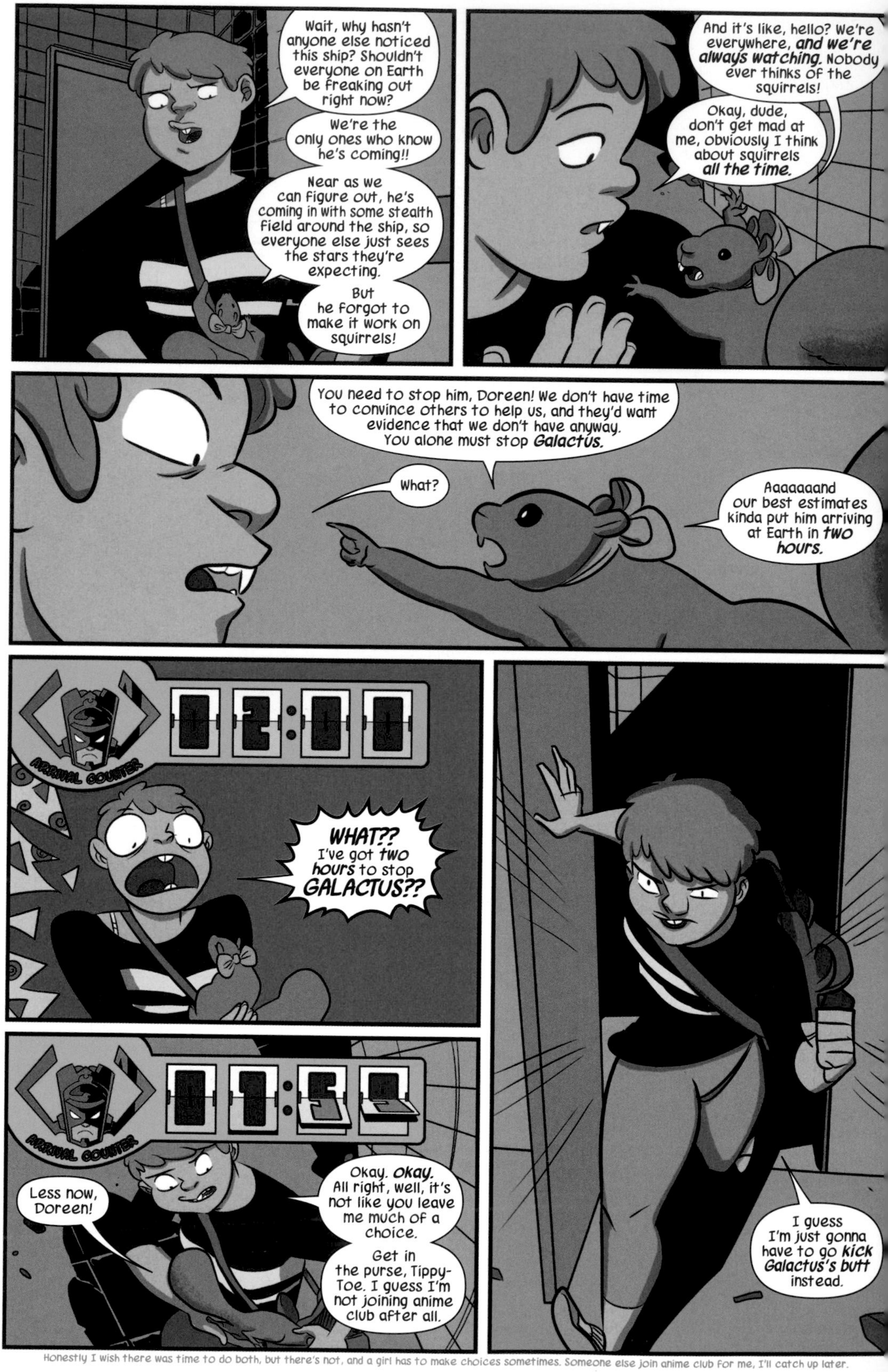
Wait, why hasn't anyone else noticed this ship? Shouldn't everyone on Earth be freaking out right now?
We're the only ones who know he's coming!!
Near as we can figure out, he's coming in with some stealth field around the ship, so everyone else just sees the stars they're expecting.
But he forgot to make it work on squirrels!
And it's like, hello? We're everywhere, **and we're always watching.** Nobody ever thinks of the squirrels!
Okay, dude, don't get mad at me, obviously I think about squirrels **all the time.**
You need to stop him, Doreen! We don't have time to convince others to help us, and they'd want evidence that we don't have anyway. You alone must stop **Galactus.**
What?
Aaaaaaand our best estimates kinda put him arriving at Earth in **two hours.**
ARRIVAL COUNTER
WHAT?? I've got **two hours** to stop **GALACTUS??**
ARRIVAL COUNTER
Less now, Doreen!
Okay. **Okay.** All right, well, it's not like you leave me much of a choice.
Get in the purse, Tippy-Toe. I guess I'm not joining anime club after all.
I guess I'm just gonna have to go **kick Galactus's butt** instead.
Honestly I wish there was time to do both, but there's not, and a girl has to make choices sometimes. Someone else join anime club for me, I'll catch up later.

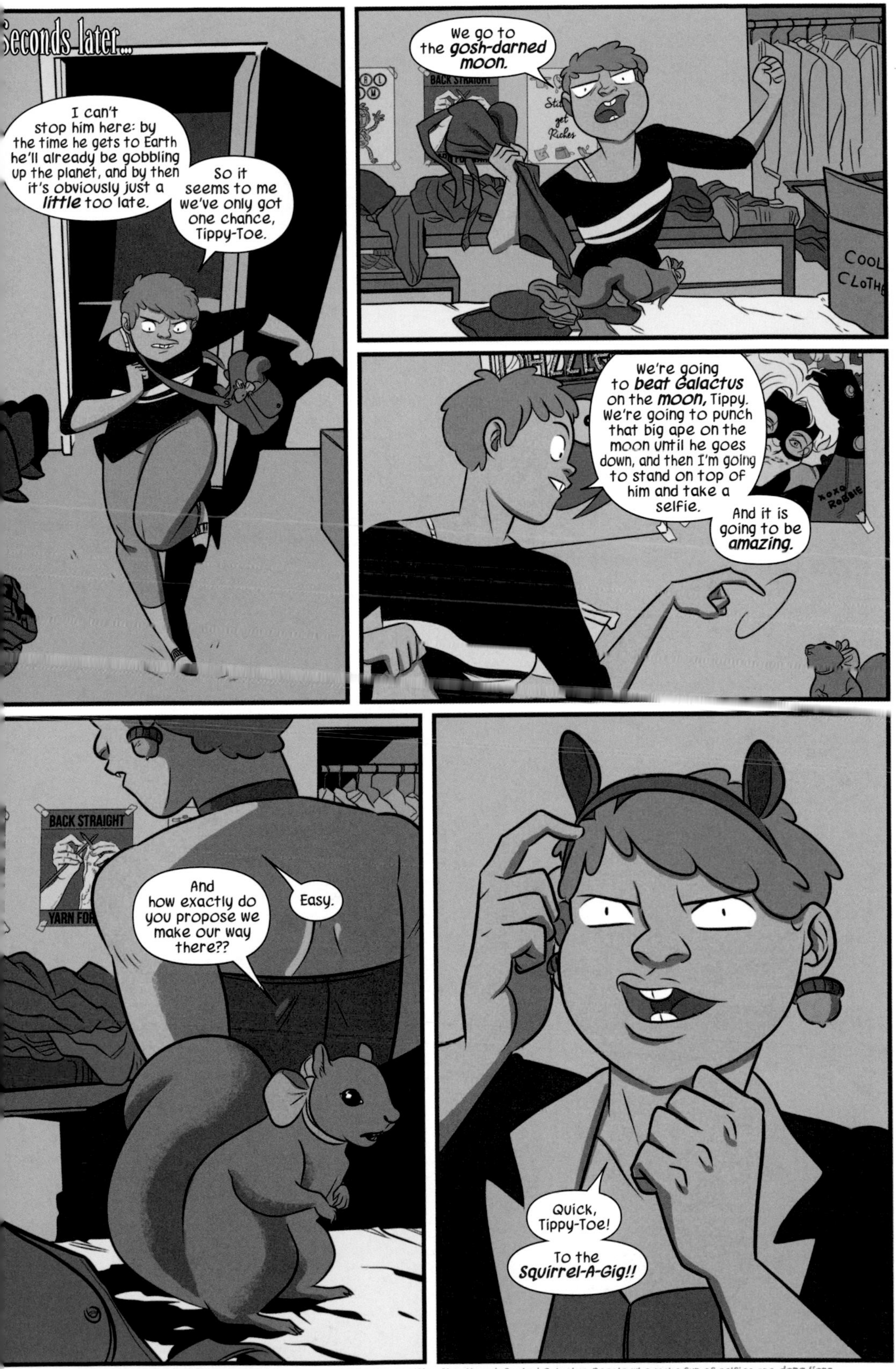
Seconds later...
I can't stop him here: by the time he gets to Earth he'll already be gobbling up the planet, and by then it's obviously just a *little* too late.
So it seems to me we've only got one chance, Tippy-Toe.
We go to the *gosh-darned moon.*
BACK STRAIGHT
COOL CLOTHES
We're going to *beat Galactus* on the *moon,* Tippy. We're going to punch that big ape on the moon until he goes down, and then I'm going to stand on top of him and take a selfie.
And it is going to be *amazing.*
XOXO ROBBIE
BACK STRAIGHT
YARN FOR
And how exactly do you propose we make our way there??
Easy.
Quick, Tippy-Toe!
To the *Squirrel-A-Gig!!*

People who make fun of selfies always act like they wouldn't take a selfie after they defeated Galactus. People who make fun of selfies are *dang liars.*

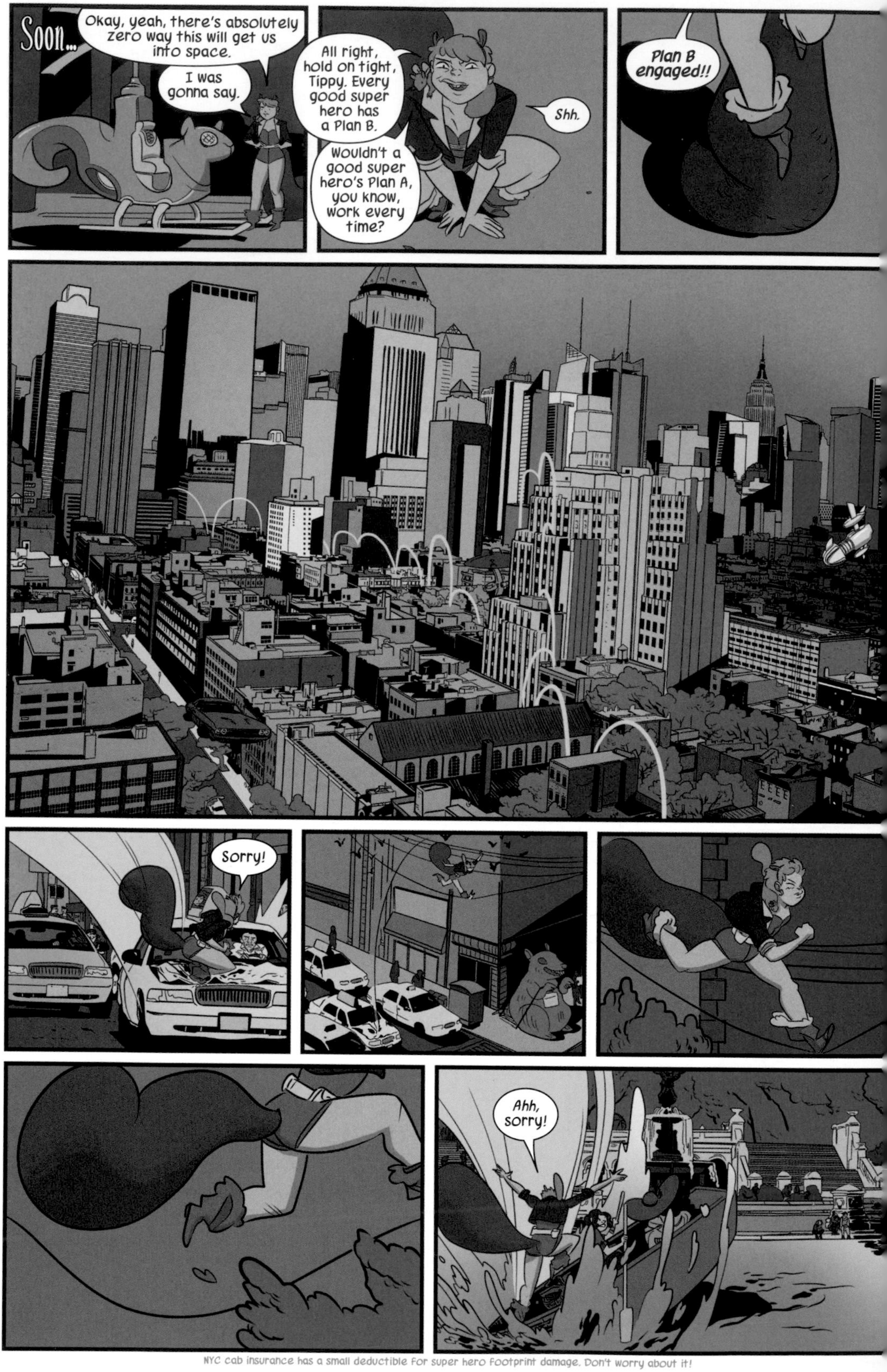
Soon...
Okay, yeah, there's absolutely zero way this will get us into space.
I was gonna say.
All right, hold on tight, Tippy. Every good super hero has a Plan B.
Wouldn't a good super hero's Plan A, you know, work every time?
Shh.
Plan B engaged!!
Sorry!
Ahh, sorry!

NYC cab insurance has a small deductible for super hero footprint damage. Don't worry about it!

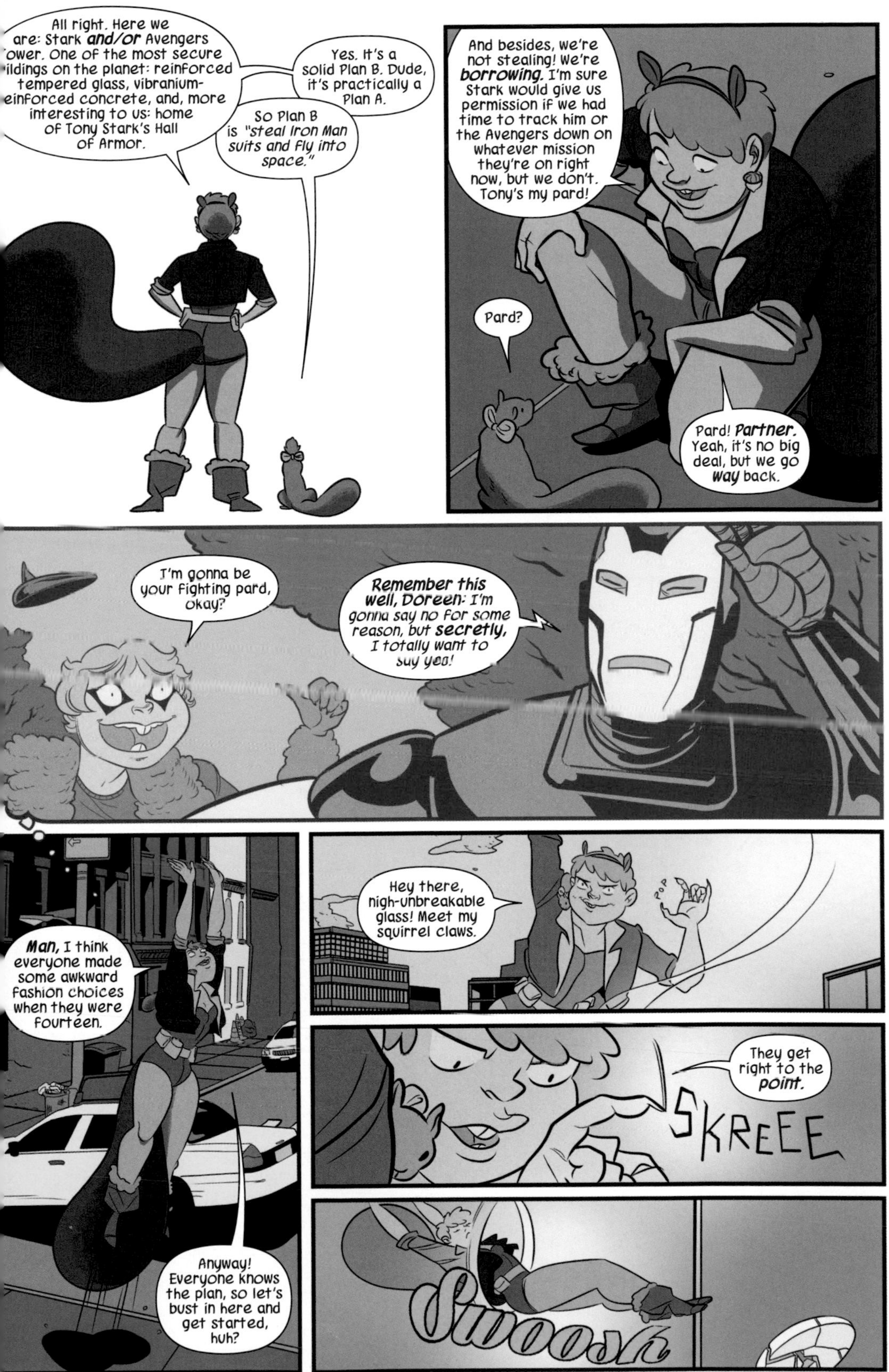
All right. Here we are: Stark and/or Avengers ower. One of the most secure ildings on the planet: reinforced tempered glass, vibranium-einforced concrete, and, more interesting to us: home of Tony Stark's Hall of Armor.
Yes. It's a solid Plan B. Dude, it's practically a Plan A.
So Plan B is "steal Iron Man suits and fly into space."
And besides, we're not stealing! We're borrowing. I'm sure Stark would give us permission if we had time to track him or the Avengers down on whatever mission they're on right now, but we don't. Tony's my pard!
Pard?
Pard! Partner. Yeah, it's no big deal, but we go way back.
I'm gonna be your fighting pard, okay?
Remember this well, Doreen: I'm gonna say no for some reason, but secretly, I totally want to say yes!
Man, I think everyone made some awkward fashion choices when they were fourteen.
Anyway! Everyone knows the plan, so let's bust in here and get started, huh?
Hey there, nigh-unbreakable glass! Meet my squirrel claws.
POP
They get right to the point.
SKREEE
SWOOSH

Shoulda paid extra to get rid of that *"nigh"* in front of *"unbreakable glass,"* Tony!

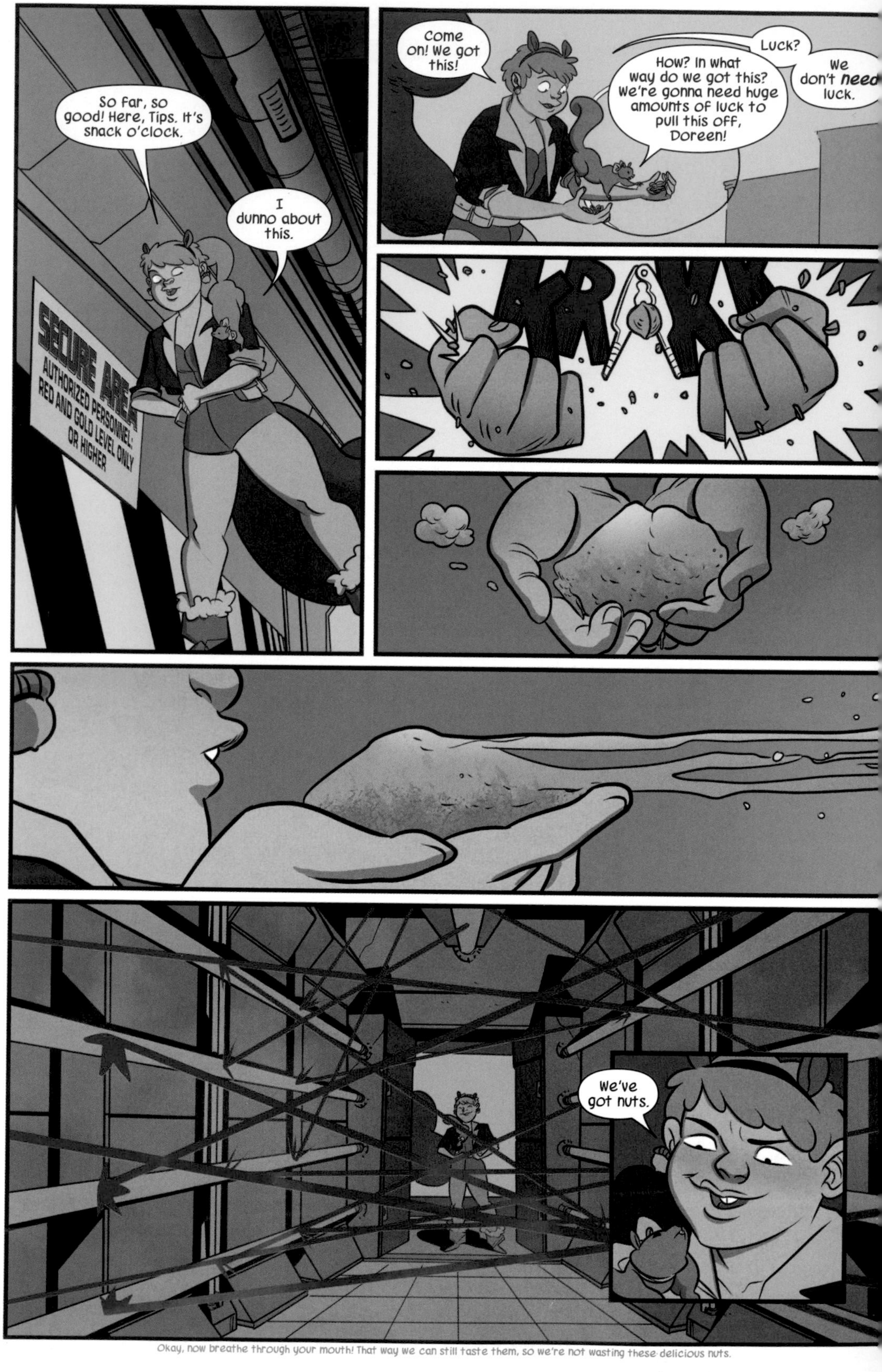
SECURE AREA
AUTHORIZED PERSONNEL: RED AND GOLD LEVEL ONLY OR HIGHER
So far, so good! Here, Tips. It's snack o'clock.
I dunno about this.
Come on! We got this!
How? In what way do we got this? We're gonna need huge amounts of luck to pull this off, Doreen!
Luck?
We don't **need** luck.
KRAK
We've got nuts.
Okay, now breathe through your mouth! That way we can still taste them, so we're not wasting these delicious nuts.

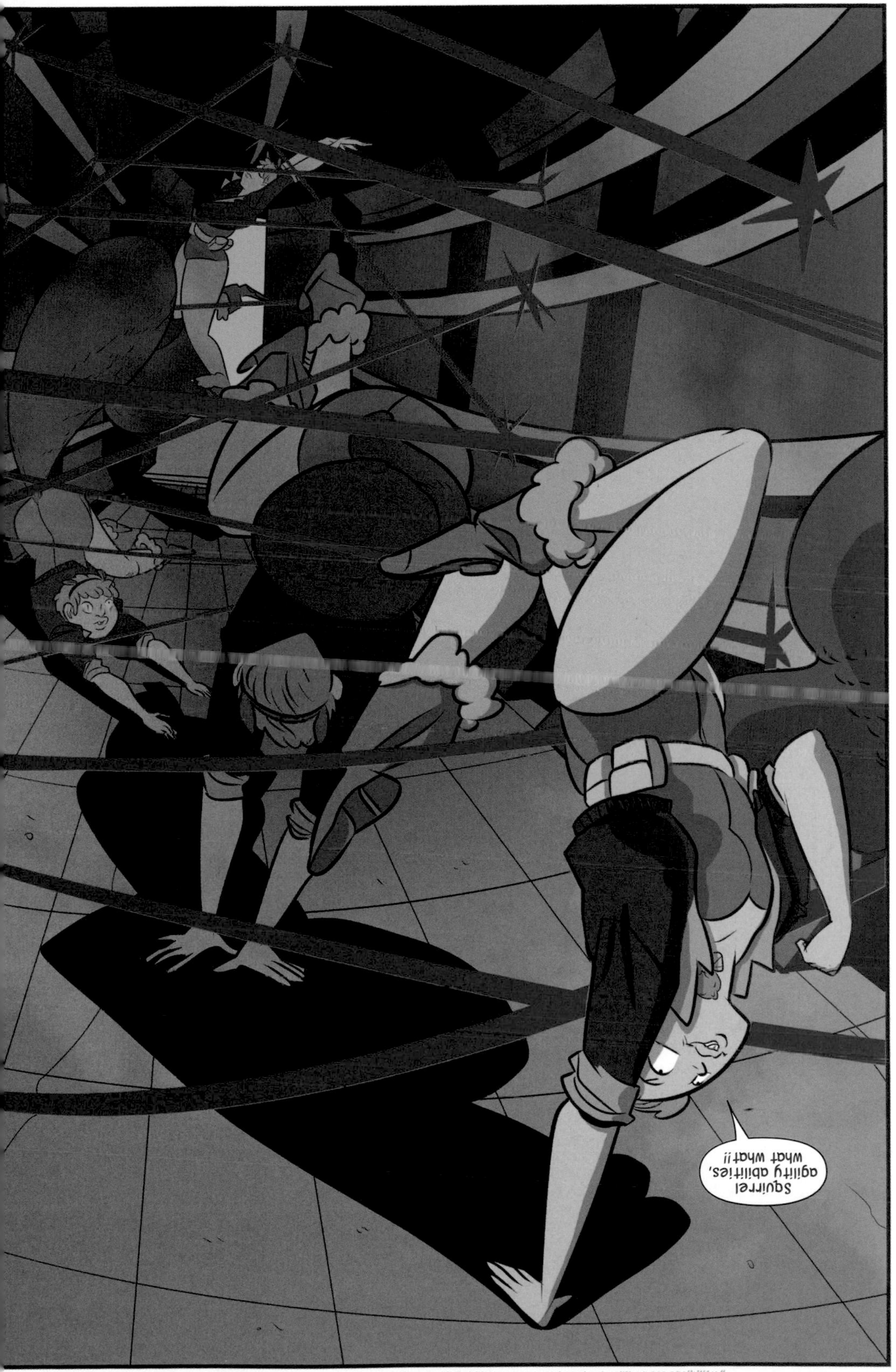
squirrel agility abilities, what what!!

As my Aunt Benjamina used to say, "With great squirrel agility ability comes great squirrel agility responsibility."

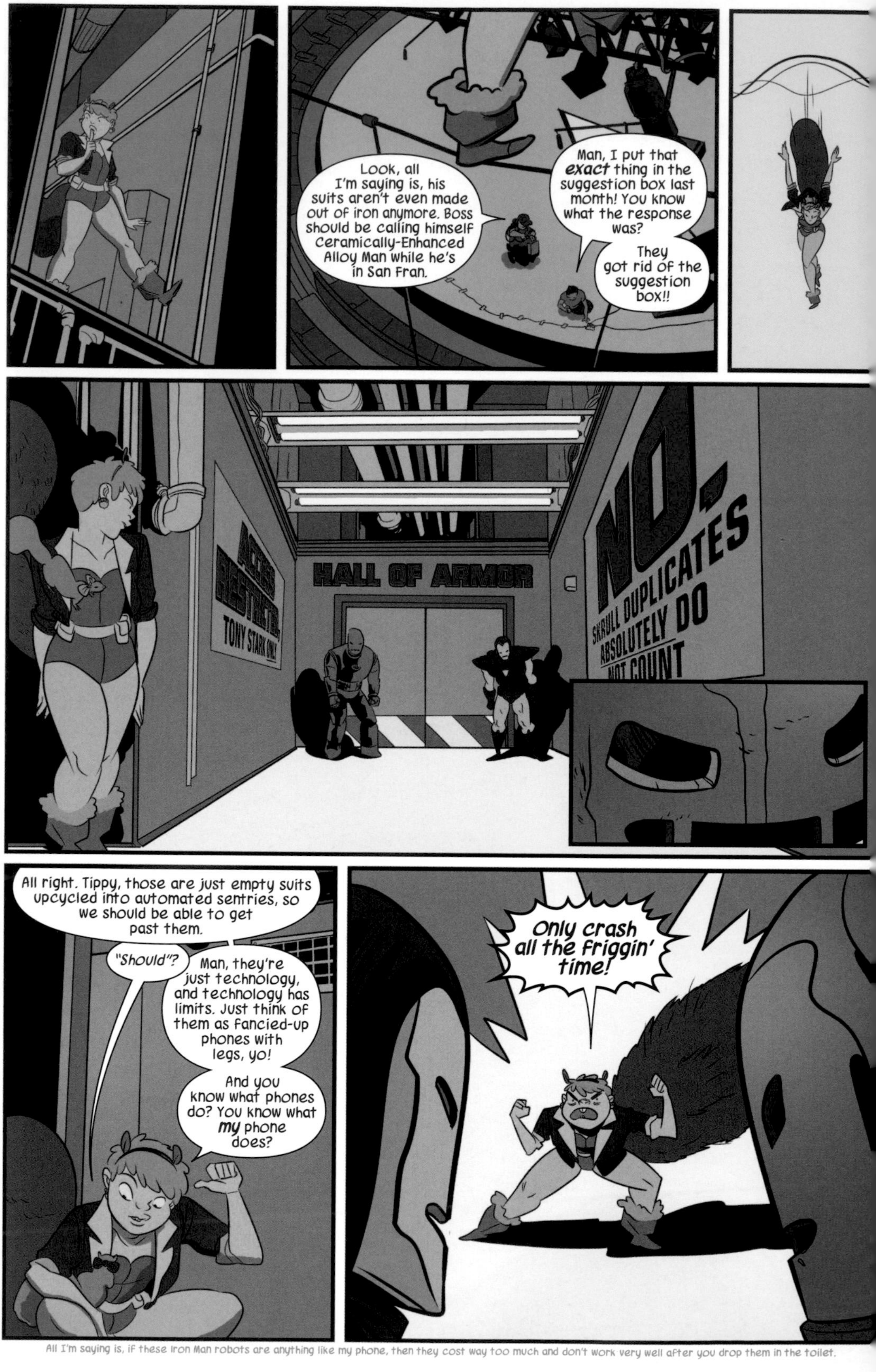
Look, all I'm saying is, his suits aren't even made out of iron anymore. Boss should be calling himself Ceramically-Enhanced Alloy Man while he's in San Fran.
Man, I put that *exact* thing in the suggestion box last month! You know what the response was?
They got rid of the suggestion box!!
ACCESS RESTRICTED. TONY STARK ONLY
HALL OF ARMOR
NO. SKRULL DUPLICATES ABSOLUTELY DO NOT COUNT
All right. Tippy, those are just empty suits upcycled into automated sentries, so we should be able to get past them.
"Should"?
Man, they're just technology, and technology has limits. Just think of them as fancied-up phones with legs, yo!
And you know what phones do? You know what *my* phone does?
Only crash all the friggin' time!

All I'm saying is, if these Iron Man robots are anything like my phone, then they cost way too much and don't work very well after you drop them in the toilet.

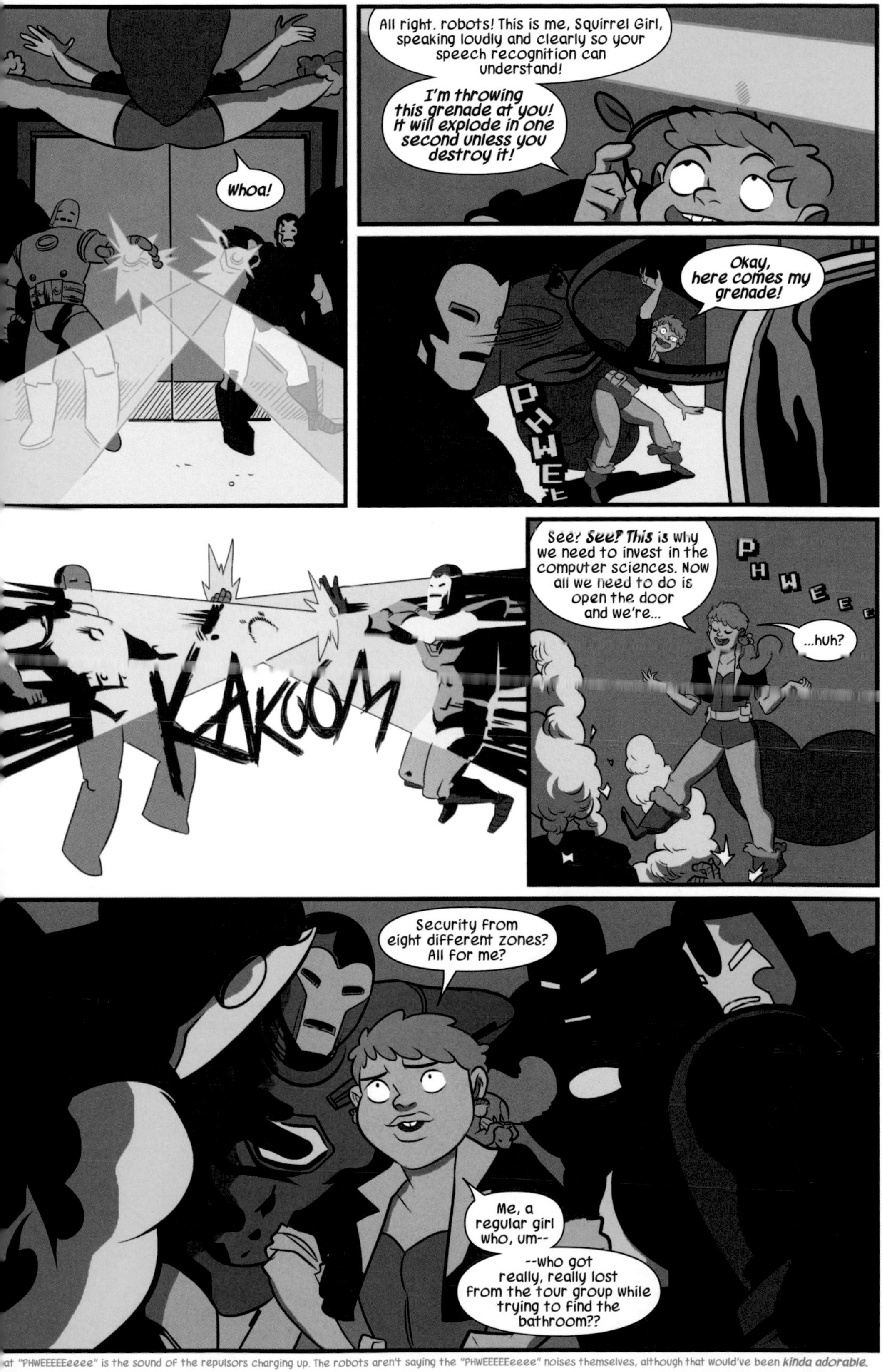
Whoa!
All right, robots! This is me, Squirrel Girl, speaking loudly and clearly so your speech recognition can understand!
I'm throwing this grenade at you! It will explode in one second unless you destroy it!
Okay, here comes my grenade!
PHWEE
KAKOOM
See? *See? This* is why we need to invest in the computer sciences. Now all we need to do is open the door and we're...
PHWEEE
...huh?
Security from eight different zones? All for me?
Me, a regular girl who, um--
--who got really, really lost from the tour group while trying to find the bathroom??

at "PHWEEEEEeeee" is the sound of the repulsors charging up. The robots aren't saying the "PHWEEEEEeeee" noises themselves, although that would've been ***kinda adorable.***

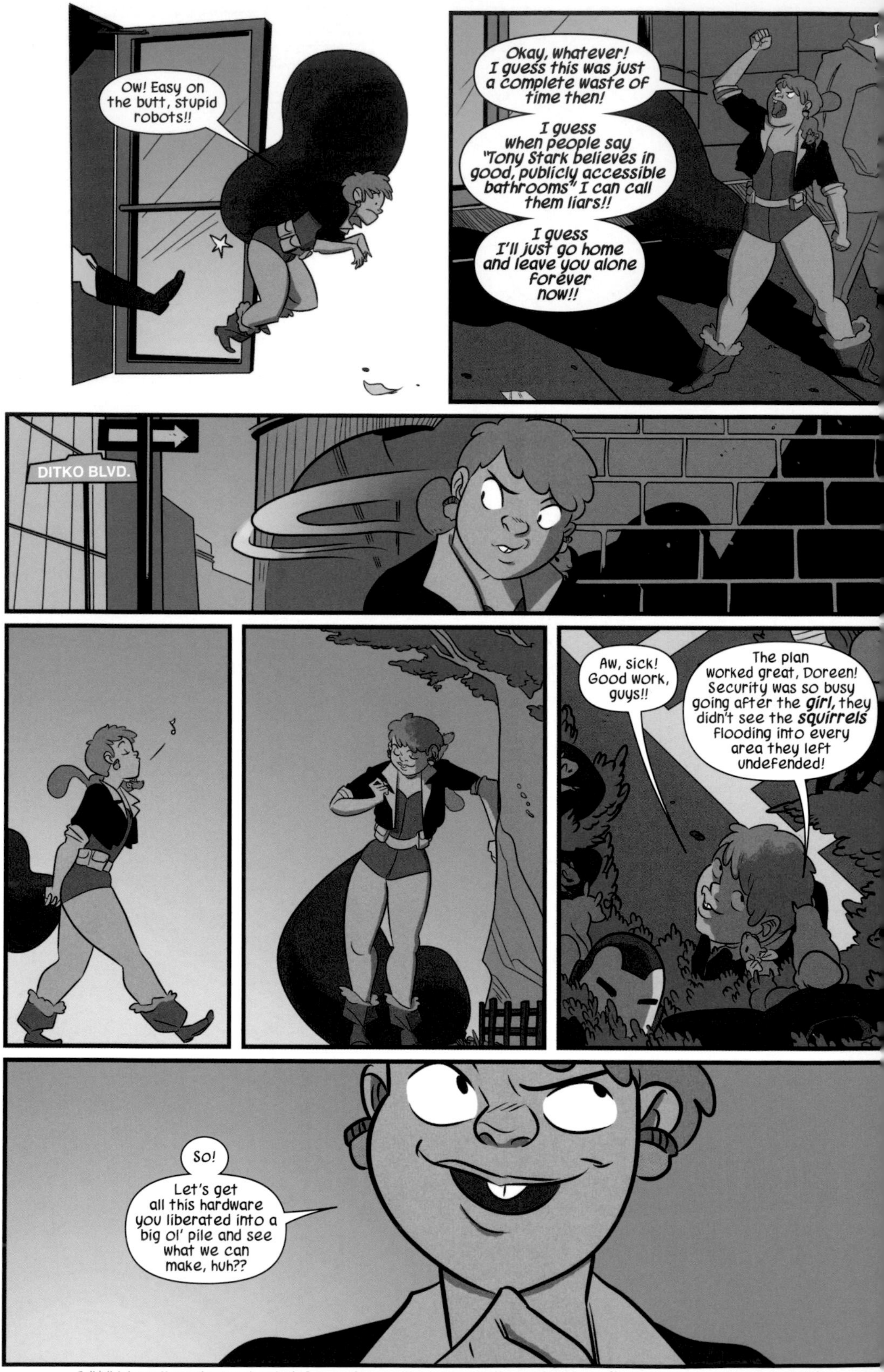

Ow! Easy on the butt, stupid robots!!
Okay, whatever! I guess this was just a complete waste of time then!
I guess when people say "Tony Stark believes in good, publicly accessible bathrooms" I can call them liars!!
I guess I'll just go home and leave you alone forever now!!
DITKO BLVD.
Aw, sick! Good work, guys!!
The plan worked great, Doreen! Security was so busy going after the girl, they didn't see the squirrels flooding into every area they left undefended!
So!
Let's get all this hardware you liberated into a big ol' pile and see what we can make, huh??

I didn't let you, the reader, know her plan before now because it's a better narrative surprise this way! ***Also:*** how do I know I can trust you, huh?? You could be ***literally anyone.***

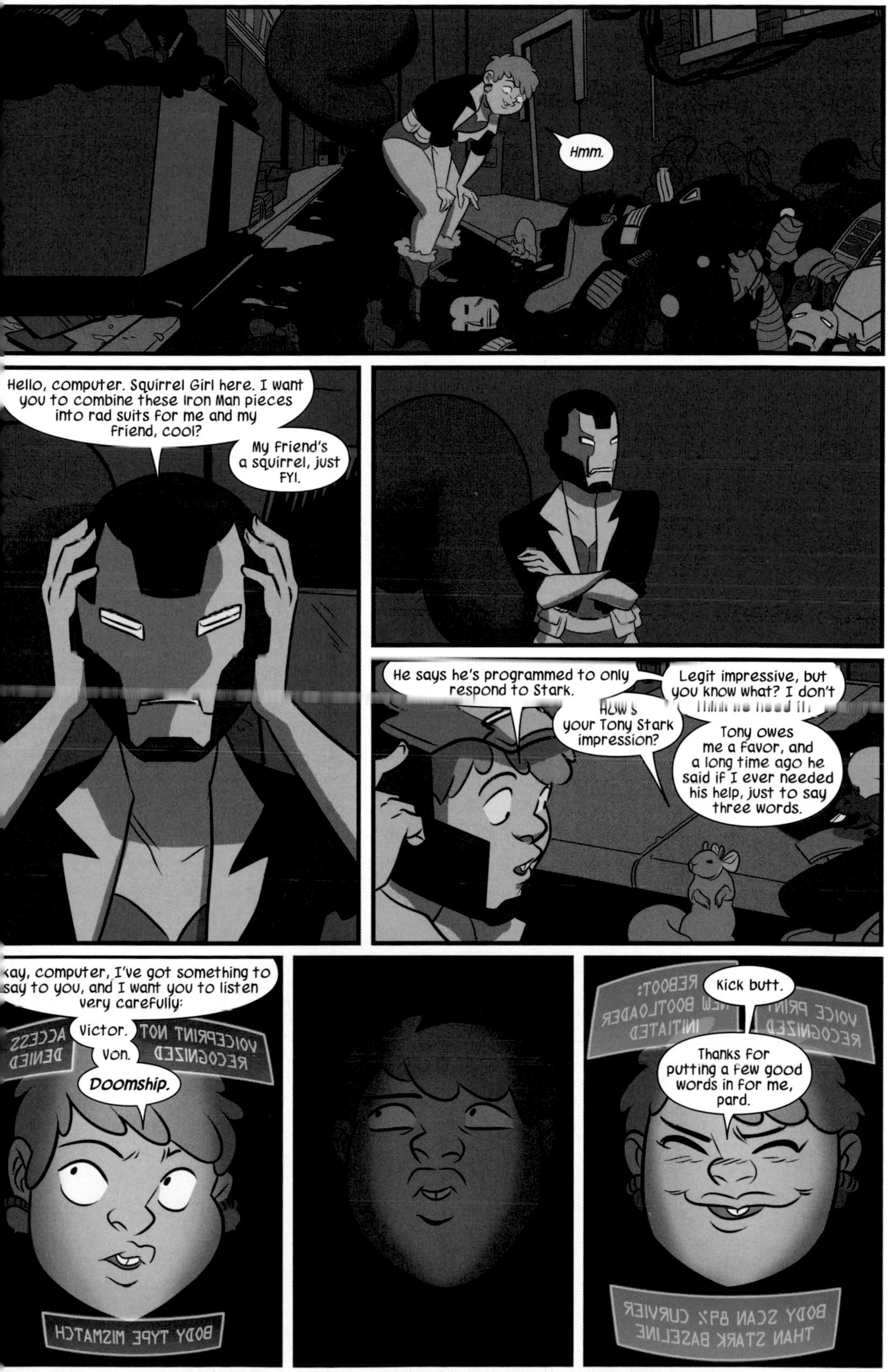
Hmm.
Hello, computer. Squirrel Girl here. I want you to combine these Iron Man pieces into rad suits for me and my friend, cool?
My friend's a squirrel, just FYI.
He says he's programmed to only respond to Stark.
How's your Tony Stark impression?
Legit impressive, but you know what? I don't
Tony owes me a favor, and a long time ago he said if I ever needed his help, just to say three words.
kay, computer, I've got something to say to you, and I want you to listen very carefully:
ACCESS DENIED
VOICEPRINT NOT RECOGNIZED
Victor.
Von.
Doomship.
BODY TYPE MISMATCH
REBOOT: NEW BOOTLOADER INITIATED
VOICE PRINT RECOGNIZED
Kick butt.
Thanks for putting a few good words in for me, pard.
BODY SCAN 89% CURVIER THAN STARK BASELINE

BODY TYPE: Rad / TAIL TYPE: Unexpected / CLAW TYPE: Geez, Tony, you really need to get these nails under control.

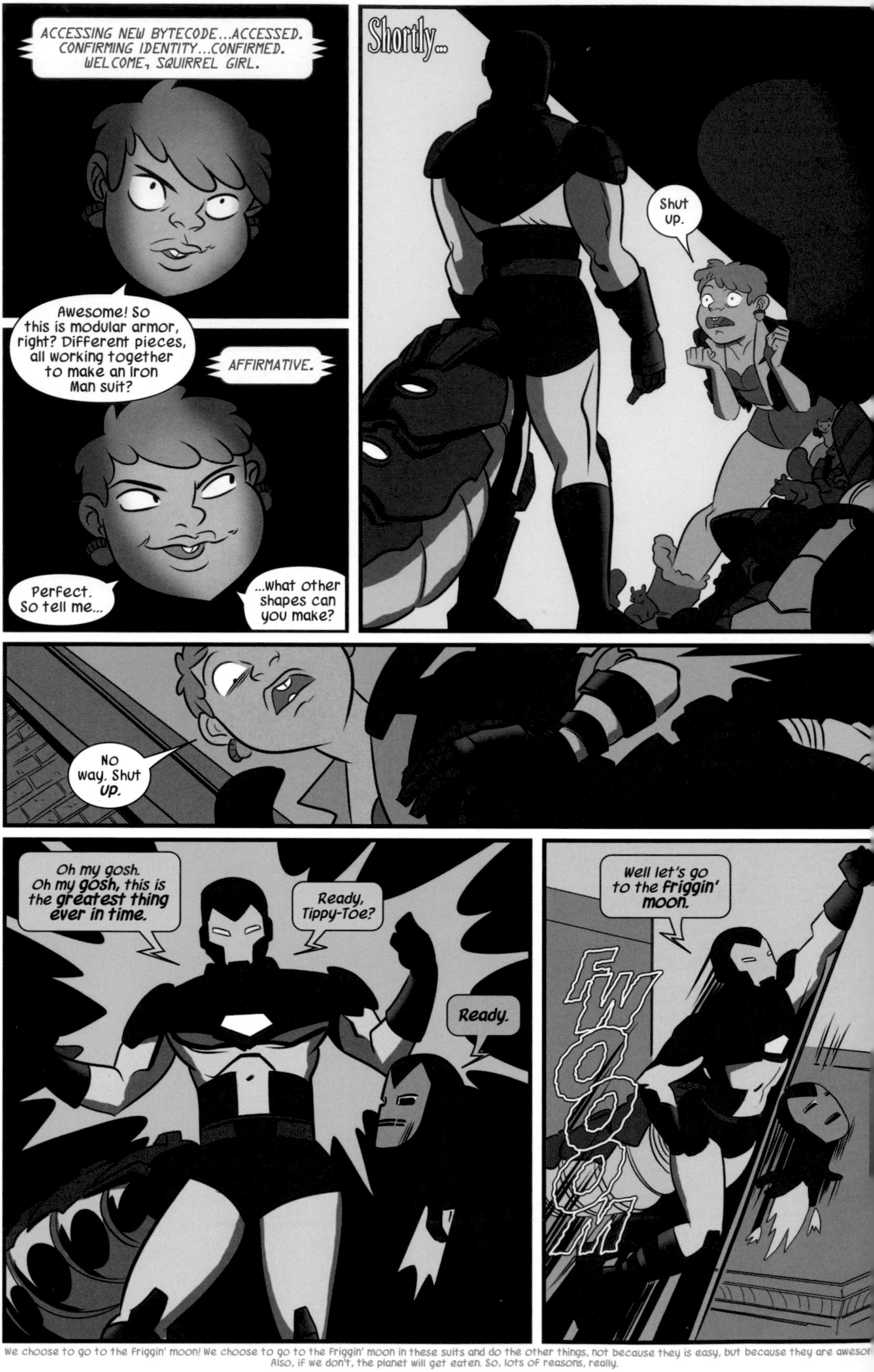
ACCESSING NEW BYTECODE...ACCESSED. CONFIRMING IDENTITY...CONFIRMED. WELCOME, SQUIRREL GIRL.
Awesome! So this is modular armor, right? Different pieces, all working together to make an Iron Man suit?
AFFIRMATIVE.
Perfect. So tell me...
...what other shapes can you make?
Shortly...
Shut up.
No way. Shut up.
Oh my gosh. Oh my gosh, this is the greatest thing ever in time.
Ready, Tippy-Toe?
Ready.
Well let's go to the friggin' moon.
FWOOOOM

We choose to go to the friggin' moon! We choose to go to the friggin' moon in these suits and do the other things, not because they is easy, but because they are awesor
Also, if we don't, the planet will get eaten. So, lots of reasons, really.

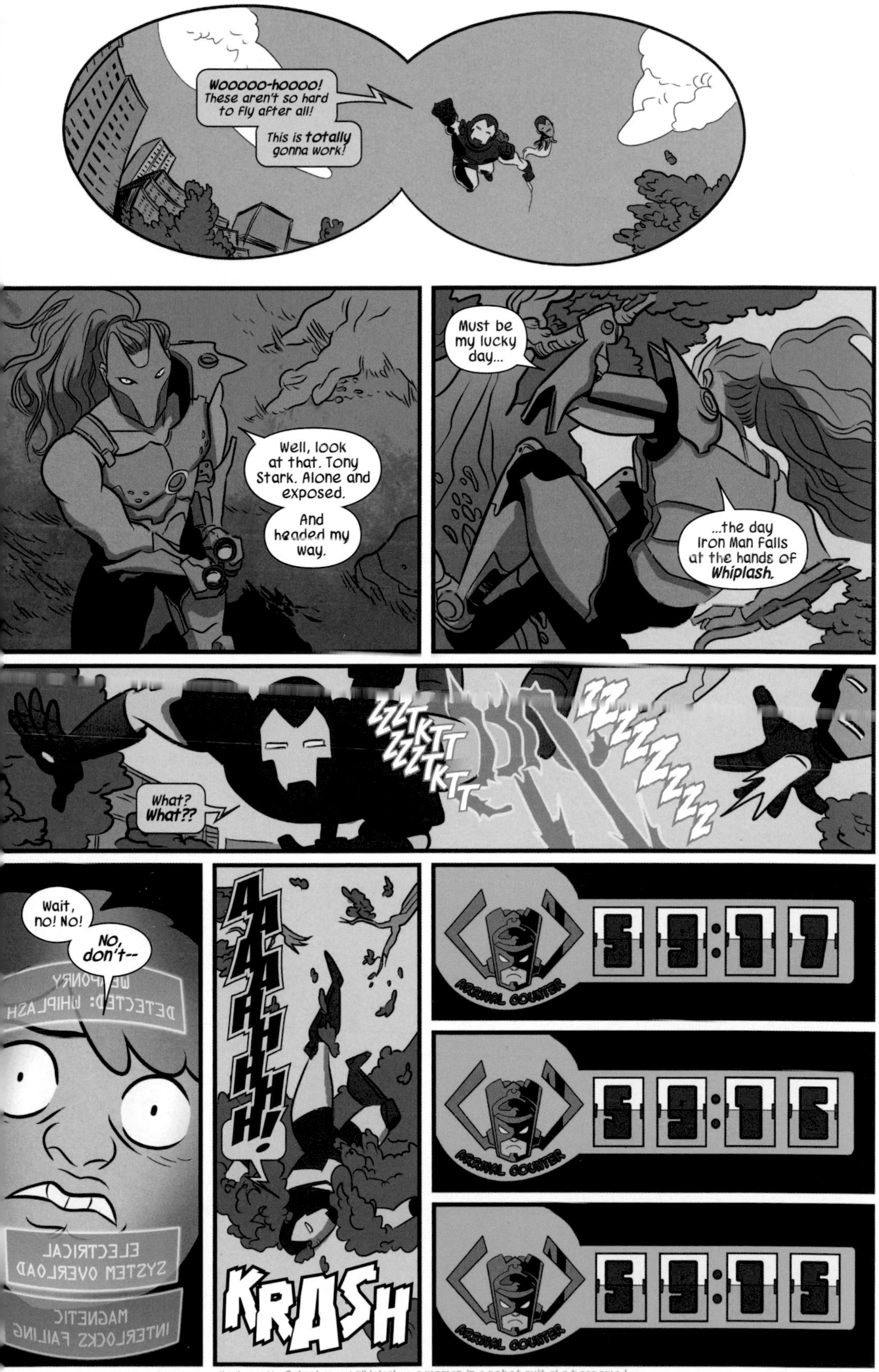
Wooooo-hoooo! These aren't so hard to fly after all!
This is totally gonna work!
Well, look at that. Tony Stark. Alone and exposed.
And headed my way.
Must be my lucky day...
...the day Iron Man falls at the hands of Whiplash.
ZZZTKTT ZZZTKTT
What? What??
Wait, no! No!
No, don't--
WEAPONRY DETECTED: WHIPLASH
ELECTRICAL SYSTEM OVERLOAD
MAGNETIC INTERLOCKS FAILING
KRASH
59:17
ARRIVAL COUNTER
59:16
ARRIVAL COUNTER
59:15
ARRIVAL COUNTER

Next month: *Galactus* and *Whiplash* vs *a woman in a robot suit she borrowed.*

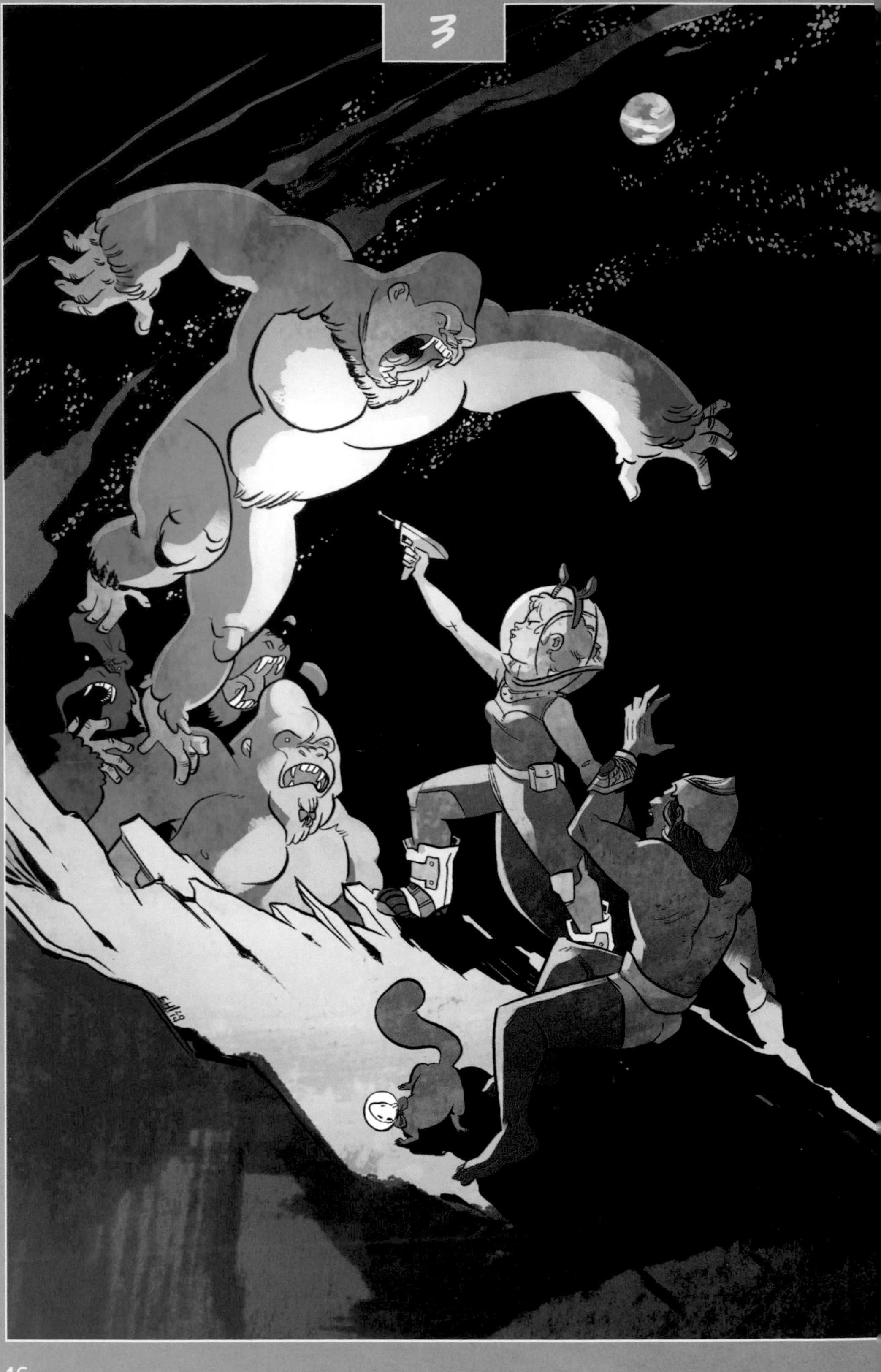
3

reen Green isn't just a first-year computer science student: she secretly also has all the powers of both squirrel and girl!
uses her amazing abilities to fight crime **and** be as awesome as possible. You know her as...**The Unbeatable Squirrel Girl!**
Let's catch up with what she's been up to until now, with...

Squirrel Girl *in a nutshell*

Squirrel Girl! @unbeatablesg
Did you guys see how I took care of Kraven the other day?

xKravenTheHunterx @unshavenkraven
NOBODY LISTEN TO @unbeatablesg, SHE DIDN'T TAKE CARE OF ME, I MERELY DECIDED TO STOP FIGHTING HER

Squirrel Girl! @unbeatablesg
@unshavenkraven hey dude did you kill any gigantos underwater like I suggested?

xKravenTheHunterx @unshavenkraven
@unbeatablesg listen

xKravenTheHunterx @unshavenkraven
@unbeatablesg these things take time

Squirrel Girl! @unbeatablesg
Apparently I'm the only one that can see that GALACTUS IS COMING TO EARTH!!

Tippy-Toe @yoitstippytoe
CHIT CHUKKA CHITTY

Squirrel Girl! @unbeatablesg
Apparently me and @yoitstippytoe are the only ones that can see GALACTUS IS COMING TO EARTH!!

Squirrel Girl! @unbeatablesg
Oh well

Squirrel Girl! @unbeatablesg
guess we'll just have to stop him ourselves then

Squirrel Girl! @unbeatablesg
ON THE FRIGGIN' MOON

Tony Stark @starkmantony
Whoever "borrowed" Iron Man armor parts from my NYC offices, please return them. Looking at you, @unbeatablesg.

Squirrel Girl! @unbeatablesg
@starkmantony Tony it's REALLY IMPORTANT. Like COSMIC important.

Squirrel Girl! @unbeatablesg
@starkmantony I don't know why I'm being coy. It's for Galactus.

Squirrel Girl! @unbeatablesg
@starkmantony I'm gonna beat up @xGALACTUSx, Tony!! ON THE MOON

Tony Stark @starkmantony
@unbeatablesg You break it, you bought it.

Whiplash @realwhiplash22
I JUST WHIPPED @STARKMANTONY OUT OF THE SKY WITH MY ENERGY WHIPS YES YES #OWNED

Tony Stark @starkmantony
Wasn't me. I'm in San Francisco, @realwhiplash22.

Whiplash @realwhiplash22
@starkmantony SORRY I CANNOT HEAR YOU OVER HOW BADLY YOU GOT #OWNED

search!

- #OWNED
- #everythingisnormalinspace
- Welcome to
- #USG
- Number Three
- Hope you like falafel jokes

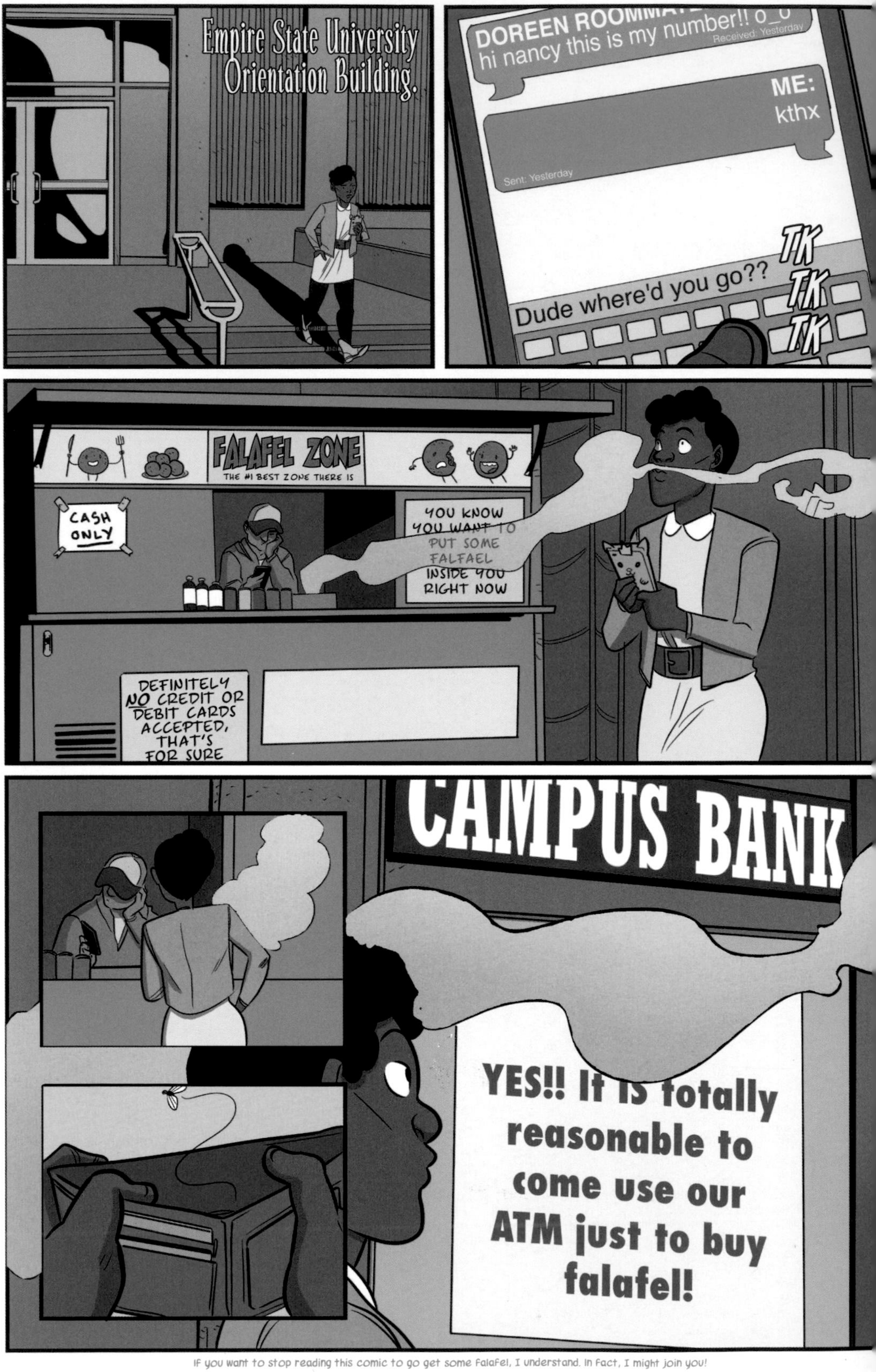
Empire State University Orientation Building.
DOREEN ROOMMATE
hi nancy this is my number!! o_o
Received: Yesterday
ME:
kthx
Sent: Yesterday
Dude where'd you go??
TK
TK
TK
FALAFEL ZONE
THE #1 BEST ZONE THERE IS
CASH ONLY
YOU KNOW YOU WANT TO PUT SOME FALFAEL INSIDE YOU RIGHT NOW
DEFINITELY NO CREDIT OR DEBIT CARDS ACCEPTED, THAT'S FOR SURE
CAMPUS BANK
YES!! It IS totally reasonable to come use our ATM just to buy falafel!

If you want to stop reading this comic to go get some falafel, I understand. In fact, I might join you!

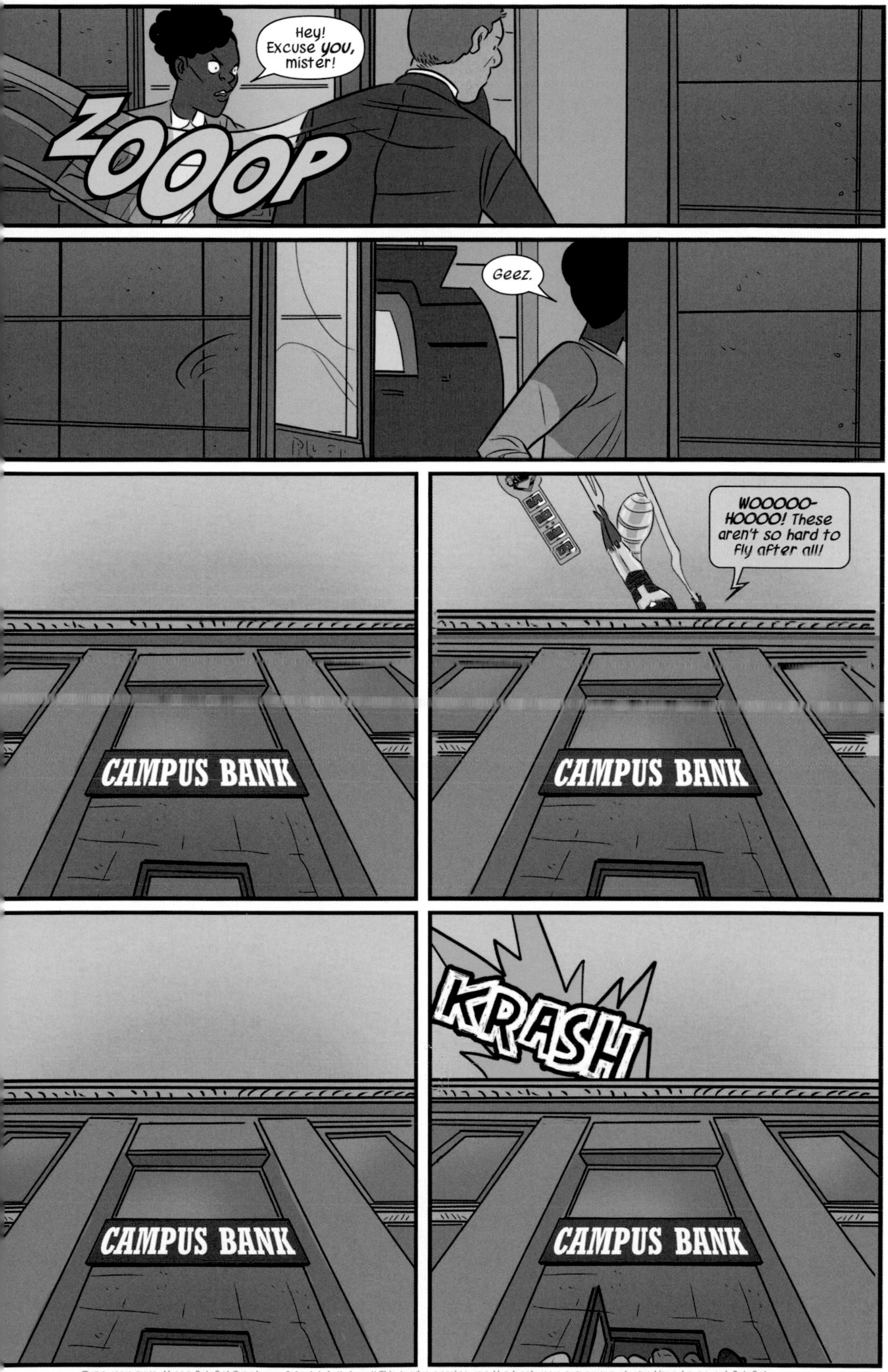
Hey! Excuse *you*, mister!
ZOOOP
Geez.
CAMPUS BANK
WOOOOO-HOOOO! These aren't so hard to fly after all!
CAMPUS BANK
CAMPUS BANK
KRASH
CAMPUS BANK

Dang, you guys, these falafel I got are friggin' delicious!! This is why comics are the best: you can pause at any time to go eat falafel, so check and mate, *all other media.* Except books, I guess. *Fine,* books are good, too.

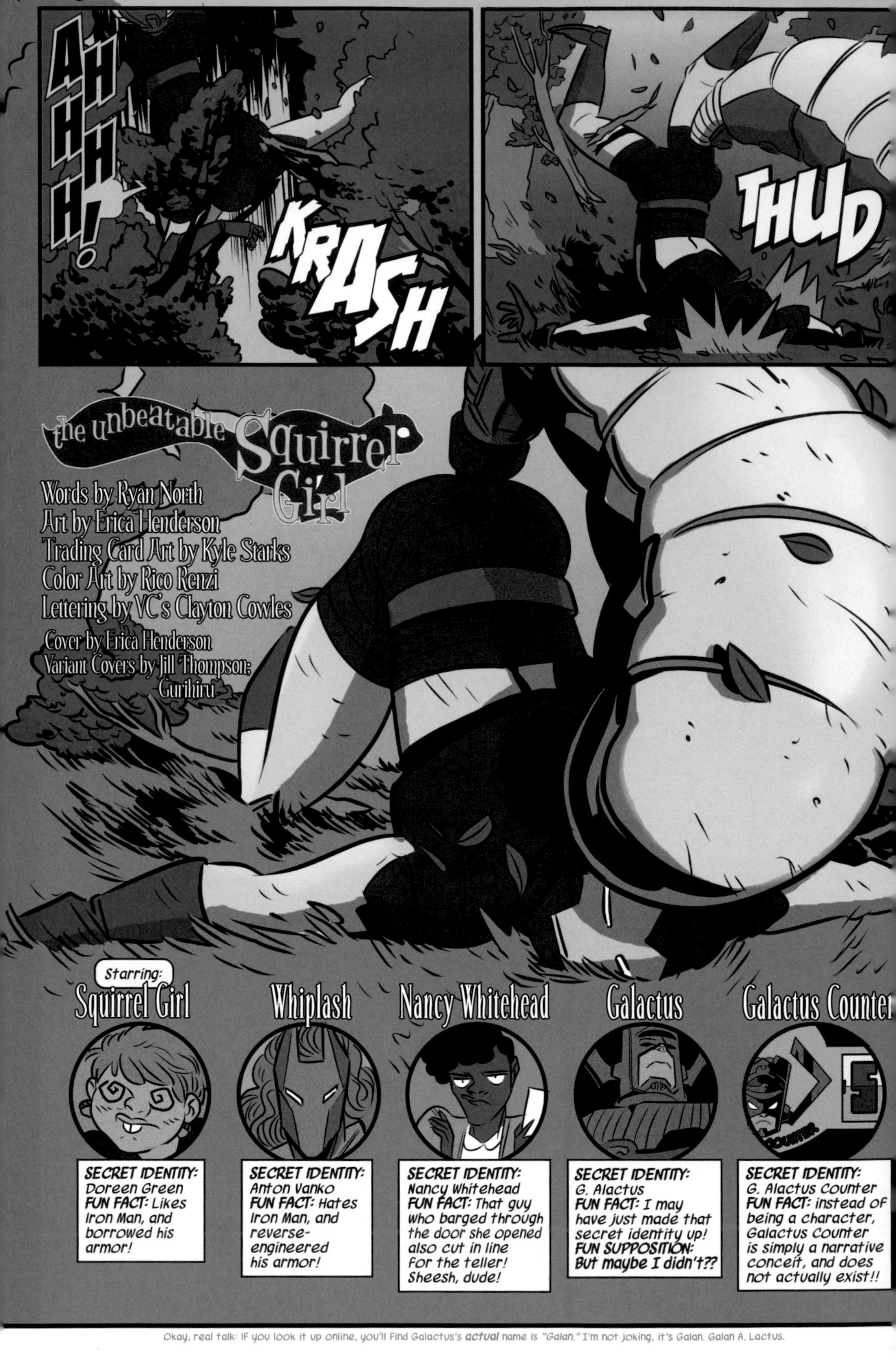
AHHHHH!
KRASH
THUD
the unbeatable Squirrel Girl
Words by Ryan North
Art by Erica Henderson
Trading Card Art by Kyle Starks
Color Art by Rico Renzi
Lettering by VC's Clayton Cowles
Cover by Erica Henderson
Variant Covers by Jill Thompson; Gurihiru
Starring:
Squirrel Girl
SECRET IDENTITY: Doreen Green
FUN FACT: Likes Iron Man, and borrowed his armor!
Whiplash
SECRET IDENTITY: Anton Vanko
FUN FACT: Hates Iron Man, and reverse-engineered his armor!
Nancy Whitehead
SECRET IDENTITY: Nancy Whitehead
FUN FACT: That guy who barged through the door she opened also cut in line for the teller! Sheesh, dude!
Galactus
SECRET IDENTITY: G. Alactus
FUN FACT: I may have just made that secret identity up!
FUN SUPPOSITION: But maybe I didn't??
Galactus Counter
SECRET IDENTITY: G. Alactus Counter
FUN FACT: instead of being a character, Galactus Counter is simply a narrative conceit, and does not actually exist!!

Okay, real talk: If you look it up online, you'll find Galactus's *actual* name is *"Galan."* I'm not joking, it's Galan. Galan A. Lactus.

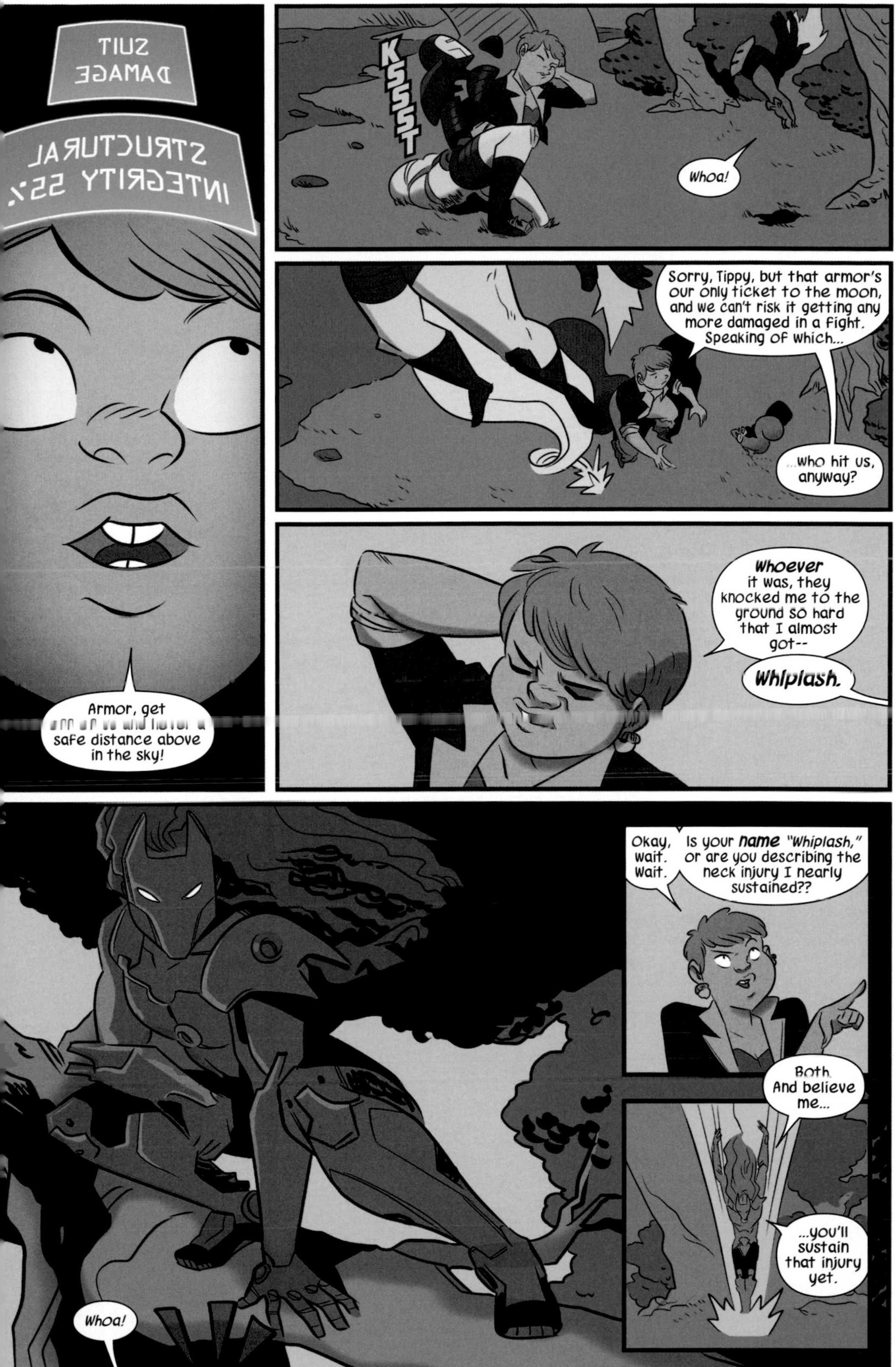
SUIT DAMAGE
STRUCTURAL INTEGRITY 55%
Armor, get
safe distance above in the sky!
KSSST
Whoa!
Sorry, Tippy, but that armor's our only ticket to the moon, and we can't risk it getting any more damaged in a fight. Speaking of which...
...who hit us, anyway?
Whoever it was, they knocked me to the ground so hard that I almost got--
Whiplash.
Okay, wait. Wait.
Is your **name** "Whiplash," or are you describing the neck injury I nearly sustained??
Both. And believe me...
...you'll sustain that injury yet.
Whoa!

it, this makes two Russian nationals that Doreen has faced off against in as many issues! Looks like these comic issues have their *own* not-so-comic issues, am I right??

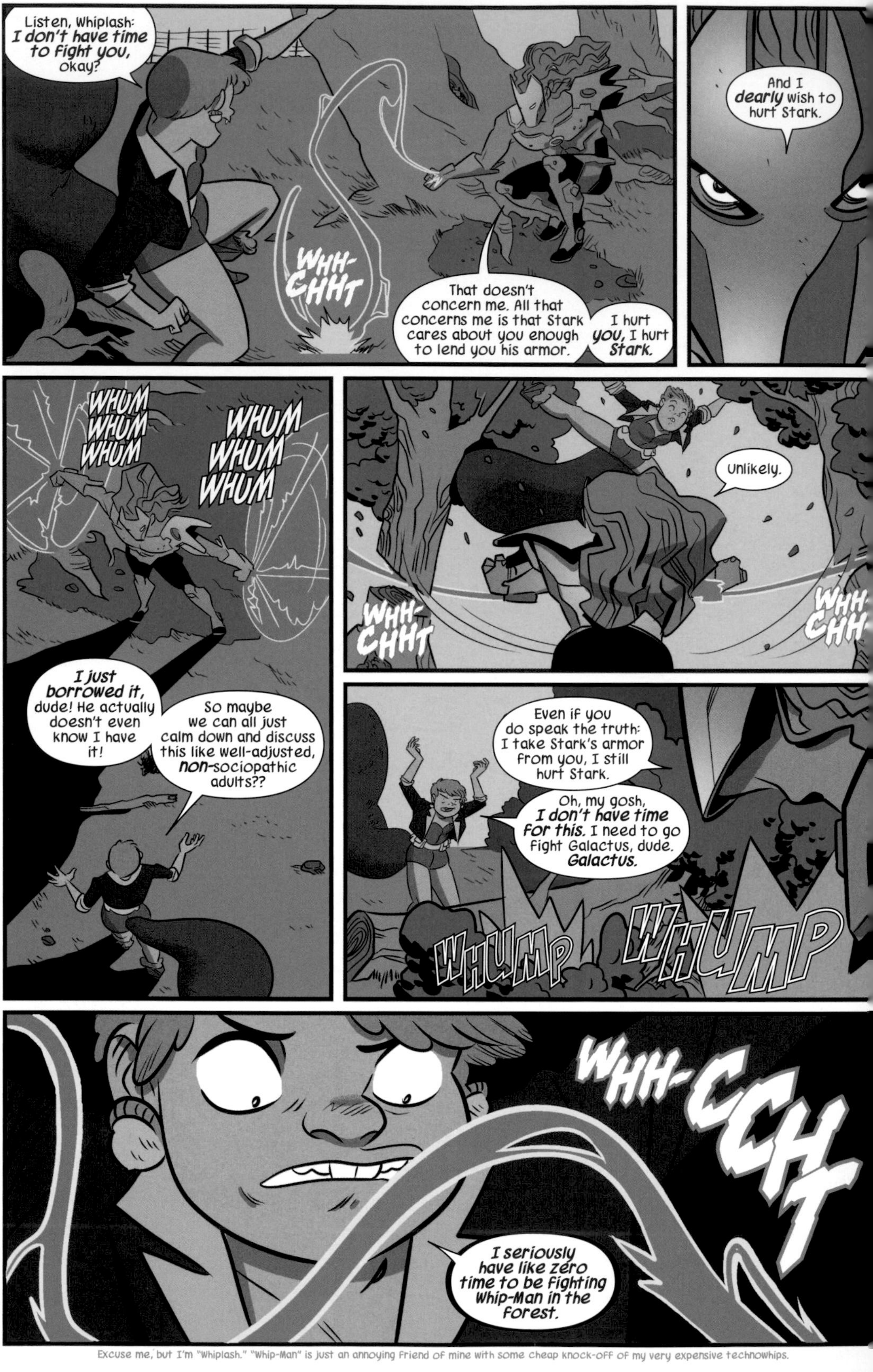

Listen, Whiplash: *I don't have time to fight you,* okay?
WHH-CHHT
That doesn't concern me. All that concerns me is that Stark cares about you enough to lend you his armor.
I hurt *you,* I hurt *Stark.*
And I *dearly* wish to hurt Stark.
WHUM WHUM WHUM
WHUM WHUM WHUM
Unlikely.
WHH-CHHT
WHH-CHH
I just borrowed it, dude! He actually doesn't even know I have it!
So maybe we can all just calm down and discuss this like well-adjusted, *non*-sociopathic adults??
Even if you do speak the truth: I take Stark's armor from you, I still hurt Stark.
Oh, my gosh, *I don't have time for this.* I need to go fight Galactus, dude. *Galactus.*
WHUMP
WHUMP
WHH-CCHT
I seriously have like zero time to be fighting Whip-Man in the forest.

Excuse me, but I'm "Whiplash." "Whip-Man" is just an annoying friend of mine with some cheap knock-off of my very expensive technowhips.

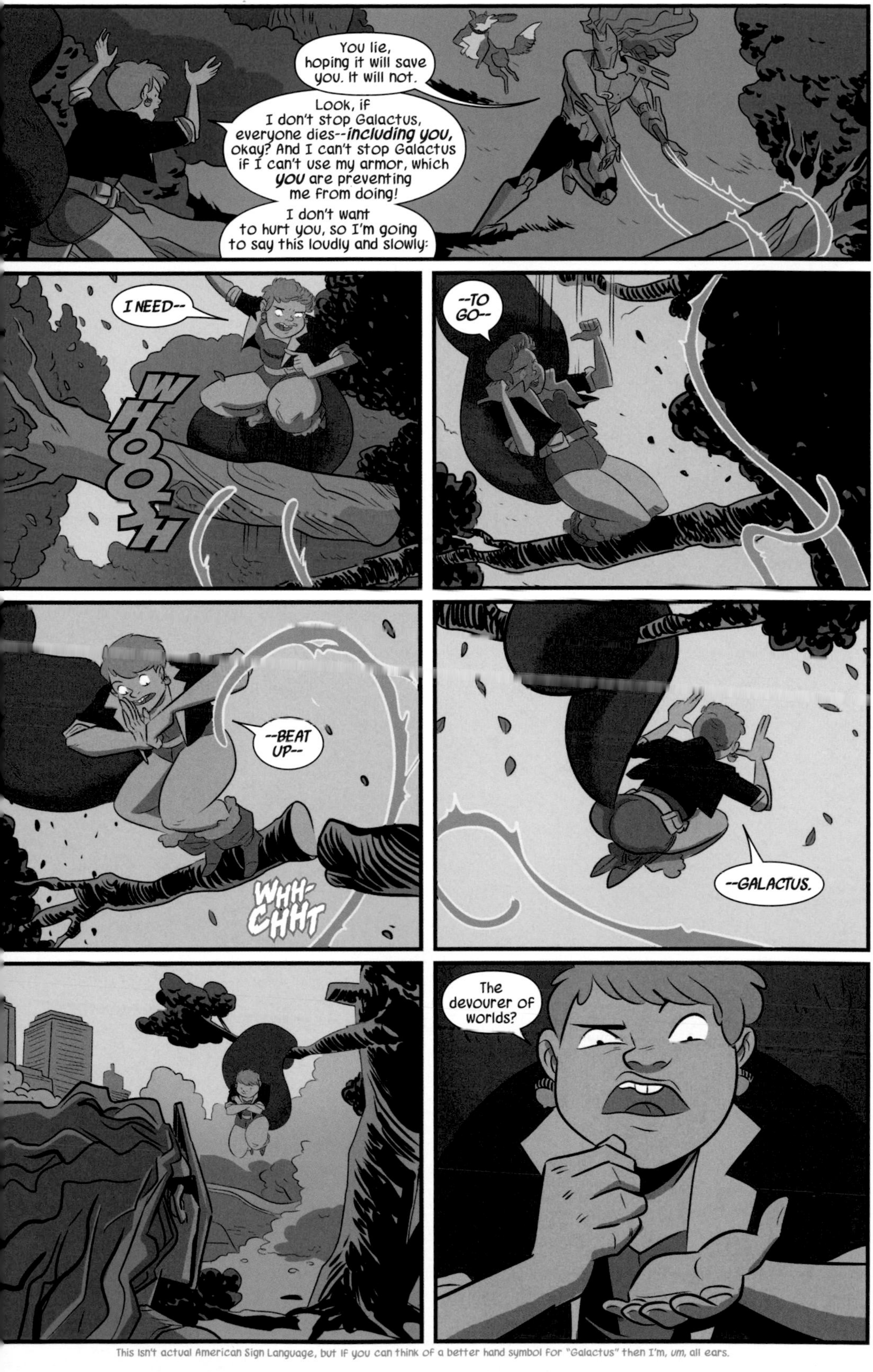
You lie, hoping it will save you. It will not.
Look, if I don't stop Galactus, everyone dies--including you, okay? And I can't stop Galactus if I can't use my armor, which you are preventing me from doing!
I don't want to hurt you, so I'm going to say this loudly and slowly:
I NEED--
WHOOOSH
--TO GO--
--BEAT UP--
WHH-CHHT
--GALACTUS.
The devourer of worlds?

This isn't actual American Sign Language, but if you can think of a better hand symbol for "Galactus" then I'm, *um,* all ears.

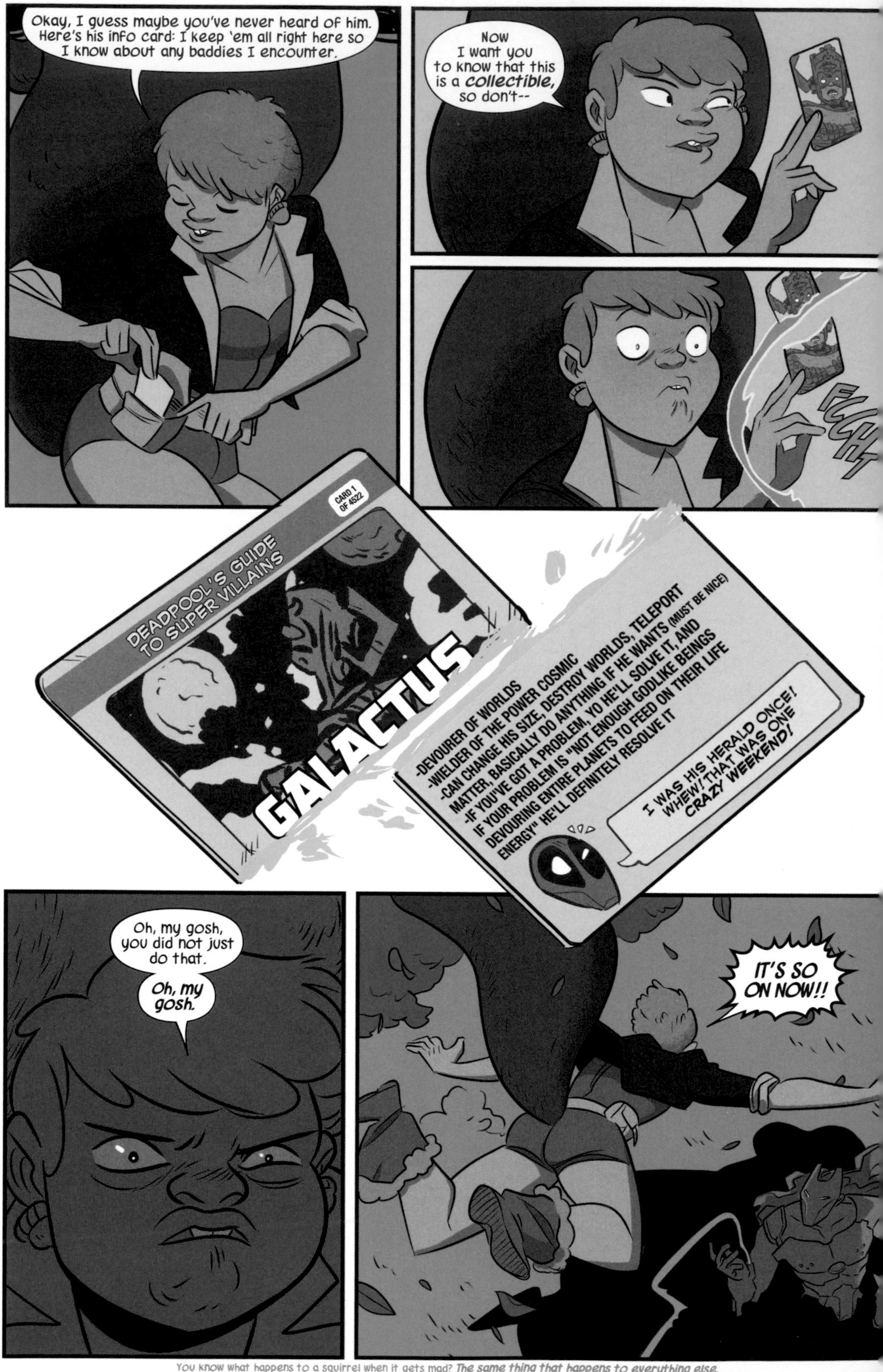
Okay, I guess maybe you've never heard of him. Here's his info card: I keep 'em all right here so I know about any baddies I encounter.
Now I want you to know that this is a *collectible*, so don't--
FCHT
DEADPOOL'S GUIDE TO SUPER VILLAINS
CARD 1 OF 4522
GALACTUS
-DEVOURER OF WORLDS
-WIELDER OF THE POWER COSMIC
-CAN CHANGE HIS SIZE, DESTROY WORLDS, TELEPORT MATTER, BASICALLY DO ANYTHING IF HE WANTS (MUST BE NICE)
-IF YOU'VE GOT A PROBLEM, YO HE'LL SOLVE IT, AND IF YOUR PROBLEM IS "NOT ENOUGH GODLIKE BEINGS DEVOURING ENTIRE PLANETS TO FEED ON THEIR LIFE ENERGY" HE'LL DEFINITELY RESOLVE IT
I WAS HIS HERALD ONCE! *WHEW!* THAT WAS ONE *CRAZY WEEKEND!*
Oh, my gosh, you did not just do that.
Oh, my gosh.
IT'S SO ON NOW!!

You know what happens to a squirrel when it gets mad? ***The same thing that happens to everything else.***
Which is to say, increased heart rate, elevated adrenaline and norepinephrine production, a lessened capacity for self-monitoring, etc., etc.

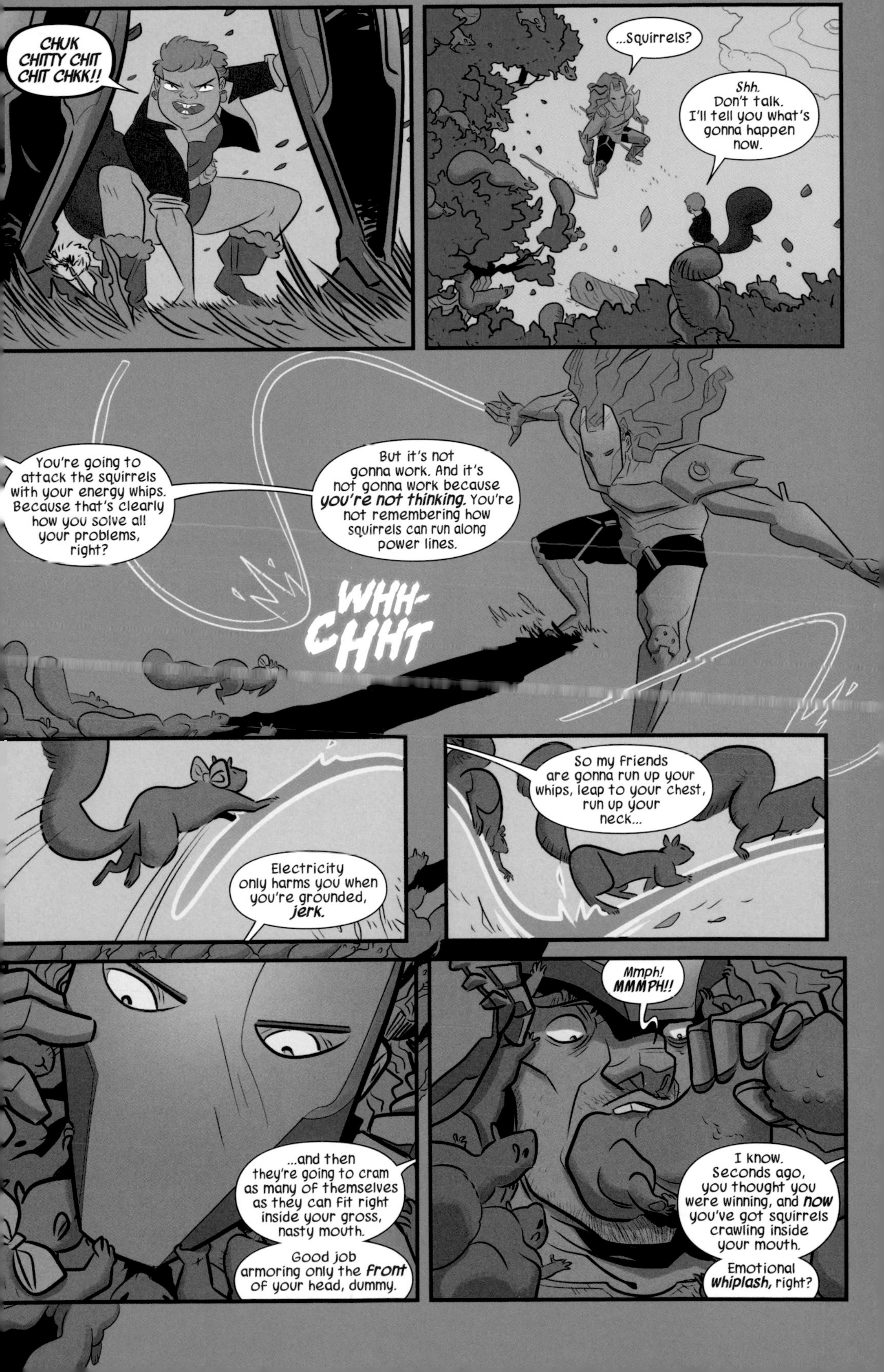
CHUK CHITTY CHIT CHIT CHKK!!
...Squirrels?
Shh. Don't talk. I'll tell you what's gonna happen now.
You're going to attack the squirrels with your energy whips. Because that's clearly how you solve all your problems, right?
But it's not gonna work. And it's not gonna work because *you're not thinking.* You're not remembering how squirrels can run along power lines.
WHH-CHHT
Electricity only harms you when you're grounded, *jerk.*
So my friends are gonna run up your whips, leap to your chest, run up your neck...
...and then they're going to cram as many of themselves as they can fit right inside your gross, nasty mouth.
Good job armoring only the *front* of your head, dummy.
Mmph! MMMPH!!
I know. Seconds ago, you thought you were winning, and *now* you've got squirrels crawling inside your mouth.
Emotional *whiplash,* right?

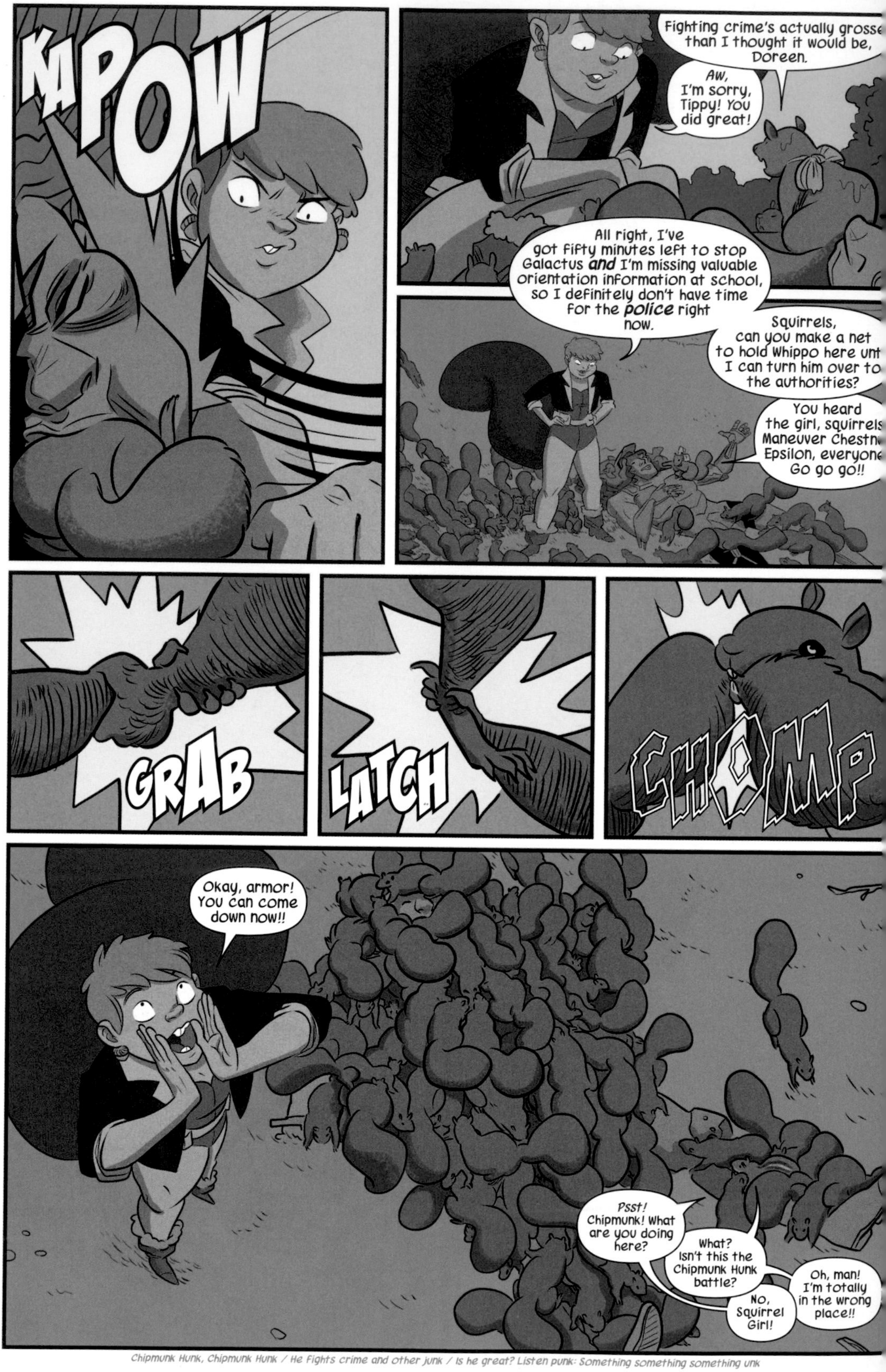
KAPOW
Fighting crime's actually grosse than I thought it would be, Doreen.
Aw, I'm sorry, Tippy! You did great!
All right, I've got fifty minutes left to stop Galactus **and** I'm missing valuable orientation information at school, so I definitely don't have time for the **police** right now.
Squirrels, can you make a net to hold Whippo here unt I can turn him over to the authorities?
You heard the girl, squirrels Maneuver Chestn Epsilon, everyone Go go go!!
GRAB
LATCH
CHOMP
Okay, armor! You can come down now!!
Psst! Chipmunk! What are you doing here?
What? Isn't this the Chipmunk Hunk battle?
No, Squirrel Girl!
Oh, man! I'm totally in the wrong place!!

Chipmunk Hunk, Chipmunk Hunk / He fights crime and other junk / Is he great? Listen punk: Something something something unk

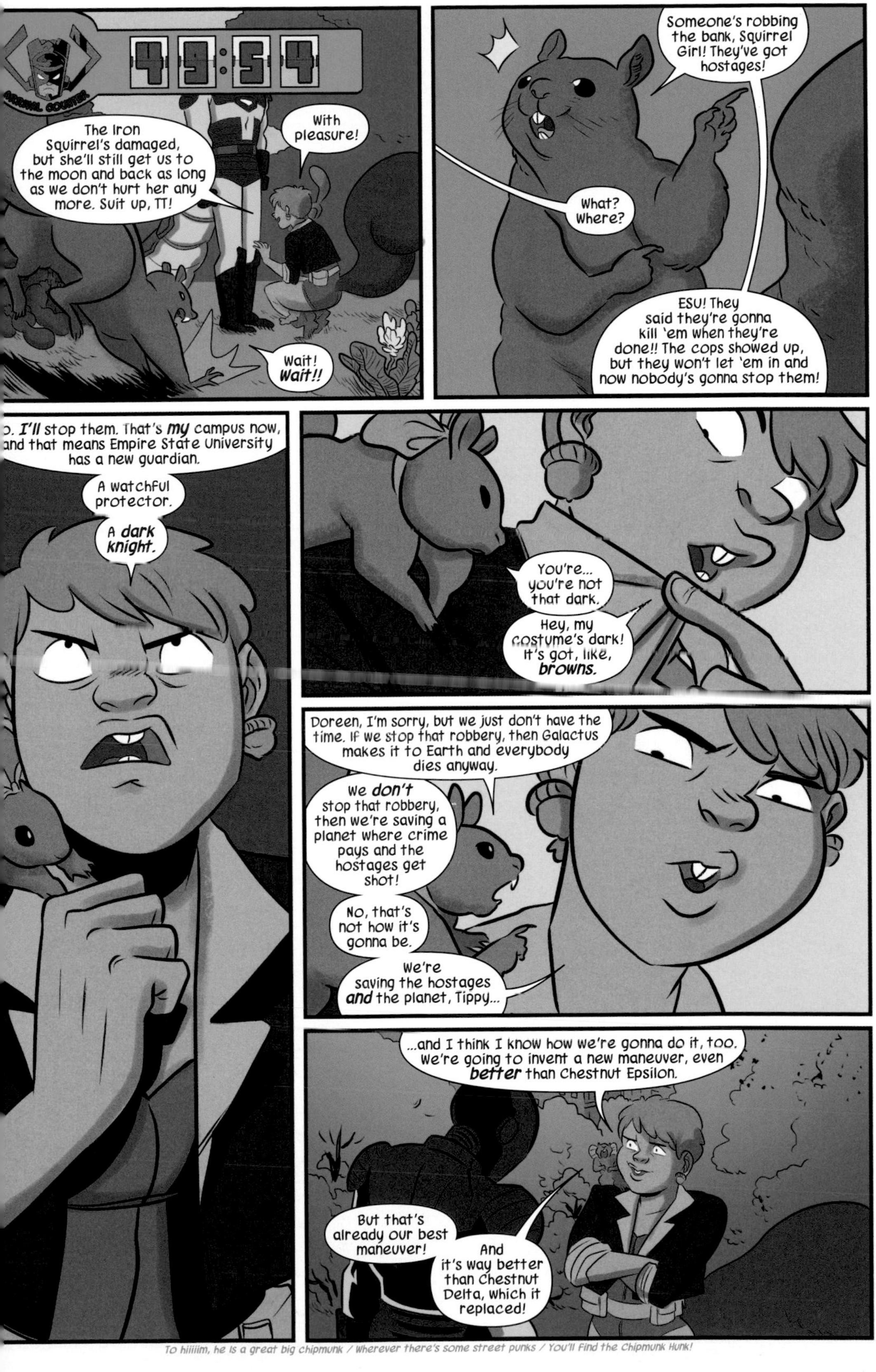
ORBITAL COUNTER
49:54
The Iron Squirrel's damaged, but she'll still get us to the moon and back as long as we don't hurt her any more. Suit up, TT!
With pleasure!
Wait! Wait!!
Someone's robbing the bank, Squirrel Girl! They've got hostages!
What? Where?
ESU! They said they're gonna kill 'em when they're done!! The cops showed up, but they won't let 'em in and now nobody's gonna stop them!
o. I'll stop them. That's my campus now, and that means Empire State University has a new guardian.
A watchful protector.
A dark knight.
You're... you're not that dark.
Hey, my costume's dark! It's got, like, browns.
Doreen, I'm sorry, but we just don't have the time. If we stop that robbery, then Galactus makes it to Earth and everybody dies anyway.
We don't stop that robbery, then we're saving a planet where crime pays and the hostages get shot!
No, that's not how it's gonna be.
We're saving the hostages and the planet, Tippy...
...and I think I know how we're gonna do it, too. We're going to invent a new maneuver, even better than Chestnut Epsilon.
But that's already our best maneuver!
And it's way better than Chestnut Delta, which it replaced!

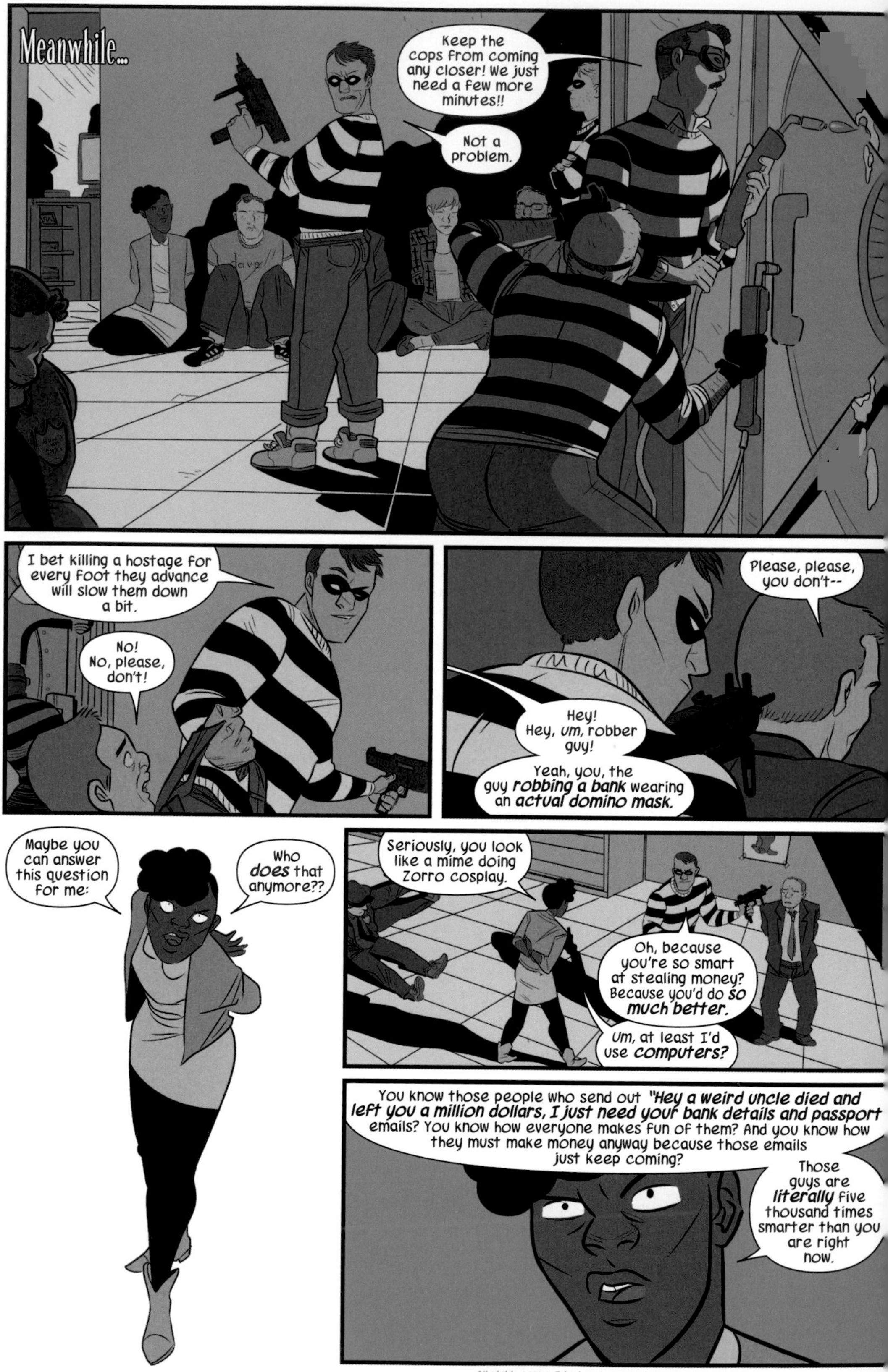
Meanwhile...
Keep the cops from coming any closer! We just need a few more minutes!!
Not a problem.
dave
I bet killing a hostage for every foot they advance will slow them down a bit.
No! No, please, don't!
Please, please, you don't--
Hey! Hey, um, robber guy!
Yeah, you, the guy robbing a bank wearing an actual domino mask.
Maybe you can answer this question for me:
Who does that anymore??
Seriously, you look like a mime doing Zorro cosplay.
Oh, because you're so smart at stealing money? Because you'd do so much better.
Um, at least I'd use computers?
You know those people who send out "Hey a weird uncle died and left you a million dollars, I just need your bank details and passport" emails? You know how everyone makes fun of them? And you know how they must make money anyway because those emails just keep coming?
Those guys are literally five thousand times smarter than you are right now.

All right, sorry, I just got excited about Chipmunk Hunk.
Back to Squirrel Girl, huh? But she's not even on this page. *Sheesh!*

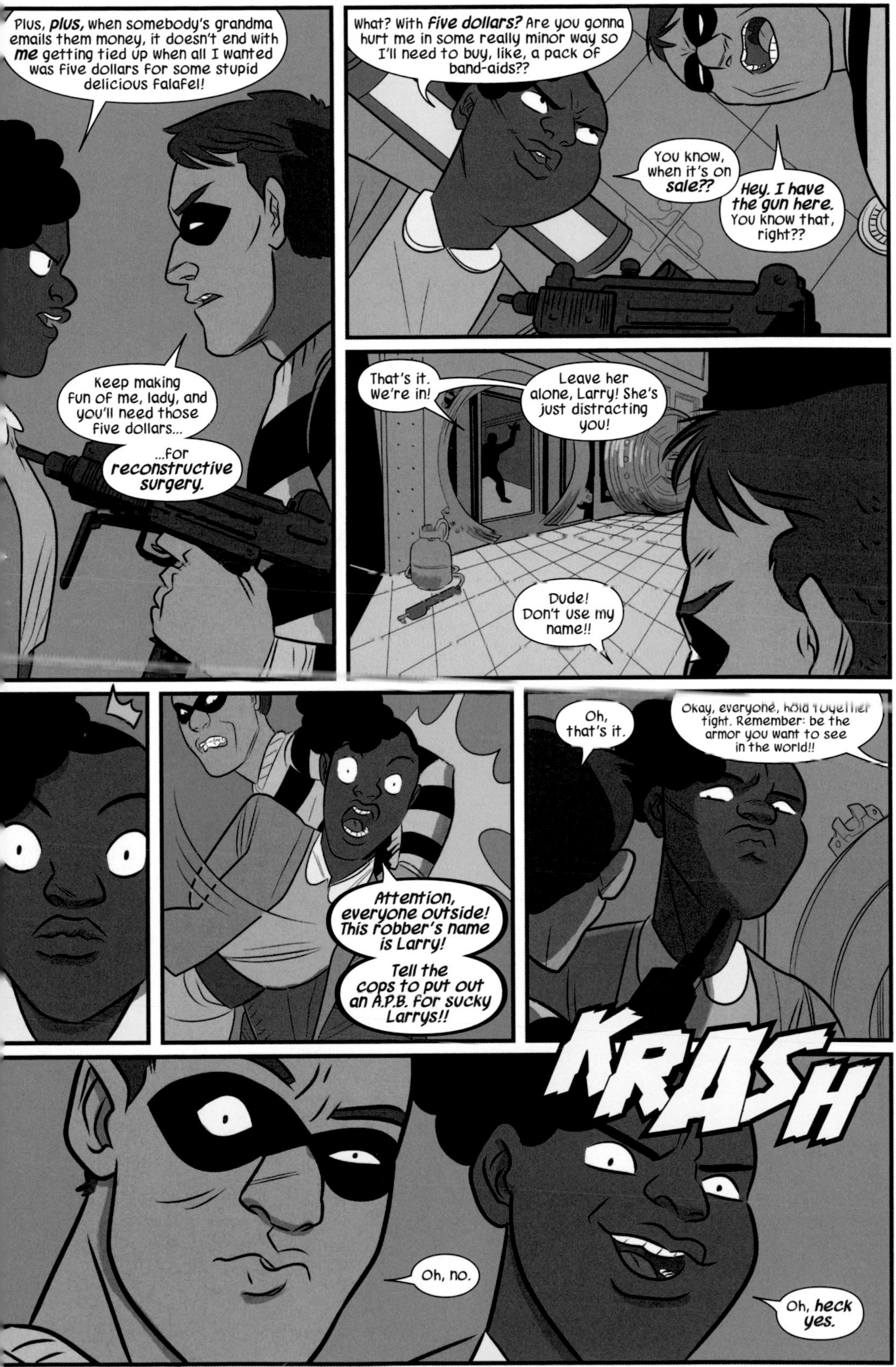
Plus, **plus**, when somebody's grandma emails them money, it doesn't end with **me** getting tied up when all I wanted was five dollars for some stupid delicious falafel!
Keep making fun of me, lady, and you'll need those five dollars...
...for **reconstructive surgery.**
What? With **five dollars?** Are you gonna hurt me in some really minor way so I'll need to buy, like, a pack of band-aids??
You know, when it's on **sale??**
Hey. I have the gun here. You know that, right??
That's it. We're in!
Leave her alone, Larry! She's just distracting you!
Dude! Don't use my name!!
Attention, everyone outside! This robber's name is Larry!
Tell the cops to put out an A.P.B. for sucky Larrys!!
Oh, that's it.
Okay, everyone, hold together tight. Remember: be the armor you want to see in the world!!
KRASH
Oh, no.
Oh, **heck yes.**

Attention, all units: be on the lookout for sucky Larrys in the area. Subjects are to be considered potentially armed and definitely sucky.

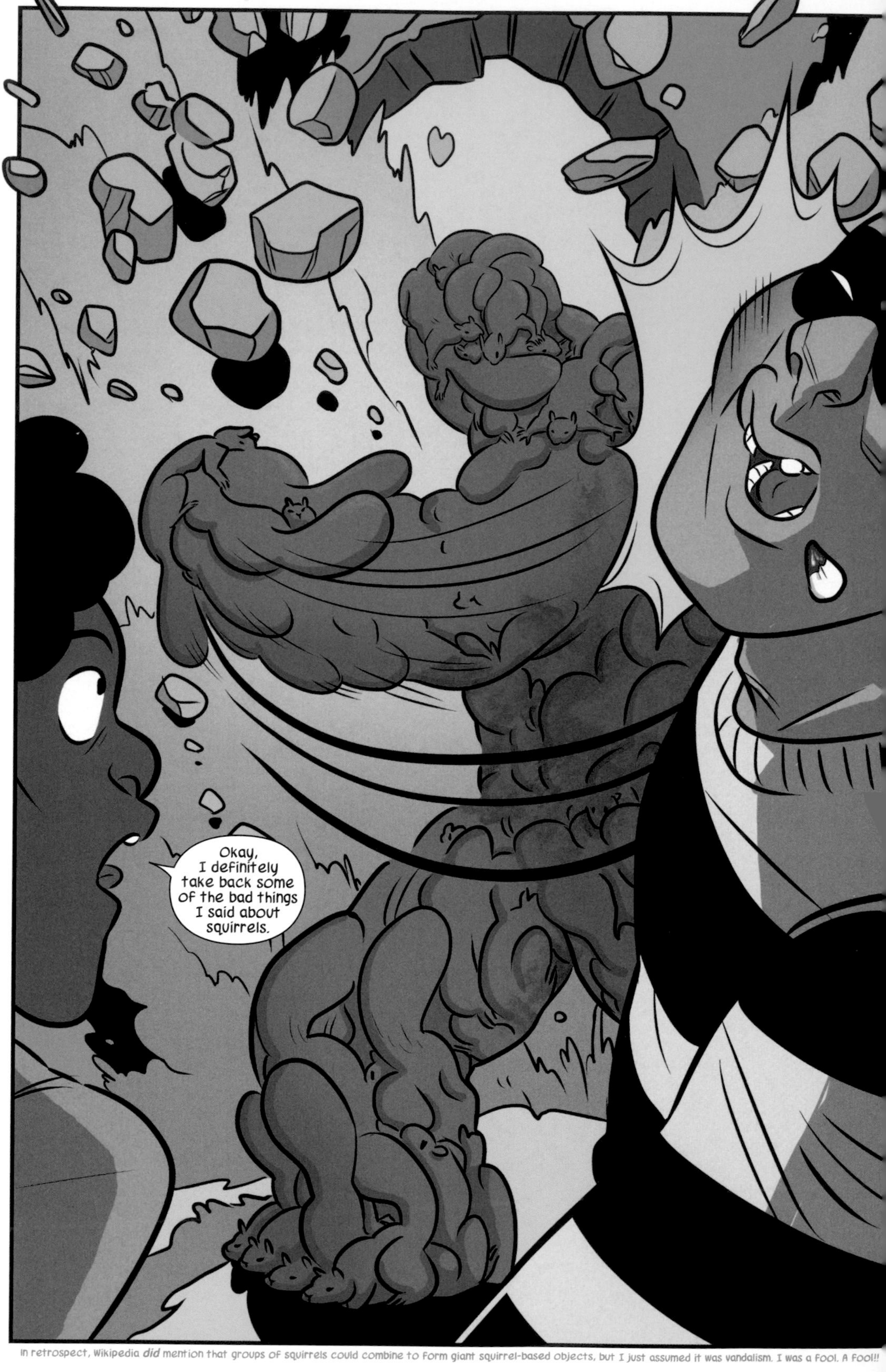
Okay, I definitely take back some of the bad things I said about squirrels.

In retrospect, Wikipedia *did* mention that groups of squirrels could combine to form giant squirrel-based objects, but I just assumed it was vandalism. I was a fool. A fool!!

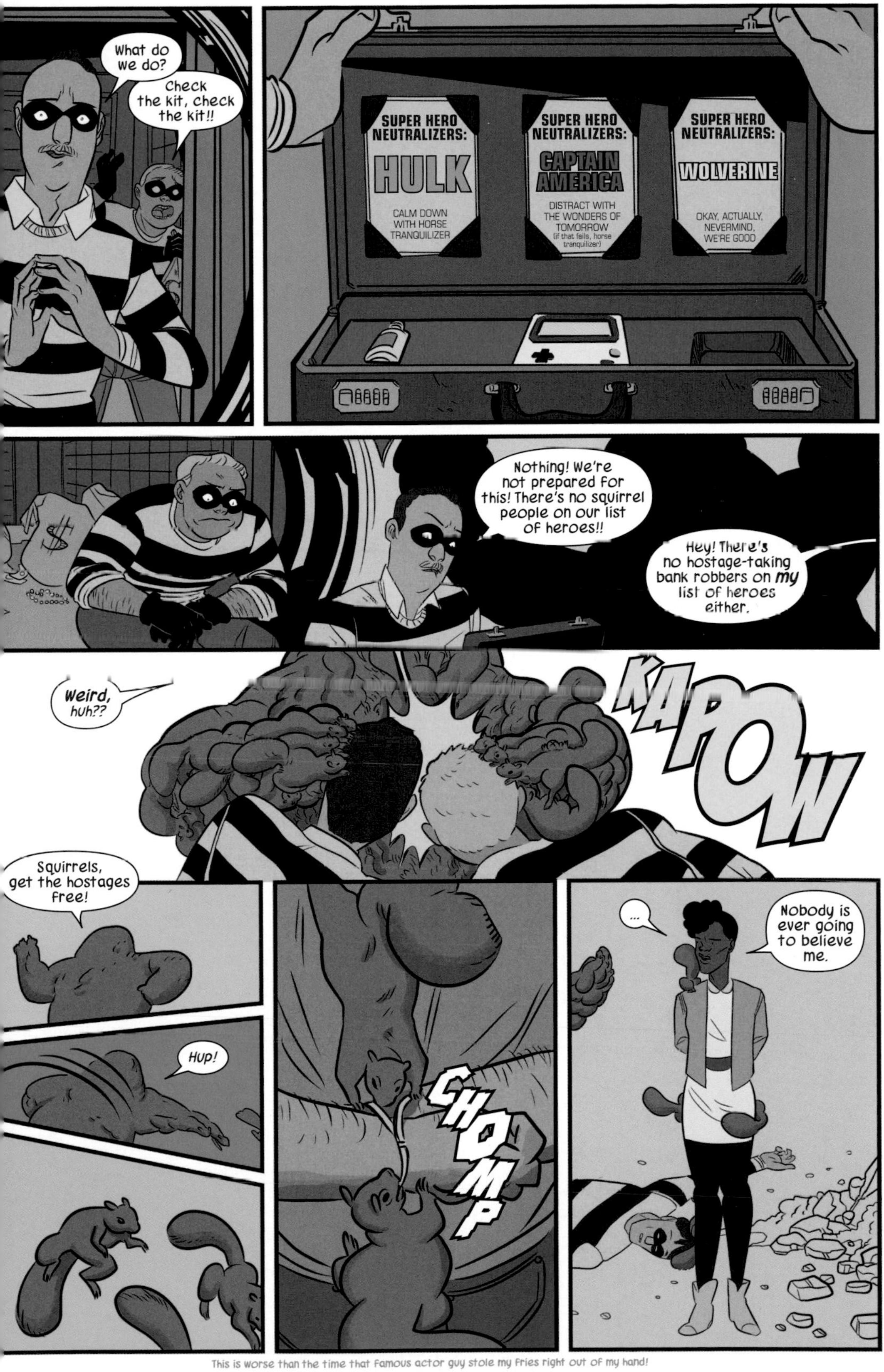

What do we do?
Check the kit, check the kit!!
SUPER HERO NEUTRALIZERS: HULK
CALM DOWN WITH HORSE TRANQUILIZER
SUPER HERO NEUTRALIZERS: CAPTAIN AMERICA
DISTRACT WITH THE WONDERS OF TOMORROW
(if that fails, horse tranquilizer)
SUPER HERO NEUTRALIZERS: WOLVERINE
OKAY, ACTUALLY, NEVERMIND, WE'RE GOOD
Nothing! We're not prepared for this! There's no squirrel people on our list of heroes!!
Hey! There's no hostage-taking bank robbers on *my* list of heroes either.
Weird, huh??
KAPOW
Squirrels, get the hostages free!
Hup!
CHOMP
...
Nobody is ever going to believe me.

This is worse than the time that famous actor guy stole my fries right out of my hand!

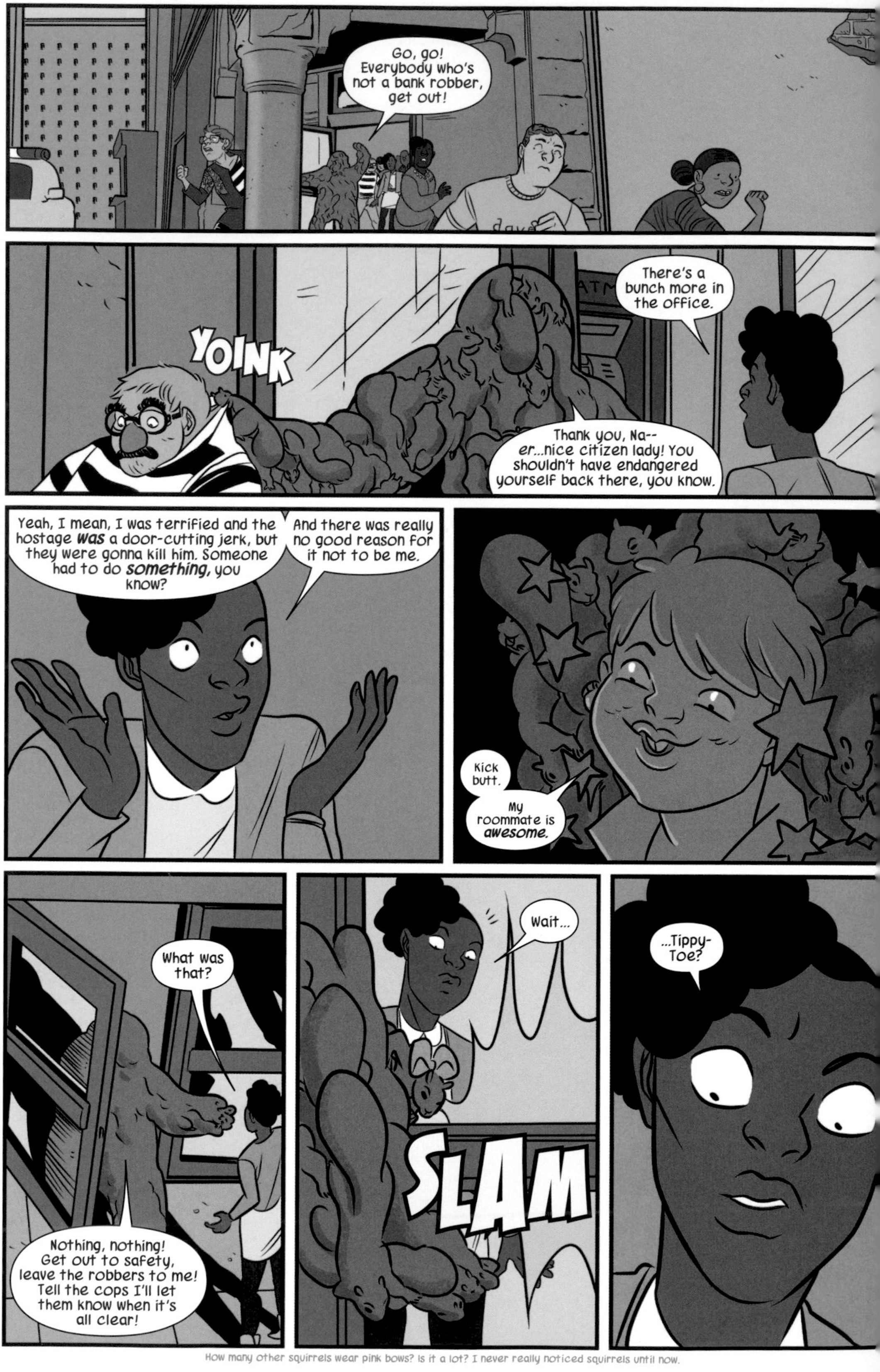
Go, go! Everybody who's not a bank robber, get out!
YOINK
There's a bunch more in the office.
Thank you, Na-- *er*...nice citizen lady! You shouldn't have endangered yourself back there, you know.
Yeah, I mean, I was terrified and the hostage **was** a door-cutting jerk, but they were gonna kill him. Someone had to do **something,** you know?
And there was really no good reason for it not to be me.
Kick butt.
My roommate is **awesome.**
What was that?
Nothing, nothing! Get out to safety, leave the robbers to me! Tell the cops I'll let them know when it's all clear!
Wait...
SLAM
...Tippy-Toe?

How many other squirrels wear pink bows? Is it a lot? I never really noticed squirrels until now.

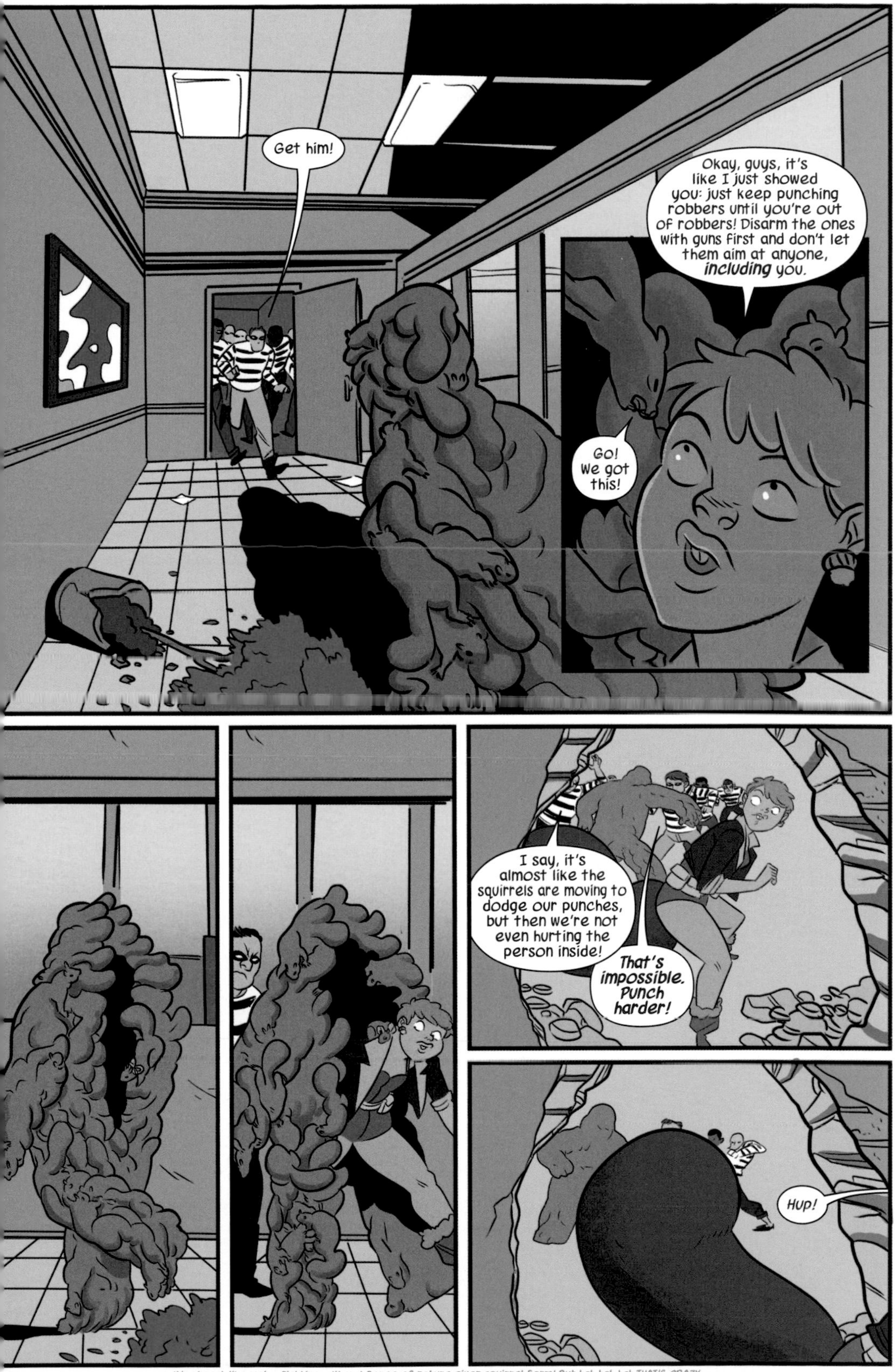

Get him!
Okay, guys, it's like I just showed you: just keep punching robbers until you're out of robbers! Disarm the ones with guns first and don't let them aim at anyone, *including* you.
Go! We got this!
I say, it's almost like the squirrels are moving to dodge our punches, but then we're not even hurting the person inside!
That's impossible. Punch harder!
Hup!

It's almost like we're fighting a literal force of nature given squirrel form! But hah hah hah THAT'S CRAZY

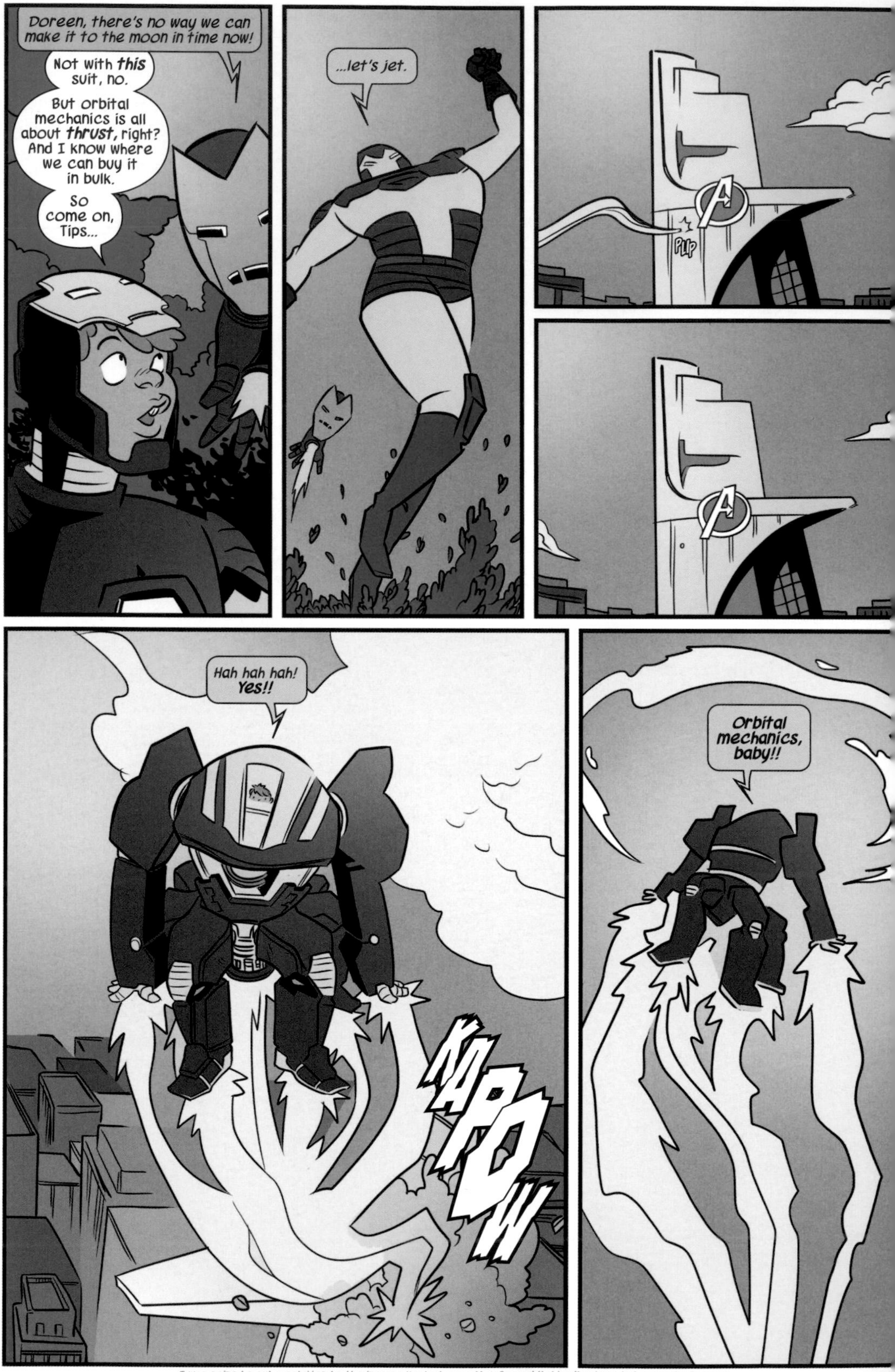
Doreen, there's no way we can make it to the moon in time now!
Not with this suit, no.
But orbital mechanics is all about thrust, right? And I know where we can buy it in bulk.
So come on, Tips...
...let's jet.
PLIP
Hah hah hah! Yes!!
KAPOW
Orbital mechanics, baby!!

I was going to put a solution to the inverse Kepler's equation for orbital bodies here but ran out of room, so you'll just have to take my word for it that the physics in my talking squirrel comic are 100% ultralegit

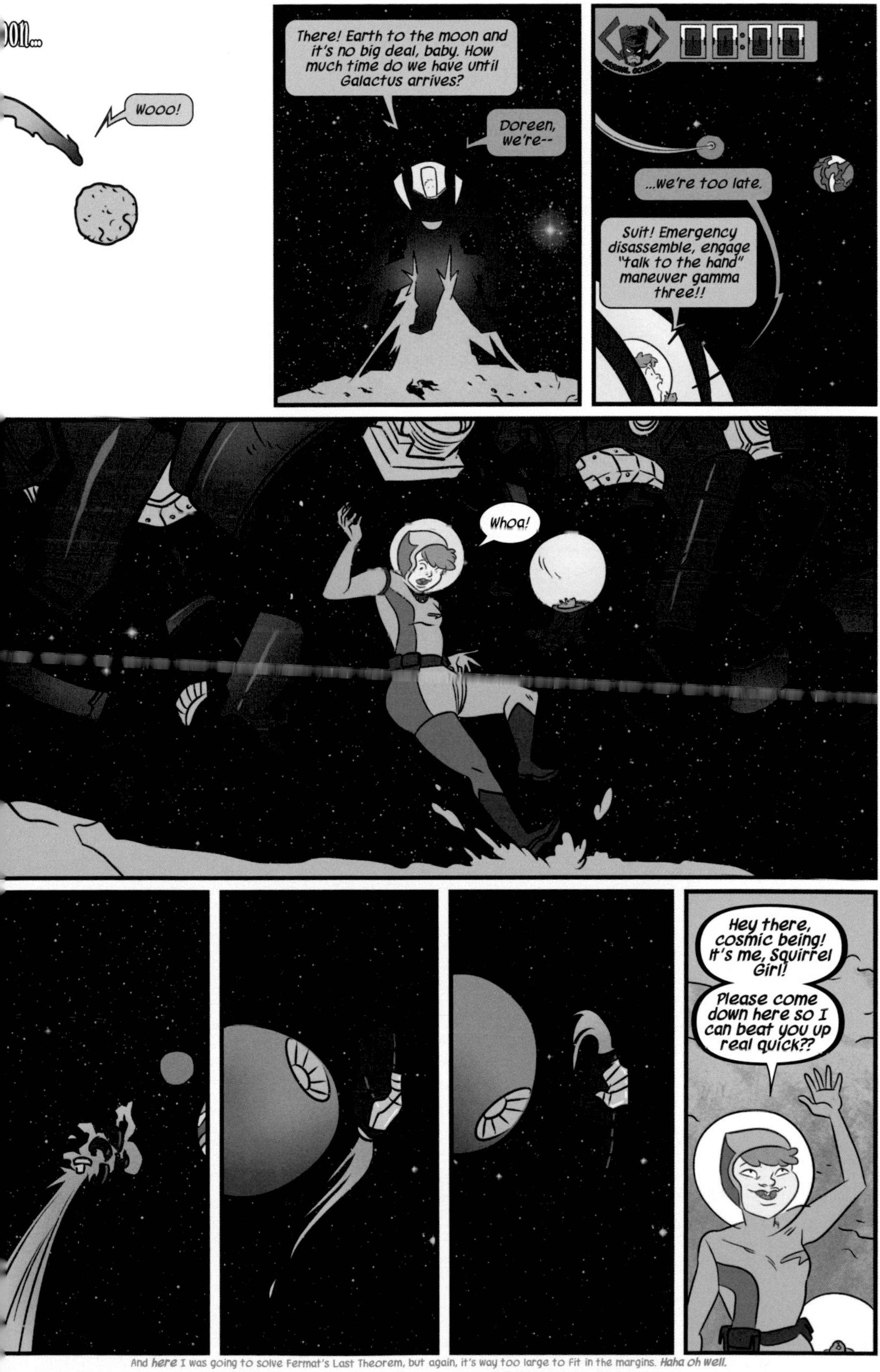
oon...
WOOO!
There! Earth to the moon and it's no big deal, baby. How much time do we have until Galactus arrives?
Doreen, we're--
00:00
...we're too late.
Suit! Emergency disassemble, engage "talk to the hand" maneuver gamma three!!
Whoa!
Hey there, cosmic being! It's me, Squirrel Girl!
Please come down here so I can beat you up real quick??

And *here* I was going to solve Fermat's Last Theorem, but again, it's way too large to fit in the margins. *Haha oh well.*

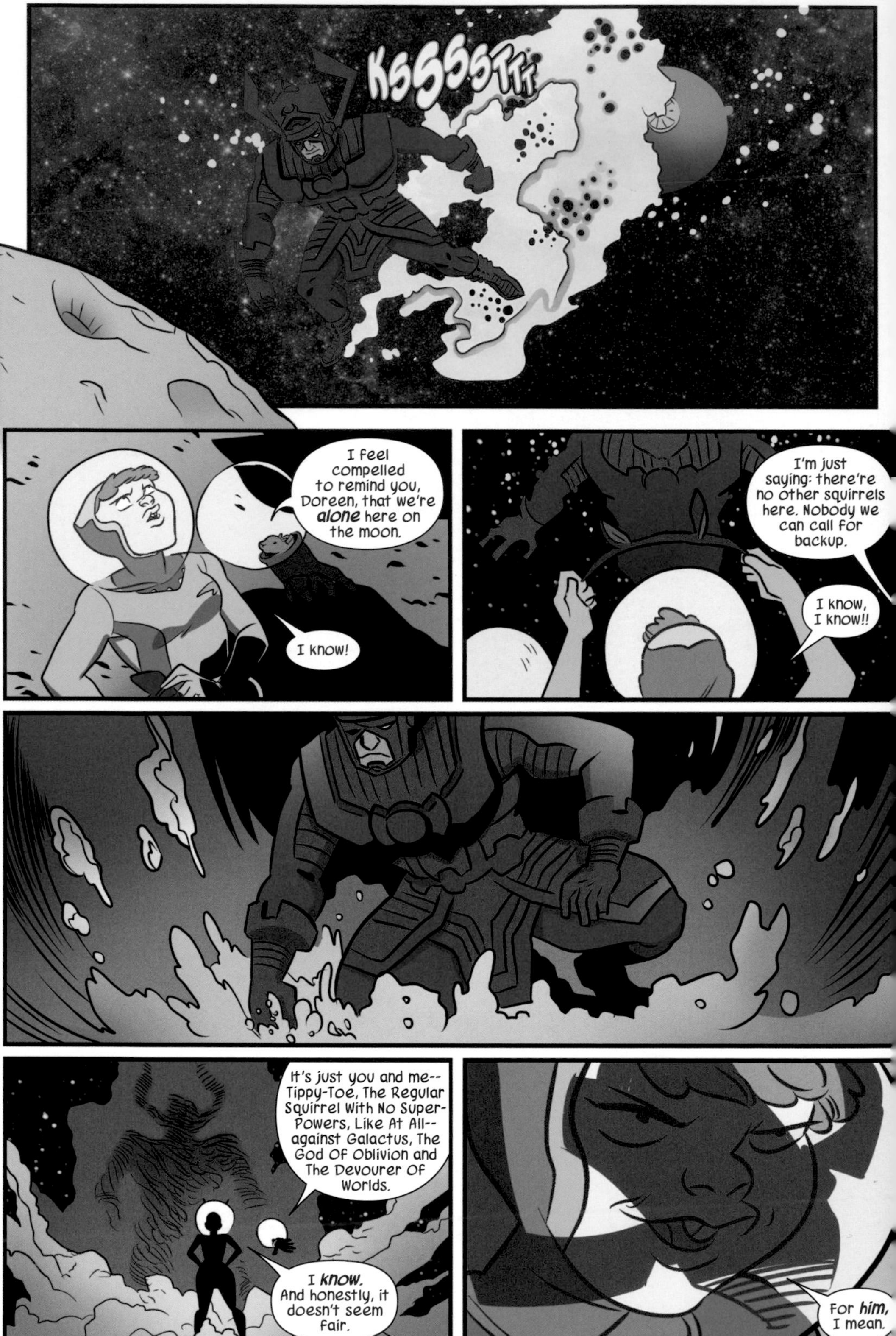
KSSSSTTT
I feel compelled to remind you, Doreen, that we're *alone* here on the moon.
I know!
I'm just saying: there're no other squirrels here. Nobody we can call for backup.
I know, I know!!
It's just you and me--Tippy-Toe, The Regular Squirrel With No Super-Powers, Like At All--against Galactus, The God Of Oblivion and The Devourer Of Worlds.
I *know.* And honestly, it doesn't seem fair.
For *him,* I mean.

What are you reading down here for? They're about to fight!!

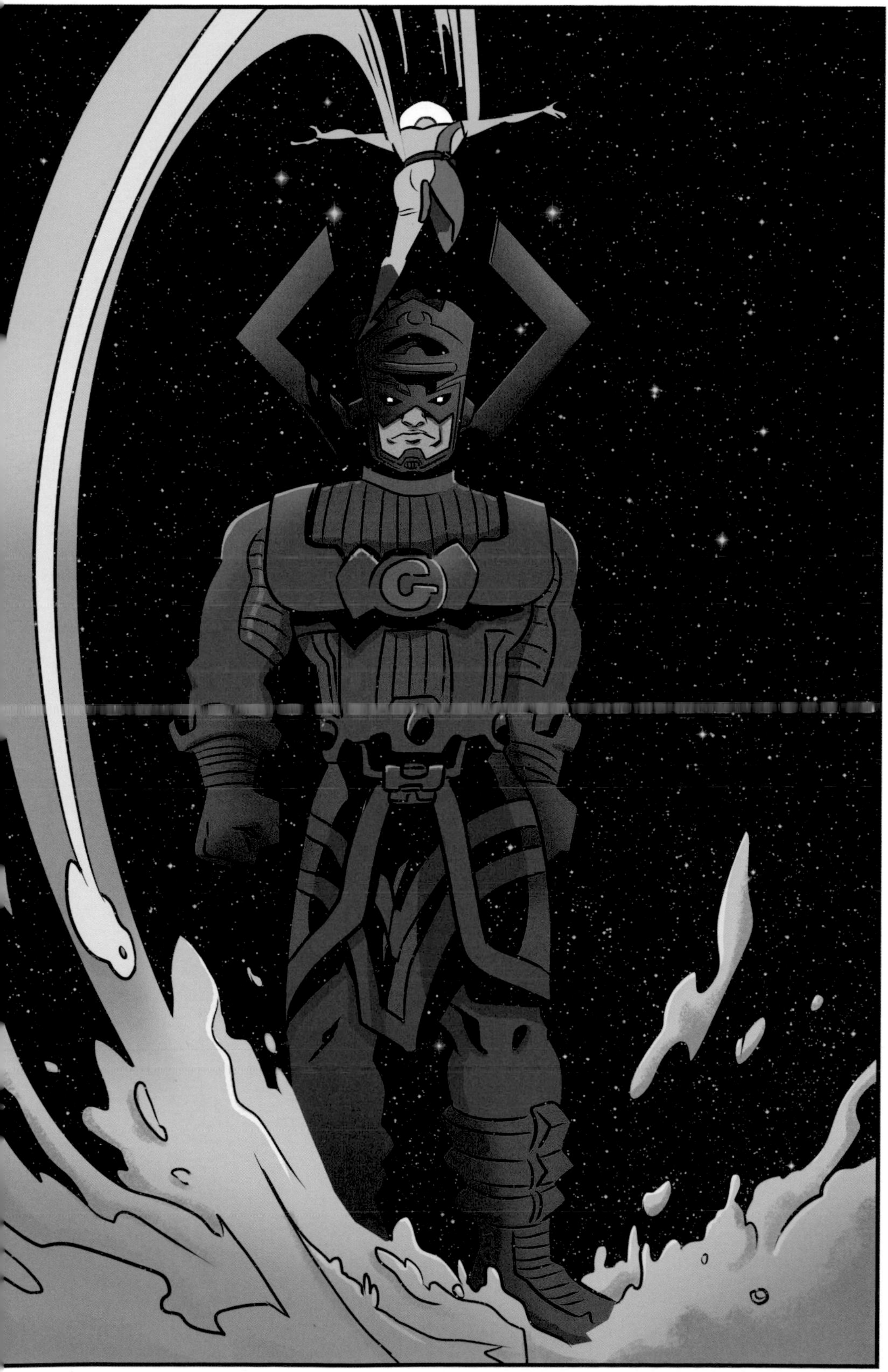

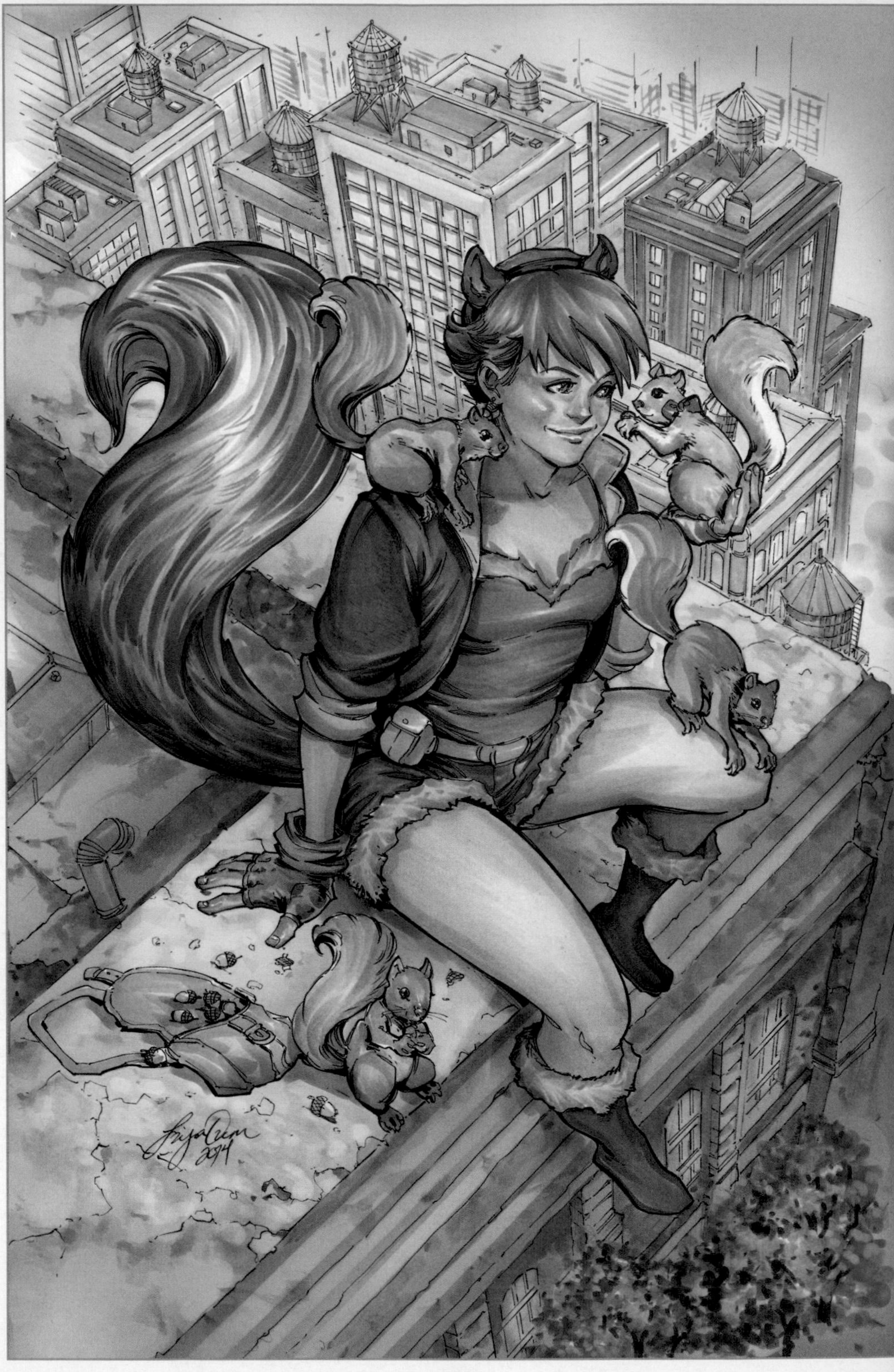

#1 VARIANT
BY SIYA OUM

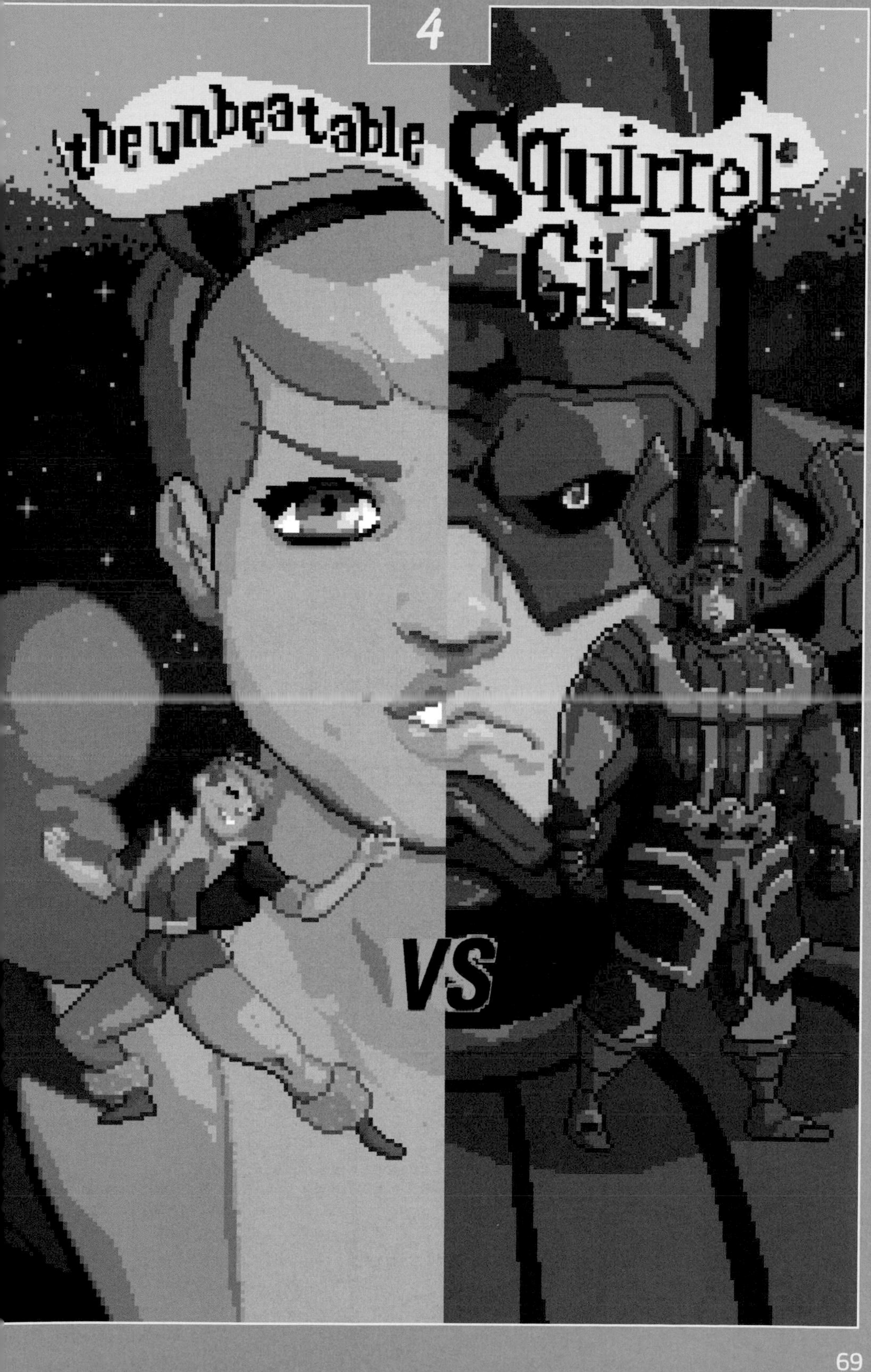
4
the unbeatable Squirrel Girl
VS

Doreen Green isn't just a first-year computer science student: she secretly also has all the powers of both squirrel and gi
She uses her amazing abilities to fight crime **and** be as awesome as possible. You know her as...*The Unbeatable Squirrel Gi*
Let's catch up with what she's been up to until now, with...

Squirrel Girl *in a nutshell*

GALACTUS @xGALACTUSx
HEY GUESS WHAT I'M COMING TO EARTH TO DEVOUR THE ENTIRE PLANET

GALACTUS @xGALACTUSx
AND NOBODY KNOWS BECAUSE I PUT MY SHIP IN A STEALTH FIELD

GALACTUS @xGALACTUSx
"BUT WAIT," YOU SAY, "AHA! NOW WE KNOW YOU'RE COMING BECAUSE YOU JUST POSTED IT ON SOCIAL MEDIA!!"

GALACTUS @xGALACTUSx
ONLY YOU AREN'T SAYING THAT BECAUSE NOBODY KNOWS I'M COMING BECAUSE NOBODY FOLLOWS ME ON THIS STUPID SITE

GALACTUS @xGALACTUSx
...

GALACTUS @xGALACTUSx
#ff @xGALACTUSx

Tony Stark @starkmantony ✓
@unbeatablesg Just heard more of my Iron Man parts have been "borrowed," and now there's a big hole in my building too. Any ideas?

Squirrel Girl! @unbeatablesg
@starkmantony Oh wow dude these suits have wifi in them??? I can go online on my way to the MOON?? Tony ur the best <3

Tony Stark @starkmantony ✓
@unbeatablesg That "wifi" works even in Mars orbit, uses proprietary Stark technology, and costs several thousand dollars a kilobyte.

Squirrel Girl! @unbeatablesg
@starkmantony um I already downloaded some songs for the trip to the moon. Sorry!!!

Tony Stark @starkmantony ✓
@unbeatablesg Don't reply to say you're sorry! That ALSO costs money!

Squirrel Girl! @unbeatablesg
@starkmantony sorry sorry!

Tony Stark @starkmantony ✓
@unbeatablesg Don't reply! Stop replying!

Squirrel Girl! @unbeatablesg
@starkmantony whoooooooooooooooooooooooooooops

Nancy W. @sewwiththeflow
Story time, friends. Your hero, me, thought she'd eat some delicious (cash-only) falafel. So I went to the bank.

Nancy W. @sewwiththeflow
And you know how banks are always the worst even when you're NOT being taken hostage? WELL GUESS WHAT?

Nancy W. @sewwiththeflow
Yep. But then we got saved by @unbeatablesg who appeared in SQUIRREL SUIT ARMOR MODE. Not even joking.

Nancy W. @sewwiththeflow
This really happened. I was saved by a squirrel suit Squirrel Girl. I know you don't believe me.

Nancy W. @sewwiththeflow
tl;dr: doesn't matter, ate falafel

Whiplash @realwhiplash22
I am trapped in #CentralPark and need #squirrelrepellant, PLEASE RT!!!!! #please #rt #please #rt #please #rt

---

search! 🔍

#bankrobbery

#banksnobbery

#mew

#squirrelsuitcrochetpattern

#snackcakes

#squirrelman

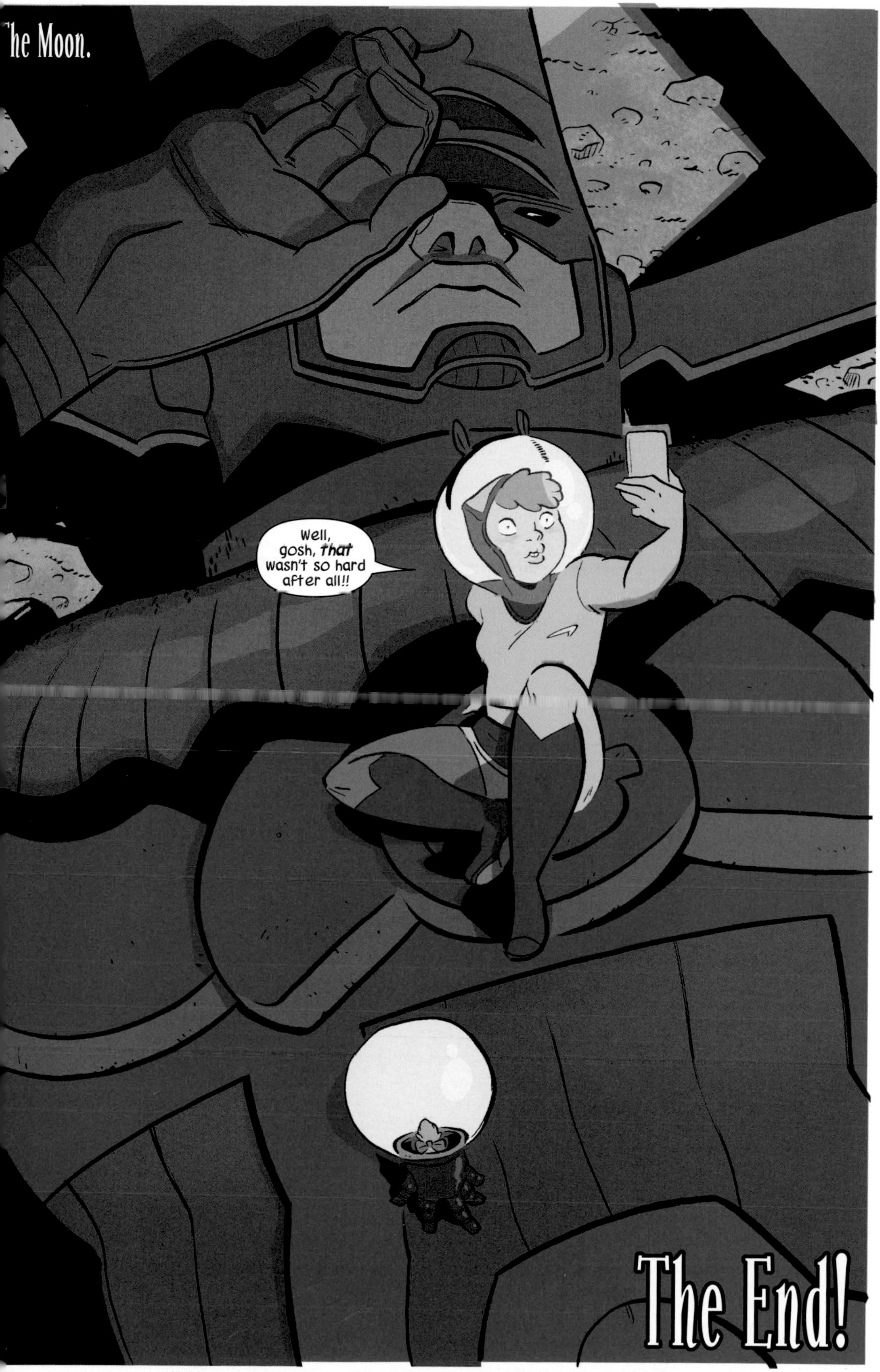
The Moon.
Well, gosh, *that* wasn't so hard after all!!
The End!

All right! Now to the letters page, and then the rest of this book is just blank pages! *Haha, oh well!!*

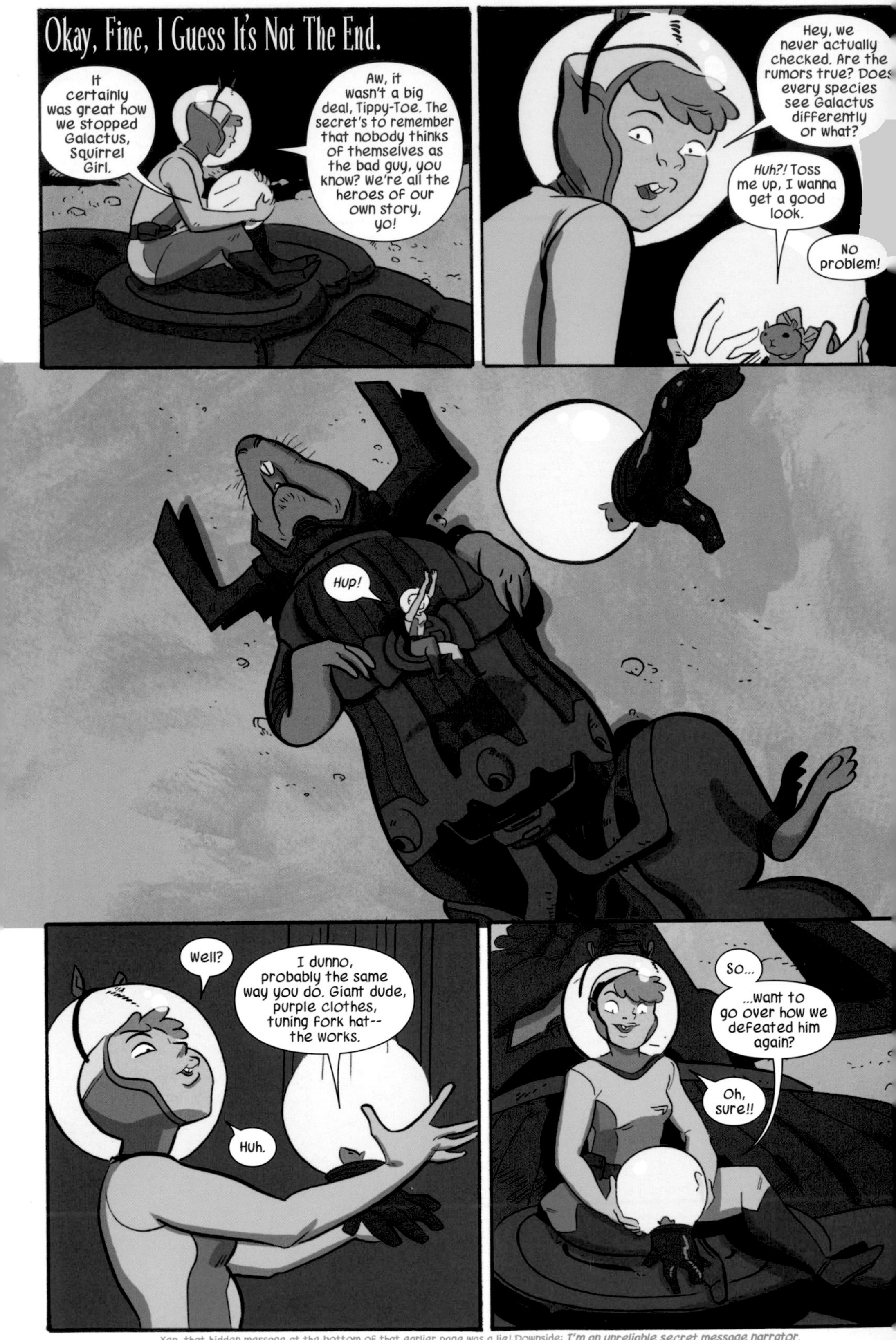
Okay, Fine, I Guess It's Not The End.
It certainly was great how we stopped Galactus, Squirrel Girl.
Aw, it wasn't a big deal, Tippy-Toe. The secret's to remember that nobody thinks of themselves as the bad guy, you know? We're all the heroes of our own story, yo!
Hey, we never actually checked. Are the rumors true? Does every species see Galactus differently or what?
Huh?! Toss me up, I wanna get a good look.
No problem!
Hup!
Well?
I dunno, probably the same way you do. Giant dude, purple clothes, tuning fork hat--the works.
Huh.
So...
...want to go over how we defeated him again?
Oh, sure!!

Yep, that hidden message at the bottom of that earlier page was a lie! Downside: *I'm an unreliable secret message narrator.*
Upside: Hey, at least this comic isn't a total ripoff now, right??

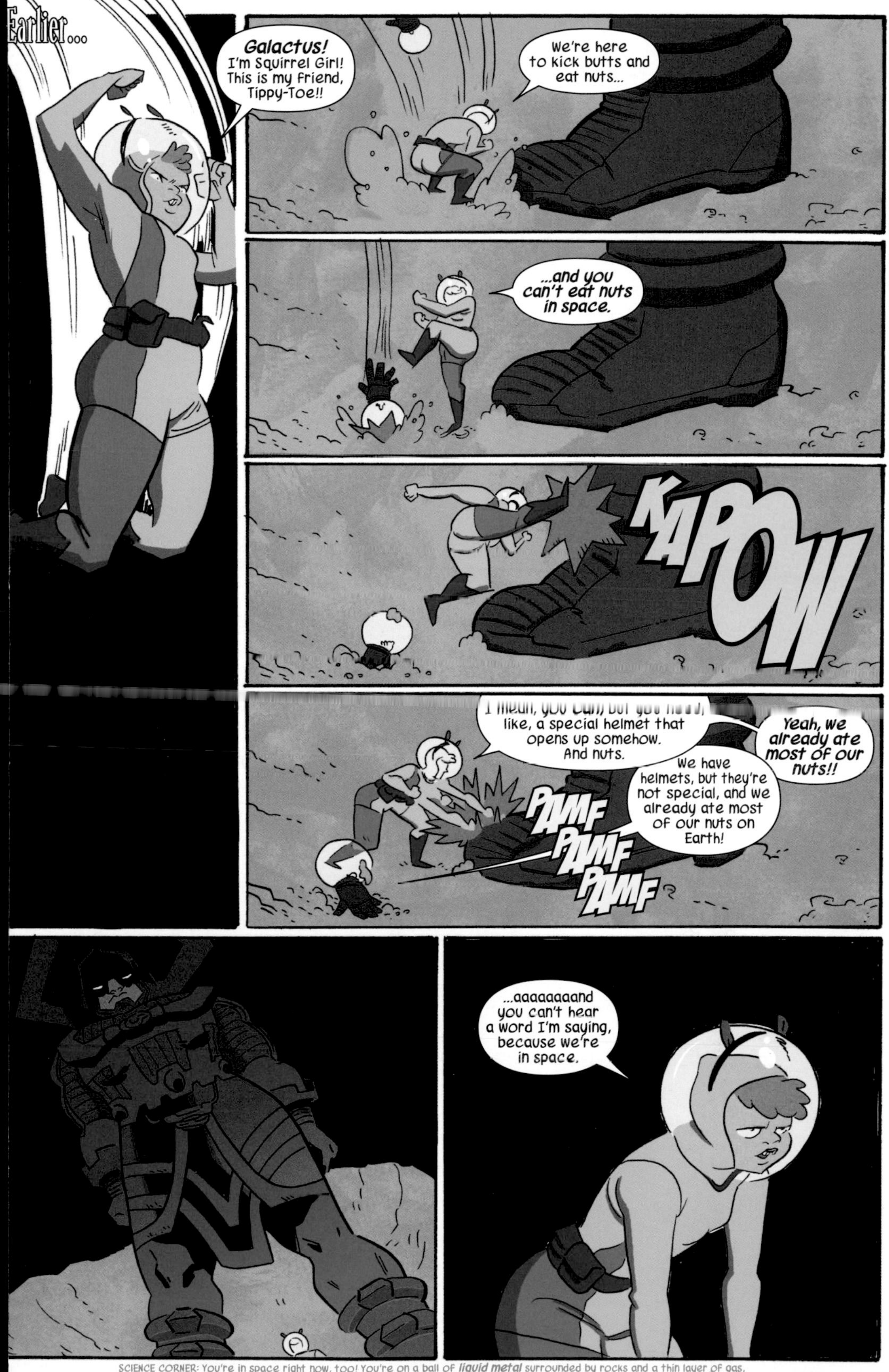

Earlier...
Galactus! I'm Squirrel Girl! This is my friend, Tippy-Toe!!
We're here to kick butts and eat nuts...
...and you can't eat nuts in space.
KAPOW
like, a special helmet that opens up somehow. And nuts.
Yeah, we already ate most of our nuts!!
We have helmets, but they're not special, and we already ate most of our nuts on Earth!
PAMF PAMF PAMF
...aaaaaaaand you can't hear a word I'm saying, because we're in space.

SCIENCE CORNER: You're in space right now, too! You're on a ball of ***liquid metal*** surrounded by rocks and a thin layer of gas, spinning wildly through the universe at thousands of kilometers per hour. Hang on tight!

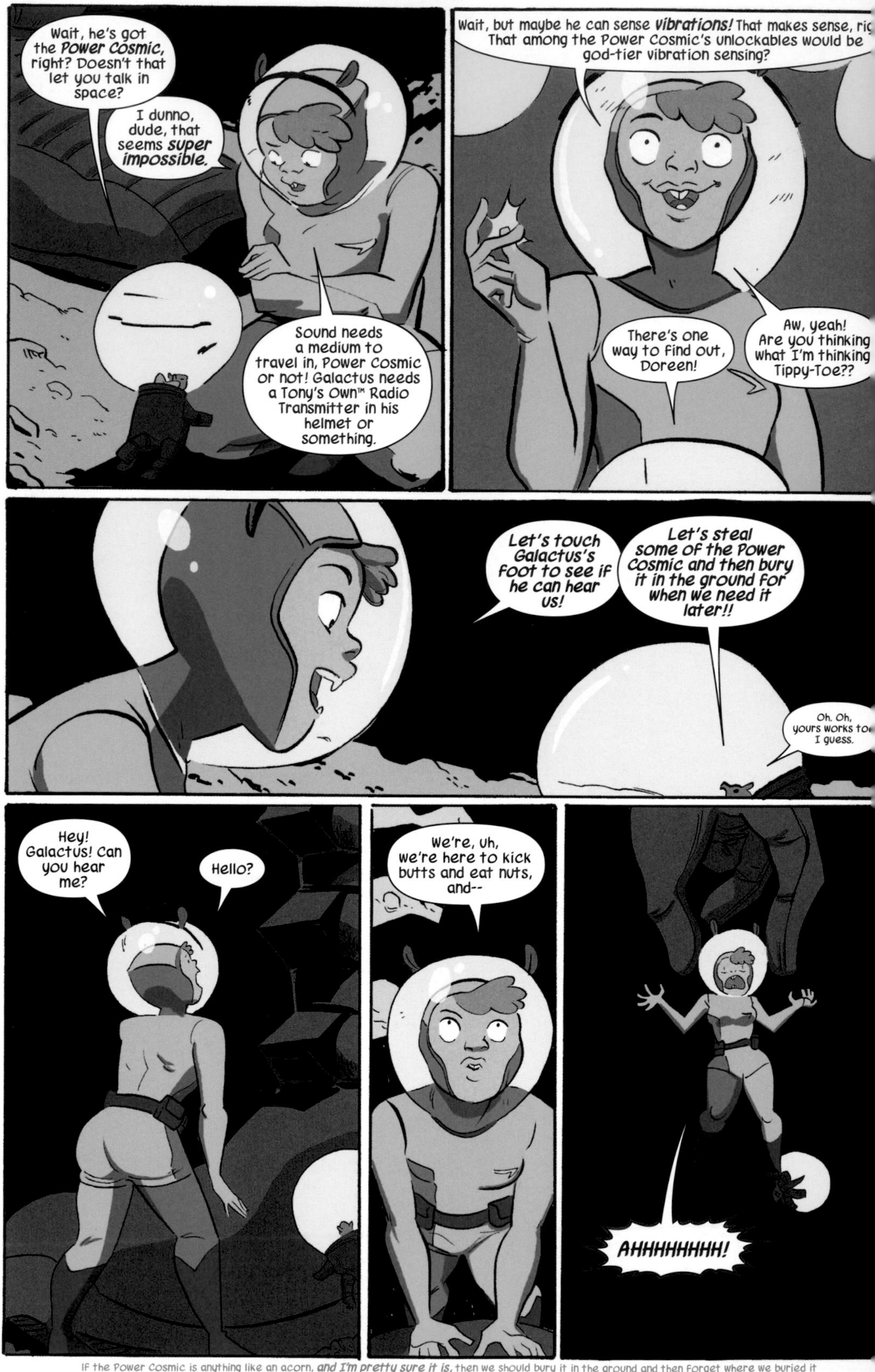
Wait, he's got the Power Cosmic, right? Doesn't that let you talk in space?
I dunno, dude, that seems super impossible.
Sound needs a medium to travel in, Power Cosmic or not! Galactus needs a Tony's Own™ Radio Transmitter in his helmet or something.
Wait, but maybe he can sense vibrations! That makes sense, rig That among the Power Cosmic's unlockables would be god-tier vibration sensing?
There's one way to find out, Doreen!
Aw, yeah! Are you thinking what I'm thinking Tippy-Toe??
Let's touch Galactus's foot to see if he can hear us!
Let's steal some of the Power Cosmic and then bury it in the ground for when we need it later!!
Oh. Oh, yours works to I guess.
Hey! Galactus! Can you hear me?
Hello?
We're, uh, we're here to kick butts and eat nuts, and--
AHHHHHHHH!

If the Power Cosmic is anything like an acorn, *and I'm pretty sure it is,* then we should bury it in the ground and then forget where we buried it and then a Power Cosmic tree will grow from that spot many years from now!

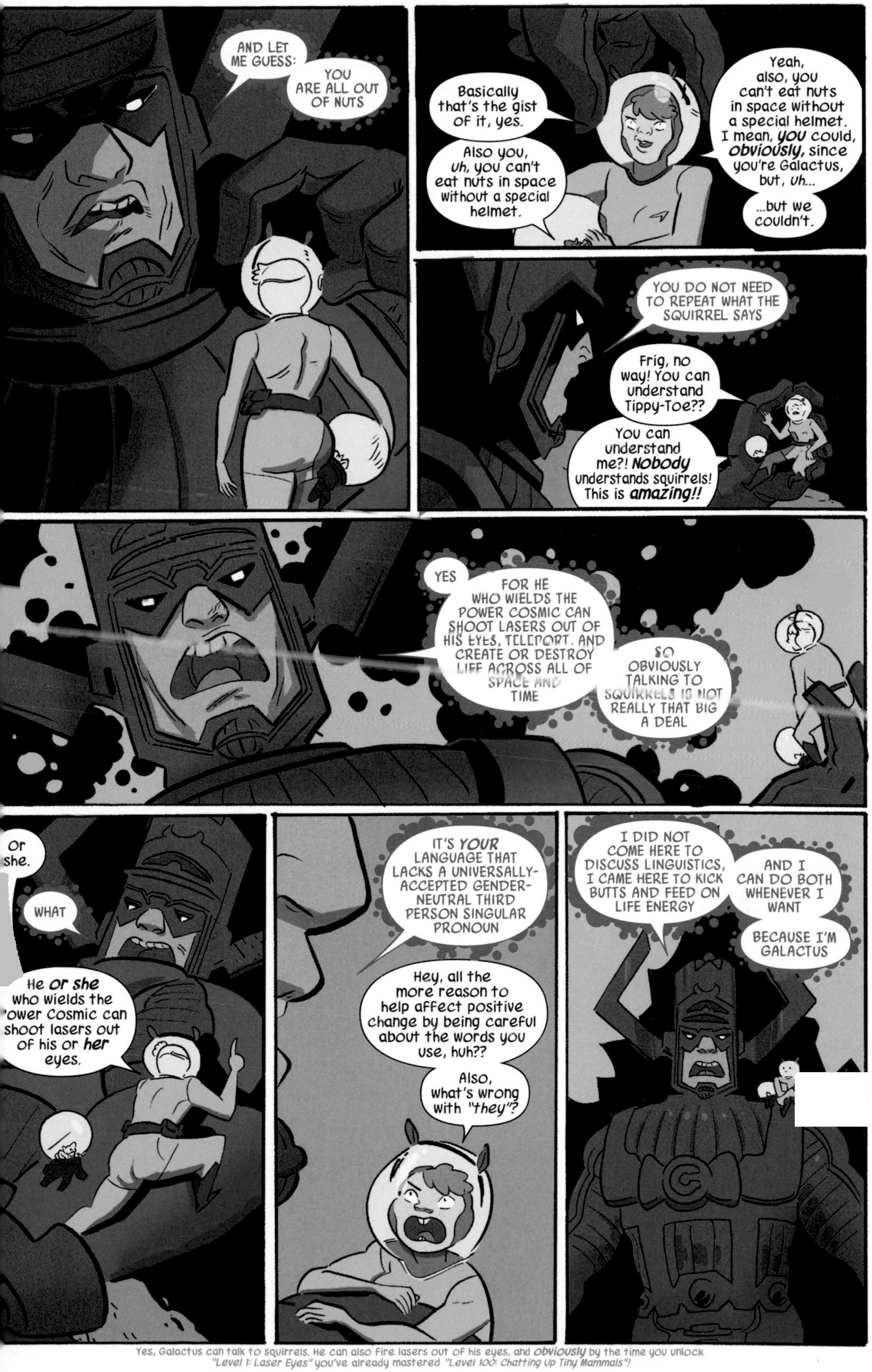
AND LET ME GUESS:
YOU ARE ALL OUT OF NUTS
Basically that's the gist of it, yes.
Also you, uh, you can't eat nuts in space without a special helmet.
Yeah, also, you can't eat nuts in space without a special helmet. I mean, YOU could, obviously, since you're Galactus, but, uh...
...but we couldn't.
YOU DO NOT NEED TO REPEAT WHAT THE SQUIRREL SAYS
Frig, no way! You can understand Tippy-Toe??
You can understand me?! Nobody understands squirrels! This is amazing!!
YES
FOR HE WHO WIELDS THE POWER COSMIC CAN SHOOT LASERS OUT OF HIS EYES, TELEPORT, AND CREATE OR DESTROY LIFE ACROSS ALL OF SPACE AND TIME
SO OBVIOUSLY TALKING TO SQUIRRELS IS NOT REALLY THAT BIG A DEAL
Or she.
WHAT
He or she who wields the Power Cosmic can shoot lasers out of his or her eyes.
IT'S YOUR LANGUAGE THAT LACKS A UNIVERSALLY-ACCEPTED GENDER-NEUTRAL THIRD PERSON SINGULAR PRONOUN
Hey, all the more reason to help affect positive change by being careful about the words you use, huh??
Also, what's wrong with "they"?
I DID NOT COME HERE TO DISCUSS LINGUISTICS, I CAME HERE TO KICK BUTTS AND FEED ON LIFE ENERGY
AND I CAN DO BOTH WHENEVER I WANT
BECAUSE I'M GALACTUS

Yes, Galactus can talk to squirrels. He can also fire lasers out of his eyes, and *obviously* by the time you unlock *"Level 1: Laser Eyes"* you've already mastered *"Level 100: Chatting Up Tiny Mammals"*!

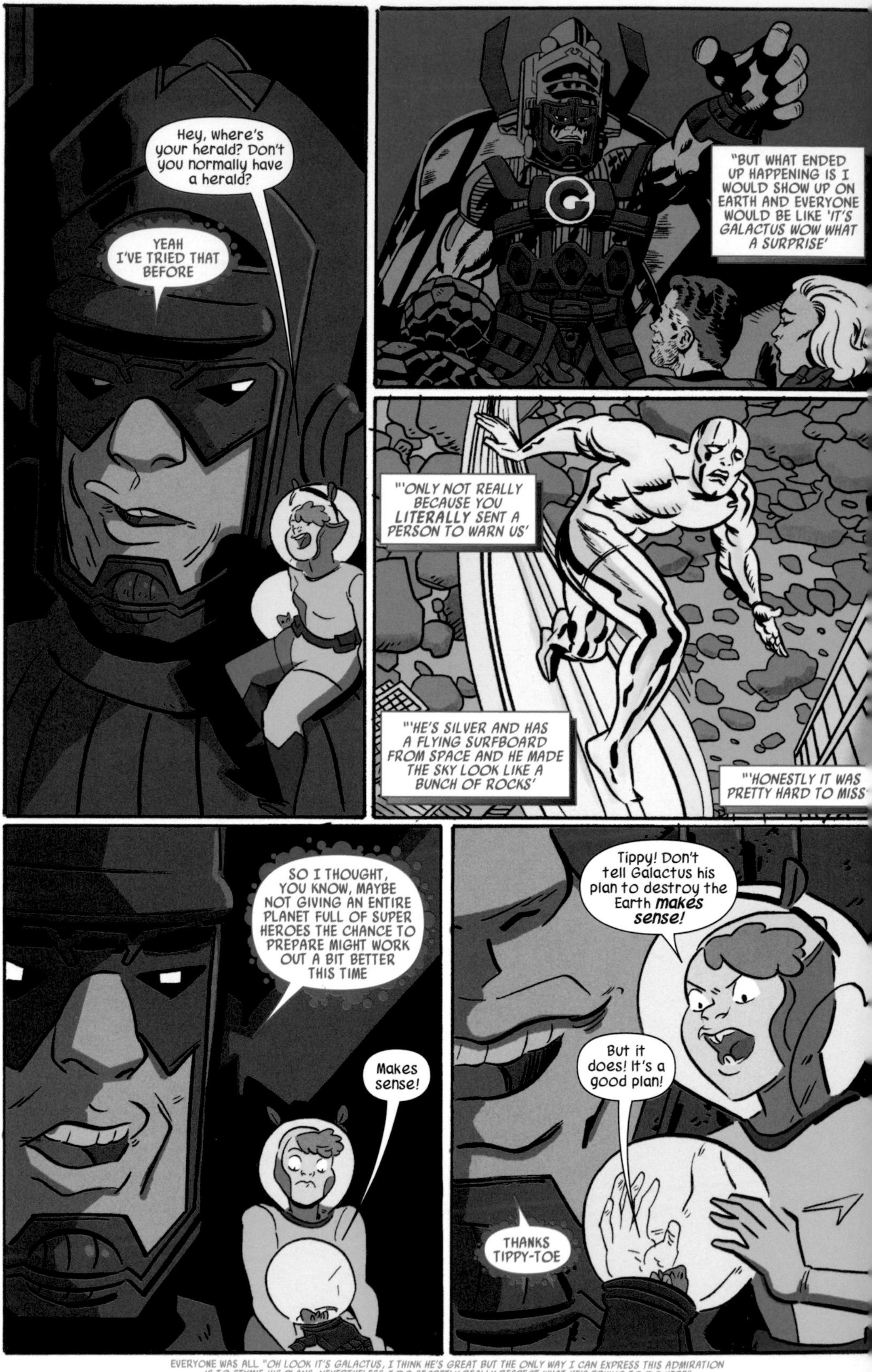
Hey, where's your herald? Don't you normally have a herald?
YEAH I'VE TRIED THAT BEFORE
"BUT WHAT ENDED UP HAPPENING IS I WOULD SHOW UP ON EARTH AND EVERYONE WOULD BE LIKE 'IT'S GALACTUS WOW WHAT A SURPRISE'
"'ONLY NOT REALLY BECAUSE YOU LITERALLY SENT A PERSON TO WARN US'
"'HE'S SILVER AND HAS A FLYING SURFBOARD FROM SPACE AND HE MADE THE SKY LOOK LIKE A BUNCH OF ROCKS'
"'HONESTLY IT WAS PRETTY HARD TO MISS'
SO I THOUGHT, YOU KNOW, MAYBE NOT GIVING AN ENTIRE PLANET FULL OF SUPER HEROES THE CHANCE TO PREPARE MIGHT WORK OUT A BIT BETTER THIS TIME
Makes sense!
Tippy! Don't tell Galactus his plan to destroy the Earth *makes sense!*
But it does! It's a good plan!
THANKS TIPPY-TOE

EVERYONE WAS ALL *"OH LOOK IT'S GALACTUS, I THINK HE'S GREAT BUT THE ONLY WAY I CAN EXPRESS THIS ADMIRATION IS TO STYMIE HIS PLANS, NEVERTHELESS I DO SECRETLY REALLY RESPECT WHAT HE'S TRYING TO DO HERE"*

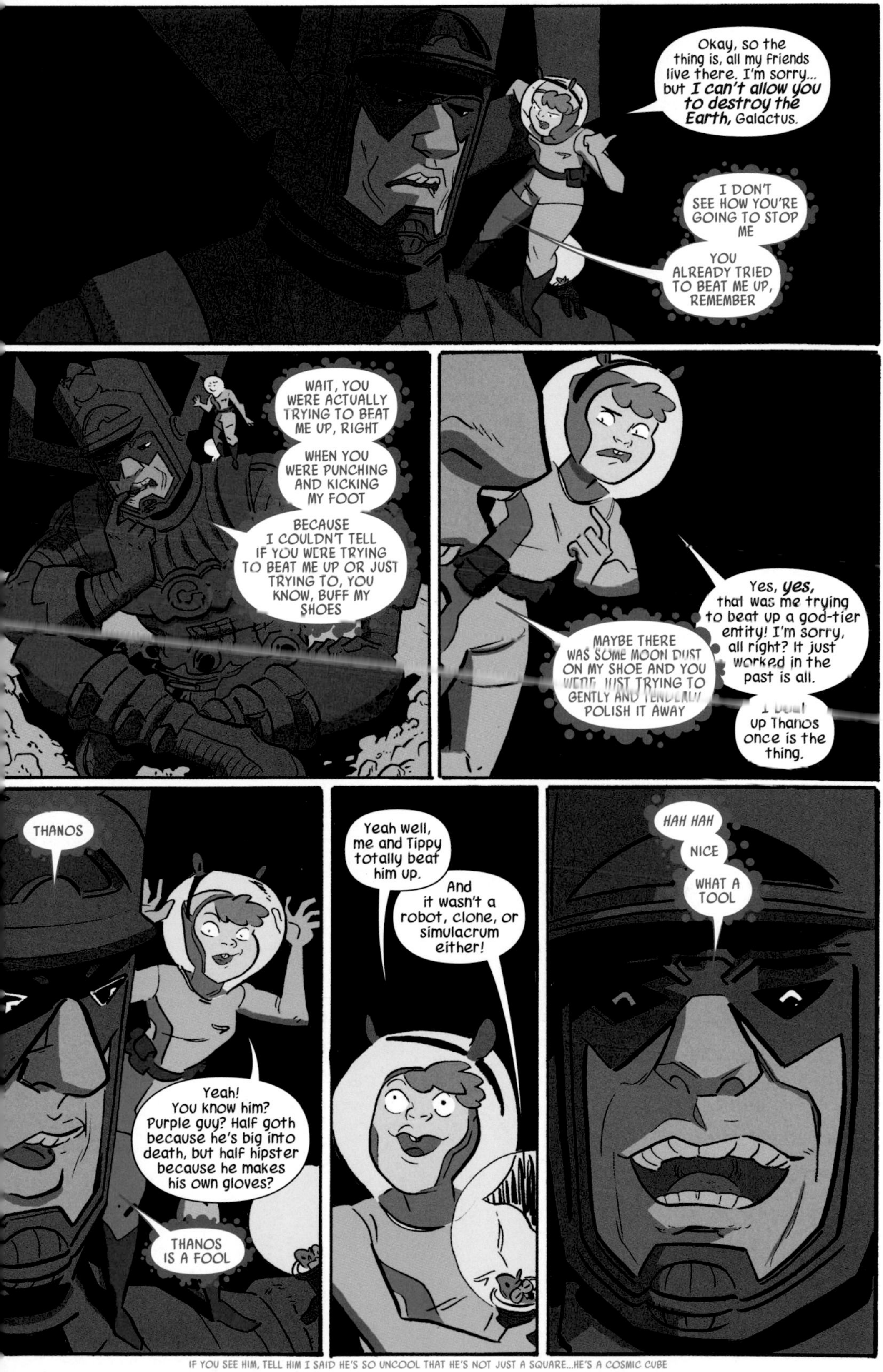
Okay, so the thing is, all my friends live there. I'm sorry... but *I can't allow you to destroy the Earth,* Galactus.
I DON'T SEE HOW YOU'RE GOING TO STOP ME
YOU ALREADY TRIED TO BEAT ME UP, REMEMBER
WAIT, YOU WERE ACTUALLY TRYING TO BEAT ME UP, RIGHT
WHEN YOU WERE PUNCHING AND KICKING MY FOOT
BECAUSE I COULDN'T TELL IF YOU WERE TRYING TO BEAT ME UP OR JUST TRYING TO, YOU KNOW, BUFF MY SHOES
MAYBE THERE WAS SOME MOON DUST ON MY SHOE AND YOU WERE JUST TRYING TO GENTLY AND TENDERLY POLISH IT AWAY
Yes, *yes,* that was me trying to beat up a god-tier entity! I'm sorry, all right? It just worked in the past is all.
up Thanos once is the thing.
THANOS
Yeah! You know him? Purple guy? Half goth because he's big into death, but half hipster because he makes his own gloves?
THANOS IS A FOOL
Yeah well, me and Tippy totally beat him up.
And it wasn't a robot, clone, or simulacrum either!
HAH HAH
NICE
WHAT A TOOL

IF YOU SEE HIM, TELL HIM I SAID HE'S SO UNCOOL THAT HE'S NOT JUST A SQUARE...HE'S A COSMIC CUBE

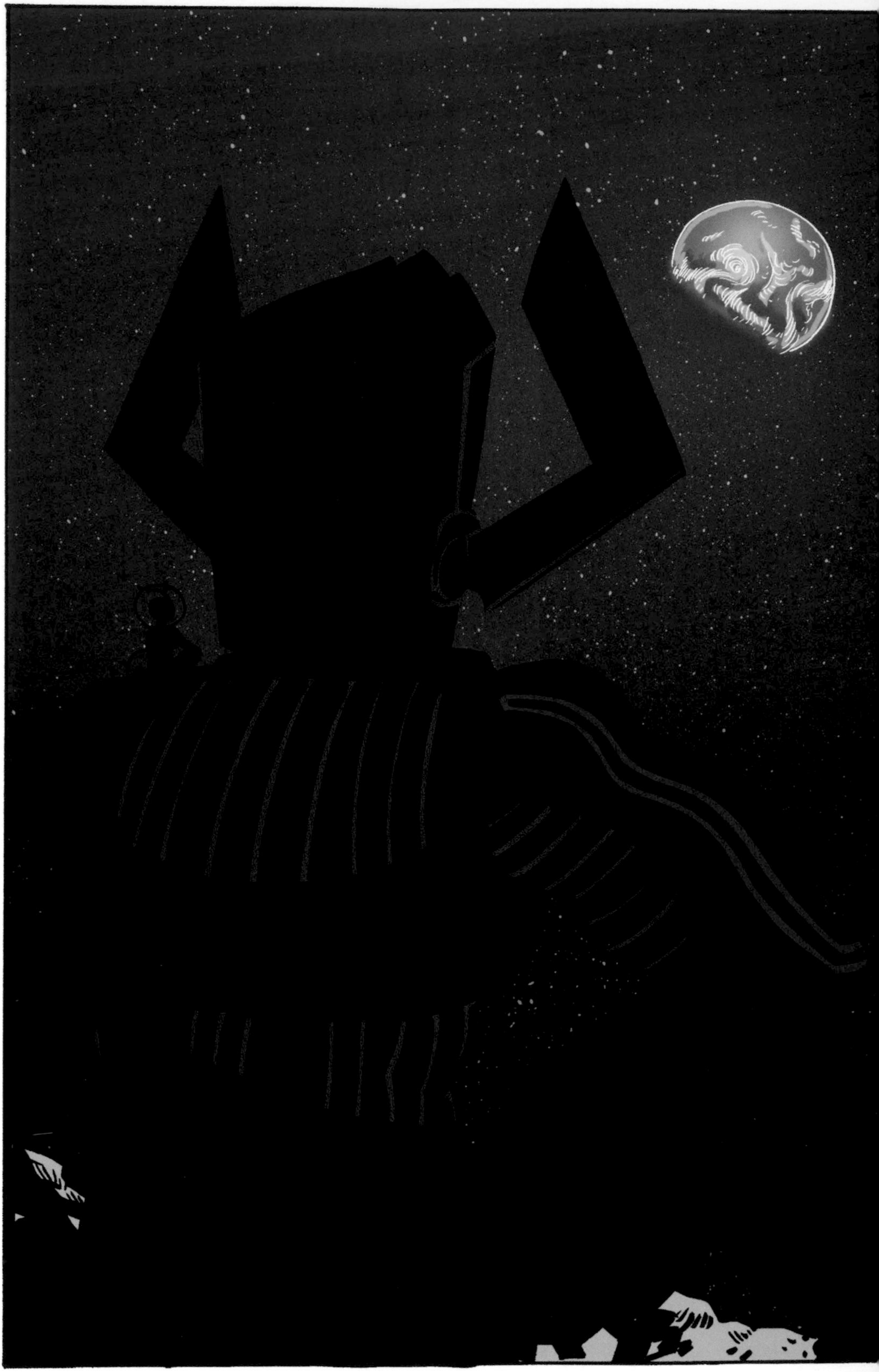

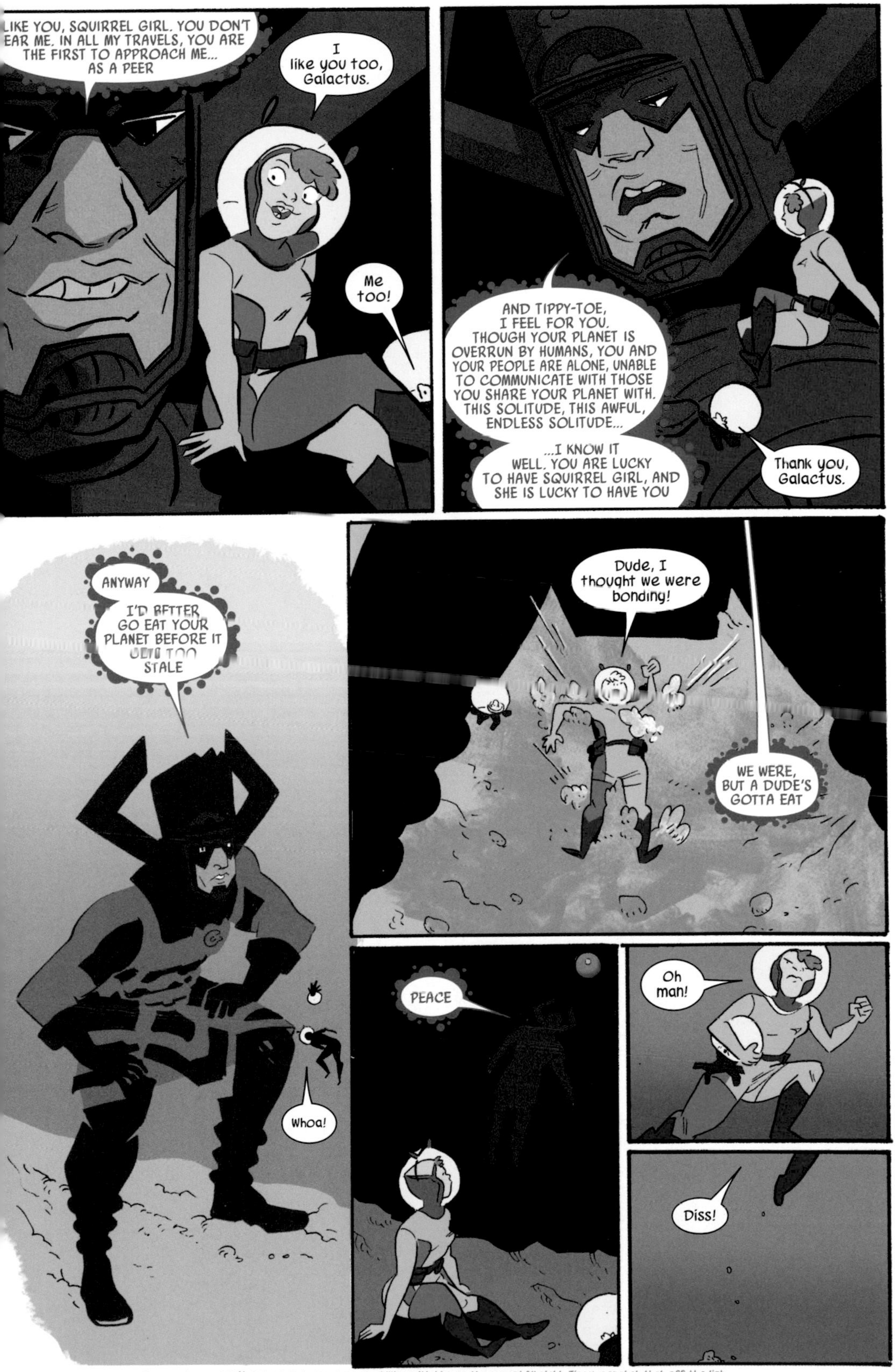
LIKE YOU, SQUIRREL GIRL. YOU DON'T
EAR ME. IN ALL MY TRAVELS, YOU ARE THE FIRST TO APPROACH ME... AS A PEER
I like you too, Galactus.
Me too!
AND TIPPY-TOE, I FEEL FOR YOU. THOUGH YOUR PLANET IS OVERRUN BY HUMANS, YOU AND YOUR PEOPLE ARE ALONE, UNABLE TO COMMUNICATE WITH THOSE YOU SHARE YOUR PLANET WITH. THIS SOLITUDE, THIS AWFUL, ENDLESS SOLITUDE...
...I KNOW IT WELL. YOU ARE LUCKY TO HAVE SQUIRREL GIRL, AND SHE IS LUCKY TO HAVE YOU
Thank you, Galactus.
ANYWAY
I'D BETTER GO EAT YOUR PLANET BEFORE IT TOO STALE
Whoa!
Dude, I thought we were bonding!
WE WERE, BUT A DUDE'S GOTTA EAT
PEACE
Oh man!
Diss!

Turns out you *can't* defeat Galactus by just chilling with him on the moon! All right, Tippy, scratch that off the list, and we'll see how well *"Fight him in orbit* ***around*** *the moon"* works out.

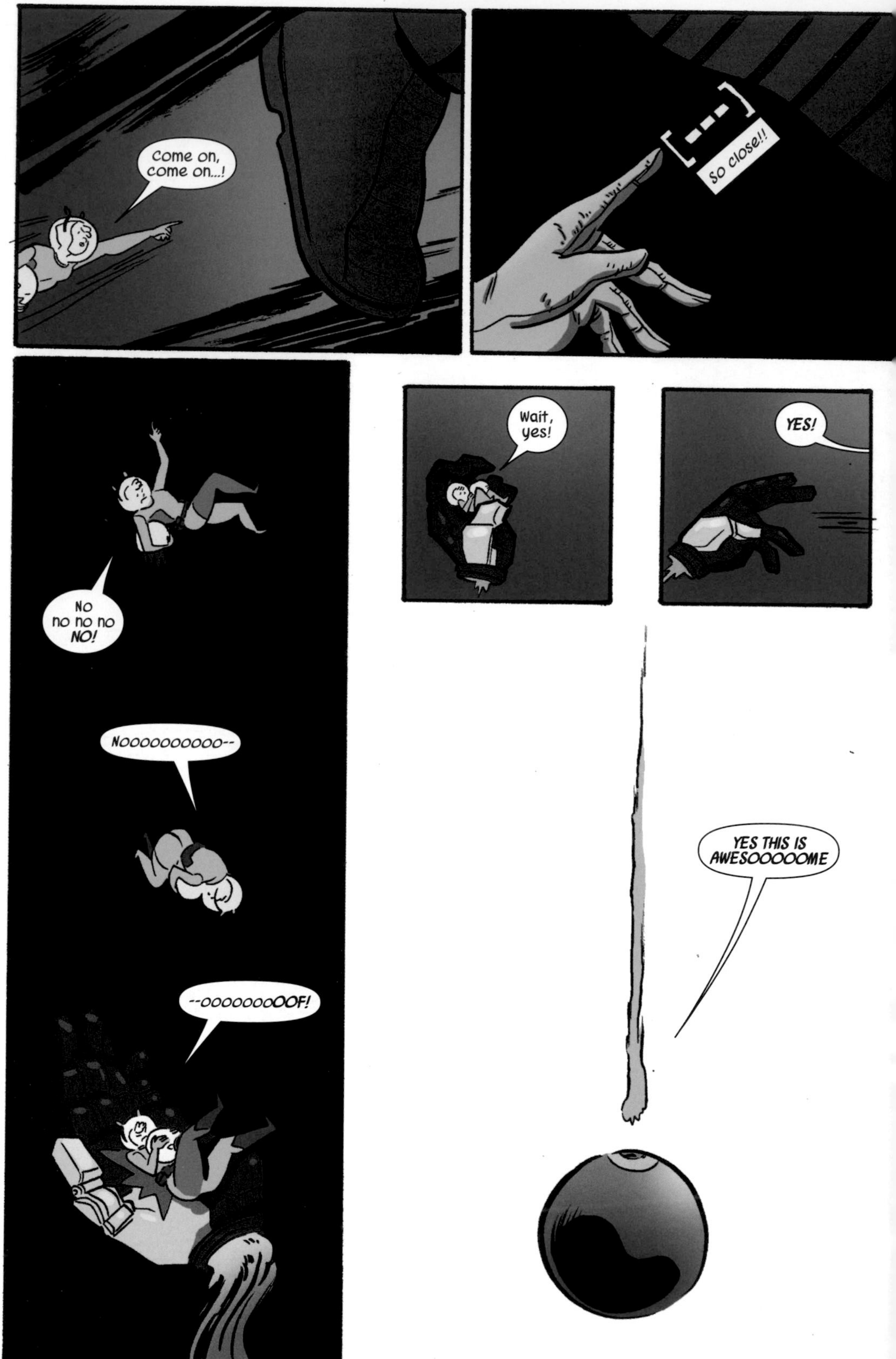
Come on, come on...!
[...]
So close!!
No no no no NO!
NOOOOOOOOOO--
--OOOOOOOOOF!
Wait, yes!
YES!
YES THIS IS AWESOOOOOME

Thanks, Iron Man suit parts! You saved the day. Come on, everyone, let's all give those suit parts...a hand??

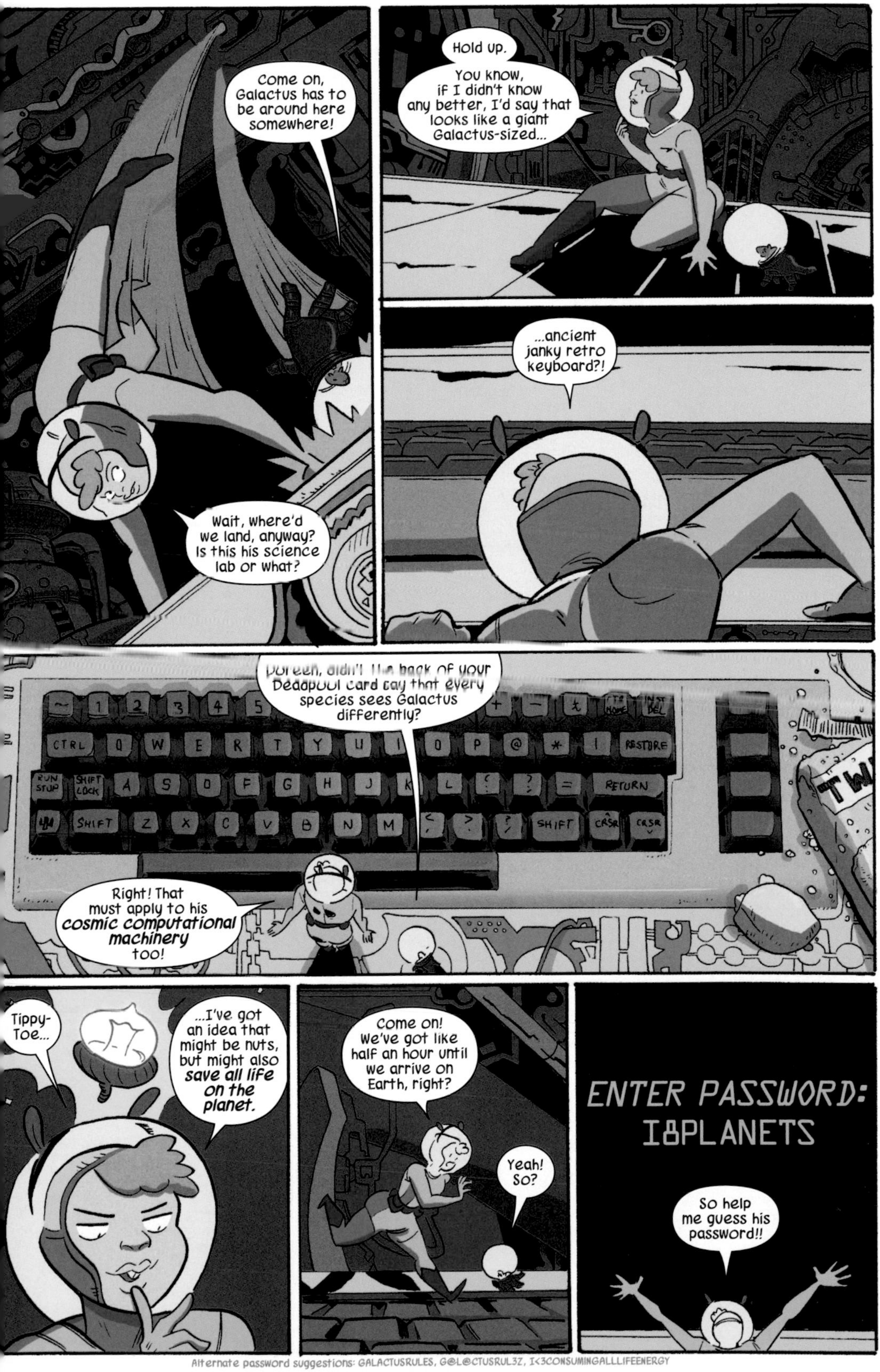
Come on, Galactus has to be around here somewhere!
Hold up.
You know, if I didn't know any better, I'd say that looks like a giant Galactus-sized...
Wait, where'd we land, anyway? Is this his science lab or what?
...ancient janky retro keyboard?!
Doreen, didn't the back of your Deadpool card say that every species sees Galactus differently?
Right! That must apply to his *cosmic computational machinery* too!
Tippy-Toe...
...I've got an idea that might be nuts, but might also *save all life on the planet.*
Come on! We've got like half an hour until we arrive on Earth, right?
Yeah! So?
ENTER PASSWORD:
I8PLANETS
So help me guess his password!!

Alternate password suggestions: GALACTUSRULES, G@L@CTUSRUL3Z, I<3CONSUMINGALLLIFEENERGY

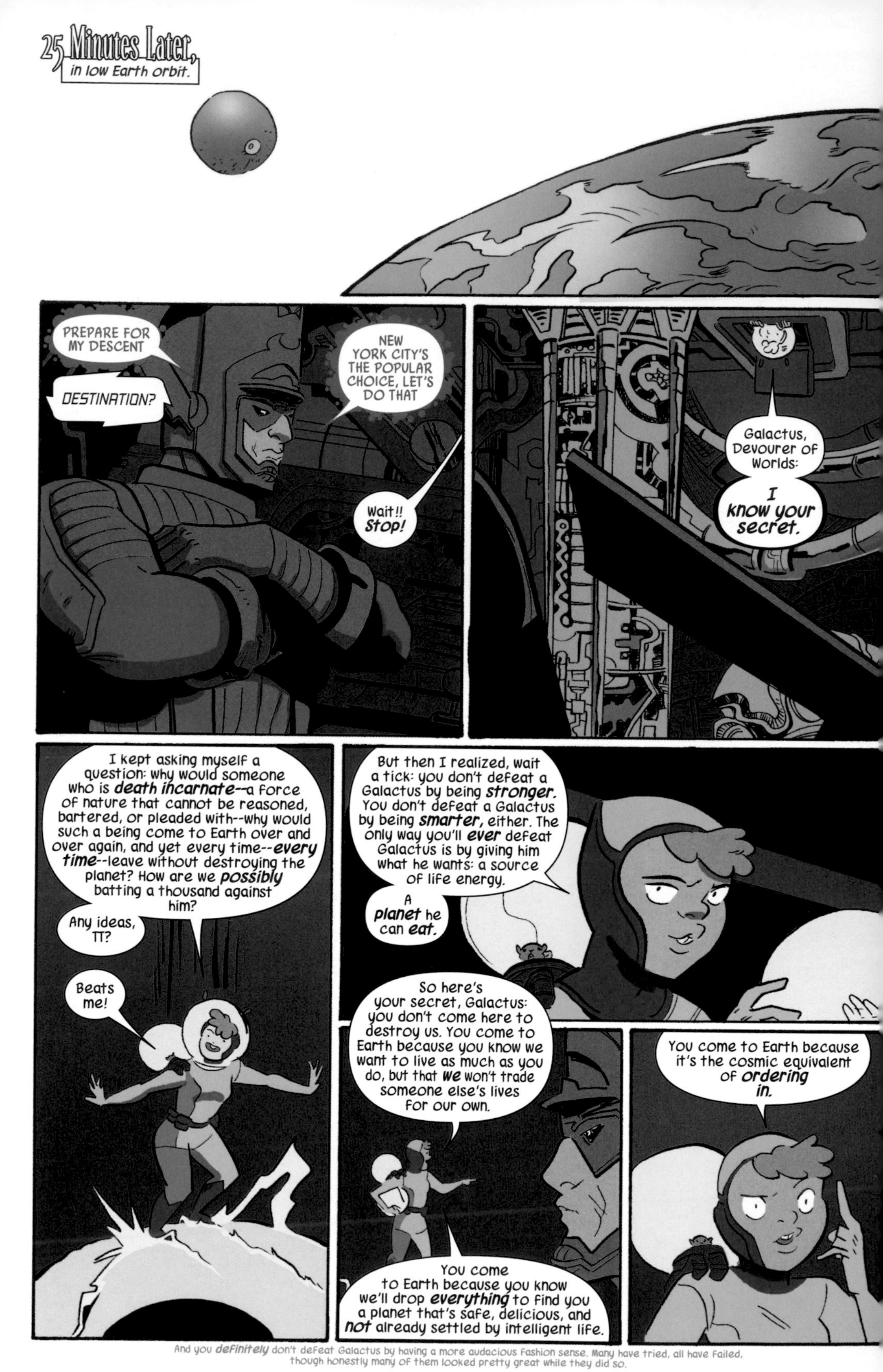
25 Minutes Later,
in low Earth orbit.
PREPARE FOR MY DESCENT
DESTINATION?
NEW YORK CITY'S THE POPULAR CHOICE, LET'S DO THAT
Wait!! Stop!
Galactus, Devourer of Worlds:
I know your secret.
I kept asking myself a question: why would someone who is death incarnate--a force of nature that cannot be reasoned, bartered, or pleaded with--why would such a being come to Earth over and over again, and yet every time--every time--leave without destroying the planet? How are we possibly batting a thousand against him?
Any ideas, TT?
Beats me!
But then I realized, wait a tick: you don't defeat a Galactus by being stronger. You don't defeat a Galactus by being smarter, either. The only way you'll ever defeat Galactus is by giving him what he wants: a source of life energy.
A planet he can eat.
So here's your secret, Galactus: you don't come here to destroy us. You come to Earth because you know we want to live as much as you do, but that we won't trade someone else's lives for our own.
You come to Earth because you know we'll drop everything to find you a planet that's safe, delicious, and not already settled by intelligent life.
You come to Earth because it's the cosmic equivalent of ordering in.

And you *definitely* don't defeat Galactus by having a more audacious fashion sense. Many have tried, all have failed, though honestly many of them looked pretty great while they did so.

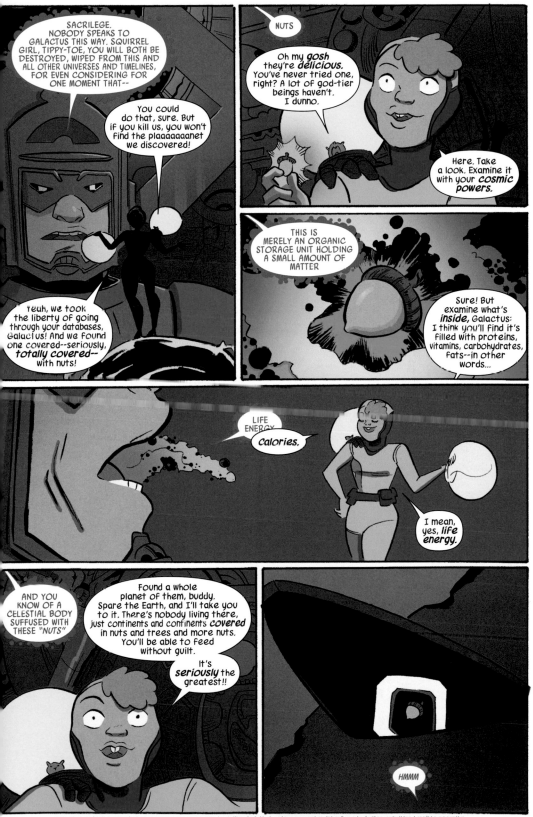

SACRILEGE. NOBODY SPEAKS TO GALACTUS THIS WAY. SQUIRREL GIRL, TIPPY-TOE, YOU WILL BOTH BE DESTROYED, WIPED FROM THIS AND ALL OTHER UNIVERSES AND TIMELINES, FOR EVEN CONSIDERING FOR ONE MOMENT THAT--

You could do that, sure. But if you kill us, you won't find the plaaaaaaanet we discovered!

Yeah, we took the liberty of going through your databases, Galactus! And we found one covered--seriously, *totally covered*-- with nuts!

NUTS

Oh my *gosh* they're *delicious.* You've never tried one, right? A lot of god-tier beings haven't. I dunno.

Here. Take a look. Examine it with your *cosmic powers.*

THIS IS MERELY AN ORGANIC STORAGE UNIT HOLDING A SMALL AMOUNT OF MATTER

Sure! But examine what's *inside,* Galactus: I think you'll find it's filled with proteins, vitamins, carbohydrates, fats--in other words...

LIFE ENERGY.

Calories.

I mean, yes, *life energy.*

AND YOU KNOW OF A CELESTIAL BODY SUFFUSED WITH THESE "NUTS"

Found a whole planet of them, buddy. Spare the Earth, and I'll take you to it. There's nobody living there, just continents and confinents *covered* in nuts and trees and more nuts. You'll be able to feed without guilt.

It's *seriously* the greatest!!

HMMM

Galactus, I don't know what your computers actually look like, but that retro computer interface had ultra-primitive terrible security. Do I thank you, or thank my imagination, or...?

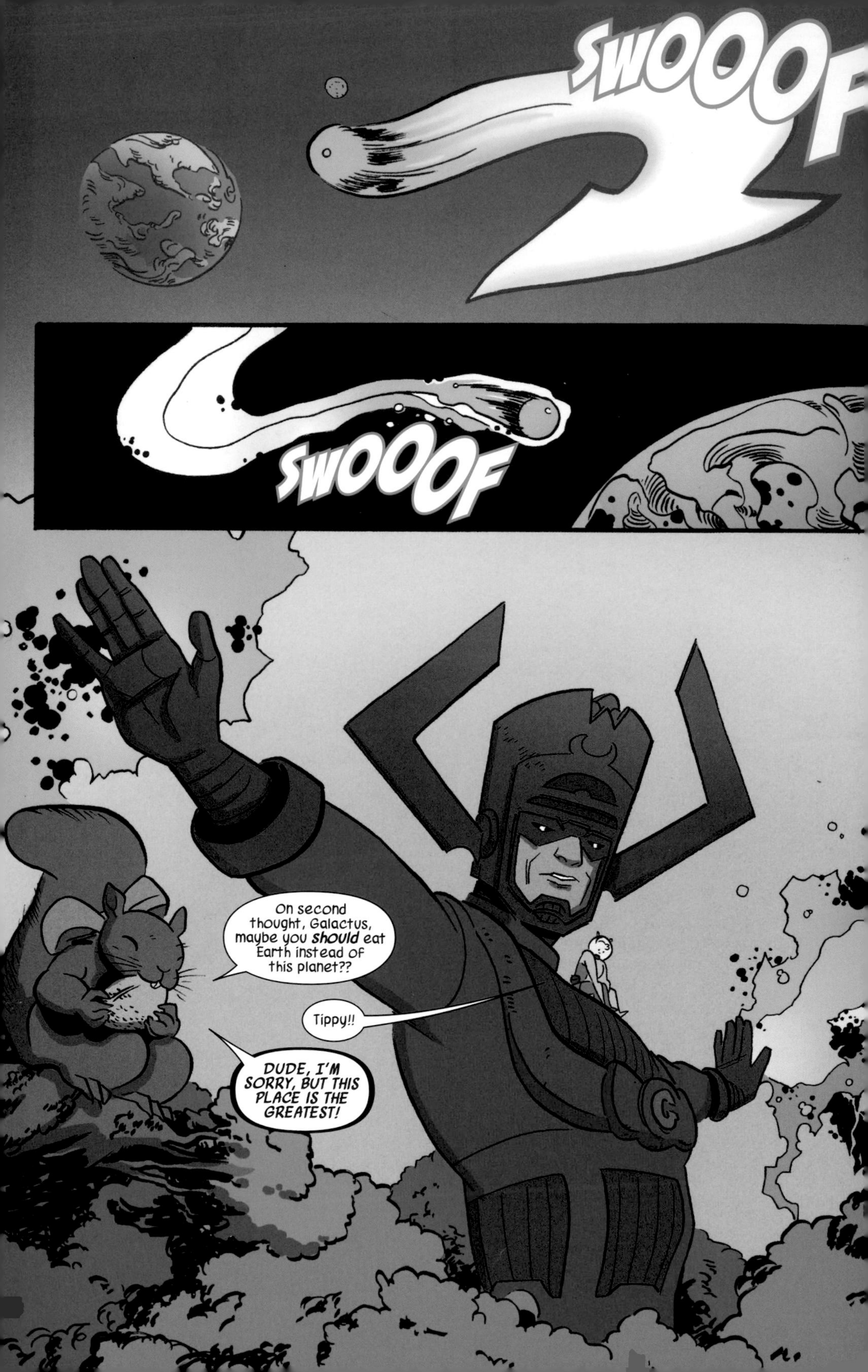
SWOOOF
SWOOOF
On second thought, Galactus, maybe you *should* eat Earth instead of this planet??
Tippy!!
DUDE, I'M SORRY, BUT THIS PLACE IS THE GREATEST!

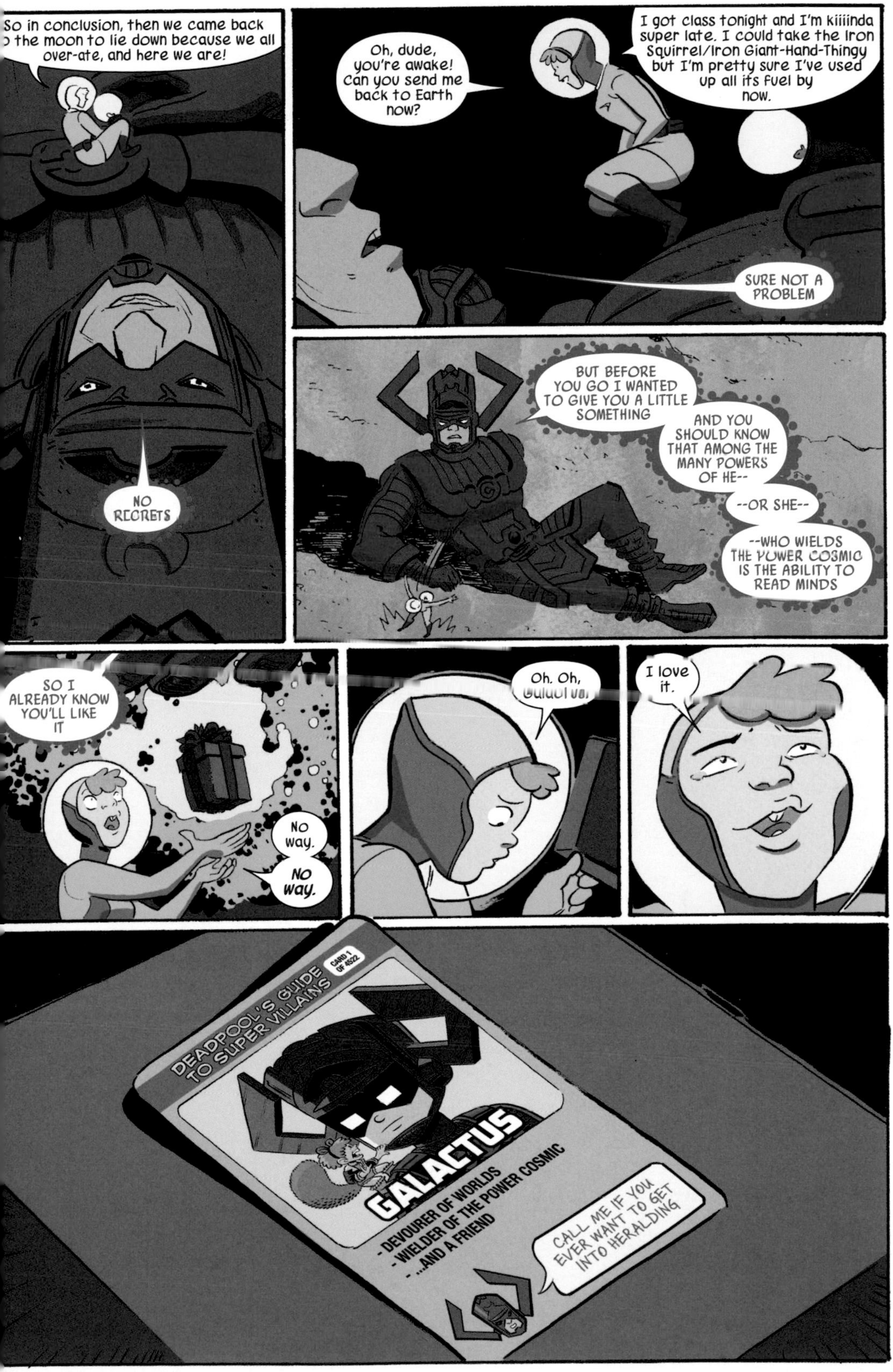

So in conclusion, then we came back o the moon to lie down because we all over-ate, and here we are!
NO REGRETS
Oh, dude, you're awake! Can you send me back to Earth now?
I got class tonight and I'm kiiiinda super late. I could take the Iron Squirrel/Iron Giant-Hand-Thingy but I'm pretty sure I've used up all its fuel by now.
SURE NOT A PROBLEM
BUT BEFORE YOU GO I WANTED TO GIVE YOU A LITTLE SOMETHING
AND YOU SHOULD KNOW THAT AMONG THE MANY POWERS OF HE--
--OR SHE--
--WHO WIELDS THE POWER COSMIC IS THE ABILITY TO READ MINDS
SO I ALREADY KNOW YOU'LL LIKE IT
No way.
No way.
Oh. Oh,
I love it.
DEADPOOL'S GUIDE TO SUPER VILLAINS
CARD 1 OF 4522
GALACTUS
- DEVOURER OF WORLDS
- WIELDER OF THE POWER COSMIC
- ...AND A FRIEND
CALL ME IF YOU EVER WANT TO GET INTO HERALDING

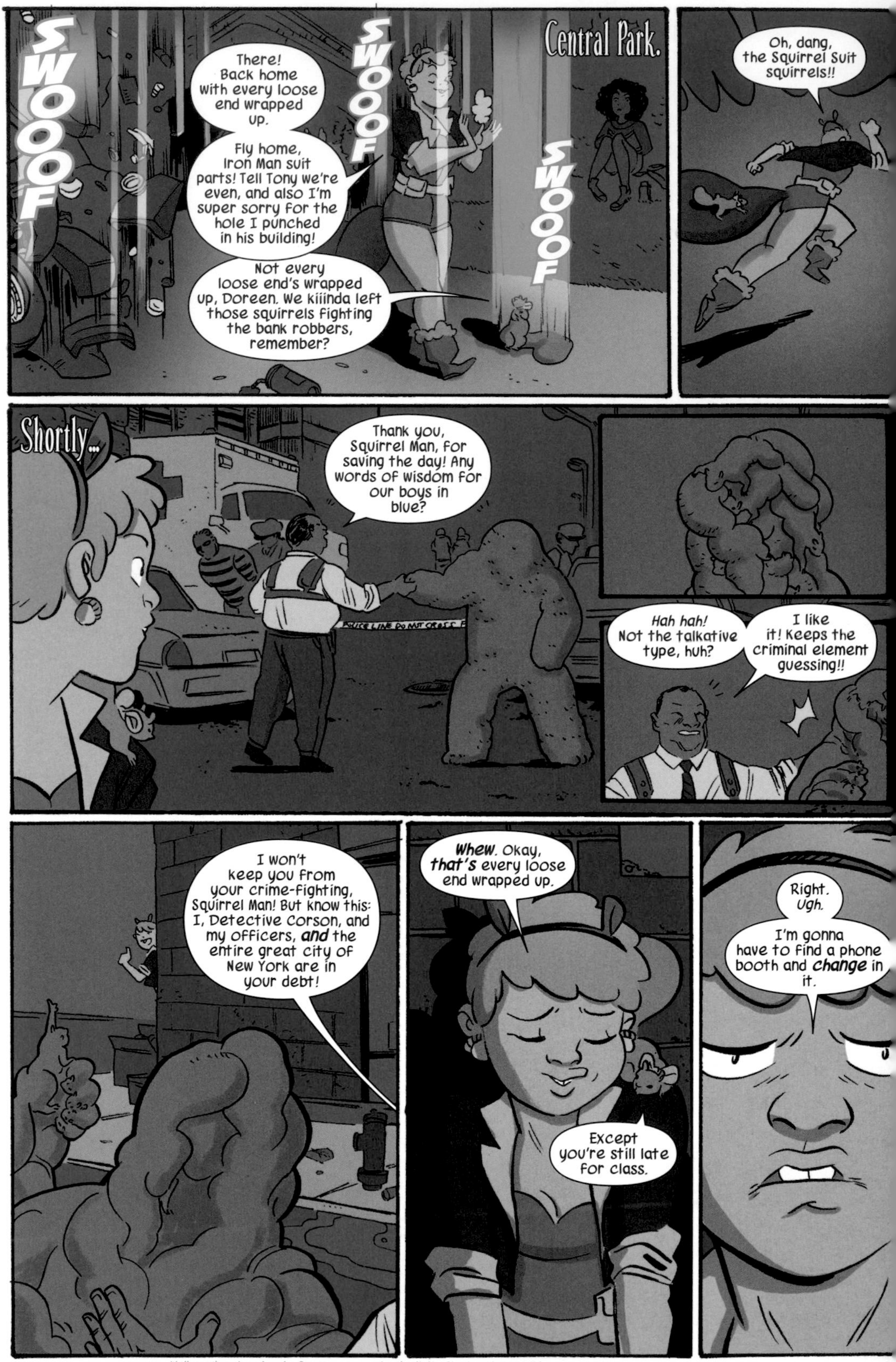
SWOOOF
SWOOOF
Central Park.
There! Back home with every loose end wrapped up.
Fly home, Iron Man suit parts! Tell Tony we're even, and also I'm super sorry for the hole I punched in his building!
SWOOOF
Not every loose end's wrapped up, Doreen. We kiiinda left those squirrels fighting the bank robbers, remember?
Oh, dang, the Squirrel Suit squirrels!!
Shortly...
Thank you, Squirrel Man, for saving the day! Any words of wisdom for our boys in blue?
Hah hah! Not the talkative type, huh?
I like it! Keeps the criminal element guessing!!
I won't keep you from your crime-fighting, Squirrel Man! But know this: I, Detective Corson, and my officers, and the entire great city of New York are in your debt!
Whew. Okay, that's every loose end wrapped up.
Except you're still late for class.
Right. Ugh.
I'm gonna have to find a phone booth and change in it.

Well, you're almost out of power, so maybe don't fly. Slowly walk or roll home, Iron Man suits!! You're free now!

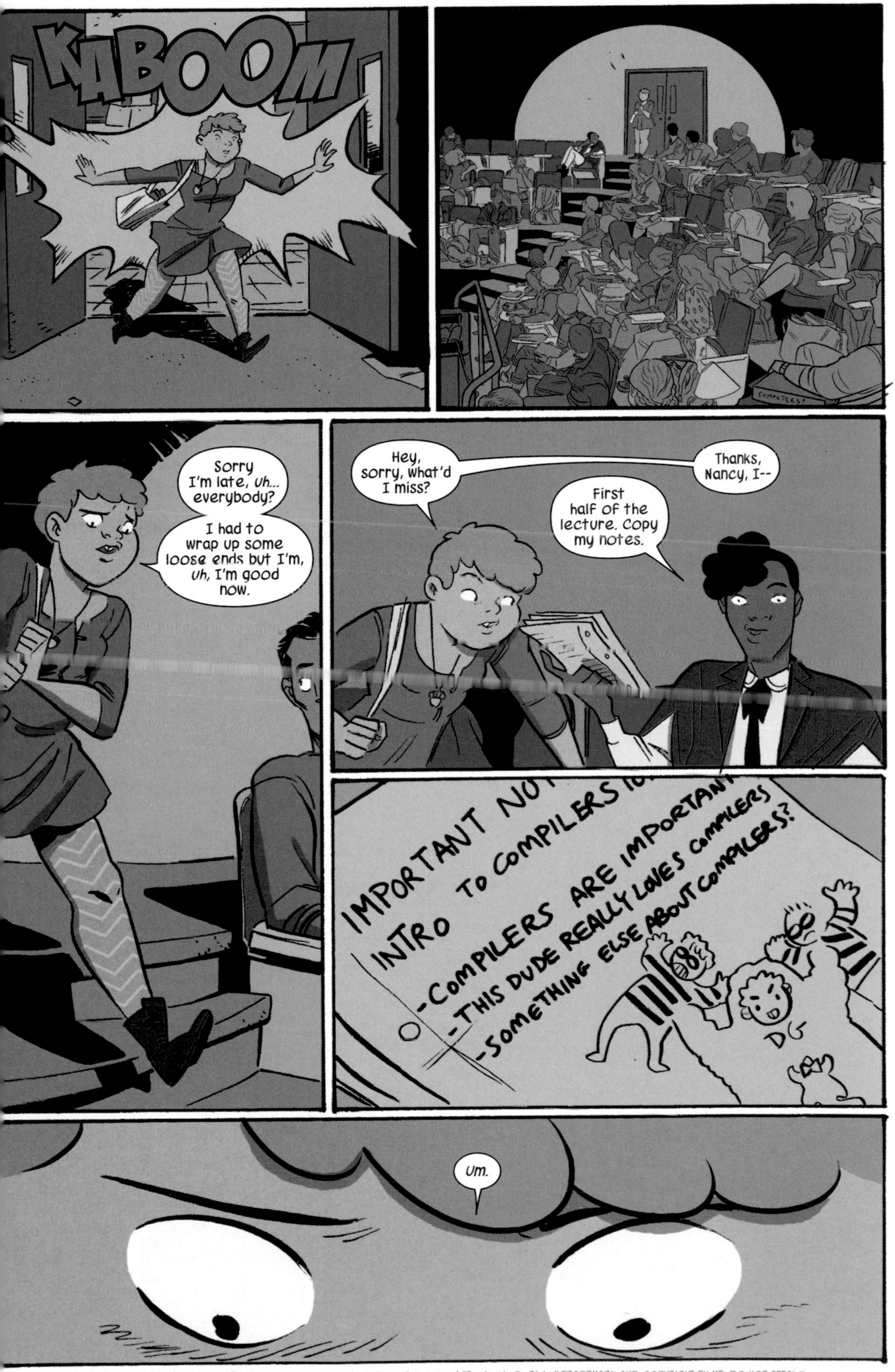
KABOOM
Sorry I'm late, uh... everybody?
I had to wrap up some loose ends but I'm, uh, I'm good now.
Hey, sorry, what'd I miss?
First half of the lecture. Copy my notes.
Thanks, Nancy, I--
IMPORTANT NO
INTRO TO COMPILERS
-COMPILERS ARE IMPORTANT
-THIS DUDE REALLY LOVES COMPILERS
-SOMETHING ELSE ABOUT COMPILERS?
DG
Um.

Oh, don't worry, that's not you! That's my new 100% original character named "Squirrely D. Girly." TRADEMARK AND COPYRIGHT BY ME, DO NOT STEAL!!

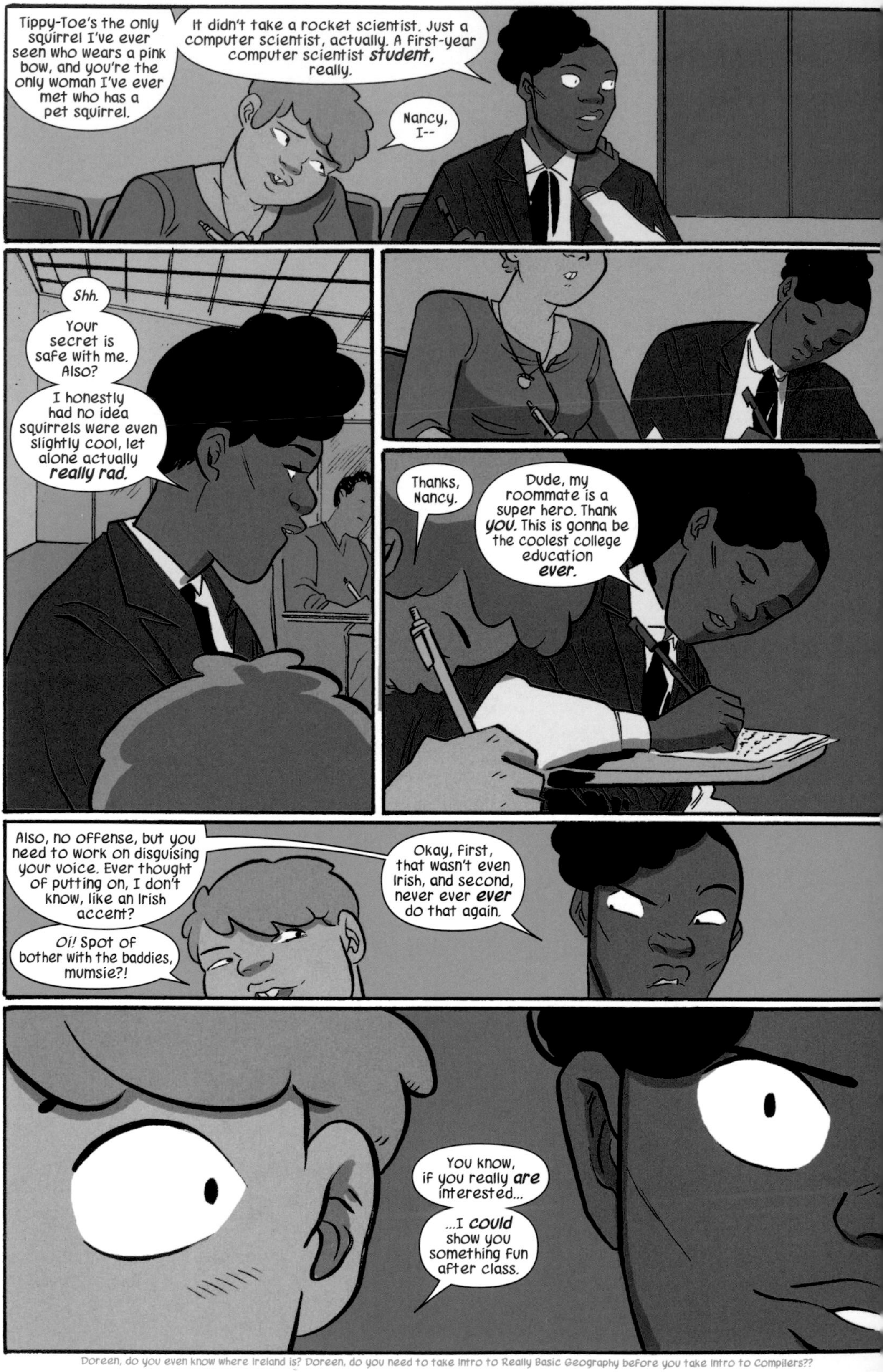
Tippy-Toe's the only squirrel I've ever seen who wears a pink bow, and you're the only woman I've ever met who has a pet squirrel.
It didn't take a rocket scientist. Just a computer scientist, actually. A first-year computer scientist *student*, really.
Nancy, I--
Shh.
Your secret is safe with me. Also?
I honestly had no idea squirrels were even slightly cool, let alone actually ***really rad.***
Thanks, Nancy.
Dude, my roommate is a super hero. Thank ***you.*** This is gonna be the coolest college education ***ever.***
Also, no offense, but you need to work on disguising your voice. Ever thought of putting on, I don't know, like an Irish accent?
Oi! Spot of bother with the baddies, mumsie?!
Okay, first, that wasn't even Irish, and second, never ever ***ever*** do that again.
You know, if you really ***are*** interested...
...I ***could*** show you something fun after class.

Doreen, do you even know where Ireland is? Doreen, do you need to take Intro to Really Basic Geography before you take Intro to Compilers??

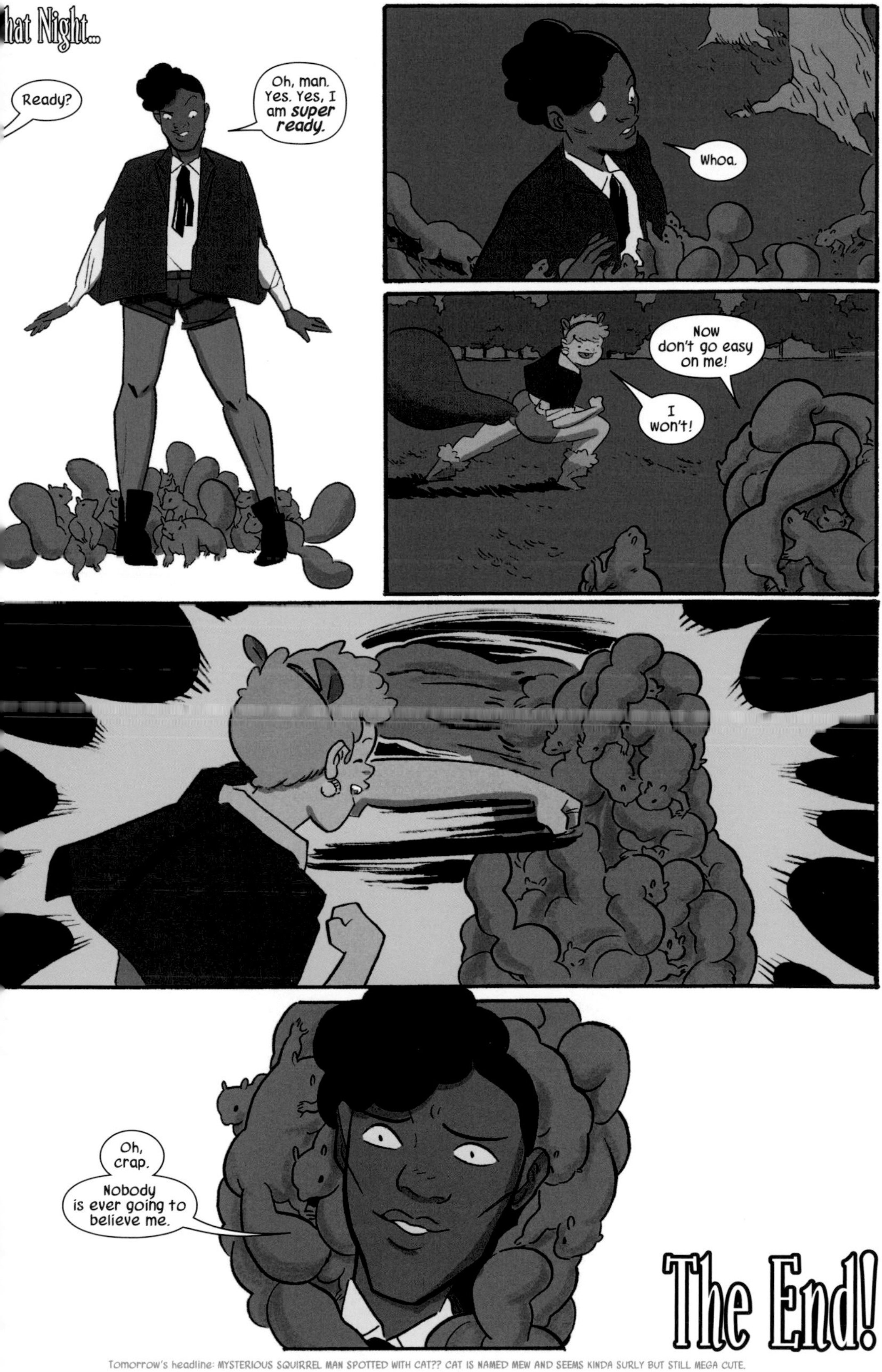
hat Night...
Ready?
Oh, man. Yes. Yes, I am super ready.
Whoa.
Now don't go easy on me!
I won't!
Oh, crap.
Nobody is ever going to believe me.
The End!
Tomorrow's headline: MYSTERIOUS SQUIRREL MAN SPOTTED WITH CAT?? CAT IS NAMED MEW AND SEEMS KINDA SURLY BUT STILL MEGA CUTE.

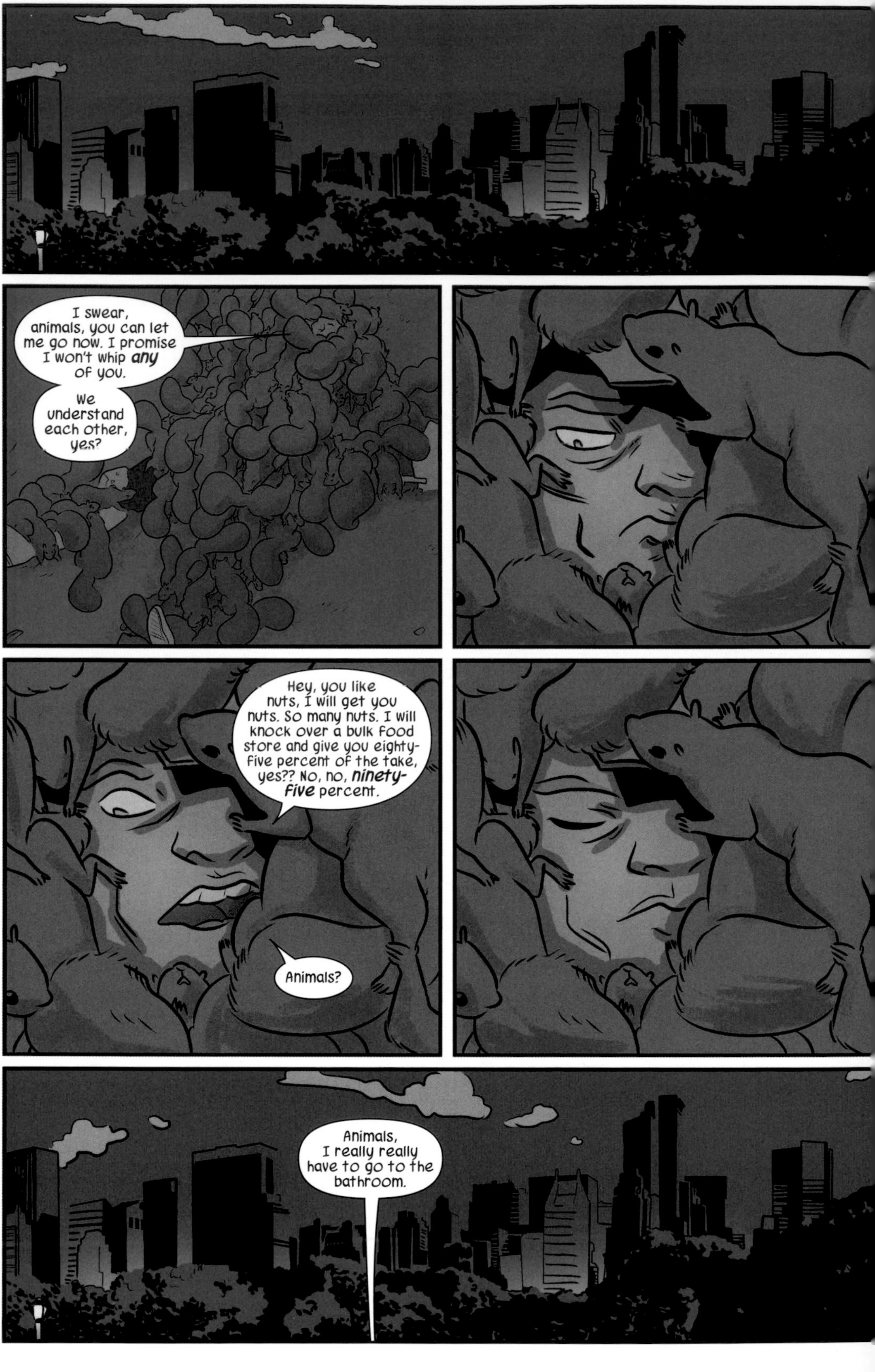
I swear, animals, you can let me go now. I promise I won't whip *any* of you.
We understand each other, yes?
Hey, you like nuts, I will get you nuts. So many nuts. I will knock over a bulk food store and give you eighty-five percent of the take, yes?? No, no, *ninety-five* percent.
Animals?
Animals, I really really have to go to the bathroom.

5

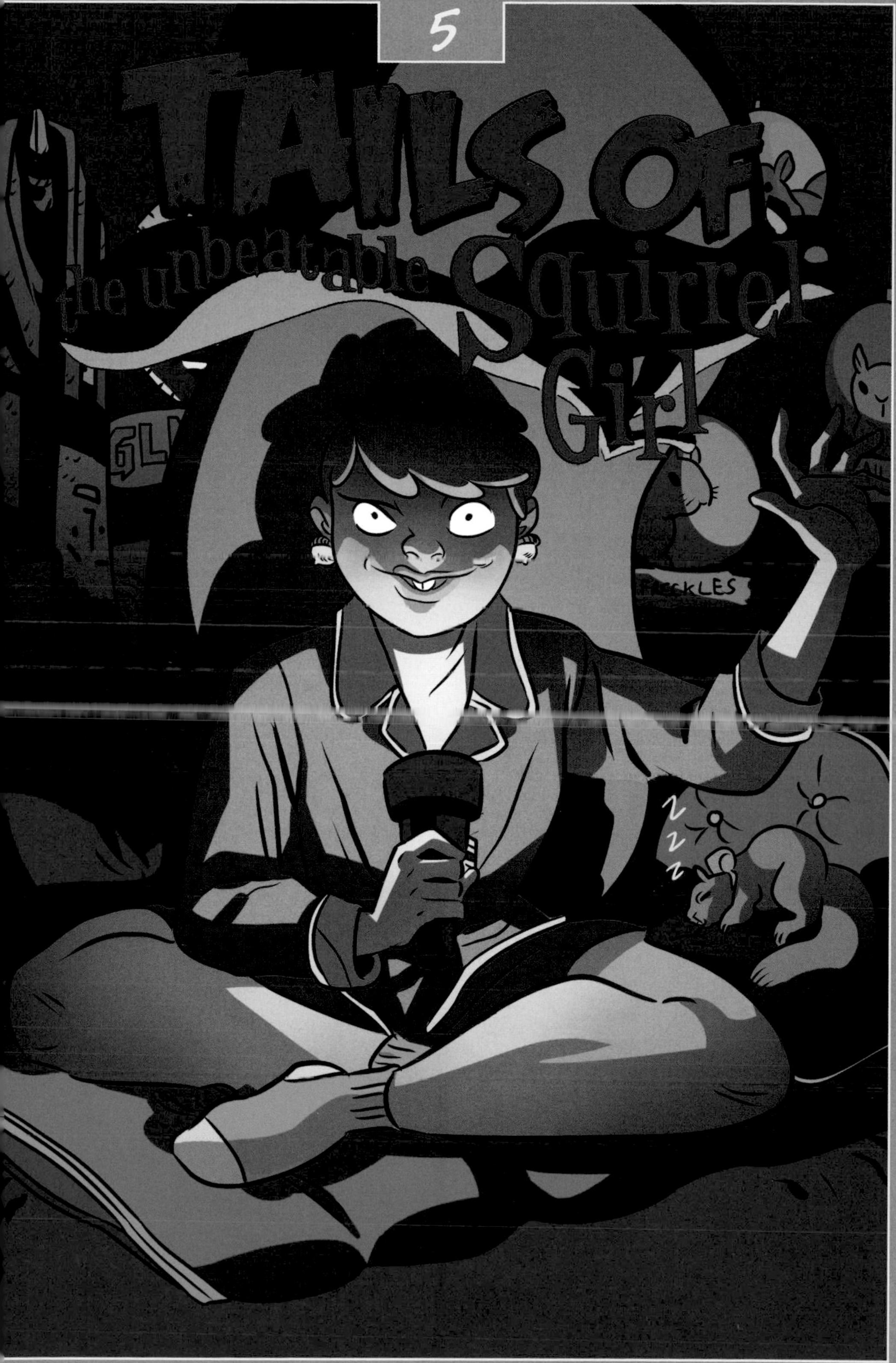
TAILS OF the unbeatable Squirrel Girl
Z
Z
Z
FRECKLES

Doreen Green isn't just a first-year computer science student: she secretly also has all the powers of both squirrel and g...
She uses her amazing abilities to fight crime **and** be as awesome as possible. You know her as...*The Unbeatable Squirrel Gir*
Let's catch up with what she's been up to until now, with...

Squirrel Girl *in a nutshell*

search! 🔍

#dinosaurs

#basslass

#clones

#acronyms

#nuthorde

#TIPPPPPPPY!!

Squirrel Girl! @unbeatablesg
@xGALACTUSx hey dude thanks for not eating the planet after all!!

GALACTUS @xGALACTUSx
@unbeatablesg NO PROBLEM THAT PLANET OF NUTS YOU FOUND WAS WAY BETTER ANYWAY

Deadpool @pooltothedead
@unbeatablesg @xGALACTUSx Wait, what? You guys weren't joking about that?

Deadpool @pooltothedead
@unbeatablesg @xGALACTUSx Galactus ACTUALLY came to Earth?? Yesterday? The ACTUAL GALACTUS was HERE??

Deadpool @pooltothedead
@unbeatablesg @xGALACTUSx dang man I spent the whole day at home watching tv in my underpants

Deadpool @pooltothedead
@unbeatablesg @xGALACTUSx CALL ME NEXT TIME!!

Tony Stark @starkmantony ✓
A bunch of my Iron Man suit parts showed up in NYC with moon dust on them. That's actually extremely valuable, so thanks @unbeatablesg.

Tippy-Toe @yoitstippytoe
@starkmantony CHITT CHUK CHITTT?

Tony Stark @starkmantony ✓
@yoitstippytoe I can't understand you. None of my translation algorithms can understand you. Probably because you are a literal squirrel.

Tippy-Toe @yoitstippytoe
@starkmantony CHUKKA.... CHITT CHUK CHITTT?

Tony Stark @starkmantony ✓
@unbeatablesg Little help?

Squirrel Girl! @unbeatablesg
@starkmantony she's asking you if you figured out that the dust came from the new moon restaurant

Tony Stark @starkmantony ✓
@unbeatablesg @yoitstippytoe What new moon restaurant?

Tippy-Toe @yoitstippytoe
@starkmantony CHUTT CHUK CHUKK CHITTY CHIT

Squirrel Girl! @unbeatablesg
@starkmantony She says "The one that just opened up! The food's good, but it doesn't have much of an ATMOSPHERE"

Squirrel Girl! @unbeatablesg
@starkmantony hahaha, that's pretty good actually!! good work @yoitstippytoe

Tony Stark @starkmantony ✓
@unbeatablesg @yoitstippytoe You guys know I'm the head of a major corporation, right?

Tony Stark @starkmantony ✓
@unbeatablesg @yoitstippytoe I shouldn't even be hanging out here as it is

Nancy W. @sewwiththeflo
I bet being covered from head to toe in a living squirrel suit doesn't smell as bad as you think it would.

Nancy W. @sewwiththeflo
IMPORTANT UPDATE:

Nancy W. @sewwiththeflo
So it turns out being covered head to toe in a living squirrel suit doesn't smell as GOOD as you think it would either

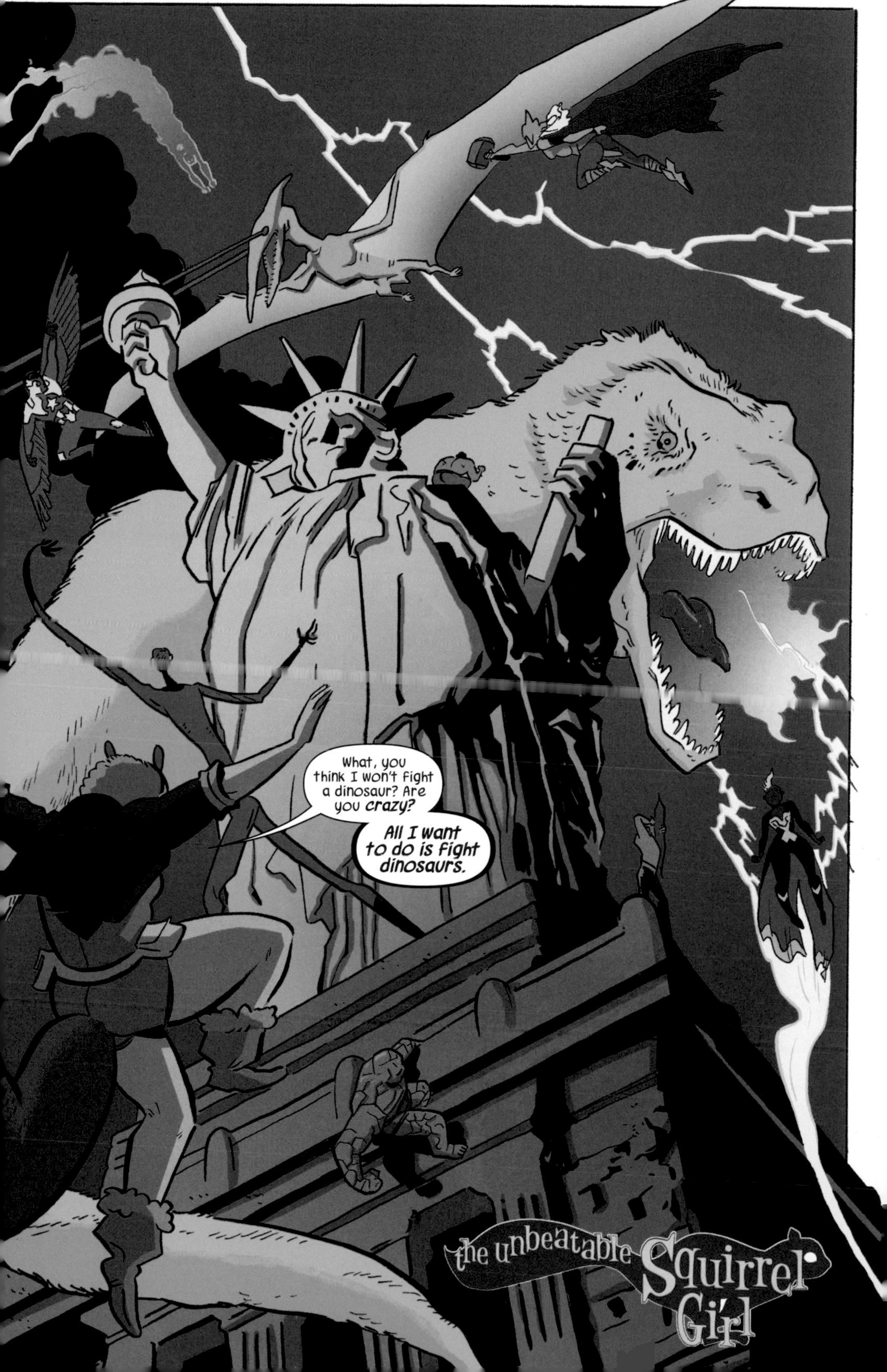
What, you think I won't fight a dinosaur? Are you *crazy*?
All I want to do is fight dinosaurs.
the unbeatable Squirrel Girl

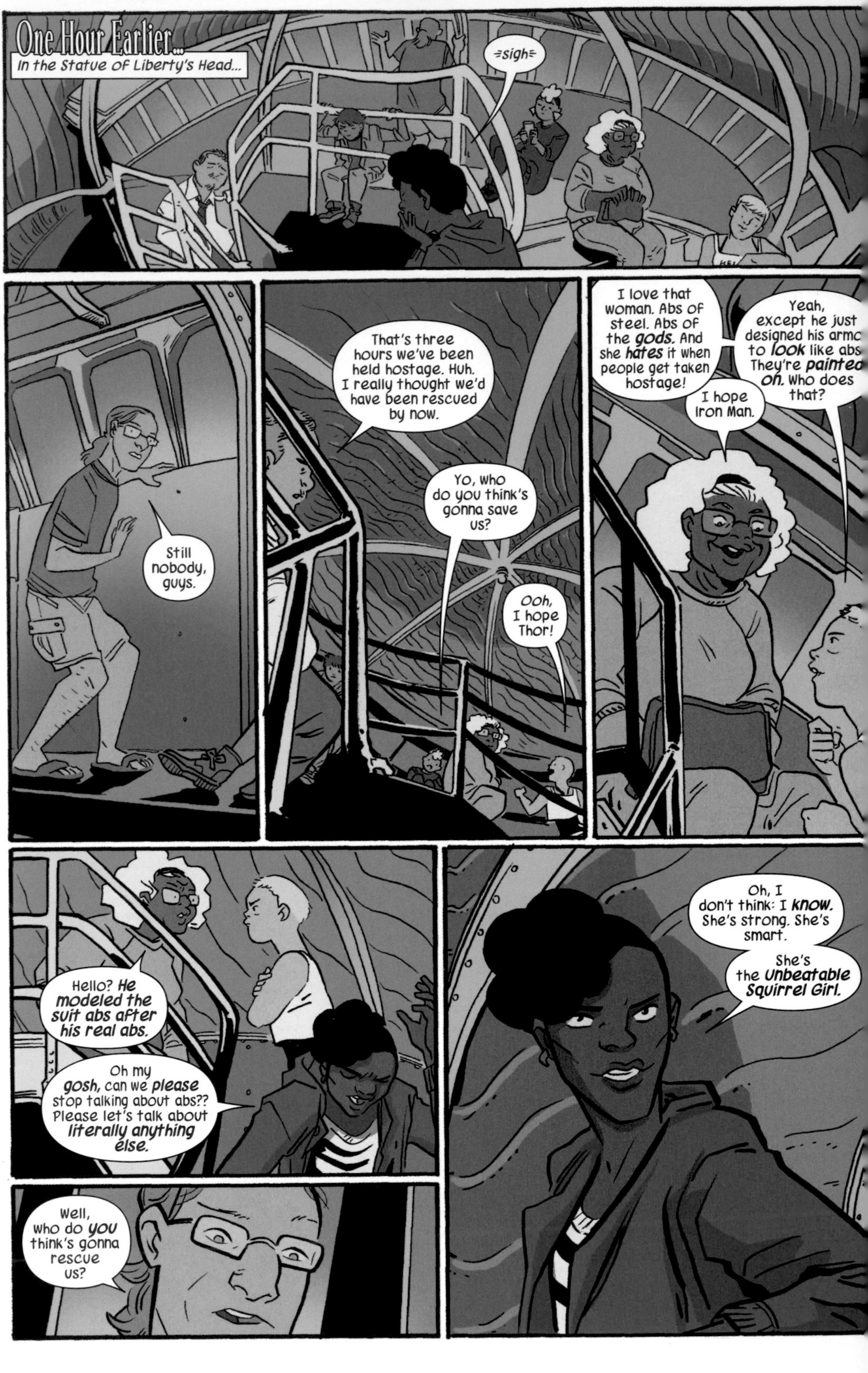

One Hour Earlier...
In the Statue of Liberty's Head...
=sigh=
Still nobody, guys.
That's three hours we've been held hostage. Huh. I really thought we'd have been rescued by now.
Yo, who do you think's gonna save us?
Ooh, I hope Thor!
I love that woman. Abs of steel. Abs of the gods. And she hates it when people get taken hostage!
I hope Iron Man.
Yeah, except he just designed his armo to look like abs They're paintea on. Who does that?
Hello? He modeled the suit abs after his real abs.
Oh my gosh, can we please stop talking about abs?? Please let's talk about literally anything else.
Well, who do you think's gonna rescue us?
Oh, I don't think: I know. She's strong. She's smart.
She's the Unbeatable Squirrel Girl.

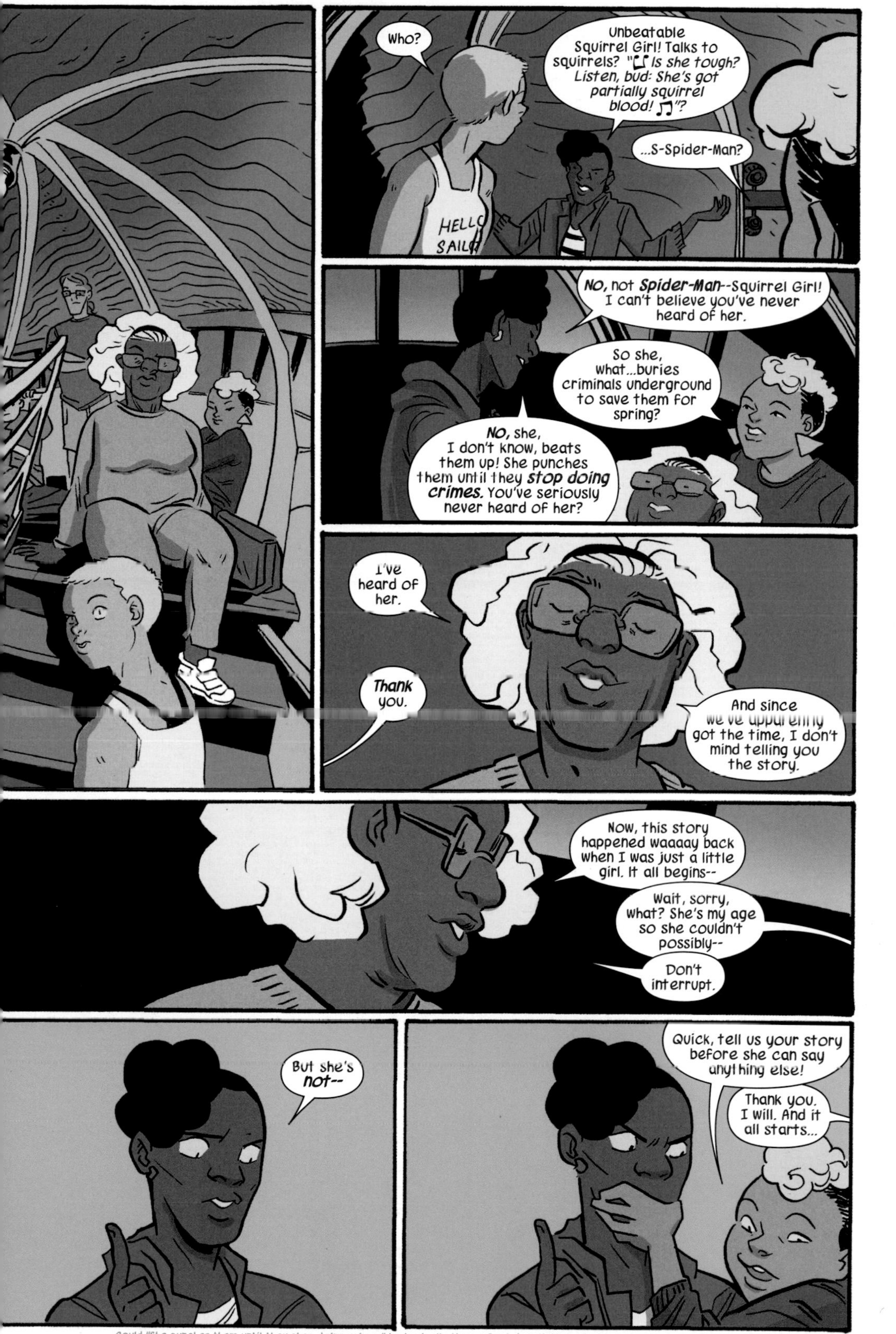
Who?
Unbeatable Squirrel Girl! Talks to squirrels? "♫ Is she tough? Listen, bud: She's got partially squirrel blood! ♫"?
...S-Spider-Man?
HELLO SAILO
NO, not Spider-Man--Squirrel Girl! I can't believe you've never heard of her.
So she, what...buries criminals underground to save them for spring?
NO, she, I don't know, beats them up! She punches them until they stop doing crimes. You've seriously never heard of her?
I've heard of her.
Thank you.
And since we've apparently got the time, I don't mind telling you the story.
Now, this story happened waaaay back when I was just a little girl. It all begins--
Wait, sorry, what? She's my age so she couldn't possibly--
Don't interrupt.
But she's not--
Quick, tell us your story before she can say anything else!
Thank you. I will. And it all starts...

Could "She punches them until they stop doing crimes" be basically the perfect description of every super hero ever?
This author who just now wrote that sentence says: yes!

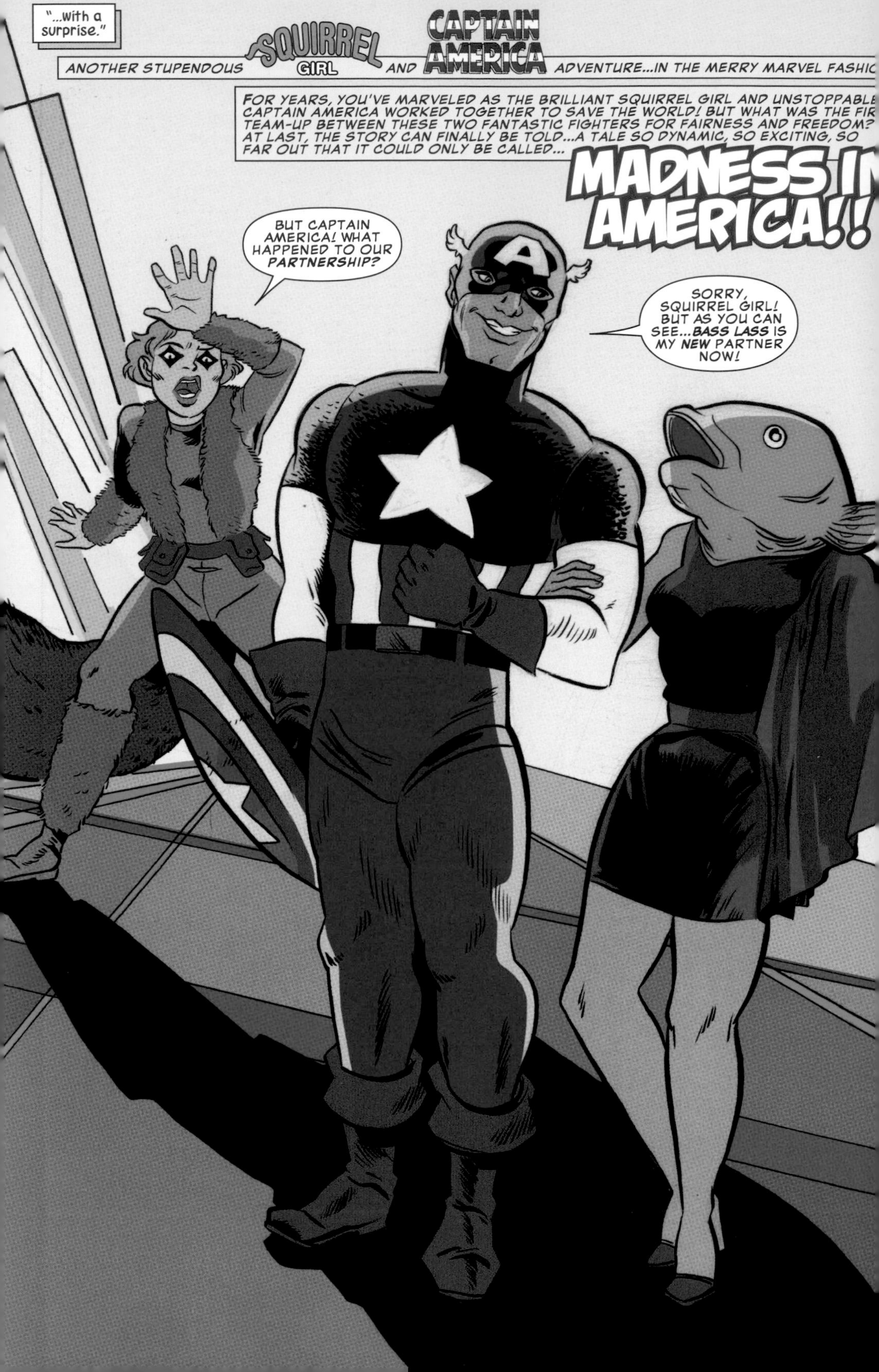
"...with a surprise."
SQUIRREL GIRL
CAPTAIN AMERICA
ANOTHER STUPENDOUS SQUIRREL GIRL AND CAPTAIN AMERICA ADVENTURE...IN THE MERRY MARVEL FASHIO
FOR YEARS, YOU'VE MARVELED AS THE BRILLIANT SQUIRREL GIRL AND UNSTOPPABLE CAPTAIN AMERICA WORKED TOGETHER TO SAVE THE WORLD! BUT WHAT WAS THE FIR TEAM-UP BETWEEN THESE TWO FANTASTIC FIGHTERS FOR FAIRNESS AND FREEDOM? AT LAST, THE STORY CAN FINALLY BE TOLD...A TALE SO DYNAMIC, SO EXCITING, SO FAR OUT THAT IT COULD ONLY BE CALLED...
MADNESS IN AMERICA!!
BUT CAPTAIN AMERICA! WHAT HAPPENED TO OUR PARTNERSHIP?
SORRY, SQUIRREL GIRL! BUT AS YOU CAN SEE...BASS LASS IS MY NEW PARTNER NOW!

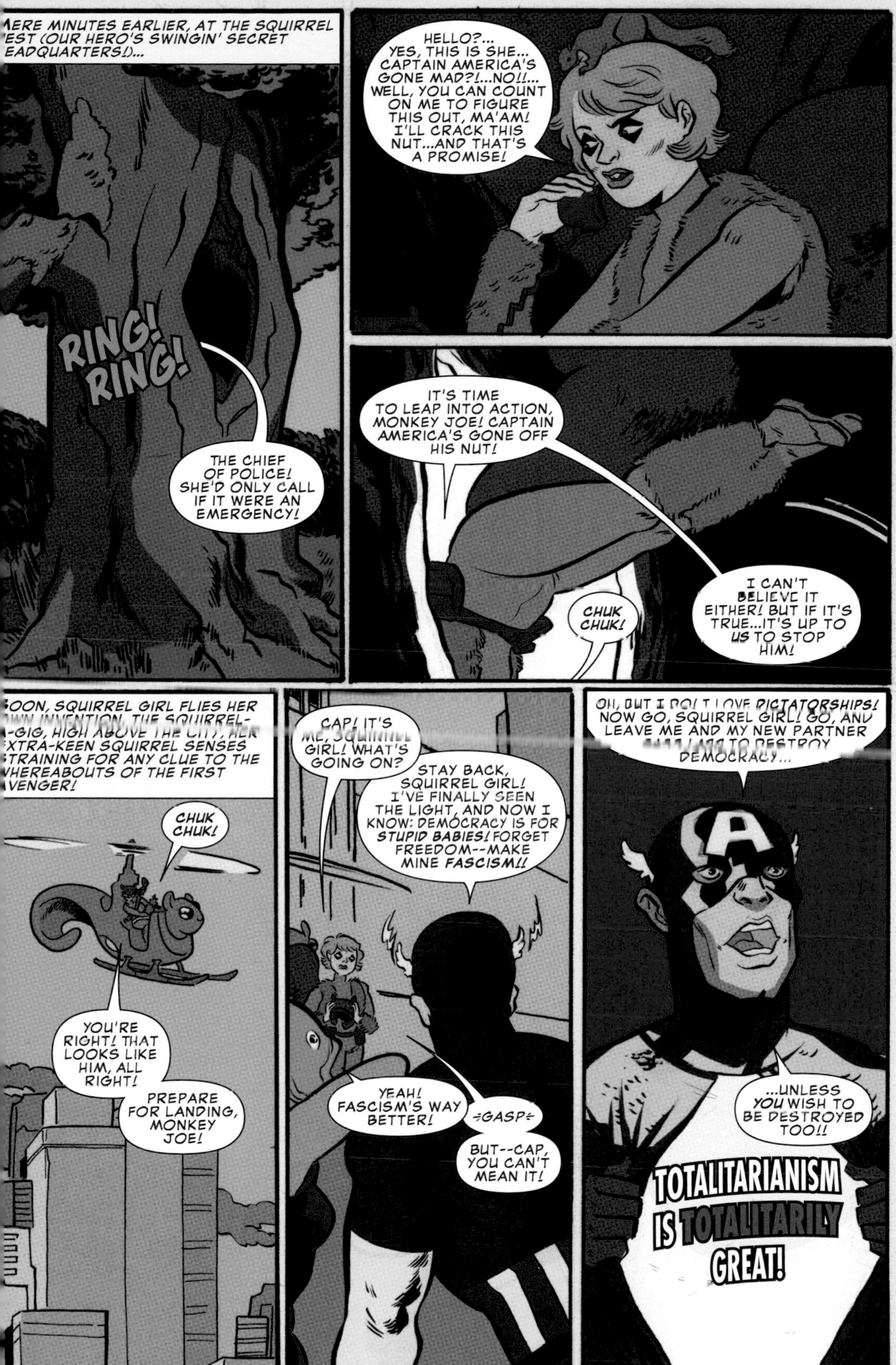
MERE MINUTES EARLIER, AT THE SQUIRREL NEST (OUR HERO'S SWINGIN' SECRET HEADQUARTERS!)...
RING! RING!
THE CHIEF OF POLICE! SHE'D ONLY CALL IF IT WERE AN EMERGENCY!
HELLO?... YES, THIS IS SHE... CAPTAIN AMERICA'S GONE MAD?!...NO!!... WELL, YOU CAN COUNT ON ME TO FIGURE THIS OUT, MA'AM! I'LL CRACK THIS NUT...AND THAT'S A PROMISE!
IT'S TIME TO LEAP INTO ACTION, MONKEY JOE! CAPTAIN AMERICA'S GONE OFF HIS NUT!
CHUK CHUK!
I CAN'T BELIEVE IT EITHER! BUT IF IT'S TRUE...IT'S UP TO US TO STOP HIM!
SOON, SQUIRREL GIRL FLIES HER OWN INVENTION, THE SQUIRREL-A-GIG, HIGH ABOVE THE CITY, HER EXTRA-KEEN SQUIRREL SENSES STRAINING FOR ANY CLUE TO THE WHEREABOUTS OF THE FIRST AVENGER!
CHUK CHUK!
YOU'RE RIGHT! THAT LOOKS LIKE HIM, ALL RIGHT!
PREPARE FOR LANDING, MONKEY JOE!
CAP! IT'S ME, SQUIRREL GIRL! WHAT'S GOING ON?
STAY BACK, SQUIRREL GIRL! I'VE FINALLY SEEN THE LIGHT, AND NOW I KNOW: DEMOCRACY IS FOR STUPID BABIES! FORGET FREEDOM--MAKE MINE FASCISM!!
YEAH! FASCISM'S WAY BETTER!
=GASP=
BUT--CAP, YOU CAN'T MEAN IT!
DICTATORSHIPS! NOW GO, SQUIRREL GIRL! GO, AND LEAVE ME AND MY NEW PARTNER
DEMOCRACY...
...UNLESS YOU WISH TO BE DESTROYED TOO!!
TOTALITARIANISM IS TOTALITARILY GREAT!

Wait, wait!! Finish reading this comic before you run off to smash the state! There's a small chance that Captain America is wrong here!

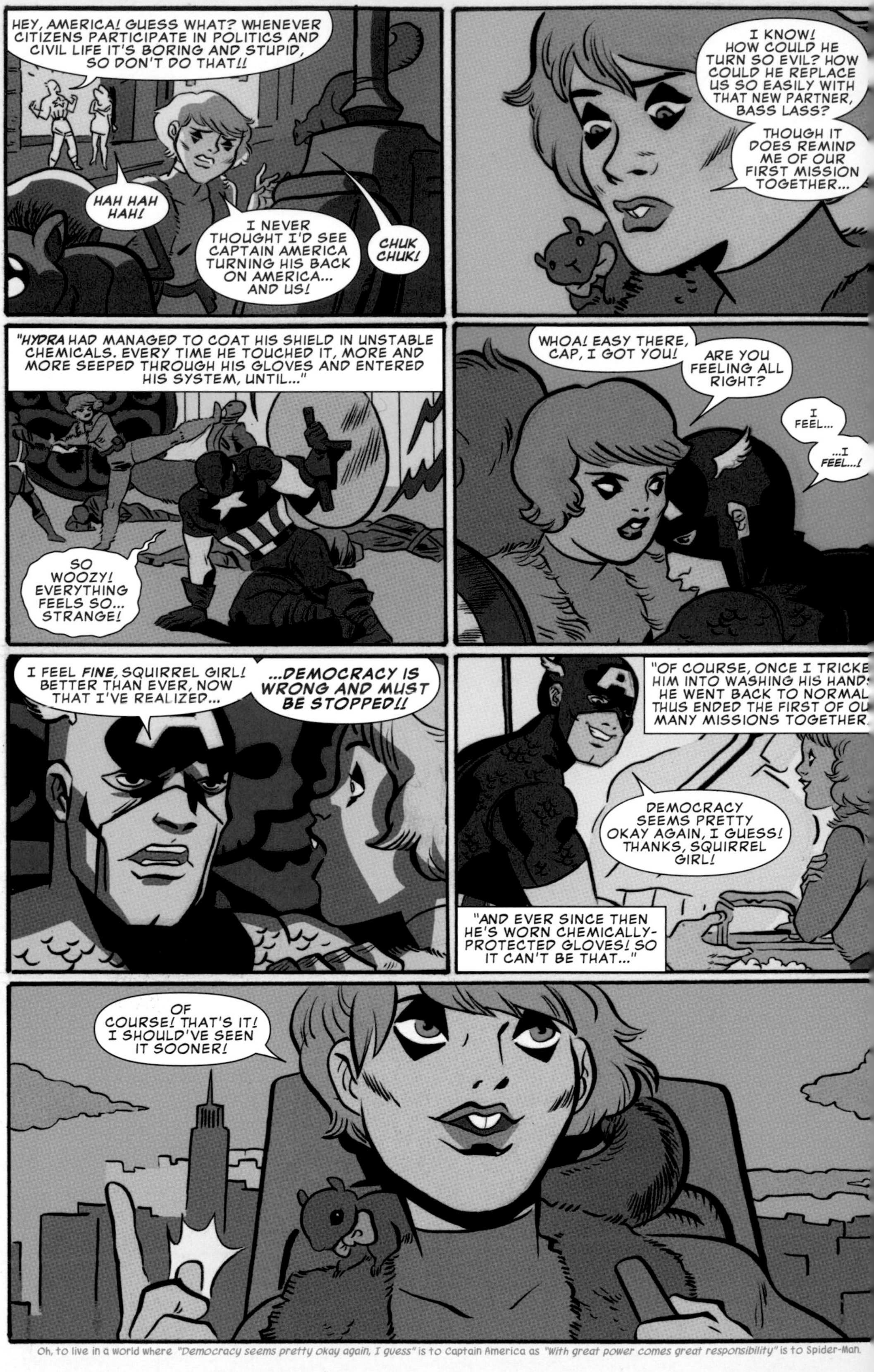

HEY, AMERICA! GUESS WHAT? WHENEVER CITIZENS PARTICIPATE IN POLITICS AND CIVIL LIFE IT'S BORING AND STUPID, SO DON'T DO THAT!!
HAH HAH HAH!
I NEVER THOUGHT I'D SEE CAPTAIN AMERICA TURNING HIS BACK ON AMERICA... AND US!
CHUK CHUK!
I KNOW! HOW COULD HE TURN SO EVIL? HOW COULD HE REPLACE US SO EASILY WITH THAT NEW PARTNER, BASS LASS?
THOUGH IT DOES REMIND ME OF OUR FIRST MISSION TOGETHER...
"HYDRA HAD MANAGED TO COAT HIS SHIELD IN UNSTABLE CHEMICALS. EVERY TIME HE TOUCHED IT, MORE AND MORE SEEPED THROUGH HIS GLOVES AND ENTERED HIS SYSTEM, UNTIL..."
SO WOOZY! EVERYTHING FEELS SO... STRANGE!
WHOA! EASY THERE, CAP, I GOT YOU!
ARE YOU FEELING ALL RIGHT?
I FEEL...
...I FEEL...!
I FEEL FINE, SQUIRREL GIRL! BETTER THAN EVER, NOW THAT I'VE REALIZED...
...DEMOCRACY IS WRONG AND MUST BE STOPPED!!
"OF COURSE, ONCE I TRICKE HIM INTO WASHING HIS HANDS HE WENT BACK TO NORMAL THUS ENDED THE FIRST OF OU MANY MISSIONS TOGETHER.
DEMOCRACY SEEMS PRETTY OKAY AGAIN, I GUESS! THANKS, SQUIRREL GIRL!
"AND EVER SINCE THEN HE'S WORN CHEMICALLY-PROTECTED GLOVES! SO IT CAN'T BE THAT..."
OF COURSE! THAT'S IT! I SHOULD'VE SEEN IT SOONER!

Oh, to live in a world where *"Democracy seems pretty okay again, I guess"* is to Captain America as *"With great power comes great responsibility"* is to Spider-Man.

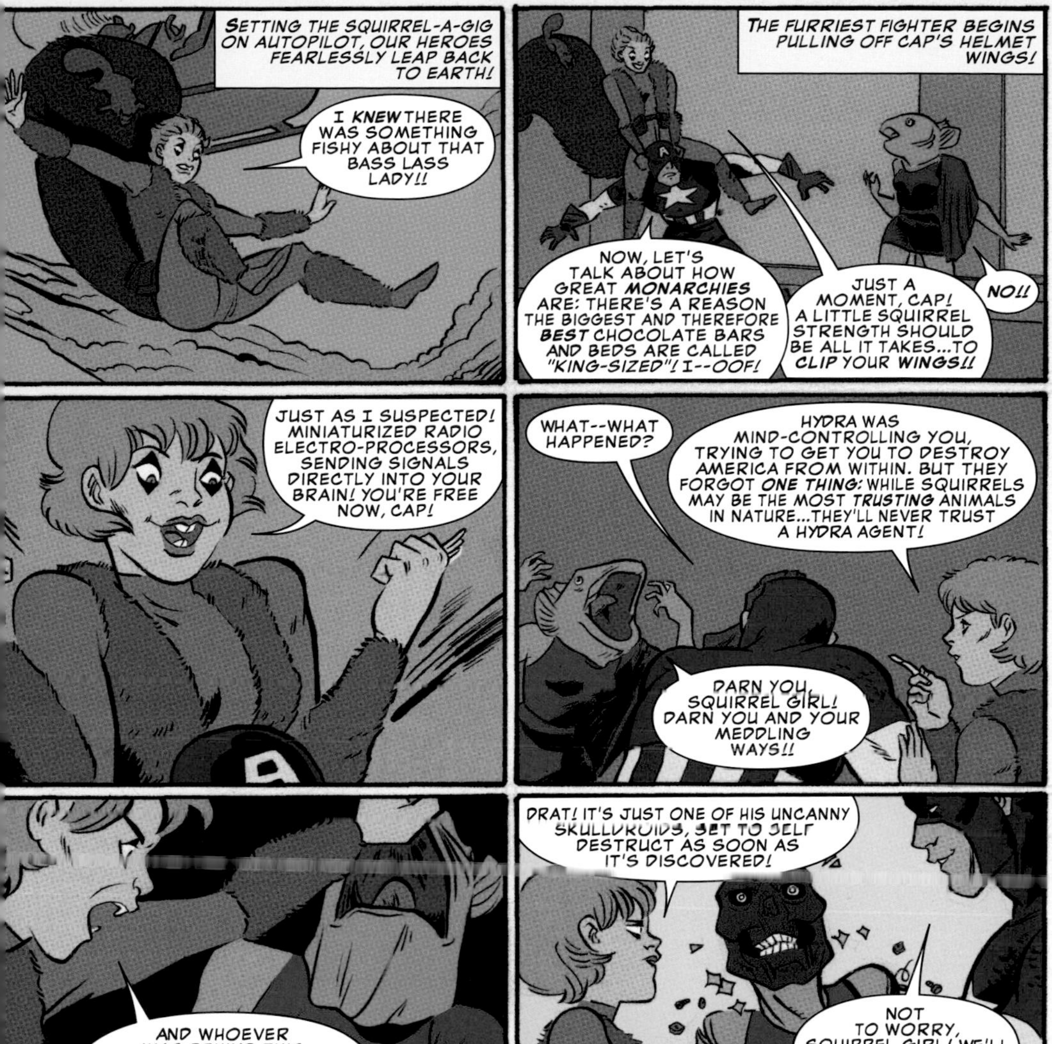
SETTING THE SQUIRREL-A-GIG ON AUTOPILOT, OUR HEROES FEARLESSLY LEAP BACK TO EARTH!
I KNEW THERE WAS SOMETHING FISHY ABOUT THAT BASS LASS LADY!!
THE FURRIEST FIGHTER BEGINS PULLING OFF CAP'S HELMET WINGS!
NOW, LET'S TALK ABOUT HOW GREAT MONARCHIES ARE: THERE'S A REASON THE BIGGEST AND THEREFORE BEST CHOCOLATE BARS AND BEDS ARE CALLED "KING-SIZED"! I--OOF!
JUST A MOMENT, CAP! A LITTLE SQUIRREL STRENGTH SHOULD BE ALL IT TAKES...TO CLIP YOUR WINGS!!
NO!!
JUST AS I SUSPECTED! MINIATURIZED RADIO ELECTRO-PROCESSORS, SENDING SIGNALS DIRECTLY INTO YOUR BRAIN! YOU'RE FREE NOW, CAP!
WHAT--WHAT HAPPENED?
HYDRA WAS MIND-CONTROLLING YOU, TRYING TO GET YOU TO DESTROY AMERICA FROM WITHIN. BUT THEY FORGOT ONE THING: WHILE SQUIRRELS MAY BE THE MOST TRUSTING ANIMALS IN NATURE...THEY'LL NEVER TRUST A HYDRA AGENT!
DARN YOU, SQUIRREL GIRL! DARN YOU AND YOUR MEDDLING WAYS!!
AND WHOEVER WAS BEHIND THIS DASTARDLY PLOT WOULD'VE HAD TO STAY CLOSE, CAP--WITHIN MICRO-BROADCASTING RANGE! IT COULD ONLY BE ONE PERSON: BASS LASS! OR SHOULD I SAY...
THE RED SKULL??
DRAT! IT'S JUST ONE OF HIS UNCANNY SKULLDROIDS, SET TO SELF DESTRUCT AS SOON AS IT'S DISCOVERED!
NOT TO WORRY, SQUIRREL GIRL! WE'LL GET HIM NEXT TIME... AND FREEDOM WILL PREVAIL!
THE END...FOR NOW!

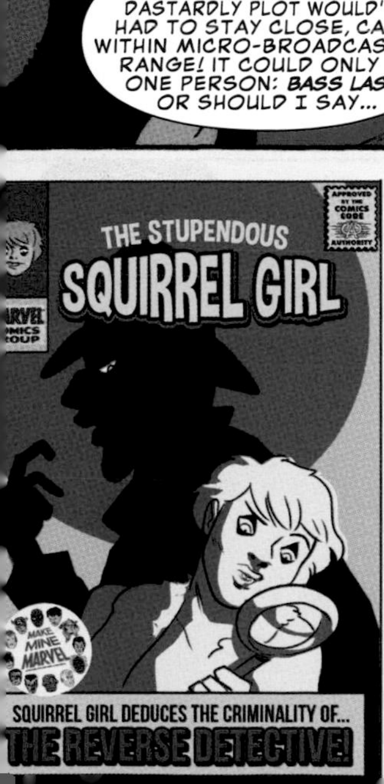
THE STUPENDOUS
SQUIRREL GIRL
APPROVED BY THE COMICS CODE AUTHORITY
MARVEL COMICS GROUP
MAKE MINE MARVEL
SQUIRREL GIRL DEDUCES THE CRIMINALITY OF...
THE REVERSE DETECTIVE!

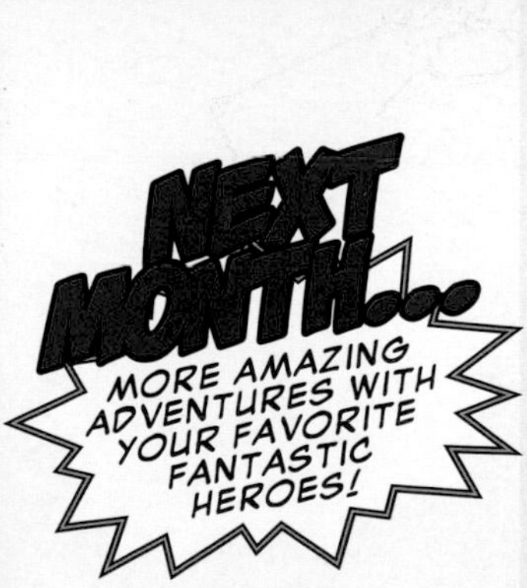
NEXT MONTH...
MORE AMAZING ADVENTURES WITH YOUR FAVORITE FANTASTIC HEROES!

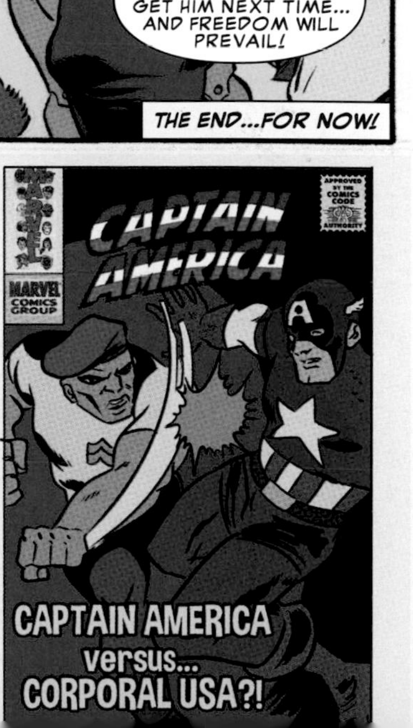
CAPTAIN AMERICA
APPROVED BY THE COMICS CODE AUTHORITY
MARVEL COMICS GROUP
CAPTAIN AMERICA versus... CORPORAL USA?!

In that comic, Captain America says *"Stand down! That's an order,* ***Corporal.****"* and then Corporal USA is all *"Um yeah so the thing is, I think it's pretty clear we're both operating outside the traditional military chain of command here??"*

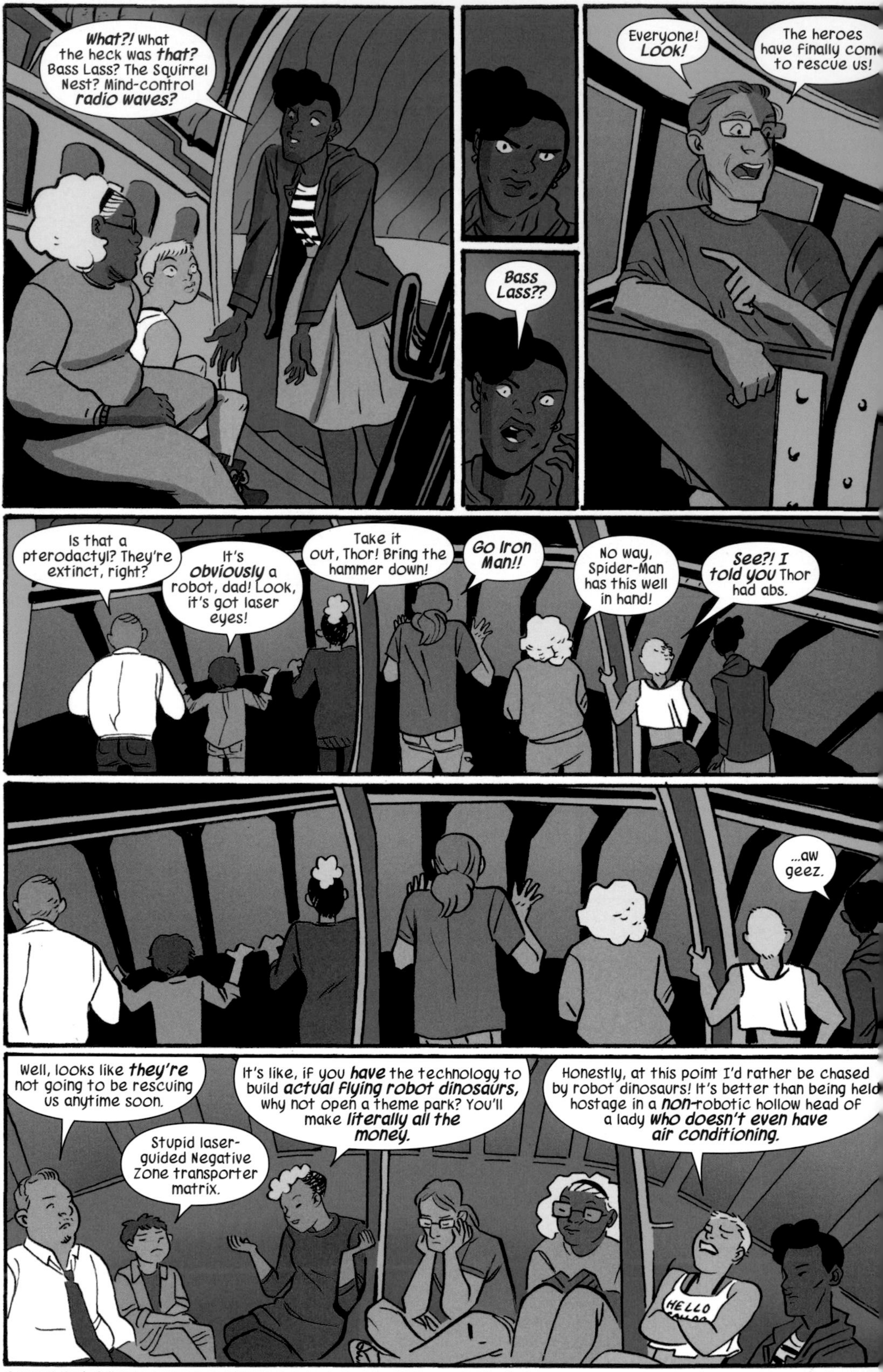
What?! What the heck was that? Bass Lass? The Squirrel Nest? Mind-control radio waves?
Bass Lass??
Everyone! LOOK!
The heroes have finally com to rescue us!
Is that a pterodactyl? They're extinct, right?
It's obviously a robot, dad! Look, it's got laser eyes!
Take it out, Thor! Bring the hammer down!
Go Iron Man!!
No way, Spider-Man has this well in hand!
See?! I told you Thor had abs.
...aw geez.
Well, looks like they're not going to be rescuing us anytime soon.
Stupid laser-guided Negative Zone transporter matrix.
It's like, if you have the technology to build actual flying robot dinosaurs, why not open a theme park? You'll make literally all the money.
Honestly, at this point I'd rather be chased by robot dinosaurs! It's better than being held hostage in a non-robotic hollow head of a lady who doesn't even have air conditioning.
HELLO

If you get tired of literally all the money and want nations to start printing *more* money just to give it to you, open up an attraction where you get to wrestle the dinosa

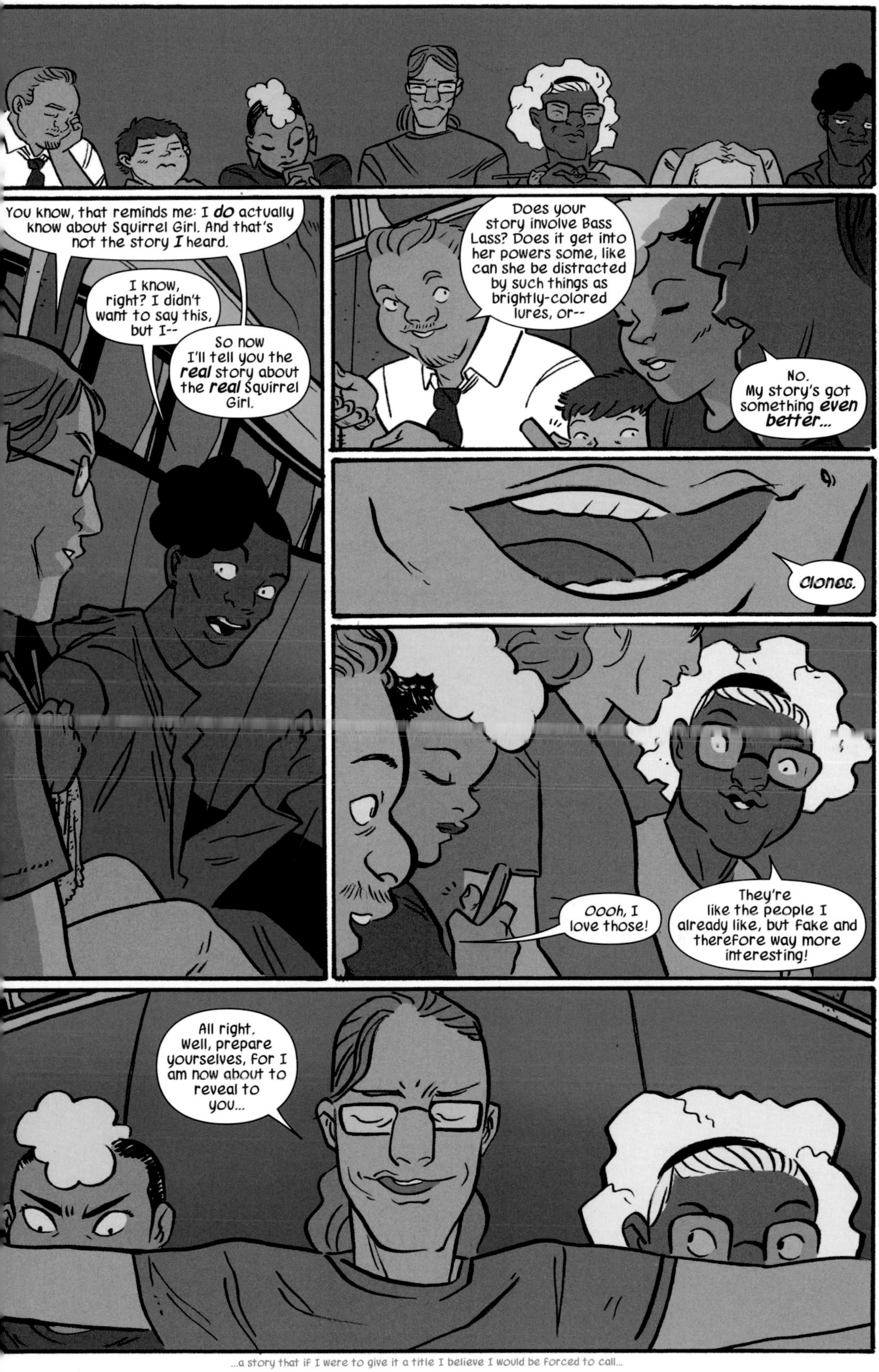
You know, that reminds me: I do actually know about Squirrel Girl. And that's not the story I heard.
I know, right? I didn't want to say this, but I--
So now I'll tell you the real story about the real Squirrel Girl.
Does your story involve Bass Lass? Does it get into her powers some, like can she be distracted by such things as brightly-colored lures, or--
No. My story's got something even better...
Clones.
They're like the people I already like, but fake and therefore way more interesting!
Oooh, I love those!
All right. Well, prepare yourselves, for I am now about to reveal to you...

...a story that if I were to give it a title I believe I would be forced to call...

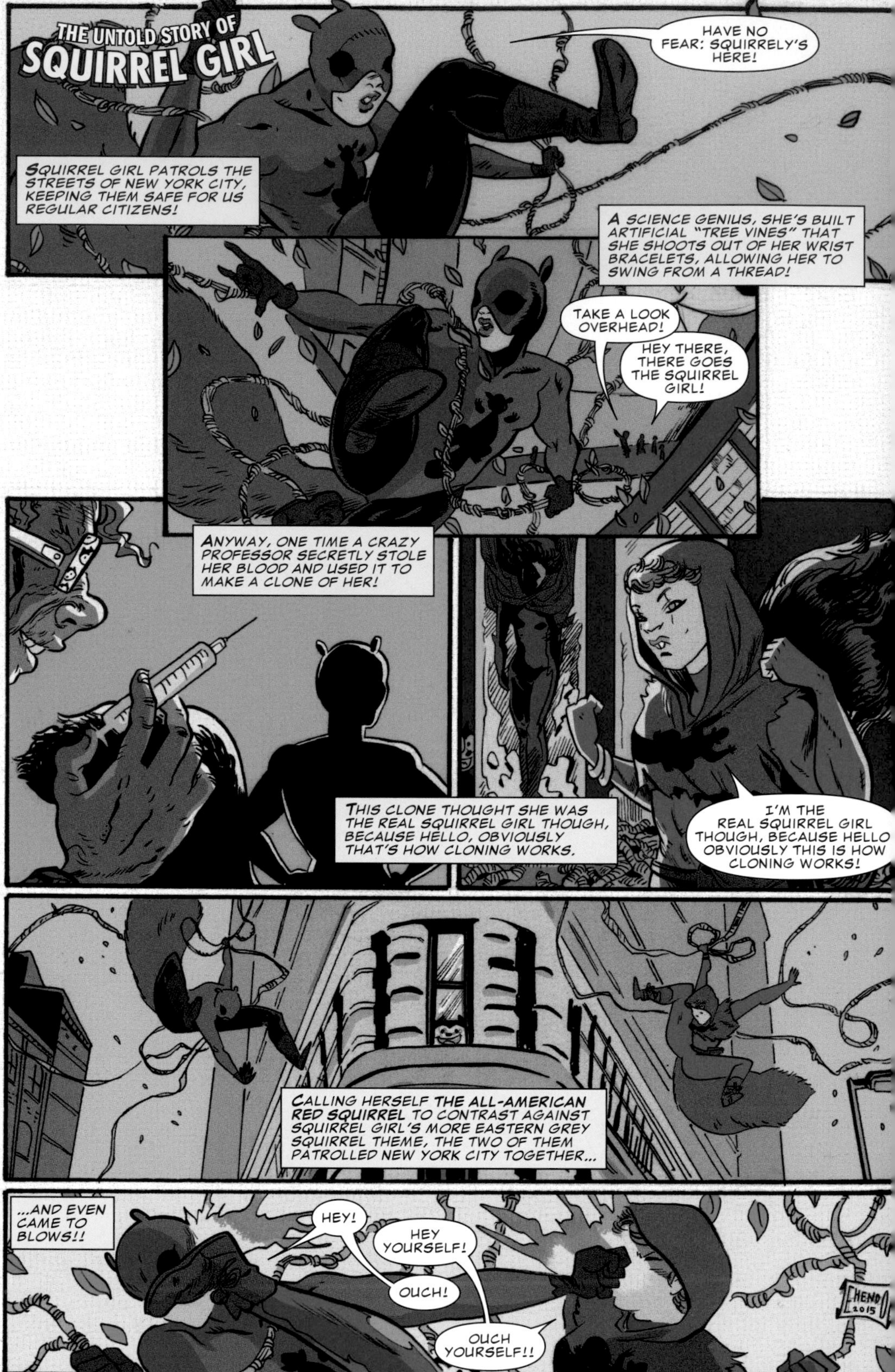
THE UNTOLD STORY OF SQUIRREL GIRL
HAVE NO FEAR: SQUIRRELY'S HERE!
SQUIRREL GIRL PATROLS THE STREETS OF NEW YORK CITY, KEEPING THEM SAFE FOR US REGULAR CITIZENS!
A SCIENCE GENIUS, SHE'S BUILT ARTIFICIAL "TREE VINES" THAT SHE SHOOTS OUT OF HER WRIST BRACELETS, ALLOWING HER TO SWING FROM A THREAD!
TAKE A LOOK OVERHEAD!
HEY THERE, THERE GOES THE SQUIRREL GIRL!
ANYWAY, ONE TIME A CRAZY PROFESSOR SECRETLY STOLE HER BLOOD AND USED IT TO MAKE A CLONE OF HER!
THIS CLONE THOUGHT SHE WAS THE REAL SQUIRREL GIRL THOUGH, BECAUSE HELLO, OBVIOUSLY THAT'S HOW CLONING WORKS.
I'M THE REAL SQUIRREL GIRL THOUGH, BECAUSE HELLO OBVIOUSLY THIS IS HOW CLONING WORKS!
CALLING HERSELF **THE ALL-AMERICAN RED SQUIRREL** TO CONTRAST AGAINST SQUIRREL GIRL'S MORE EASTERN GREY SQUIRREL THEME, THE TWO OF THEM PATROLLED NEW YORK CITY TOGETHER...
...AND EVEN CAME TO BLOWS!!
HEY!
HEY YOURSELF!
OUCH!
OUCH YOURSELF!!
HENO 2015

Hey, this reminds me: with great power doesn't come great responsibility! With great power *actually* comes great joules per second, or *"watts,"* the integral of which over time measures the work performed. Librarians: please go ahead and file this comic in the *"WOW! SCIENCE FACTS"* section of the library.

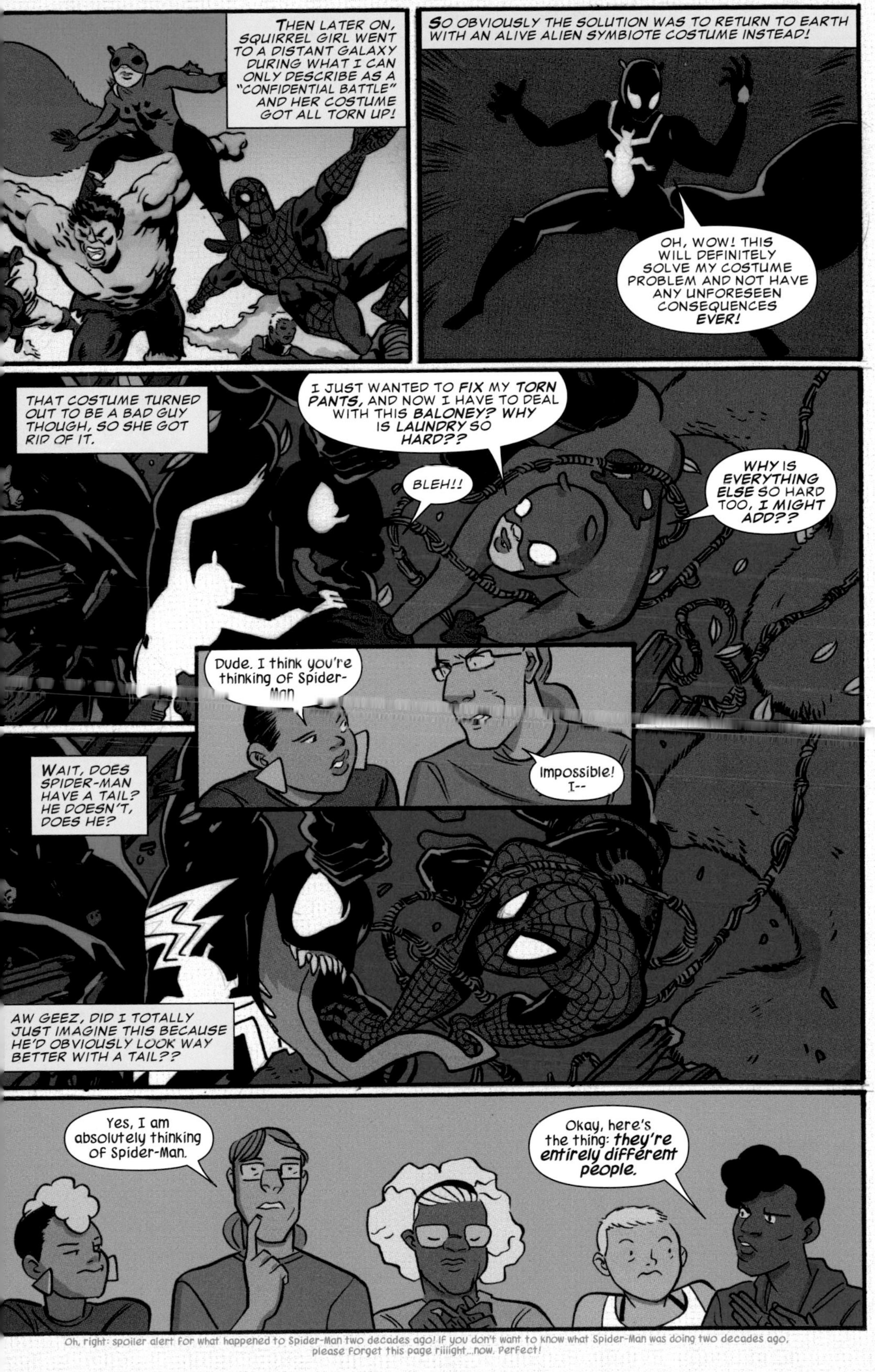

THEN LATER ON, SQUIRREL GIRL WENT TO A DISTANT GALAXY DURING WHAT I CAN ONLY DESCRIBE AS A "CONFIDENTIAL BATTLE" AND HER COSTUME GOT ALL TORN UP!
SO OBVIOUSLY THE SOLUTION WAS TO RETURN TO EARTH WITH AN ALIVE ALIEN SYMBIOTE COSTUME INSTEAD!
OH, WOW! THIS WILL DEFINITELY SOLVE MY COSTUME PROBLEM AND NOT HAVE ANY UNFORESEEN CONSEQUENCES EVER!
THAT COSTUME TURNED OUT TO BE A BAD GUY THOUGH, SO SHE GOT RID OF IT.
I JUST WANTED TO FIX MY TORN PANTS, AND NOW I HAVE TO DEAL WITH THIS BALONEY? WHY IS LAUNDRY SO HARD??
BLEH!!
WHY IS EVERYTHING ELSE SO HARD TOO, I MIGHT ADD??
Dude. I think you're thinking of Spider-Man
Impossible! I--
WAIT, DOES SPIDER-MAN HAVE A TAIL? HE DOESN'T, DOES HE?
AW GEEZ, DID I TOTALLY JUST IMAGINE THIS BECAUSE HE'D OBVIOUSLY LOOK WAY BETTER WITH A TAIL??
Yes, I am absolutely thinking of Spider-Man.
Okay, here's the thing: they're entirely different people.

Oh, right: spoiler alert for what happened to Spider-Man two decades ago! If you don't want to know what Spider-Man was doing two decades ago, please forget this page riiiight...now. Perfect!

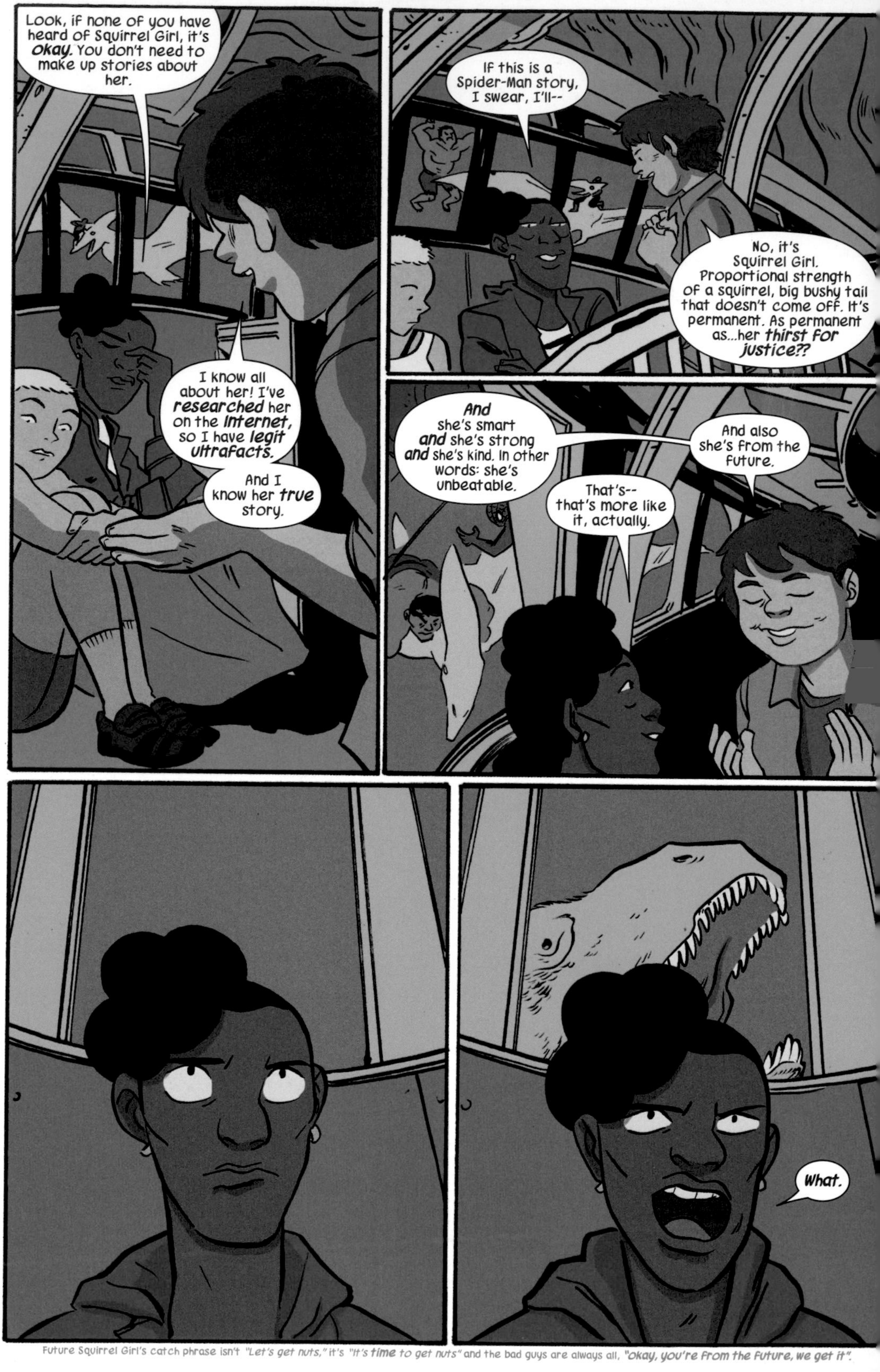
Look, if none of you have heard of Squirrel Girl, it's okay. You don't need to make up stories about her.
I know all about her! I've researched her on the Internet, so I have legit ultrafacts.
And I know her true story.
If this is a Spider-Man story, I swear, I'll--
No, it's Squirrel Girl. Proportional strength of a squirrel, big bushy tail that doesn't come off. It's permanent. As permanent as...her thirst for justice??
And she's smart and she's strong and she's kind. In other words: she's unbeatable.
And also she's from the future.
That's-- that's more like it, actually.
What.

Future Squirrel Girl's catch phrase isn't *"Let's get nuts,"* it's *"It's* ***time*** *to get nuts"* and the bad guys are always all, *"Okay, you're from the future, we get it"*.

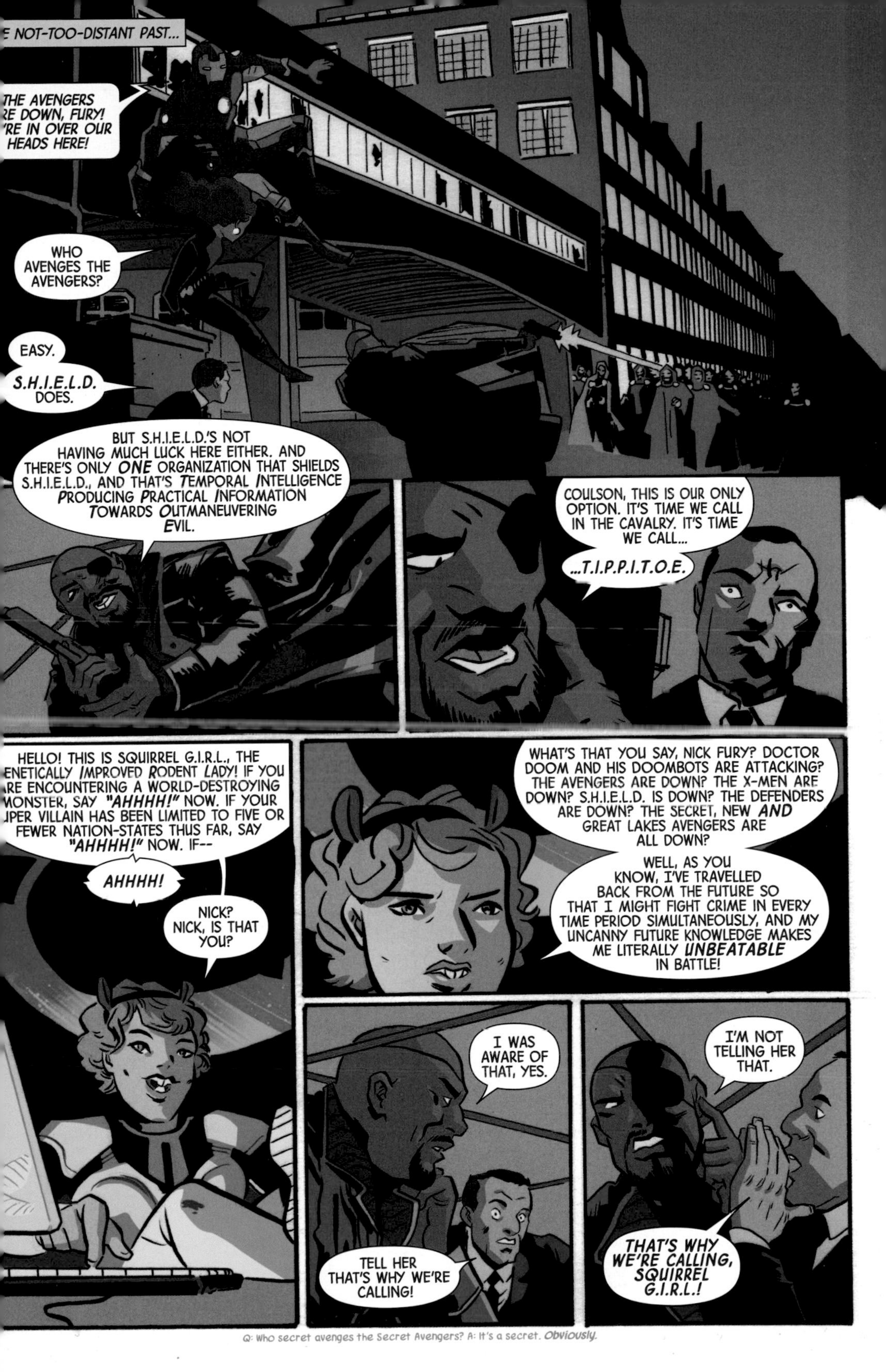
E NOT-TOO-DISTANT PAST...
THE AVENGERS
RE DOWN, FURY!
'RE IN OVER OUR
HEADS HERE!
WHO AVENGES THE AVENGERS?
EASY.
S.H.I.E.L.D. DOES.
BUT S.H.I.E.L.D.'S NOT HAVING MUCH LUCK HERE EITHER. AND THERE'S ONLY ONE ORGANIZATION THAT SHIELDS S.H.I.E.L.D., AND THAT'S TEMPORAL INTELLIGENCE PRODUCING PRACTICAL INFORMATION TOWARDS OUTMANEUVERING EVIL.
COULSON, THIS IS OUR ONLY OPTION. IT'S TIME WE CALL IN THE CAVALRY. IT'S TIME WE CALL...
...T.I.P.P.I.T.O.E.
HELLO! THIS IS SQUIRREL G.I.R.L., THE
ENETICALLY IMPROVED RODENT LADY! IF YOU
RE ENCOUNTERING A WORLD-DESTROYING
MONSTER, SAY "AHHHH!" NOW. IF YOUR
JPER VILLAIN HAS BEEN LIMITED TO FIVE OR
FEWER NATION-STATES THUS FAR, SAY
"AHHHH!" NOW. IF--
AHHHH!
NICK? NICK, IS THAT YOU?
WHAT'S THAT YOU SAY, NICK FURY? DOCTOR DOOM AND HIS DOOMBOTS ARE ATTACKING? THE AVENGERS ARE DOWN? THE X-MEN ARE DOWN? S.H.I.E.L.D. IS DOWN? THE DEFENDERS ARE DOWN? THE SECRET, NEW AND GREAT LAKES AVENGERS ARE ALL DOWN?
WELL, AS YOU KNOW, I'VE TRAVELLED BACK FROM THE FUTURE SO THAT I MIGHT FIGHT CRIME IN EVERY TIME PERIOD SIMULTANEOUSLY, AND MY UNCANNY FUTURE KNOWLEDGE MAKES ME LITERALLY UNBEATABLE IN BATTLE!
I WAS AWARE OF THAT, YES.
TELL HER THAT'S WHY WE'RE CALLING!
I'M NOT TELLING HER THAT.
THAT'S WHY WE'RE CALLING, SQUIRREL G.I.R.L.!

Q: Who secret avenges the Secret Avengers? A: It's a secret. *Obviously.*

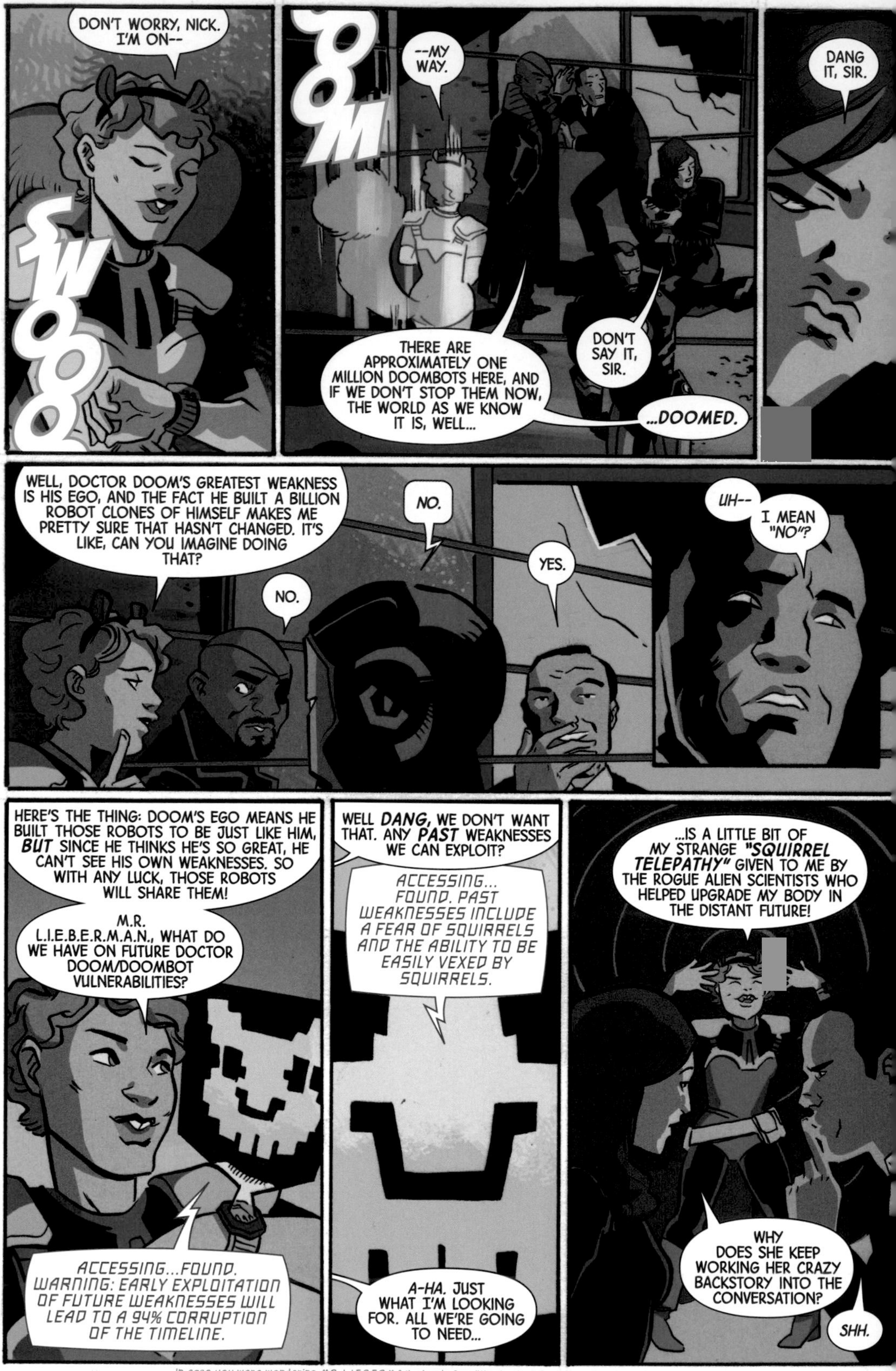
DON'T WORRY, NICK. I'M ON--
FWOOOM
--MY WAY.
THERE ARE APPROXIMATELY ONE MILLION DOOMBOTS HERE, AND IF WE DON'T STOP THEM NOW, THE WORLD AS WE KNOW IT IS, WELL...
DON'T SAY IT, SIR.
...DOOMED.
DANG IT, SIR.
WELL, DOCTOR DOOM'S GREATEST WEAKNESS IS HIS EGO, AND THE FACT HE BUILT A BILLION ROBOT CLONES OF HIMSELF MAKES ME PRETTY SURE THAT HASN'T CHANGED. IT'S LIKE, CAN YOU IMAGINE DOING THAT?
NO.
NO.
YES.
UH--
I MEAN "NO"?
HERE'S THE THING: DOOM'S EGO MEANS HE BUILT THOSE ROBOTS TO BE JUST LIKE HIM, BUT SINCE HE THINKS HE'S SO GREAT, HE CAN'T SEE HIS OWN WEAKNESSES. SO WITH ANY LUCK, THOSE ROBOTS WILL SHARE THEM!
M.R. L.I.E.B.E.R.M.A.N., WHAT DO WE HAVE ON FUTURE DOCTOR DOOM/DOOMBOT VULNERABILITIES?
ACCESSING...FOUND. WARNING: EARLY EXPLOITATION OF FUTURE WEAKNESSES WILL LEAD TO A 94% CORRUPTION OF THE TIMELINE.
WELL DANG, WE DON'T WANT THAT. ANY PAST WEAKNESSES WE CAN EXPLOIT?
ACCESSING... FOUND. PAST WEAKNESSES INCLUDE A FEAR OF SQUIRRELS AND THE ABILITY TO BE EASILY VEXED BY SQUIRRELS.
A-HA. JUST WHAT I'M LOOKING FOR. ALL WE'RE GOING TO NEED...
...IS A LITTLE BIT OF MY STRANGE "SQUIRREL TELEPATHY" GIVEN TO ME BY THE ROGUE ALIEN SCIENTISTS WHO HELPED UPGRADE MY BODY IN THE DISTANT FUTURE!
WHY DOES SHE KEEP WORKING HER CRAZY BACKSTORY INTO THE CONVERSATION?
SHH.

In case you were wondering, M.R. L.I.E.B.E.R.M.A.N. stands for "Mechanical Resource For Locating Inefficiencies, Efficiencies, Battle-Exploitable Resources, and Machinery; Also Nuts."

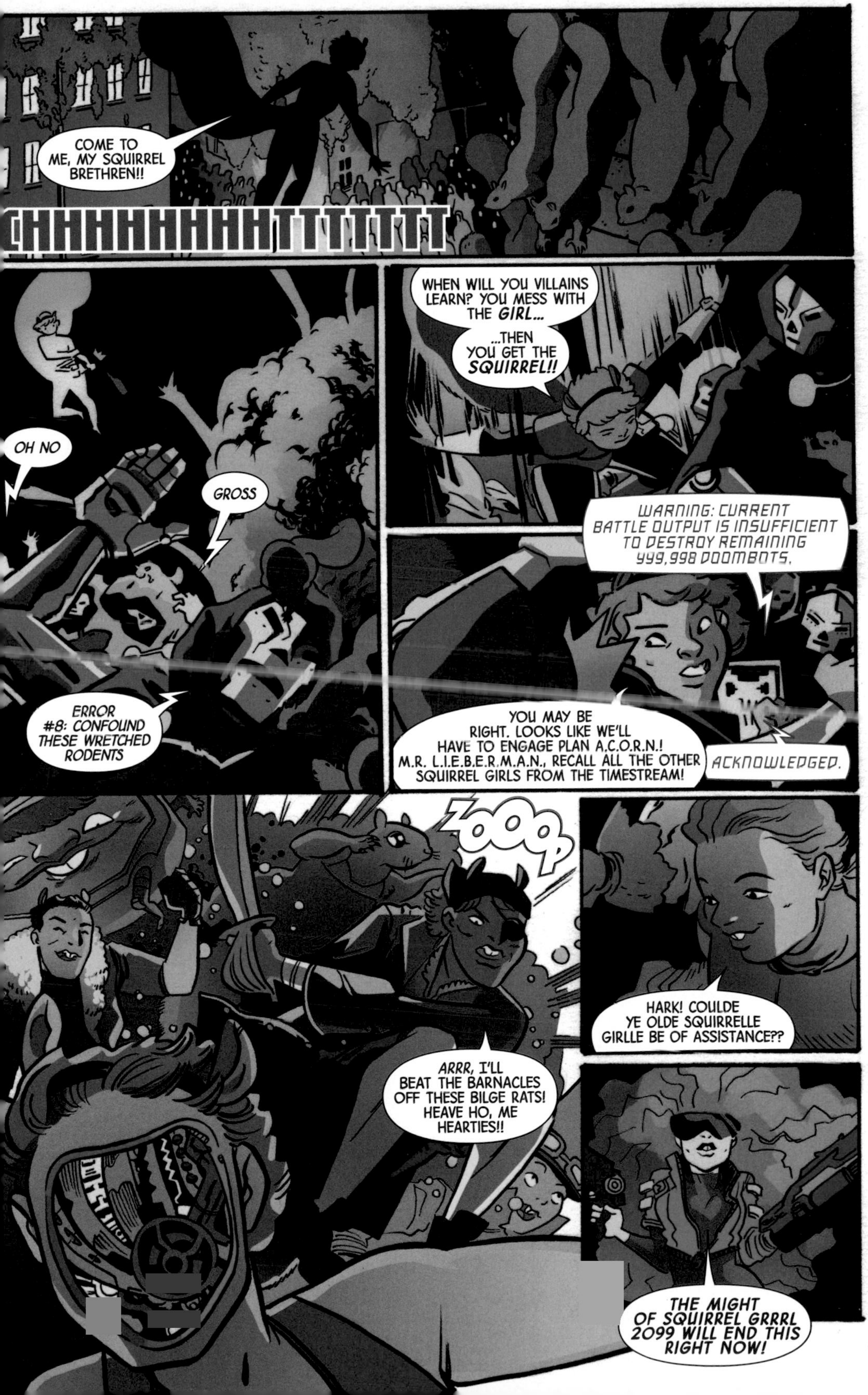
COME TO ME, MY SQUIRREL BRETHREN!!
CHHHHHHHTTTTTTT
OH NO
GROSS
ERROR #8: CONFOUND THESE WRETCHED RODENTS
WHEN WILL YOU VILLAINS LEARN? YOU MESS WITH THE GIRL...
...THEN YOU GET THE SQUIRREL!!
WARNING: CURRENT BATTLE OUTPUT IS INSUFFICIENT TO DESTROY REMAINING 999,998 DOOMBOTS.
YOU MAY BE RIGHT. LOOKS LIKE WE'LL HAVE TO ENGAGE PLAN A.C.O.R.N.! M.R. L.I.E.B.E.R.M.A.N., RECALL ALL THE OTHER SQUIRREL GIRLS FROM THE TIMESTREAM!
ACKNOWLEDGED.
ZOOOP
ARRR, I'LL BEAT THE BARNACLES OFF THESE BILGE RATS! HEAVE HO, ME HEARTIES!!
HARK! COULDE YE OLDE SQUIRRELLE GIRLLE BE OF ASSISTANCE??
THE MIGHT OF SQUIRREL GRRRL 2099 WILL END THIS RIGHT NOW!

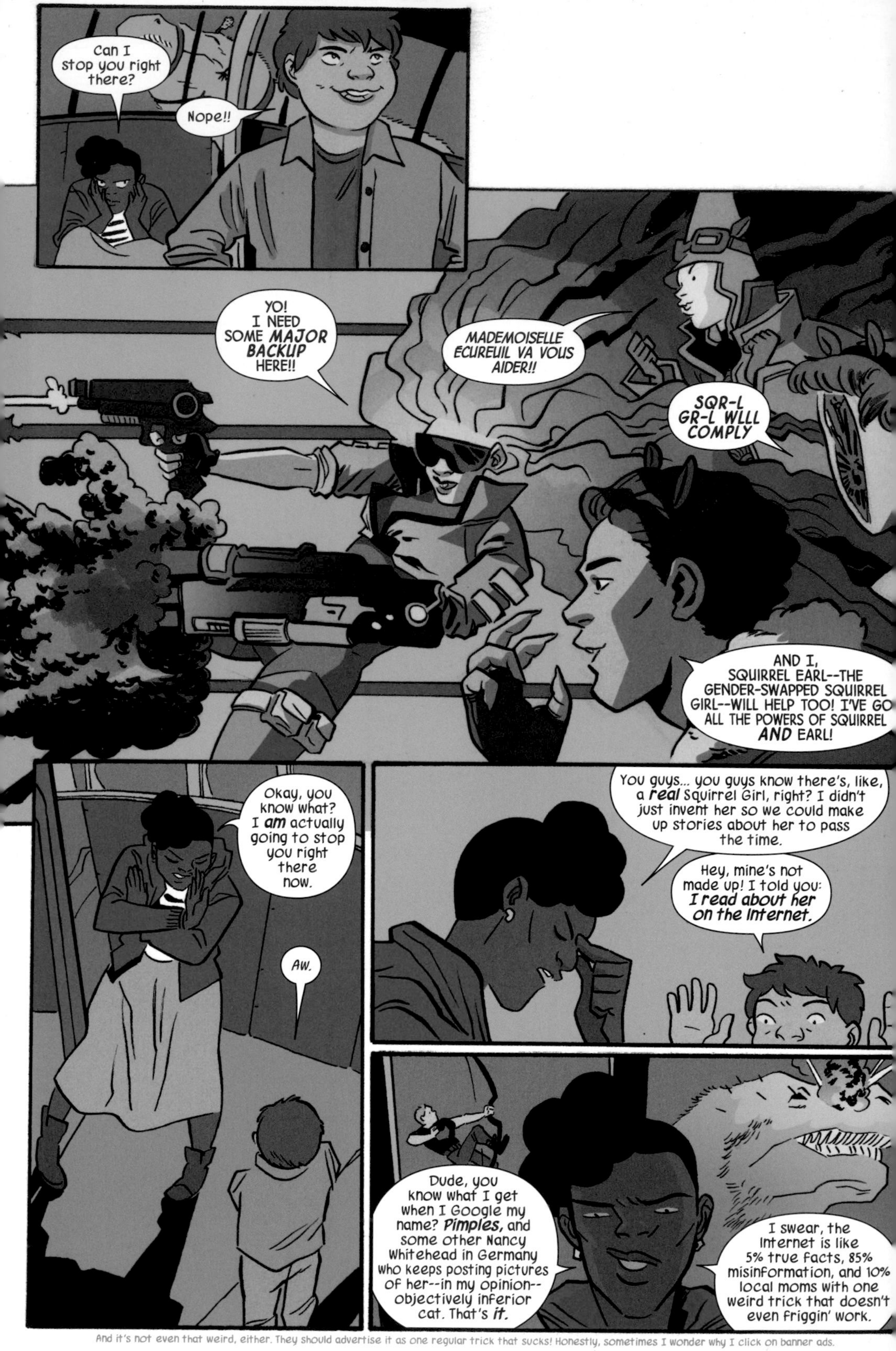
Can I stop you right there?
Nope!!
YO! I NEED SOME MAJOR BACKUP HERE!!
MADEMOISELLE ECUREUIL VA VOUS AIDER!!
SQR-L GR-L WLLL COMPLY
AND I, SQUIRREL EARL--THE GENDER-SWAPPED SQUIRREL GIRL--WILL HELP TOO! I'VE GO ALL THE POWERS OF SQUIRREL AND EARL!
Okay, you know what? I am actually going to stop you right there now.
Aw.
You guys... you guys know there's, like, a real Squirrel Girl, right? I didn't just invent her so we could make up stories about her to pass the time.
Hey, mine's not made up! I told you: I read about her on the Internet.
Dude, you know what I get when I Google my name? Pimples, and some other Nancy Whitehead in Germany who keeps posting pictures of her--in my opinion--objectively inferior cat. That's it.
I swear, the Internet is like 5% true facts, 85% misinformation, and 10% local moms with one weird trick that doesn't even friggin' work.

And it's not even that weird, either. They should advertise it as one regular trick that sucks! Honestly, sometimes I wonder why I click on banner ads.

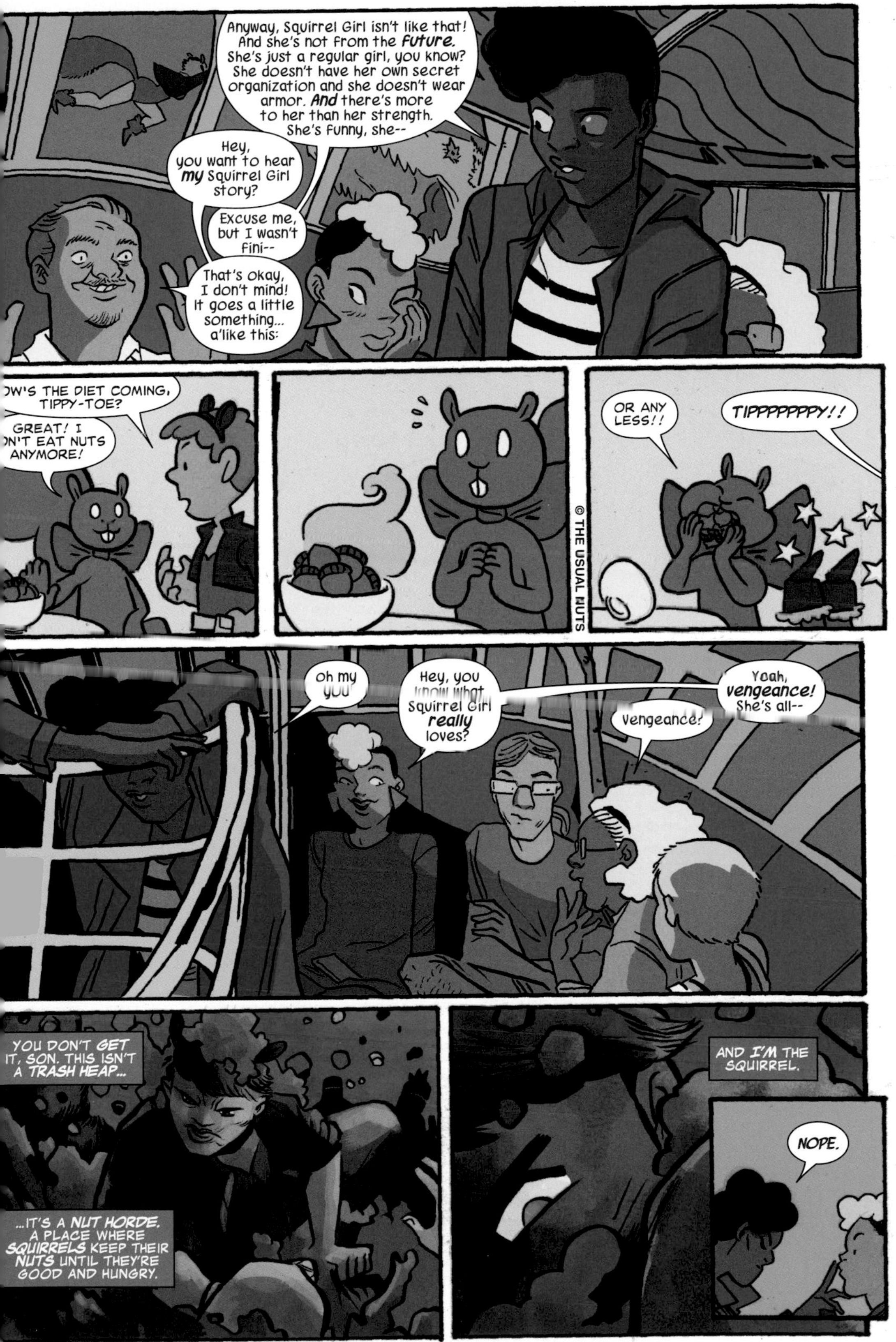

Anyway, Squirrel Girl isn't like that! And she's not from the *future.* She's just a regular girl, you know? She doesn't have her own secret organization and she doesn't wear armor. *And* there's more to her than her strength. She's funny, she--
Hey, you want to hear *my* Squirrel Girl story?
Excuse me, but I wasn't fini--
That's okay, I don't mind! It goes a little something... a'like this:
OW'S THE DIET COMING, TIPPY-TOE?
GREAT! I ON'T EAT NUTS ANYMORE!
© THE USUAL NUTS
OR ANY LESS!!
TIPPPPPPPY!!
Oh my
Hey, you
Squirrel Girl *really* loves?
Vengeance!
Yeah, *vengeance!* She's all--
YOU DON'T *GET* IT, SON. THIS ISN'T A *TRASH HEAP*...
...IT'S A *NUT HORDE.* A PLACE WHERE *SQUIRRELS* KEEP THEIR *NUTS* UNTIL THEY'RE GOOD AND HUNGRY.
AND *I'M* THE SQUIRREL.
NOPE.

I've got squirrels. Lots of squirrels. Sometimes I count them just to make myself feel crazy.

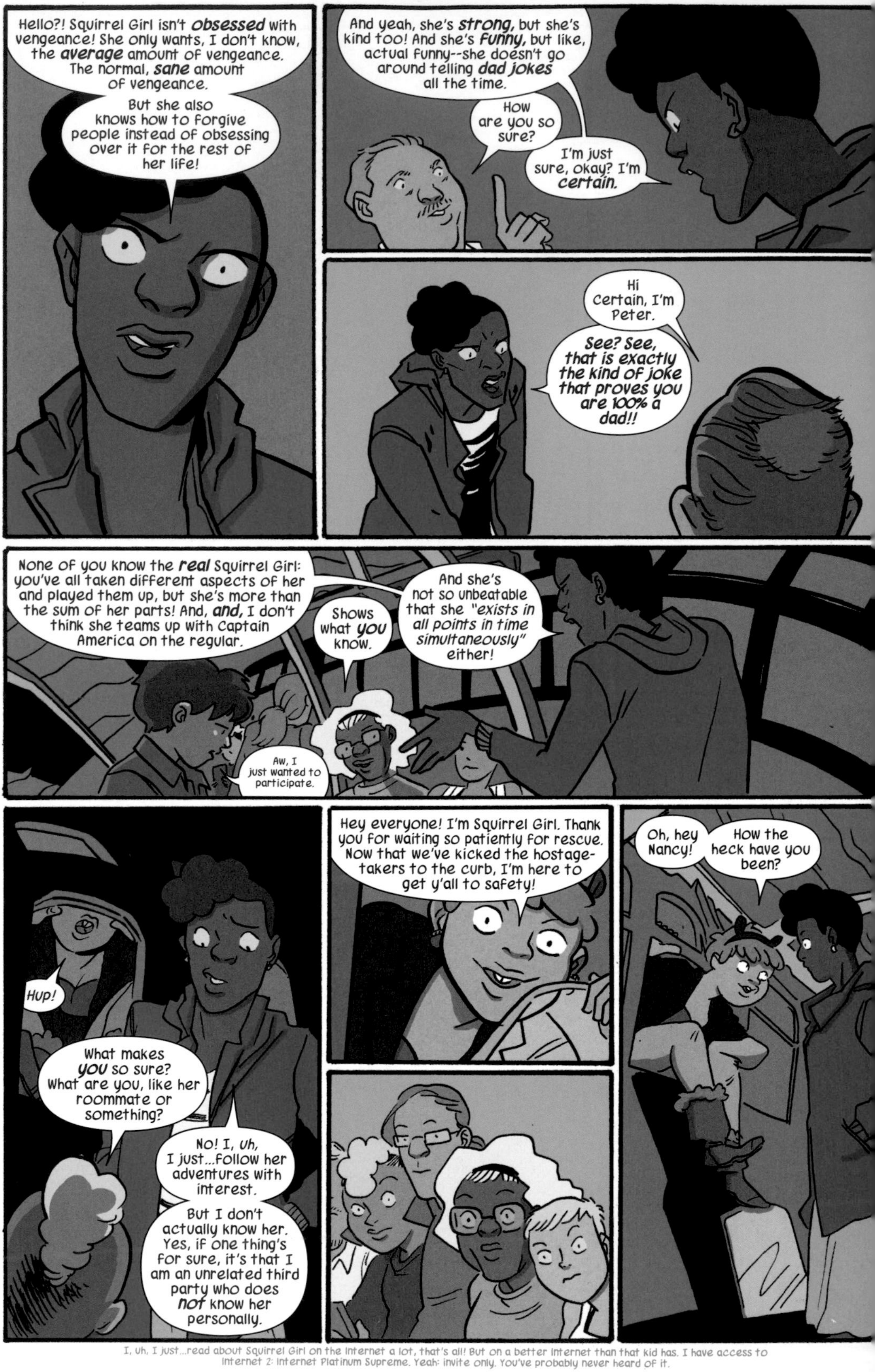
Hello?! Squirrel Girl isn't obsessed with vengeance! She only wants, I don't know, the average amount of vengeance. The normal, sane amount of vengeance.
But she also knows how to forgive people instead of obsessing over it for the rest of her life!
And yeah, she's strong, but she's kind too! And she's funny, but like, actual funny--she doesn't go around telling dad jokes all the time.
How are you so sure?
I'm just sure, okay? I'm certain.
Hi Certain, I'm Peter.
See? See, that is exactly the kind of joke that proves you are 100% a dad!!
None of you know the real Squirrel Girl: you've all taken different aspects of her and played them up, but she's more than the sum of her parts! And, and, I don't think she teams up with Captain America on the regular.
Shows what you know.
And she's not so unbeatable that she "exists in all points in time simultaneously" either!
Aw, I just wanted to participate.
Hup!
What makes you so sure? What are you, like her roommate or something?
No! I, uh, I just...follow her adventures with interest.
But I don't actually know her. Yes, if one thing's for sure, it's that I am an unrelated third party who does not know her personally.
Hey everyone! I'm Squirrel Girl. Thank you for waiting so patiently for rescue. Now that we've kicked the hostage-takers to the curb, I'm here to get y'all to safety!
Oh, hey Nancy!
How the heck have you been?

I, uh, I just...read about Squirrel Girl on the internet a lot, that's all! But on a better internet than that kid has. I have access to Internet 2: Internet Platinum Supreme. Yeah: invite only. You've probably never heard of it.

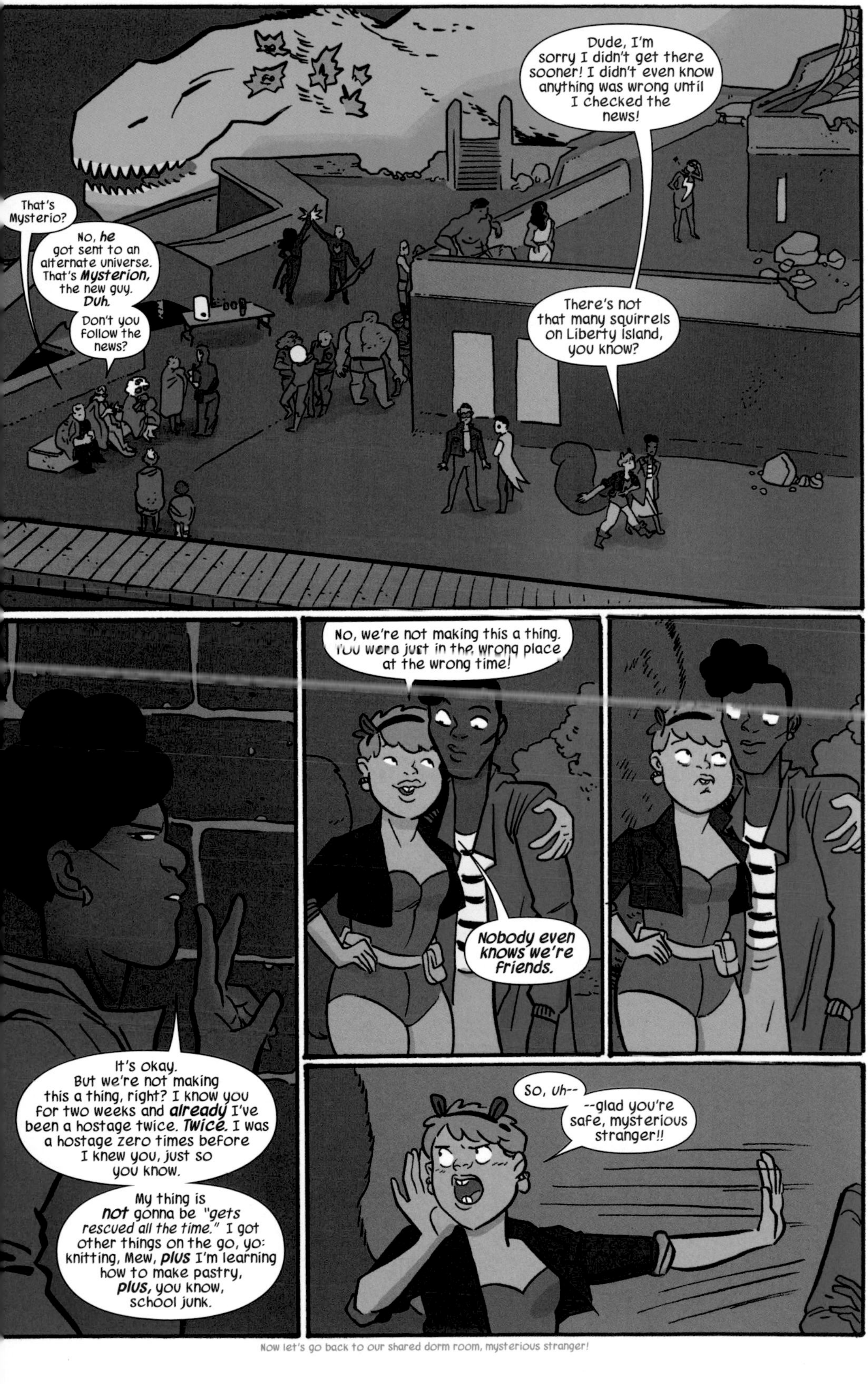

That's Mysterio?
No, he got sent to an alternate universe. That's Mysterion, the new guy. Duh.
Don't you follow the news?
Dude, I'm sorry I didn't get there sooner! I didn't even know anything was wrong until I checked the news!
There's not that many squirrels on Liberty Island, you know?
It's okay. But we're not making this a thing, right? I know you for two weeks and already I've been a hostage twice. Twice. I was a hostage zero times before I knew you, just so you know.
My thing is not gonna be "gets rescued all the time." I got other things on the go, yo: knitting, Mew, plus I'm learning how to make pastry, plus, you know, school junk.
No, we're not making this a thing. You were just in the wrong place at the wrong time!
Nobody even knows we're friends.
So, uh--
--glad you're safe, mysterious stranger!!

Now let's go back to our shared dorm room, mysterious stranger!

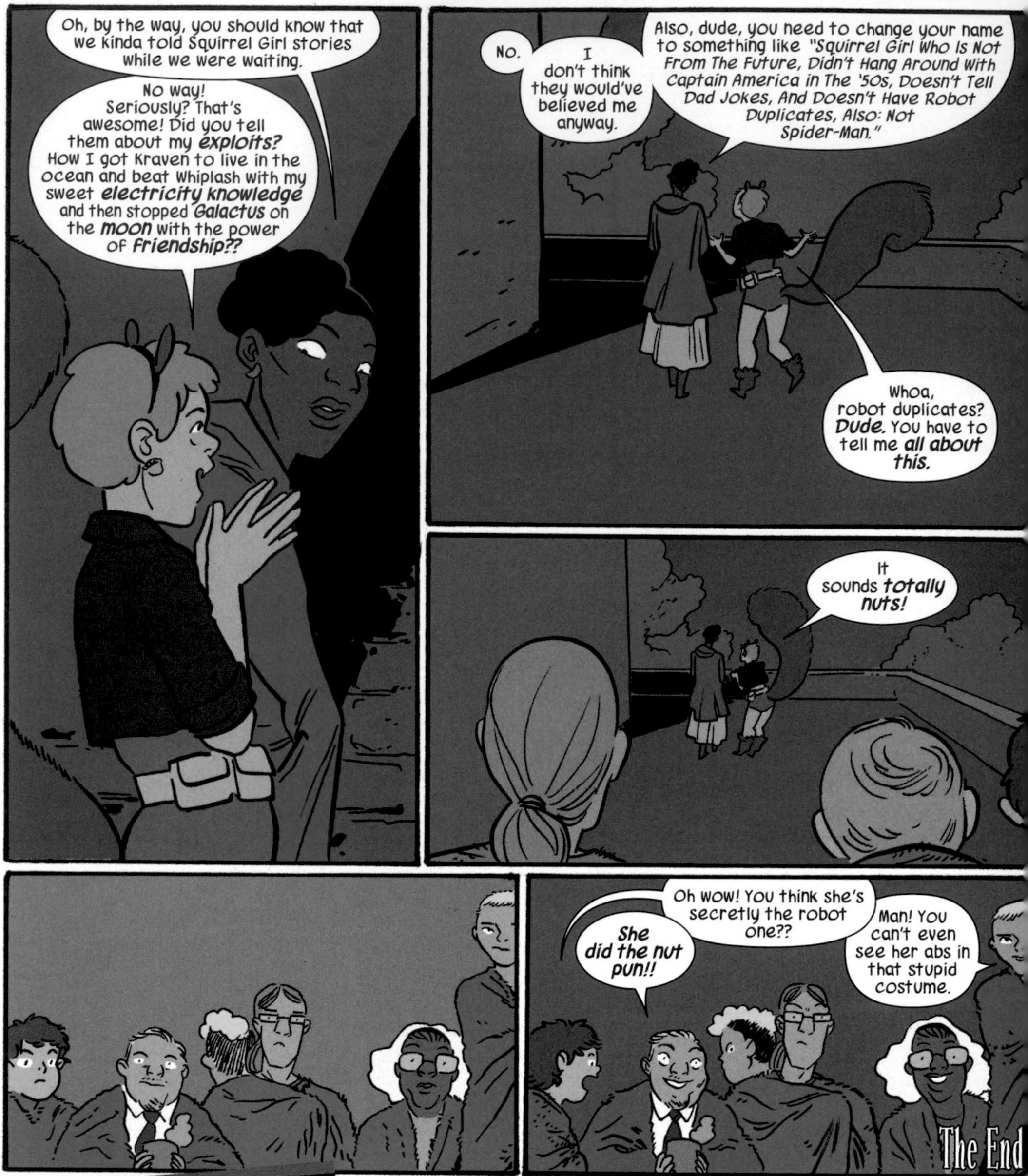
Oh, by the way, you should know that we kinda told Squirrel Girl stories while we were waiting.
No way! Seriously? That's awesome! Did you tell them about my *exploits?* How I got Kraven to live in the ocean and beat Whiplash with my sweet *electricity knowledge* and then stopped *Galactus* on the *moon* with the power of *friendship??*
No.
I don't think they would've believed me anyway.
Also, dude, you need to change your name to something like *"Squirrel Girl Who Is Not From The Future, Didn't Hang Around With Captain America in The '50s, Doesn't Tell Dad Jokes, And Doesn't Have Robot Duplicates, Also: Not Spider-Man."*
Whoa, robot duplicates? *Dude.* You have to tell me *all about this.*
It sounds *totally nuts!*
She did the nut pun!!
Oh WOW! You think she's secretly the robot one??
Man! You can't even see her abs in that stupid costume.
The End

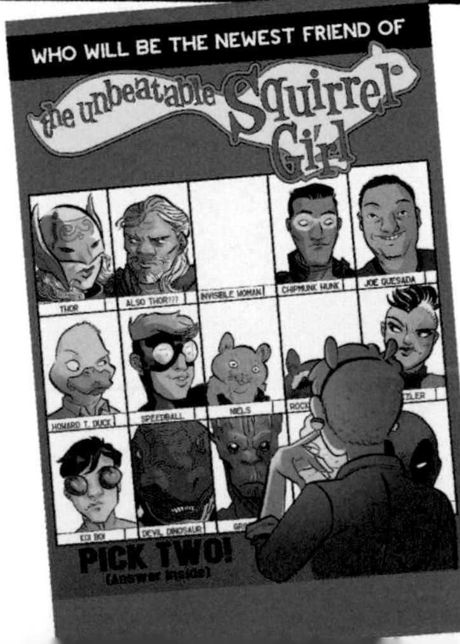
WHO WILL BE THE NEWEST FRIEND OF
the unbeatable Squirrel Girl
THOR
ALSO THOR???
INVISIBLE WOMAN
CHIPMUNK HUNK
JOE QUESADA
HOWARD T. DUCK
SPEEDBALL
NIELS
KOI BOI
DEVIL DINOSAUR
PICK TWO!
(Answer inside)

NEXT MONTH...

MORE AMAZING ADVENTURES WITH YOUR FAVORITE FANTASTIC HEROES!

♫ S.G.W.I.N.F.T.F.D.H.A.W.C.A.I.T.5.D.T.D.J.A.D.H.R.D.A.N.S.M., S.G.W.I.N.F.T.F.D.H.A.W.C.A.I.T.5.D.T.D.J.A.D.H.R.D.A.N.S.M., powers of both S.G.W.I.N.F.T.F.D.H.A.W.C.A.I.T.5.D.T.D.J.A.D.H.R.D.A.N.S.M. and girl. ♫

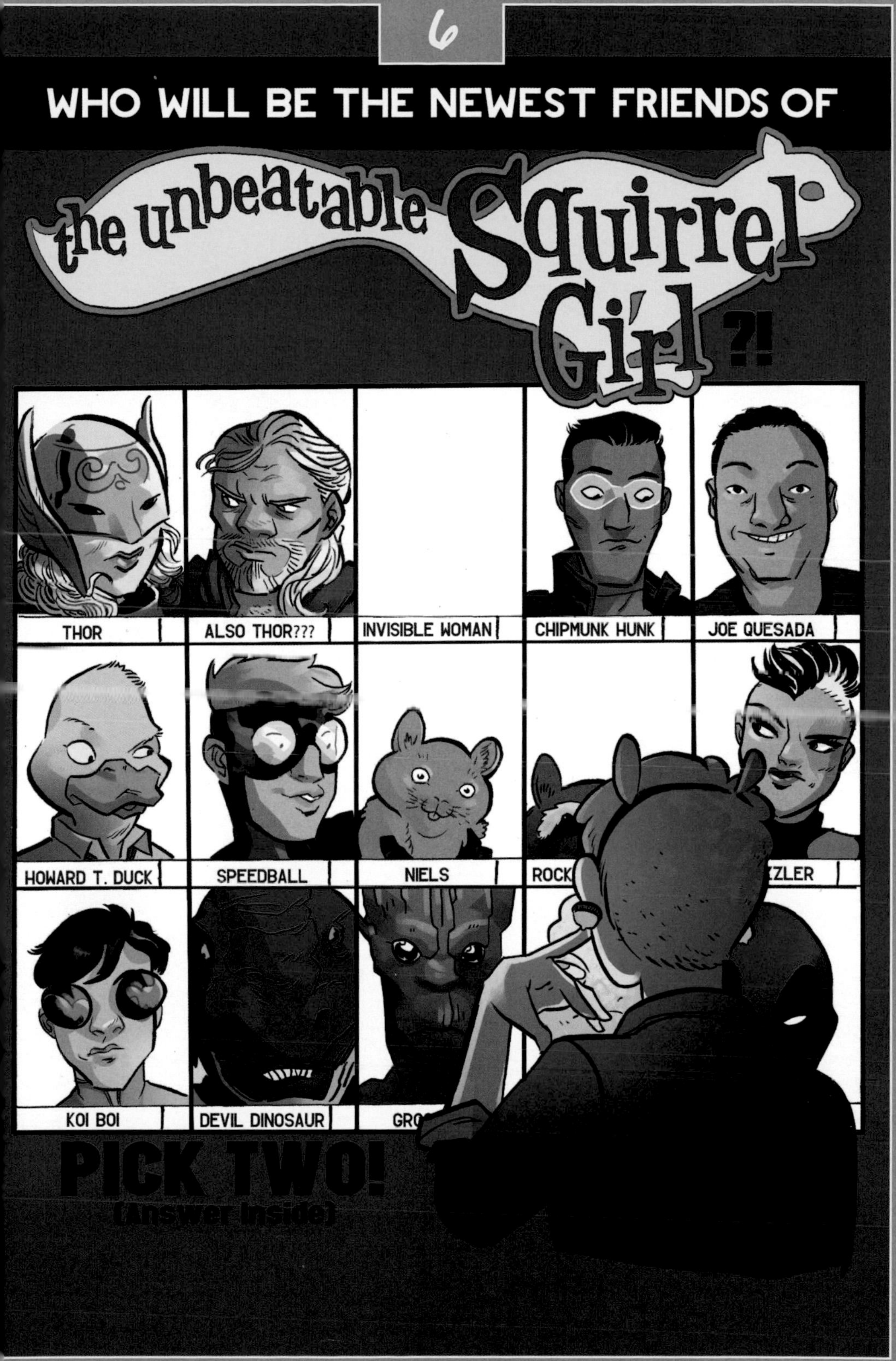
6
WHO WILL BE THE NEWEST FRIENDS OF
the unbeatable Squirrel Girl ?!
THOR
ALSO THOR???
INVISIBLE WOMAN
CHIPMUNK HUNK
JOE QUESADA
HOWARD T. DUCK
SPEEDBALL
NIELS
ROCK
KOI BOI
DEVIL DINOSAUR
GRO
PICK TWO!
(Answer Inside)

Doreen Green isn't just a first-year computer science student: she secretly also has all the powers of both squirrel and gi
She uses her amazing abilities to fight crime **and** be as awesome as possible. You know her as...**The Unbeatable Squirrel Gi**
Let's catch up with what she's been up to until now, with...

Squirrel Girl in a nutshell

Squirrel Girl! @unbeatablesg
RT if you helped defeat Mysterion and his ROBOT DINOSAURS and saved the statue of liberty!!

Squirrel Girl! @unbeatablesg
RT @unbeatablesg: RT if you helped defeat Mysterion and his ROBOT DINOSAURS and saved the statue of liberty!!

Squirrel Girl! @unbeatablesg
Yes I did just retweet myself

Squirrel Girl! @unbeatablesg
PROBABLY because I totally just helped defeat Mysterion and his ROBOT DINOSAURS and saved the STATUE OF LIBERTY??

Squirrel Girl! @unbeatablesg
@HULKYSMASHY hey thanks for the RT!

HULK @HULKYSMASHY
@unbeatablesg HULK SMASH PUNY DINOSAUR!!

Squirrel Girl! @unbeatablesg
@HULKYSMASHY haha we sure did!!

HULK @HULKYSMASHY
@unbeatablesg HULK GLAD WHEN SOCIOLOGICAL PROBLEMS CAN BE SOLVED BY SMASHING

Squirrel Girl! @unbeatablesg
@HULKYSMASHY yeah it's always nice when things work out that way actually

CampusBank @campusbank
Good news! We've fixed the giant squirrel-suit-shaped hole in our wall. CampusBank: We've Got Class Too™.

Squirrel Girl! @unbeatablesg
@campusbank okay but let's not forget the only reason that hole is there is because i saved all the hostages

CampusBank @campusbank
We think you'll be INTERESTed in our new savings account fee schedules. CampusBank: We've Got Class Too™.

Squirrel Girl! @unbeatablesg
@campusbank cool pun bro but can we at least acknowledge how i saved all the hostages

CampusBank @campusbank
We can't take all the CREDIT for our new student charge card plans. CampusBank: We've Got Class Too™.

Squirrel Girl! @unbeatablesg
@campusbank sometimes i wonder why i follow so many #brands on social media

Squirrel Girl! @unbeatablesg
Okay everyone, HONESTLY, tell me this wall doesn't look WAY BETTER with a hole:

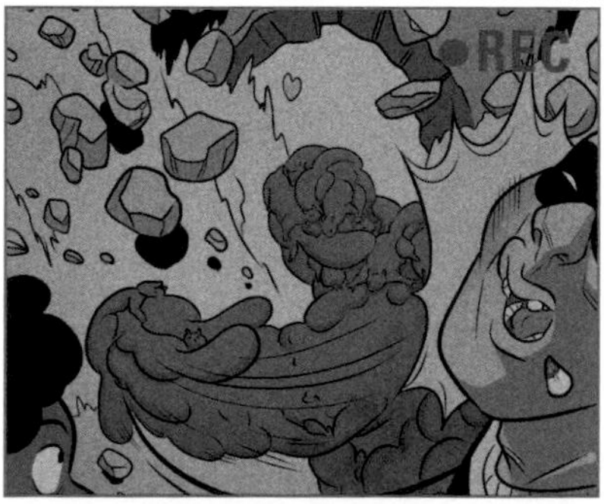
REC

search!

#hippothehippo

#imwithskrull

#liontomeetyou

#squirrelgirl

#kicksbuttseatsnuts

Oh that poor narrator

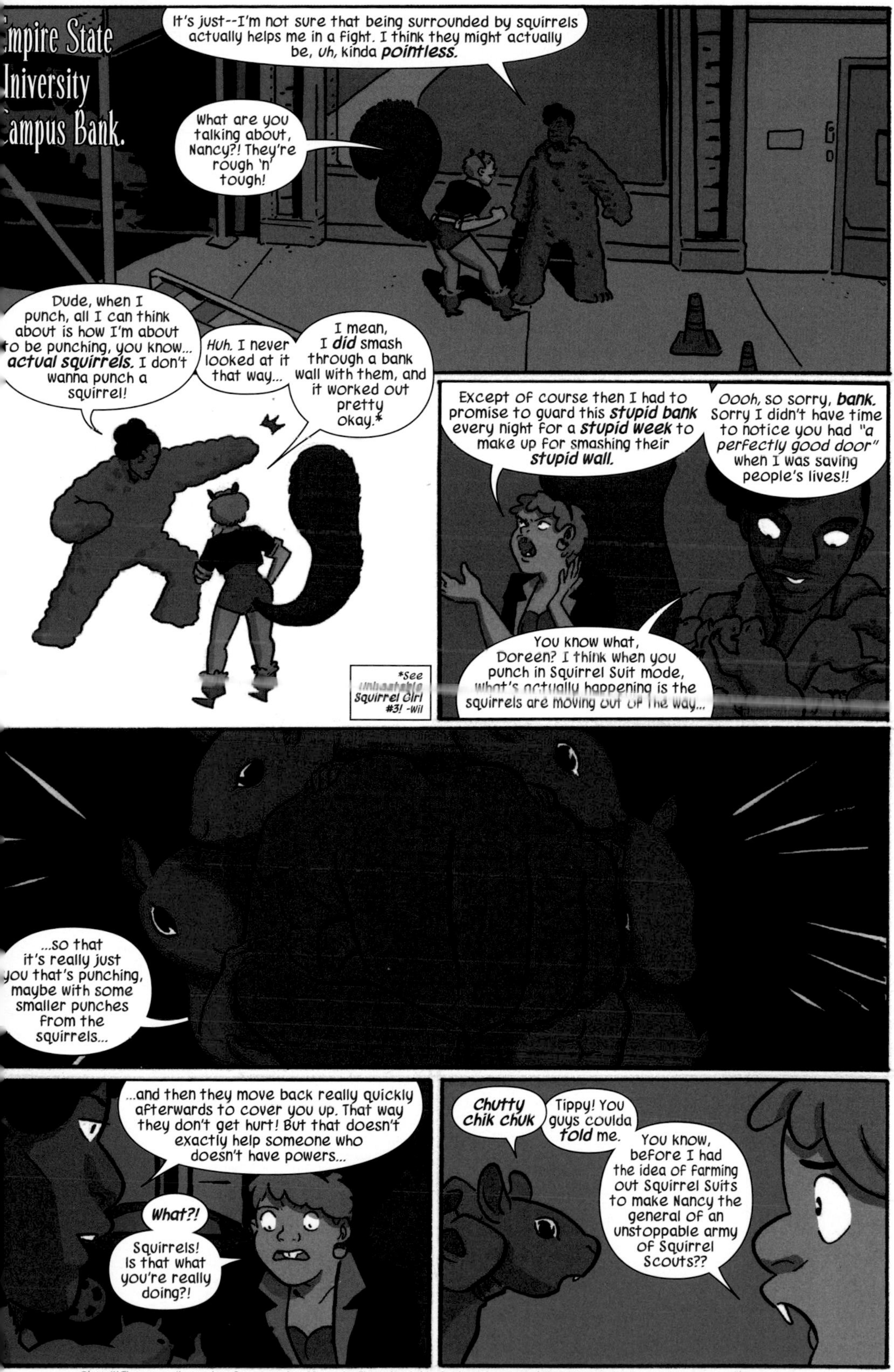
Empire State University Campus Bank.
It's just--I'm not sure that being surrounded by squirrels actually helps me in a fight. I think they might actually be, uh, kinda pointless.
What are you talking about, Nancy?! They're rough 'n' tough!
Dude, when I punch, all I can think about is how I'm about to be punching, you know... actual squirrels. I don't wanna punch a squirrel!
Huh. I never looked at it that way...
I mean, I did smash through a bank wall with them, and it worked out pretty okay.*
*See Unbeatable Squirrel Girl #3! -Wil
Except of course then I had to promise to guard this stupid bank every night for a stupid week to make up for smashing their stupid wall.
Oooh, so sorry, bank. Sorry I didn't have time to notice you had "a perfectly good door" when I was saving people's lives!!
You know what, Doreen? I think when you punch in Squirrel Suit mode, what's actually happening is the squirrels are moving out of the way...
...so that it's really just you that's punching, maybe with some smaller punches from the squirrels...
...and then they move back really quickly afterwards to cover you up. That way they don't get hurt! But that doesn't exactly help someone who doesn't have powers...
What?!
Squirrels! Is that what you're really doing?!
Chutty chik chuk
Tippy! You guys coulda told me.
You know, before I had the idea of farming out Squirrel Suits to make Nancy the general of an unstoppable army of Squirrel Scouts??

Oh well! There go all our plans for our spin-off comic: The Unbeatable Squirrel Scouts And Their Warm And Soft, Yet Also Furry, Battle Suits.

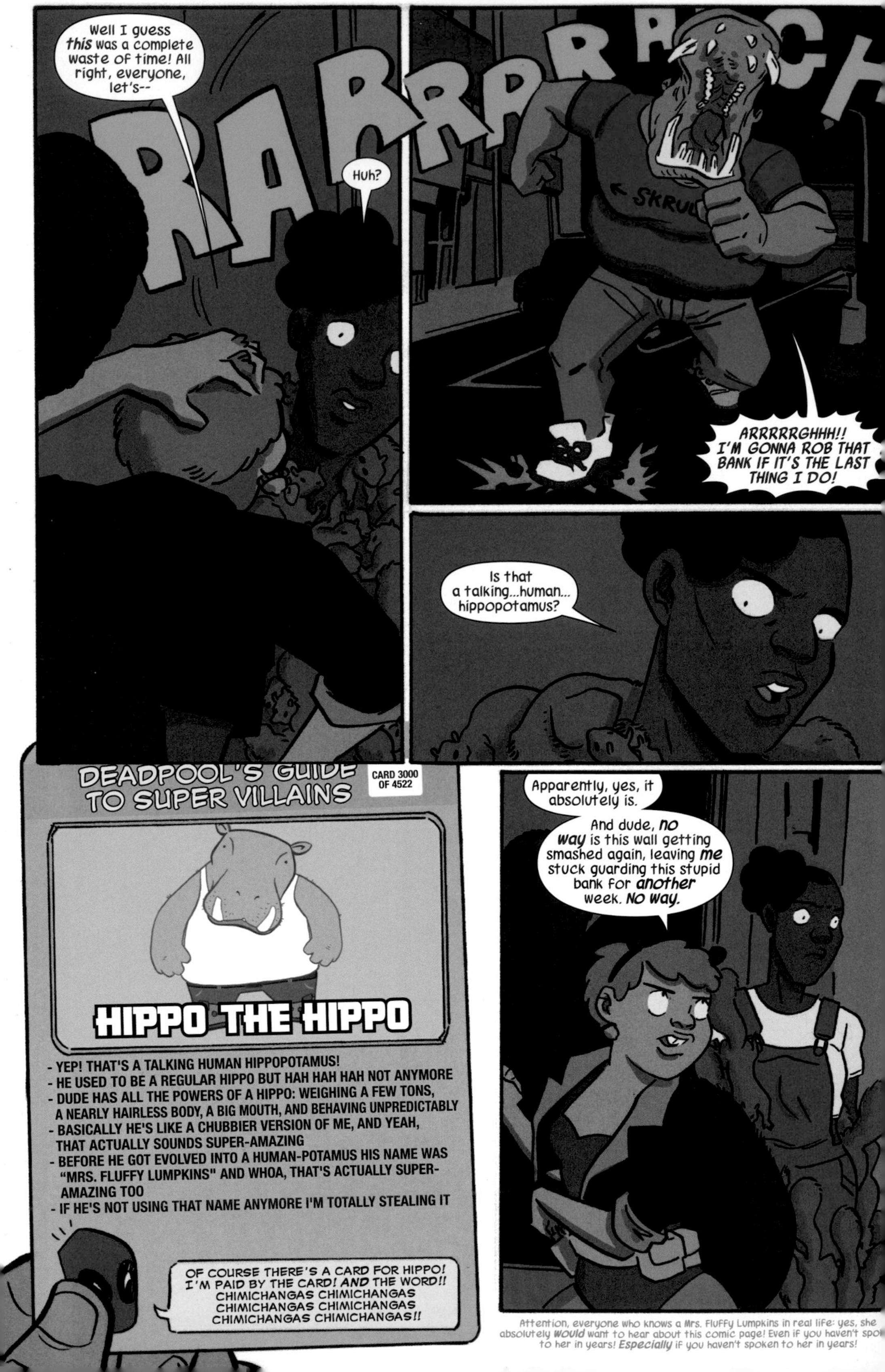

Well I guess *this* was a complete waste of time! All right, everyone, let's--
RAARRRRAACK
Huh?
SKRULL
ARRRRRGHHH!! I'M GONNA ROB THAT BANK IF IT'S THE LAST THING I DO!
Is that a talking...human... hippopotamus?
DEADPOOL'S GUIDE TO SUPER VILLAINS
CARD 3000 OF 4522
HIPPO THE HIPPO
- YEP! THAT'S A TALKING HUMAN HIPPOPOTAMUS!
- HE USED TO BE A REGULAR HIPPO BUT HAH HAH HAH NOT ANYMORE
- DUDE HAS ALL THE POWERS OF A HIPPO: WEIGHING A FEW TONS, A NEARLY HAIRLESS BODY, A BIG MOUTH, AND BEHAVING UNPREDICTABLY
- BASICALLY HE'S LIKE A CHUBBIER VERSION OF ME, AND YEAH, THAT ACTUALLY SOUNDS SUPER-AMAZING
- BEFORE HE GOT EVOLVED INTO A HUMAN-POTAMUS HIS NAME WAS "MRS. FLUFFY LUMPKINS" AND WHOA, THAT'S ACTUALLY SUPER-AMAZING TOO
- IF HE'S NOT USING THAT NAME ANYMORE I'M TOTALLY STEALING IT
OF COURSE THERE'S A CARD FOR HIPPO! I'M PAID BY THE CARD! *AND* THE WORD!! CHIMICHANGAS CHIMICHANGAS CHIMICHANGAS CHIMICHANGAS CHIMICHANGAS CHIMICHANGAS!!
Apparently, yes, it absolutely is.
And dude, ***no way*** is this wall getting smashed again, leaving ***me*** stuck guarding this stupid bank for ***another*** week. ***No way.***
Attention, everyone who knows a Mrs. Fluffy Lumpkins in real life: yes, she absolutely ***would*** want to hear about this comic page! Even if you haven't spo to her in years! ***Especially*** if you haven't spoken to her in years!

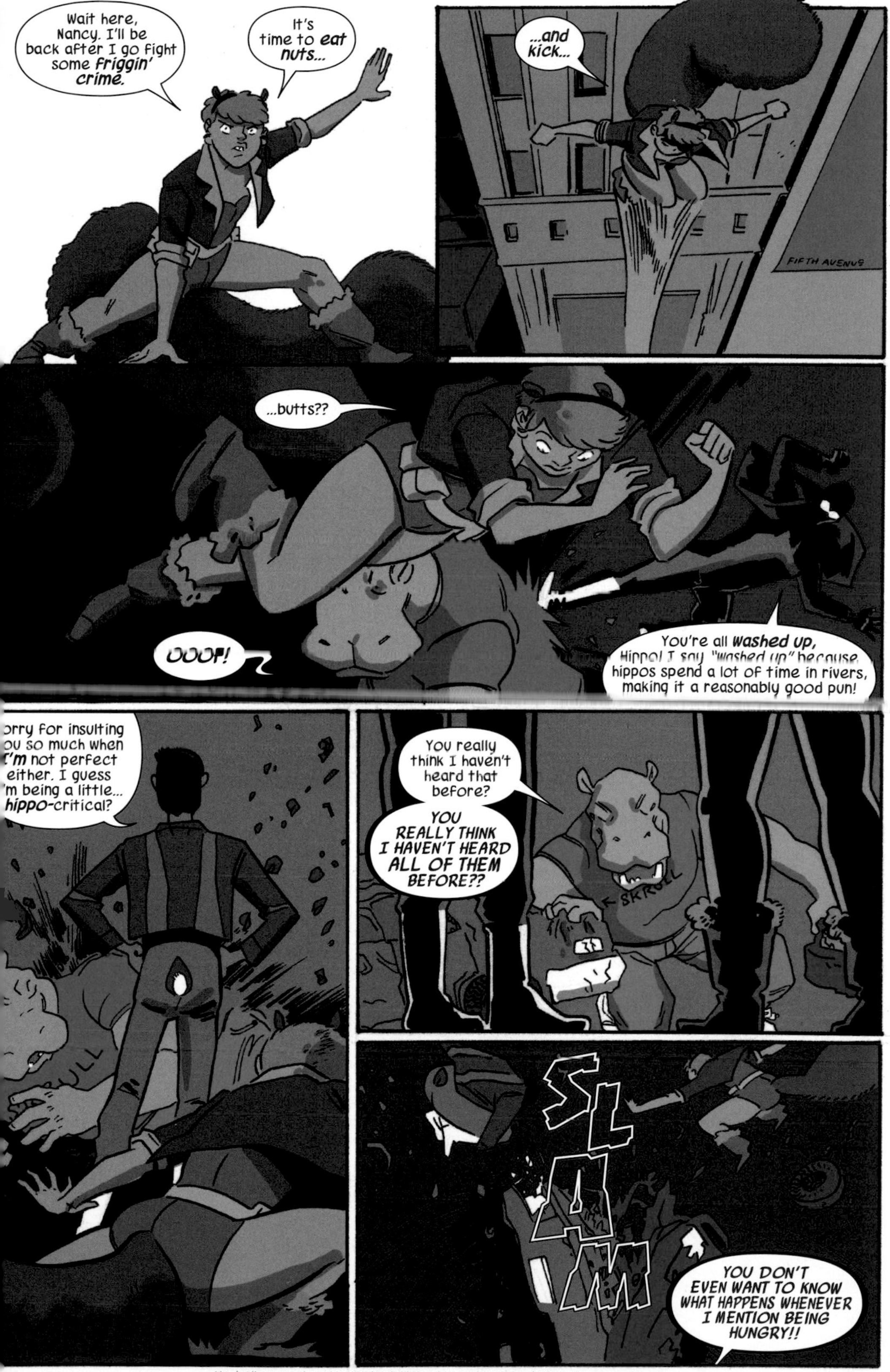

Wait here, Nancy. I'll be back after I go fight some friggin' crime.
It's time to eat nuts...
...and kick...
FIFTH AVENUE
...butts??
OOOF!
You're all washed up, Hippo! I say "washed up" because hippos spend a lot of time in rivers, making it a reasonably good pun!
orry for insulting ou so much when I'm not perfect either. I guess 'm being a little... hippo-critical?
You really think I haven't heard that before?
YOU REALLY THINK I HAVEN'T HEARD ALL OF THEM BEFORE??
SKRULL
SLAM
YOU DON'T EVEN WANT TO KNOW WHAT HAPPENS WHENEVER I MENTION BEING HUNGRY!!

We don't even eat marbles! We've *never* eaten marbles!! Who designs these games?

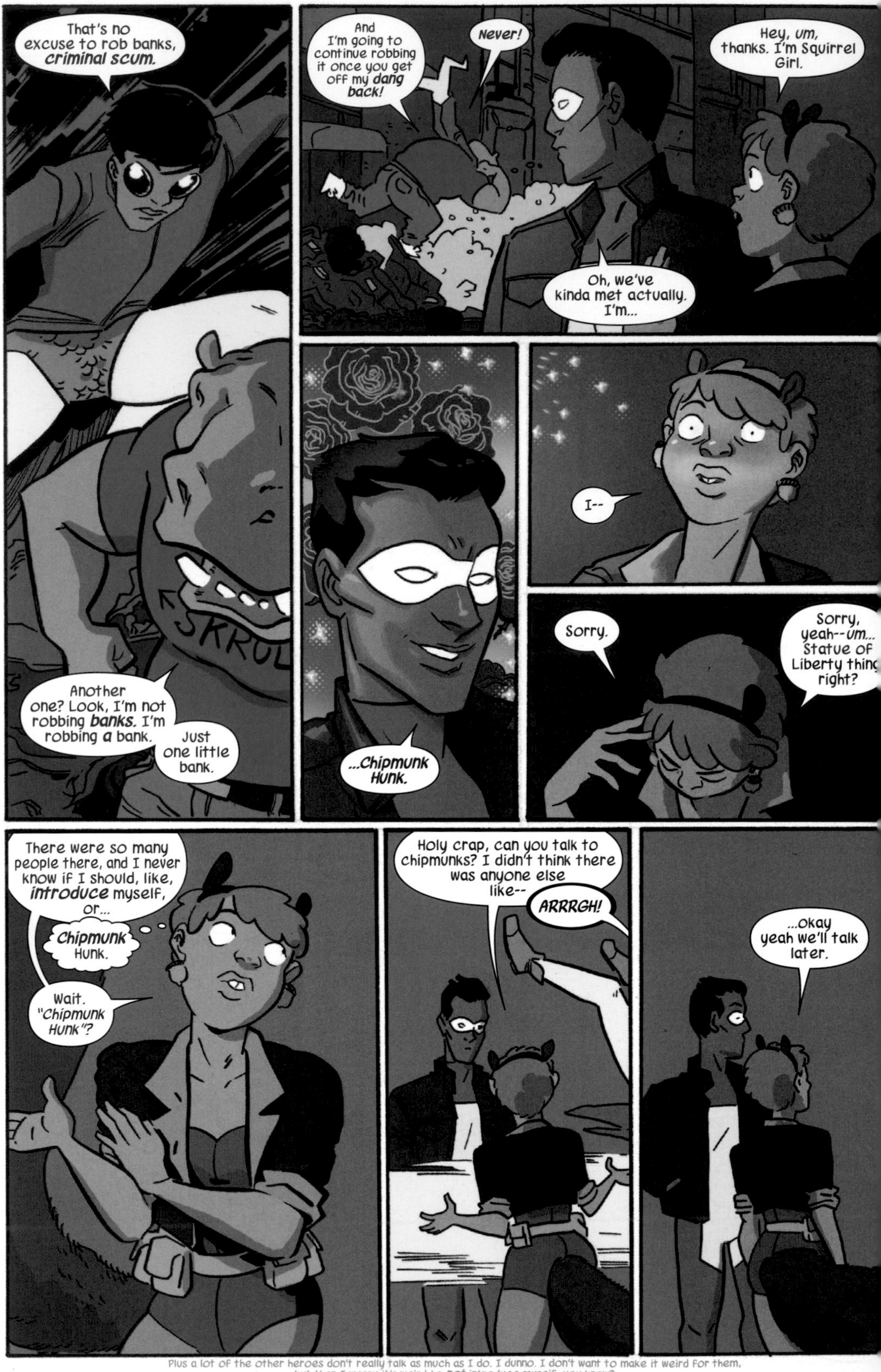
That's no excuse to rob banks, criminal scum.
Another one? Look, I'm not robbing banks. I'm robbing a bank.
Just one little bank.
SKRULL
And I'm going to continue robbing it once you get off my dang back!
Never!
Hey, um, thanks. I'm Squirrel Girl.
Oh, we've kinda met actually. I'm...
...Chipmunk Hunk.
I--
Sorry.
Sorry, yeah--um... Statue of Liberty thing right?
There were so many people there, and I never know if I should, like, introduce myself, or...
Chipmunk Hunk.
Wait. "Chipmunk Hunk"?
Holy crap, can you talk to chipmunks? I didn't think there was anyone else like--
ARRRGH!
...okay yeah we'll talk later.

Plus a lot of the other heroes don't really talk as much as I do. I dunno. I don't want to make it weird for them, but then I worry it's weird to *not* introduce myself, you know?

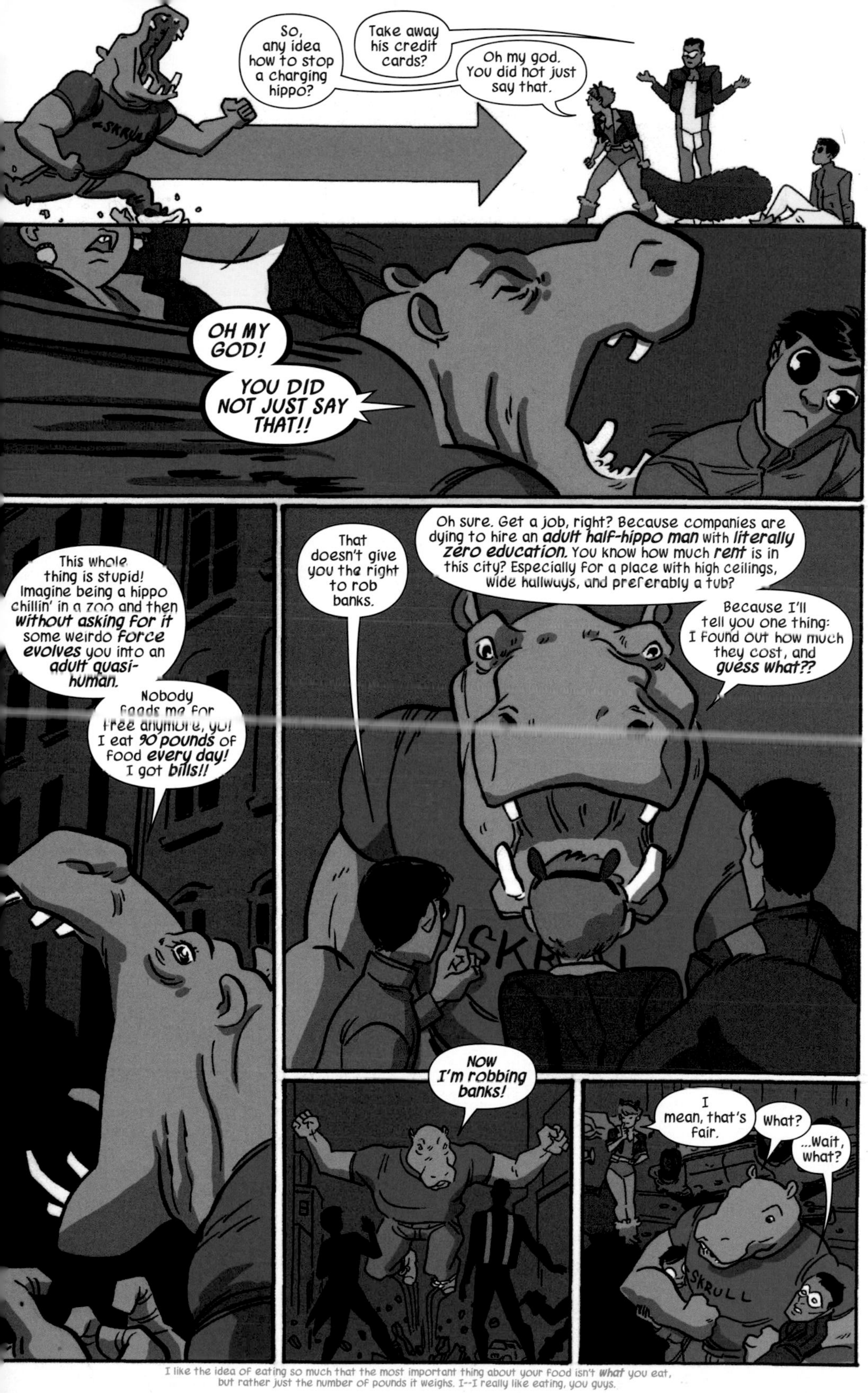
So, any idea how to stop a charging hippo?
Take away his credit cards?
Oh my god. You did not just say that.
OH MY GOD!
YOU DID NOT JUST SAY THAT!!
This whole thing is stupid! Imagine being a hippo chillin' in a zoo and then without asking for it some weirdo force evolves you into an adult quasi-human.
Nobody feeds me for free anymore, yo! I eat 90 pounds of food every day! I got bills!!
That doesn't give you the right to rob banks.
Oh sure. Get a job, right? Because companies are dying to hire an adult half-hippo man with literally zero education. You know how much rent is in this city? Especially for a place with high ceilings, wide hallways, and preferably a tub?
Because I'll tell you one thing: I found out how much they cost, and guess what??
SKRULL
NOW I'm robbing banks!
I mean, that's fair.
What?
...Wait, what?
SKRULL

I like the idea of eating so much that the most important thing about your food isn't *what* you eat, but rather just the number of pounds it weighs. I--I really like eating, you guys.

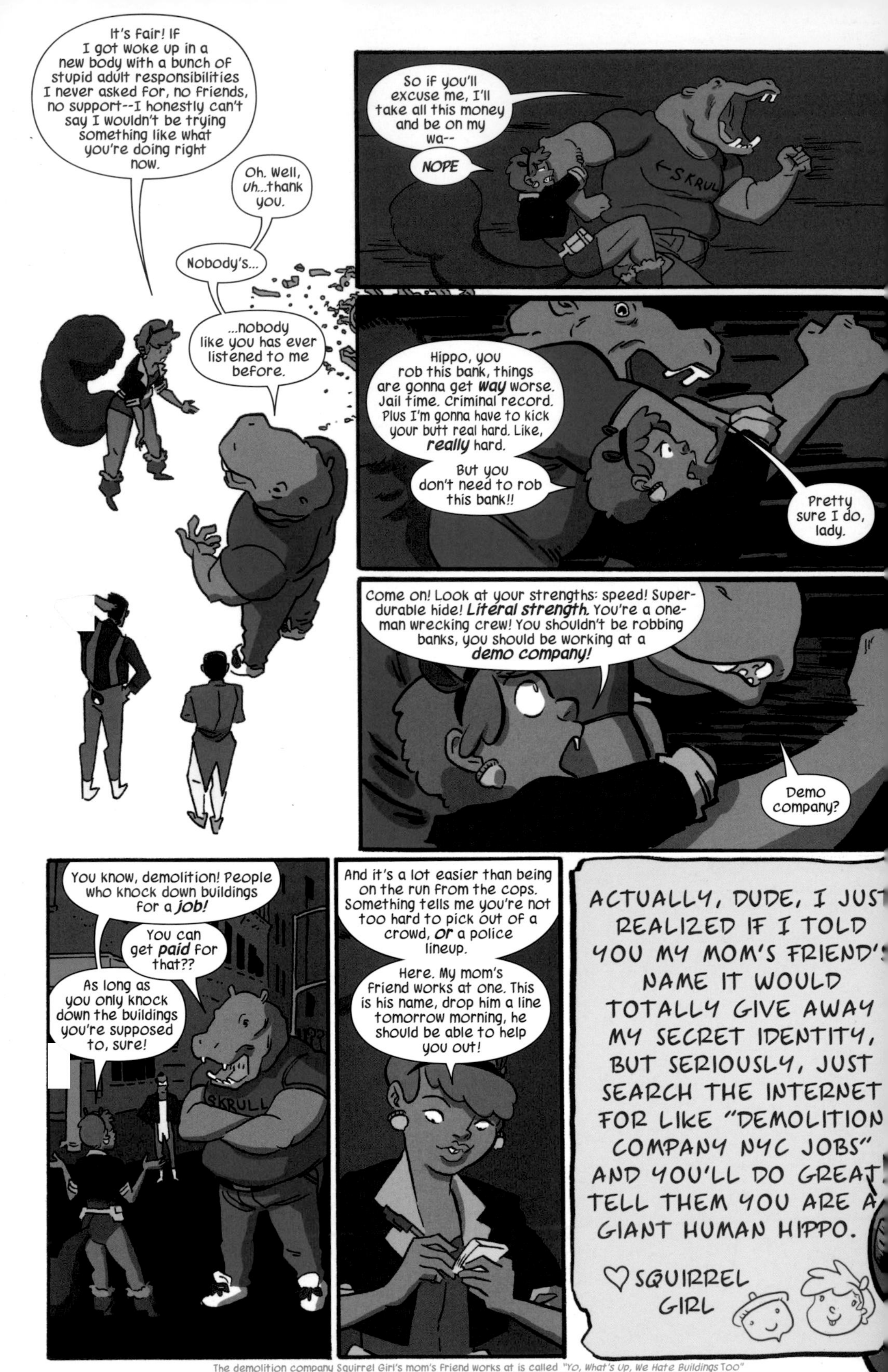
It's fair! If I got woke up in a new body with a bunch of stupid adult responsibilities I never asked for, no friends, no support--I honestly can't say I wouldn't be trying something like what you're doing right now.
Oh. Well, uh...thank you.
Nobody's...
...nobody like you has ever listened to me before.
So if you'll excuse me, I'll take all this money and be on my wa--
NOPE
SKRULL
Hippo, you rob this bank, things are gonna get way worse. Jail time. Criminal record. Plus I'm gonna have to kick your butt real hard. Like, really hard.
But you don't need to rob this bank!!
Pretty sure I do, lady.
Come on! Look at your strengths: speed! Super-durable hide! Literal strength. You're a one-man wrecking crew! You shouldn't be robbing banks, you should be working at a demo company!
Demo company?
You know, demolition! People who knock down buildings for a job!
You can get paid for that??
As long as you only knock down the buildings you're supposed to, sure!
SKRULL
And it's a lot easier than being on the run from the cops. Something tells me you're not too hard to pick out of a crowd, or a police lineup.
Here. My mom's friend works at one. This is his name, drop him a line tomorrow morning, he should be able to help you out!
ACTUALLY, DUDE, I JUST REALIZED IF I TOLD YOU MY MOM'S FRIEND'S NAME IT WOULD TOTALLY GIVE AWAY MY SECRET IDENTITY, BUT SERIOUSLY, JUST SEARCH THE INTERNET FOR LIKE "DEMOLITION COMPANY NYC JOBS" AND YOU'LL DO GREAT. TELL THEM YOU ARE A GIANT HUMAN HIPPO.
♡ SQUIRREL GIRL

The demolition company Squirrel Girl's mom's friend works at is called *"Yo, What's Up, We Hate Buildings Too"* because who wouldn't hire a demo company with that name? The answer: nobody.

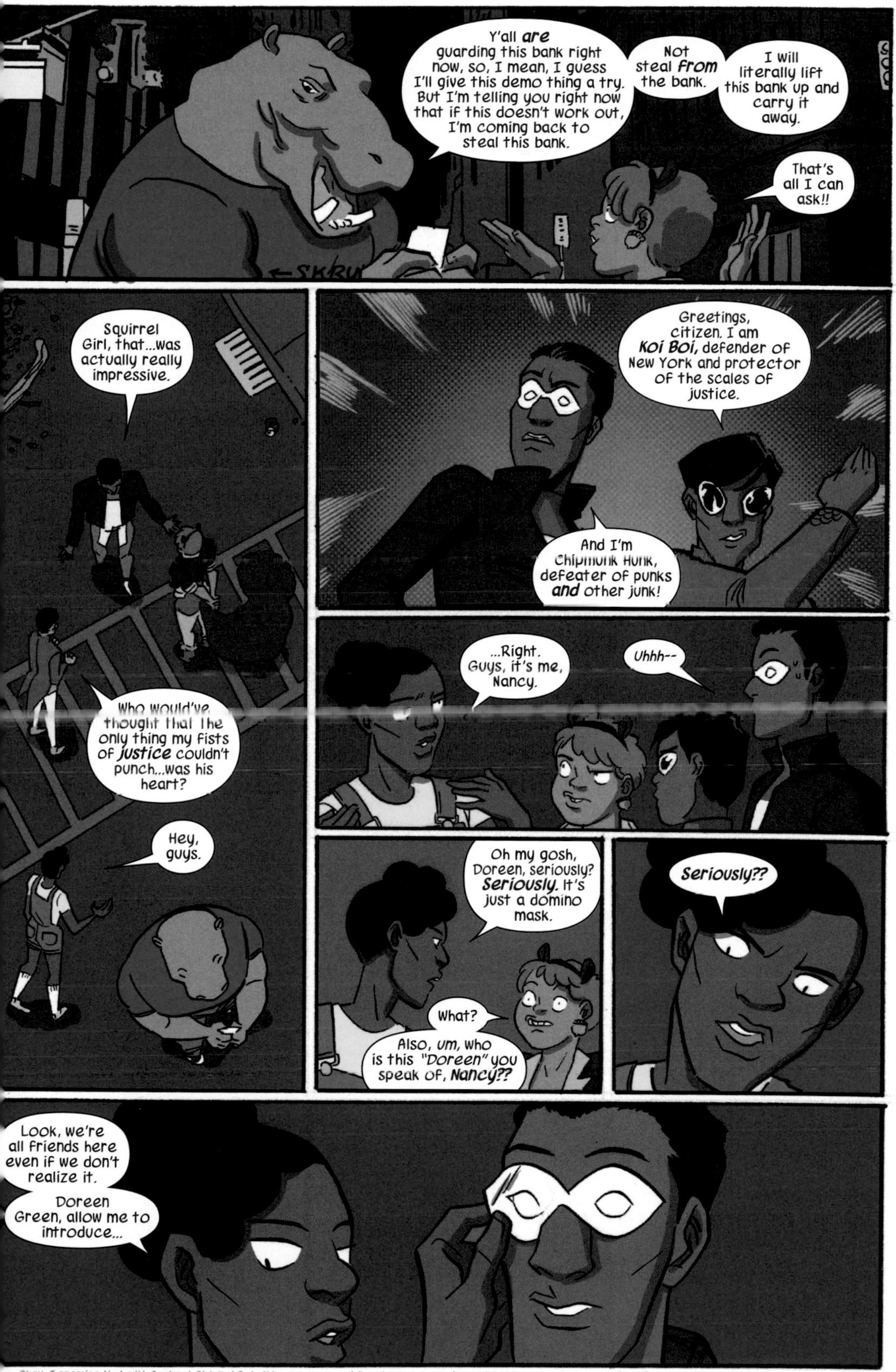
Y'all *are* guarding this bank right now, so, I mean, I guess I'll give this demo thing a try. But I'm telling you right now that if this doesn't work out, I'm coming back to steal this bank.
Not steal *from* the bank.
I will literally lift this bank up and carry it away.
That's all I can ask!!
Squirrel Girl, that...was actually really impressive.
Who would've thought that the only thing my fists of *justice* couldn't punch...was his heart?
Hey, guys.
Greetings, citizen. I am *Koi Boi,* defender of New York and protector of the scales of justice.
And I'm Chipmunk Hunk, defeater of punks *and* other junk!
...Right. Guys, it's me, Nancy.
Uhhh--
Oh my gosh, Doreen, seriously? *Seriously.* It's just a domino mask.
What?
Also, *um,* who is this *"Doreen"* you speak of, *Nancy??*
Seriously??
Look, we're all friends here even if we don't realize it.
Doreen Green, allow me to introduce...

Okay, I promise that with Squirrel Girl, Koi Boi, Chipmunk Hunk, and Bass Lass, we are done with animal rhyming names. *Promise.* For at least the next eleven pages.

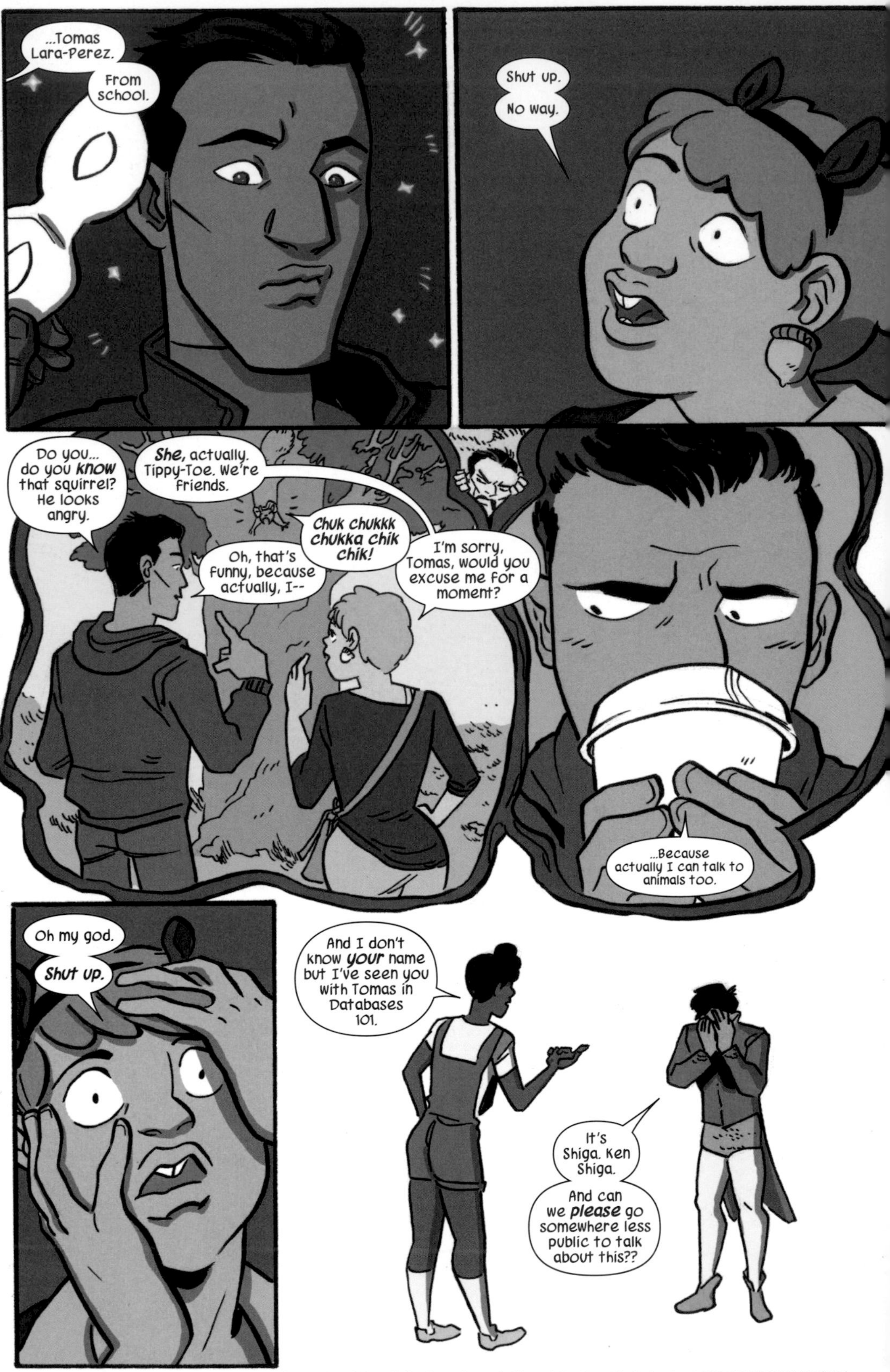
...Tomas Lara-Perez.
From school.
Shut up.
No way.
Do you... do you **know** that squirrel? He looks angry.
She, actually. Tippy-Toe. We're friends.
Chuk chukkk chukka chik chik!
Oh, that's funny, because actually, I--
I'm sorry, Tomas, would you excuse me for a moment?
...Because actually I can talk to animals too.
Oh my god.
Shut up.
And I don't know ***your*** name but I've seen you with Tomas in Databases 101.
It's Shiga. Ken Shiga.
And can we ***please*** go somewhere less public to talk about this??

This flashback is from our first issue, and if you haven't bought it yet, good news: holding out for six months just got you ***two*** panels from it for free! At this rate you'll be able to read the whole first issue in several dozen years!

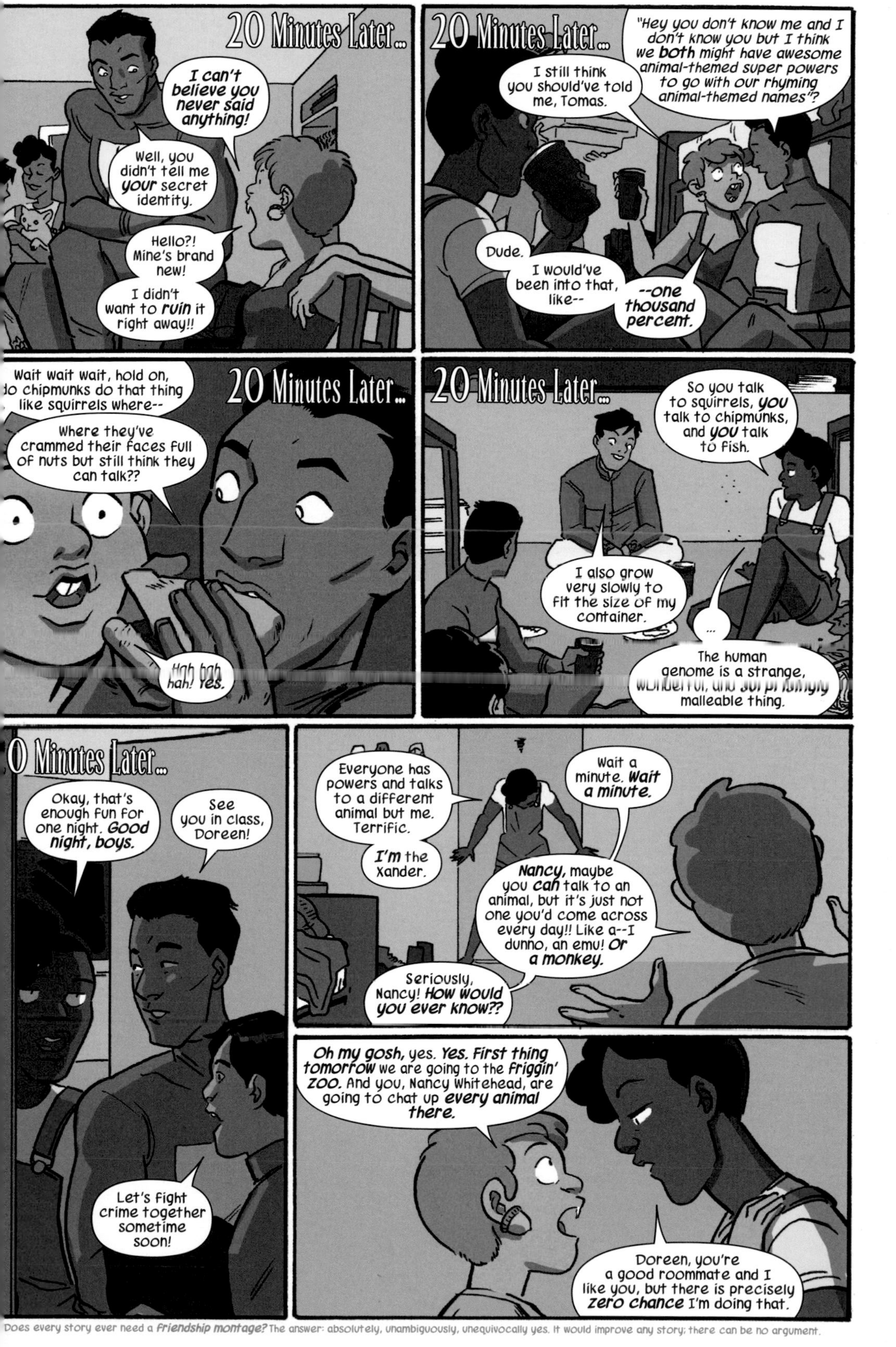
20 Minutes Later...
I can't believe you never said anything!
Well, you didn't tell me your secret identity.
Hello?! Mine's brand new!
I didn't want to ruin it right away!!
20 Minutes Later...
I still think you should've told me, Tomas.
"Hey you don't know me and I don't know you but I think we both might have awesome animal-themed super powers to go with our rhyming animal-themed names"?
Dude.
I would've been into that, like--
--one thousand percent.
Wait wait wait, hold on, do chipmunks do that thing like squirrels where--
Where they've crammed their faces full of nuts but still think they can talk??
20 Minutes Later...
Hah hah hah! Yes.
20 Minutes Later...
So you talk to squirrels, you talk to chipmunks, and you talk to fish.
I also grow very slowly to fit the size of my container.
...
The human genome is a strange, wonderful, and surprisingly malleable thing.
0 Minutes Later...
Okay, that's enough fun for one night. Good night, boys.
See you in class, Doreen!
Let's fight crime together sometime soon!
Everyone has powers and talks to a different animal but me. Terrific.
I'm the Xander.
Wait a minute. Wait a minute.
Nancy, maybe you can talk to an animal, but it's just not one you'd come across every day!! Like a--I dunno, an emu! Or a monkey.
Seriously, Nancy! How would you ever know??
Oh my gosh, yes. Yes. First thing tomorrow we are going to the friggin' zoo. And you, Nancy Whitehead, are going to chat up every animal there.
Doreen, you're a good roommate and I like you, but there is precisely zero chance I'm doing that.

Does every story ever need a *friendship montage?* The answer: absolutely, unambiguously, unequivocally yes. It would improve any story; there can be no argument.

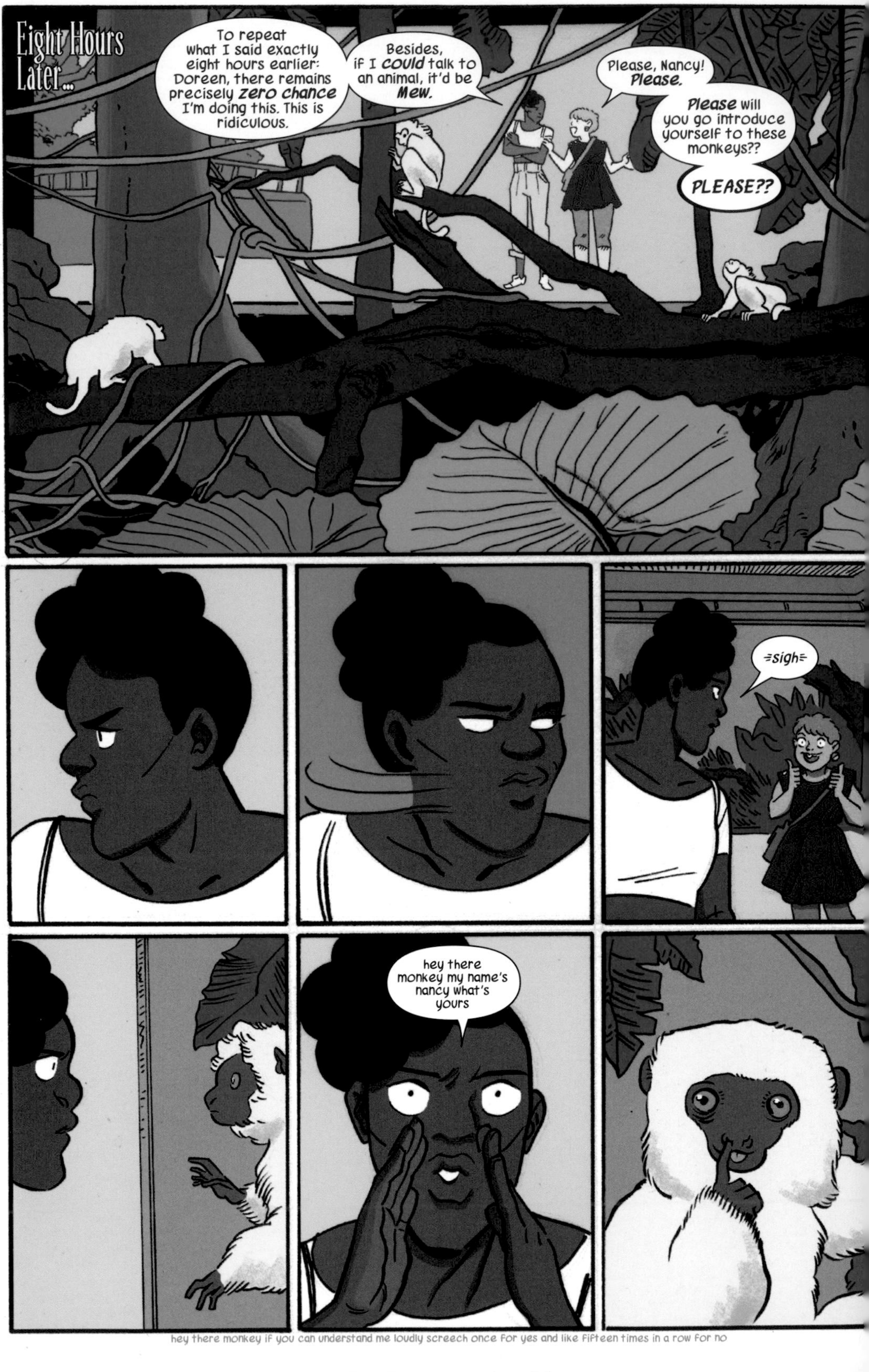
Eight Hours Later...
To repeat what I said exactly eight hours earlier: Doreen, there remains precisely zero chance I'm doing this. This is ridiculous.
Besides, if I could talk to an animal, it'd be Mew.
Please, Nancy! Please.
Please will you go introduce yourself to these monkeys??
PLEASE??
sigh
hey there monkey my name's nancy what's yours
hey there monkey if you can understand me loudly screech once for yes and like fifteen times in a row for no

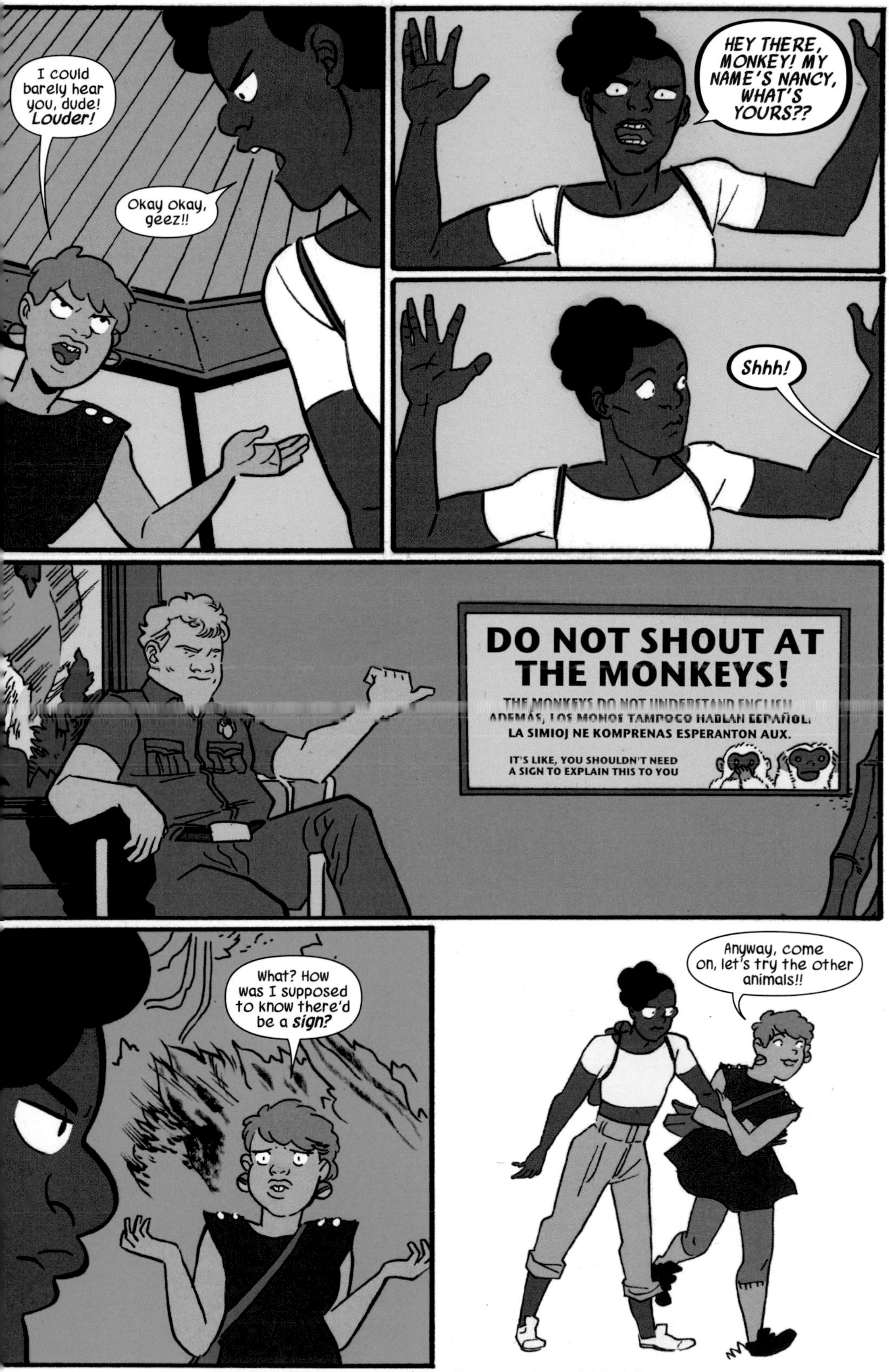
I could barely hear you, dude! *Louder!*
Okay okay, geez!!
HEY THERE, MONKEY! MY NAME'S NANCY, WHAT'S YOURS??
Shhh!
DO NOT SHOUT AT THE MONKEYS!
THE MONKEYS DO NOT UNDERSTAND ENGLISH.
ADEMÁS, LOS MONOS TAMPOCO HABLAN ESPAÑOL.
LA SIMIOJ NE KOMPRENAS ESPERANTON AUX.
IT'S LIKE, YOU SHOULDN'T NEED A SIGN TO EXPLAIN THIS TO YOU
What? How was I supposed to know there'd be a *sign?*
Anyway, come on, let's try the other animals!!

Okay, secretly the monkeys have taught themselves some sign language but that's *it*.

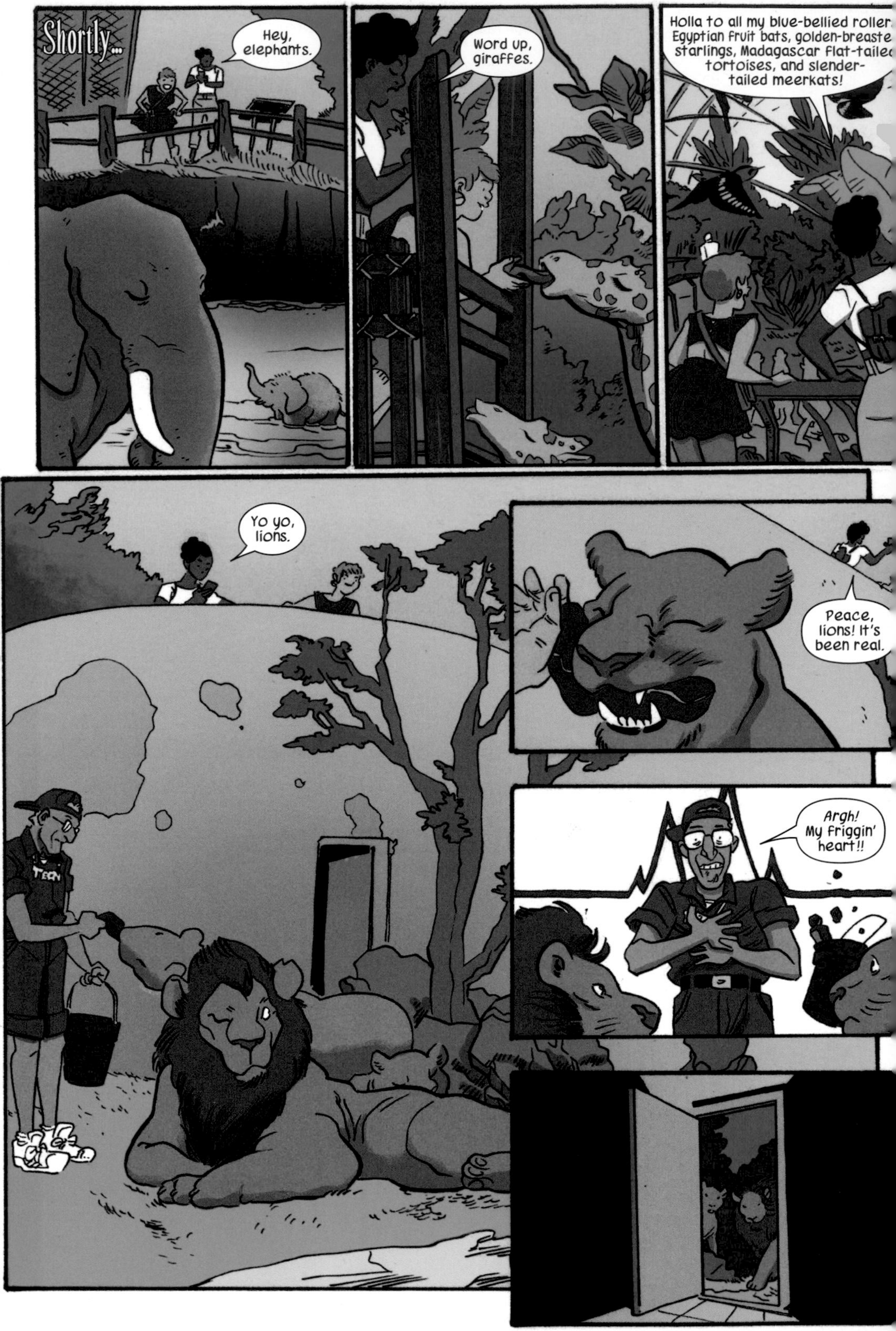
Shortly...
Hey, elephants.
Word up, giraffes.
Holla to all my blue-bellied rollers, Egyptian fruit bats, golden-breasted starlings, Madagascar flat-tailed tortoises, and slender-tailed meerkats!
Yo yo, lions.
Peace, lions! It's been real.
Argh! My friggin' heart!!

See, this is exactly why zoo regulations *clearly* state to close all lion doors *before* having a medical emergency.

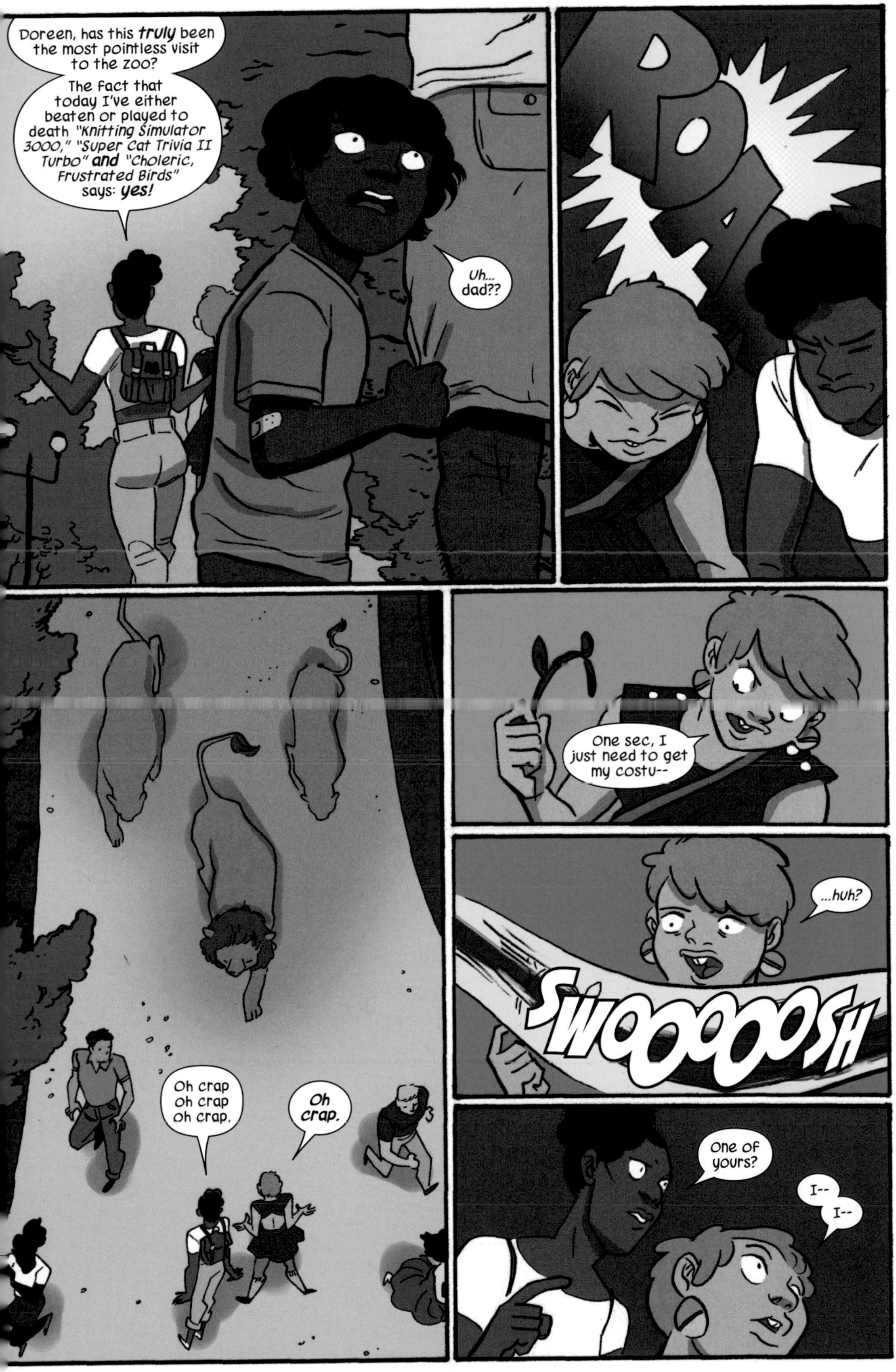
Doreen, has this truly been the most pointless visit to the zoo?
The fact that today I've either beaten or played to death "Knitting Simulator 3000," "Super Cat Trivia II Turbo" and "Choleric, Frustrated Birds" says: yes!
Uh... dad??
POW
One sec, I just need to get my costu--
...huh?
SWOOOOOSH
Oh crap oh crap oh crap.
Oh crap.
One of yours?
I--
I--

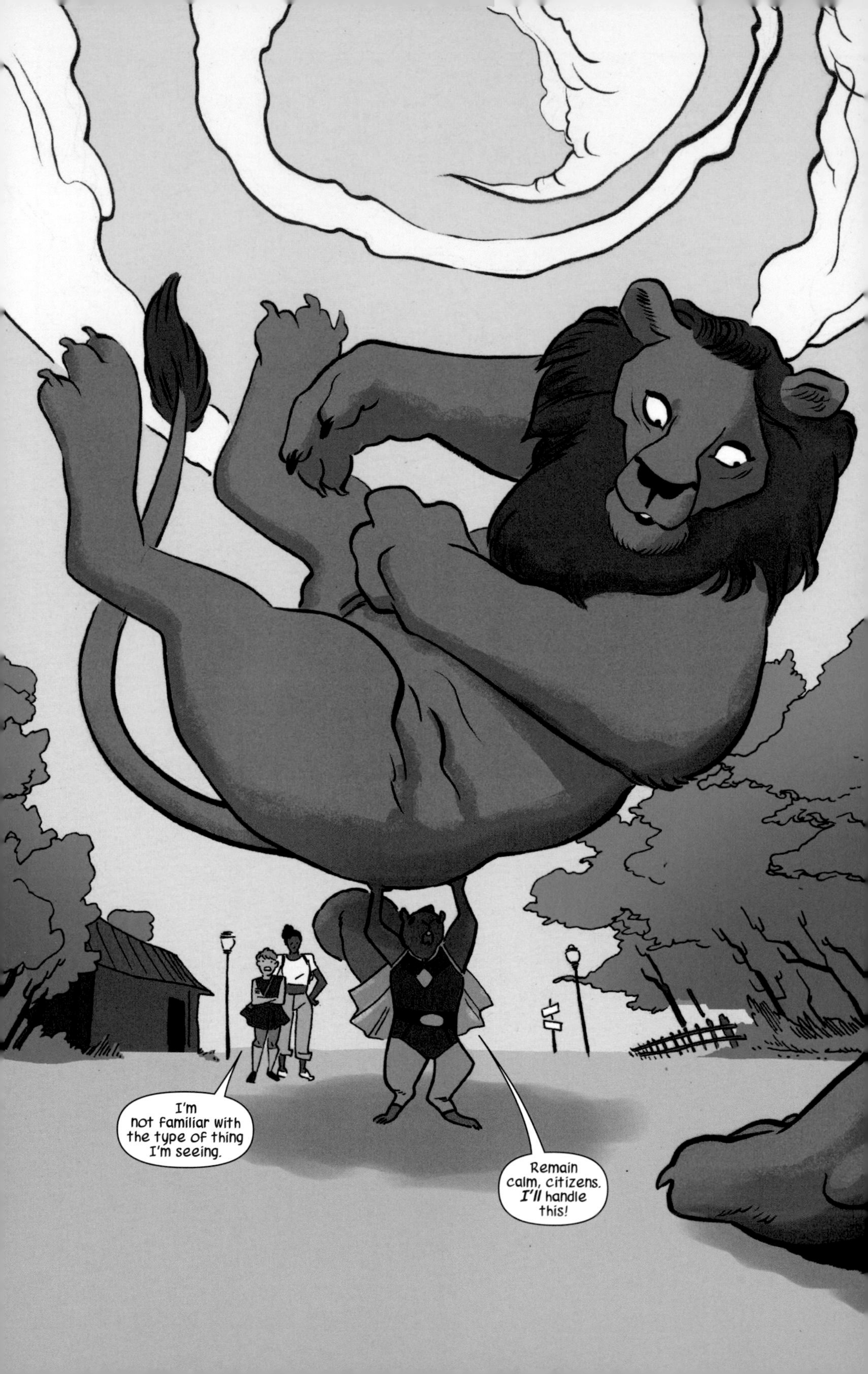
I'm not familiar with the type of thing I'm seeing.
Remain calm, citizens. *I'll* handle this!

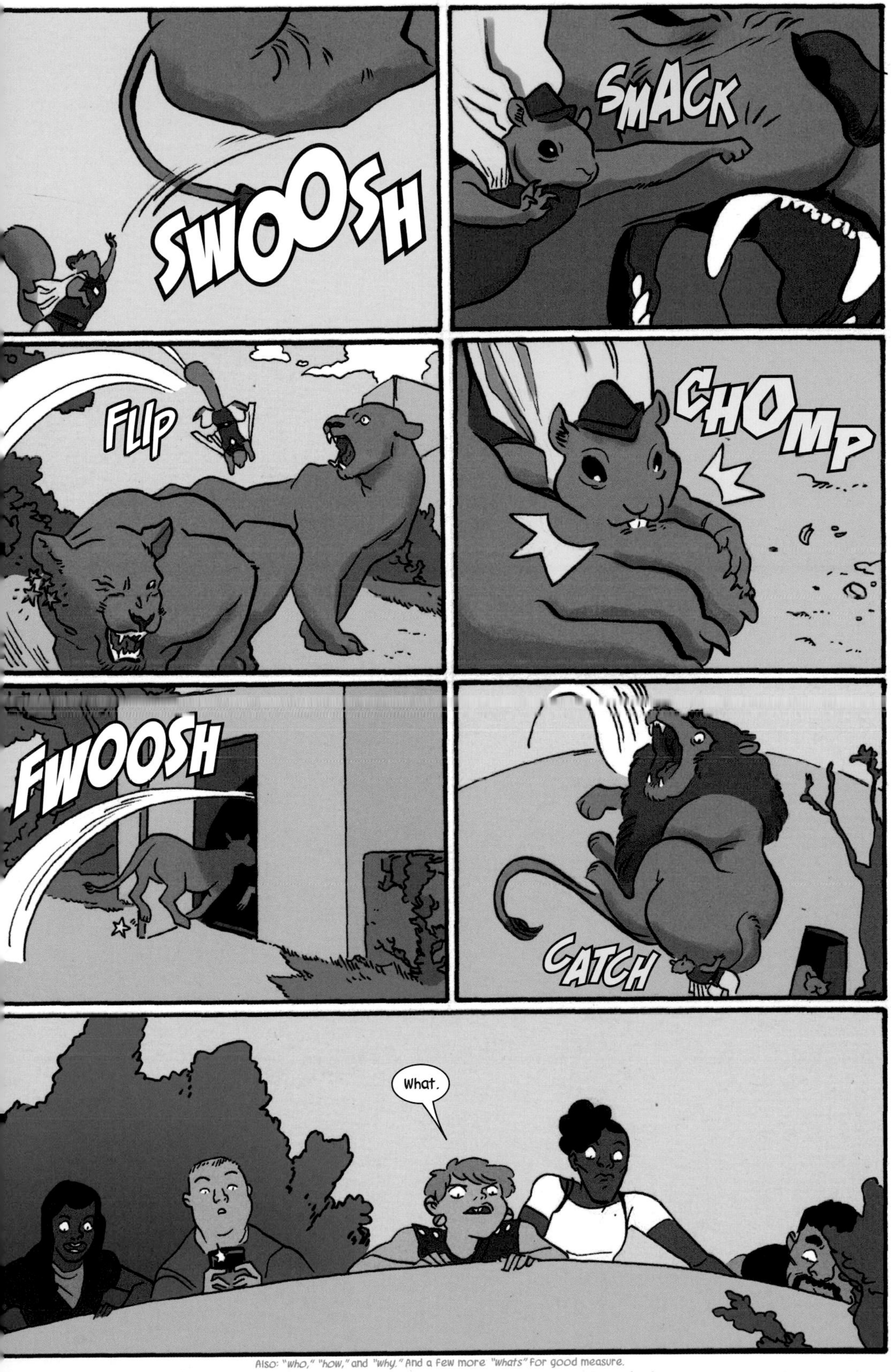
SWOOSH
SMACK
FLIP
CHOMP
FWOOSH
CATCH
What.

Also: "who," "how," and "why." And a few more "whats" for good measure.

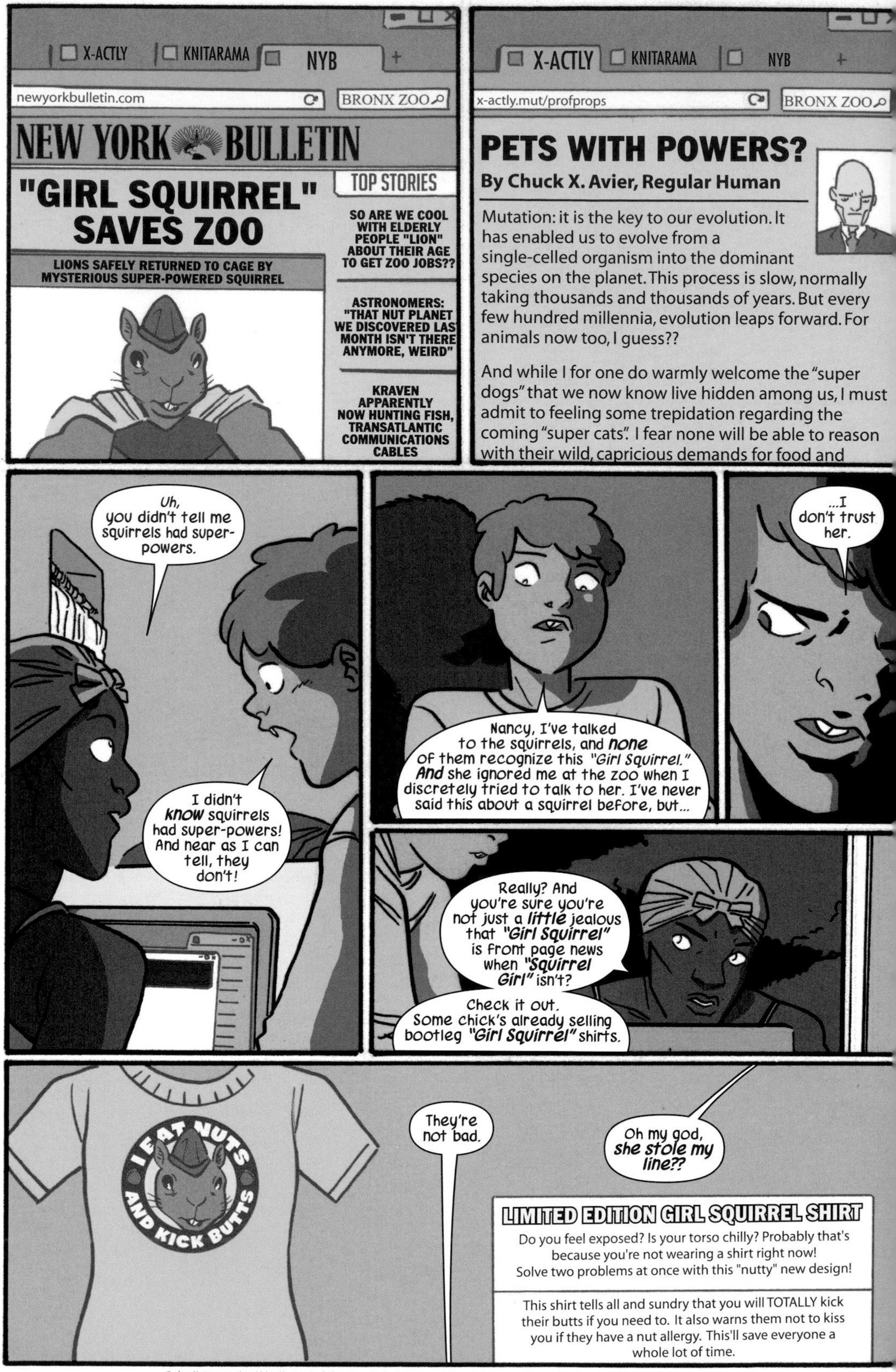
X-ACTLY
KNITARAMA
NYB
newyorkbulletin.com
BRONX ZOO
NEW YORK BULLETIN
"GIRL SQUIRREL" SAVES ZOO
LIONS SAFELY RETURNED TO CAGE BY MYSTERIOUS SUPER-POWERED SQUIRREL
TOP STORIES
SO ARE WE COOL WITH ELDERLY PEOPLE "LION" ABOUT THEIR AGE TO GET ZOO JOBS??
ASTRONOMERS: "THAT NUT PLANET WE DISCOVERED LAST MONTH ISN'T THERE ANYMORE, WEIRD"
KRAVEN APPARENTLY NOW HUNTING FISH, TRANSATLANTIC COMMUNICATIONS CABLES
X-ACTLY
KNITARAMA
NYB
x-actly.mut/profprops
BRONX ZOO
PETS WITH POWERS?
By Chuck X. Avier, Regular Human
Mutation: it is the key to our evolution. It has enabled us to evolve from a single-celled organism into the dominant species on the planet. This process is slow, normally taking thousands and thousands of years. But every few hundred millennia, evolution leaps forward. For animals now too, I guess??
And while I for one do warmly welcome the "super dogs" that we now know live hidden among us, I must admit to feeling some trepidation regarding the coming "super cats". I fear none will be able to reason with their wild, capricious demands for food and
Uh, you didn't tell me squirrels had super-powers.
I didn't KNOW squirrels had super-powers! And near as I can tell, they don't!
Nancy, I've talked to the squirrels, and NONE of them recognize this "Girl Squirrel." AND she ignored me at the zoo when I discretely tried to talk to her. I've never said this about a squirrel before, but...
...I don't trust her.
Really? And you're sure you're not just a little jealous that "Girl Squirrel" is front page news when "Squirrel Girl" isn't?
Check it out. Some chick's already selling bootleg "Girl Squirrel" shirts.
I EAT NUTS AND KICK BUTTS
They're not bad.
Oh my god, she stole my line??
LIMITED EDITION GIRL SQUIRREL SHIRT
Do you feel exposed? Is your torso chilly? Probably that's because you're not wearing a shirt right now! Solve two problems at once with this "nutty" new design!
This shirt tells all and sundry that you will TOTALLY kick their butts if you need to. It also warns them not to kiss you if they have a nut allergy. This'll save everyone a whole lot of time.

I don't know who this Chuck X. Avier guy is, but he sure likes talking up this School for Gifted Youngsters! Weird!!

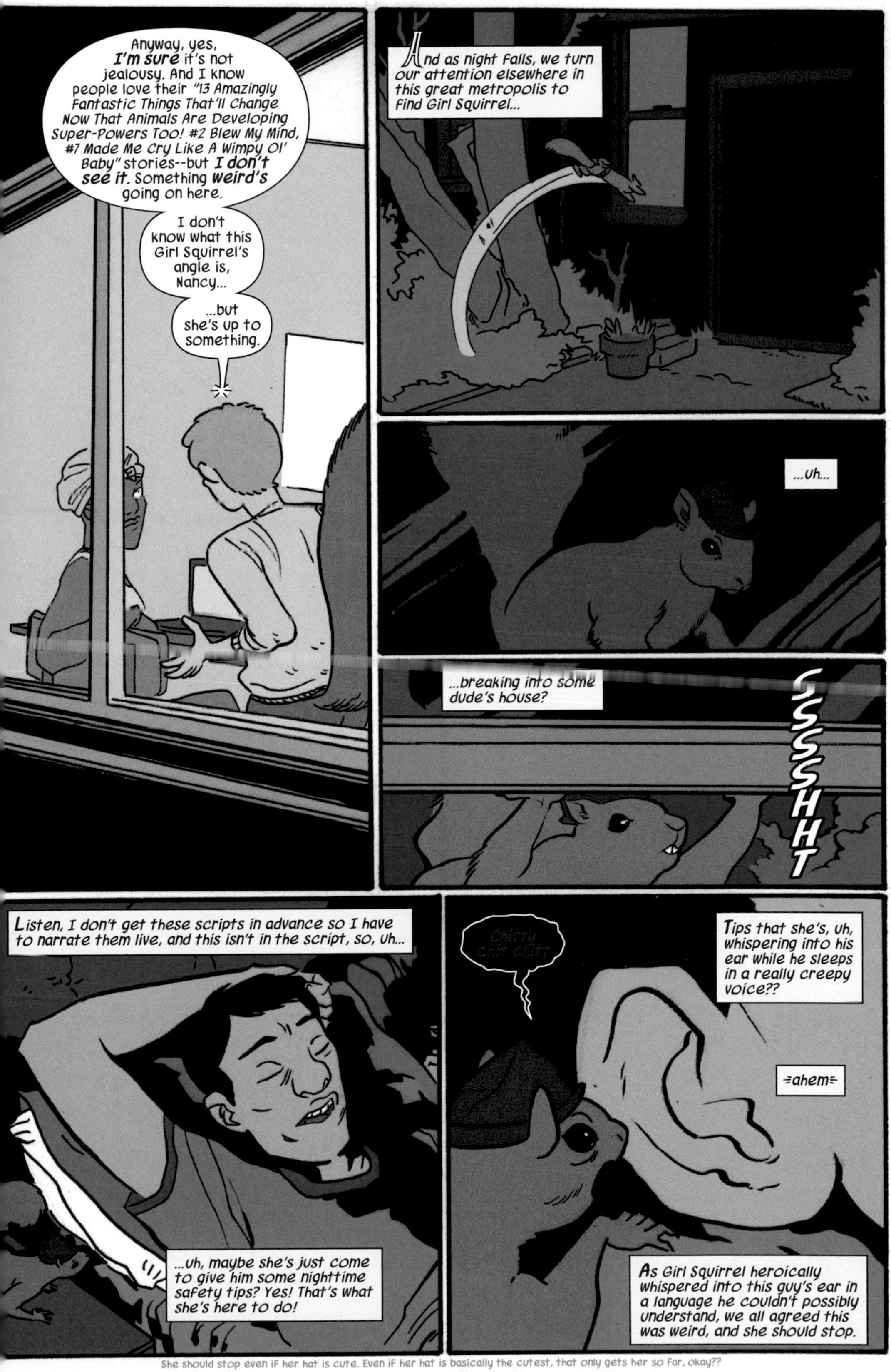
Anyway, yes, I'm sure it's not jealousy. And I know people love their "13 Amazingly Fantastic Things That'll Change Now That Animals Are Developing Super-Powers Too! #2 Blew My Mind, #7 Made Me Cry Like A Wimpy Ol' Baby" stories--but I don't see it. Something weird's going on here.
I don't know what this Girl Squirrel's angle is, Nancy...
...but she's up to something.
And as night falls, we turn our attention elsewhere in this great metropolis to find Girl Squirrel...
...uh...
...breaking into some dude's house?
SSSSHHT
Listen, I don't get these scripts in advance so I have to narrate them live, and this isn't in the script, so, uh...
...uh, maybe she's just come to give him some nighttime safety tips? Yes! That's what she's here to do!
Chitty chit chitt
Tips that she's, uh, whispering into his ear while he sleeps in a really creepy voice??
=ahem=
As Girl Squirrel heroically whispered into this guy's ear in a language he couldn't possibly understand, we all agreed this was weird, and she should stop.

She should stop even if her hat is cute. Even if her hat is basically the cutest, that only gets her so far, okay??

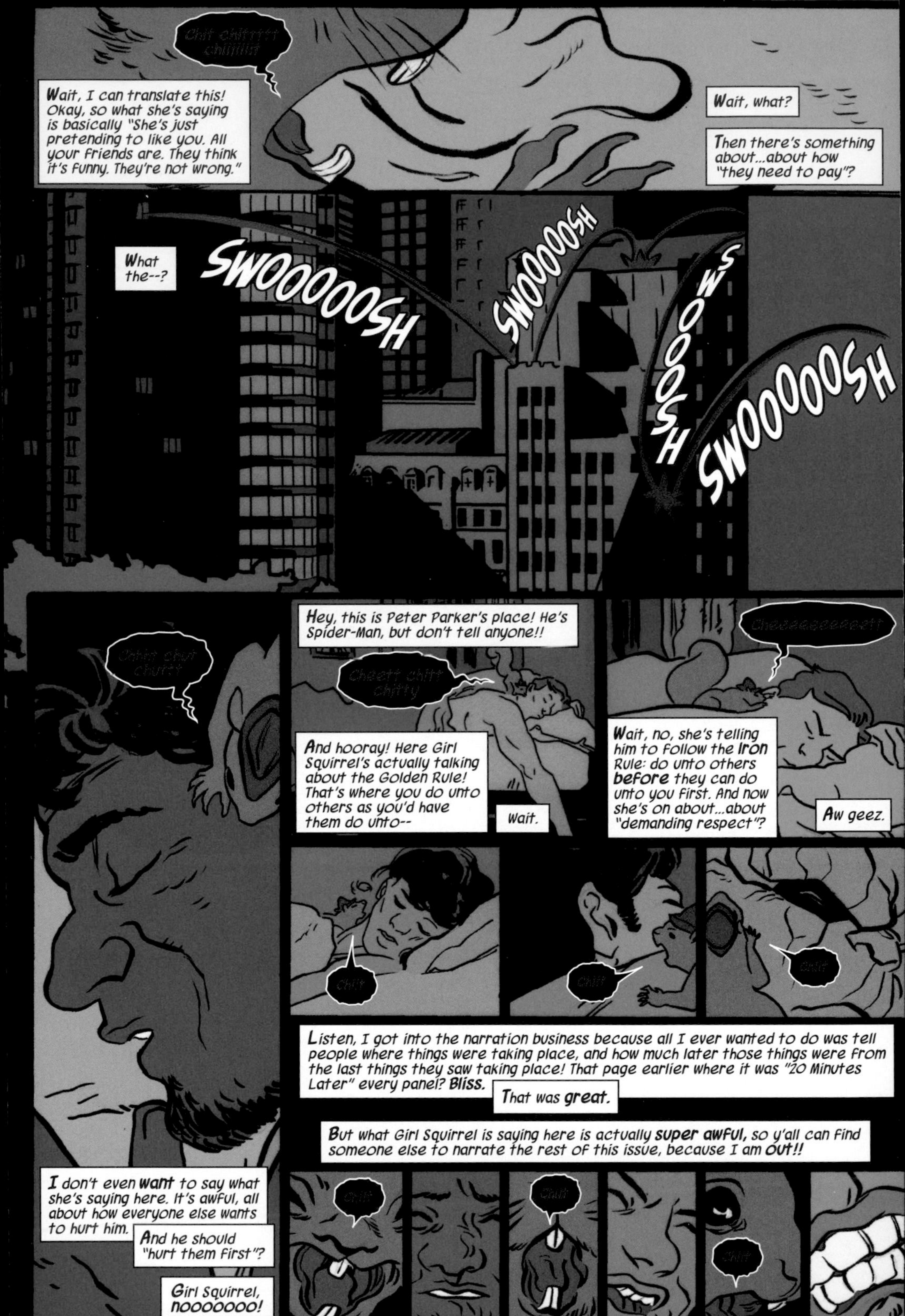
Wait, I can translate this! Okay, so what she's saying is basically "She's just pretending to like you. All your friends are. They think it's funny. They're not wrong."
Wait, what?
Then there's something about...about how "they need to pay"?
What the--?
SWOOOOOOSH
SWOOOOOSH
SWOOOOSH
SWOOOOOSH
Hey, this is Peter Parker's place! He's Spider-Man, but don't tell anyone!!
And hooray! Here Girl Squirrel's actually talking about the Golden Rule! That's where you do unto others as you'd have them do unto--
Wait.
Wait, no, she's telling him to follow the Iron Rule: do unto others before they can do unto you first. And now she's on about..."demanding respect"?
Aw geez.
Listen, I got into the narration business because all I ever wanted to do was tell people where things were taking place, and how much later those things were from the last things they saw taking place! That page earlier where it was "20 Minutes Later" every panel? Bliss.
That was great.
But what Girl Squirrel is saying here is actually super awful, so y'all can find someone else to narrate the rest of this issue, because I am out!!
I don't even want to say what she's saying here. It's awful, all about how everyone else wants to hurt him.
And he should "hurt them first"?
Girl Squirrel, nooooooo!

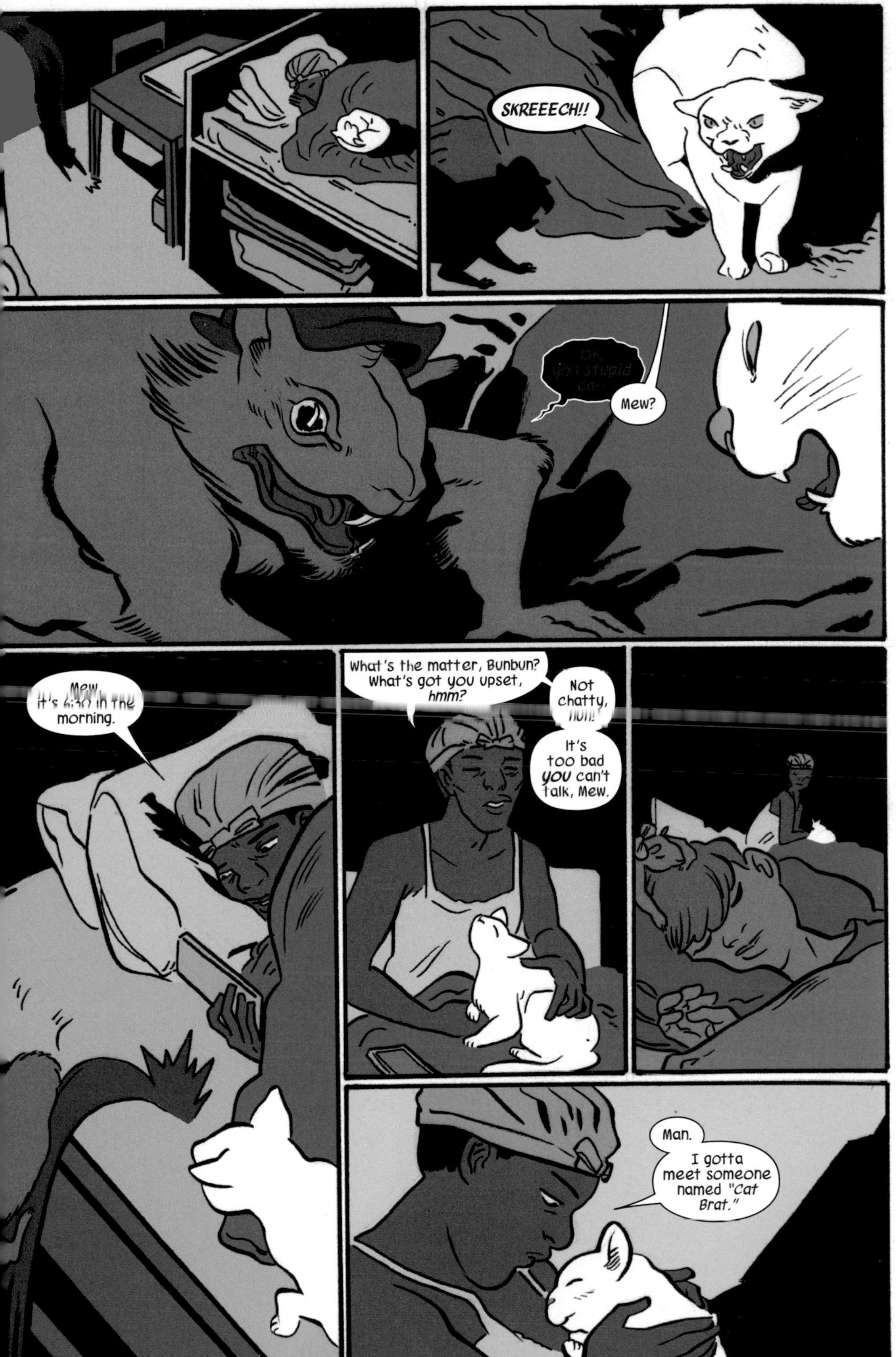
SKREEECH!!
Oh, you stupid ca--
Mew?
Mew, it's 6:30 in the morning.
What's the matter, Bunbun? What's got you upset, hmm?
Not chatty, huh?
It's too bad YOU can't talk, Mew.
Man.
I gotta meet someone named "Cat Brat."

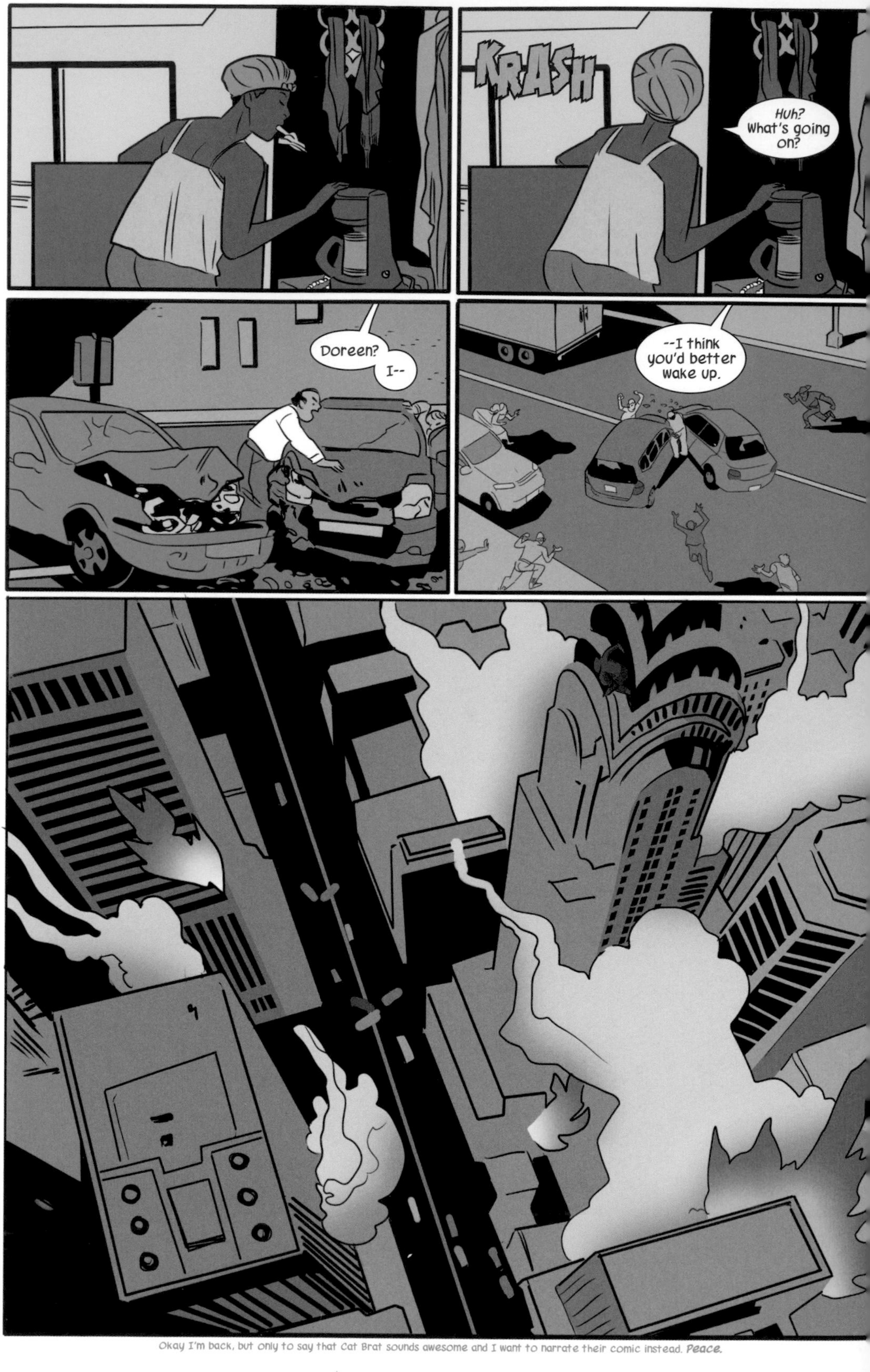
KRASH
Huh? What's going on?
Doreen? I--
--I think you'd better wake up.

Okay I'm back, but only to say that Cat Brat sounds awesome and I want to narrate their comic instead. *Peace.*

7

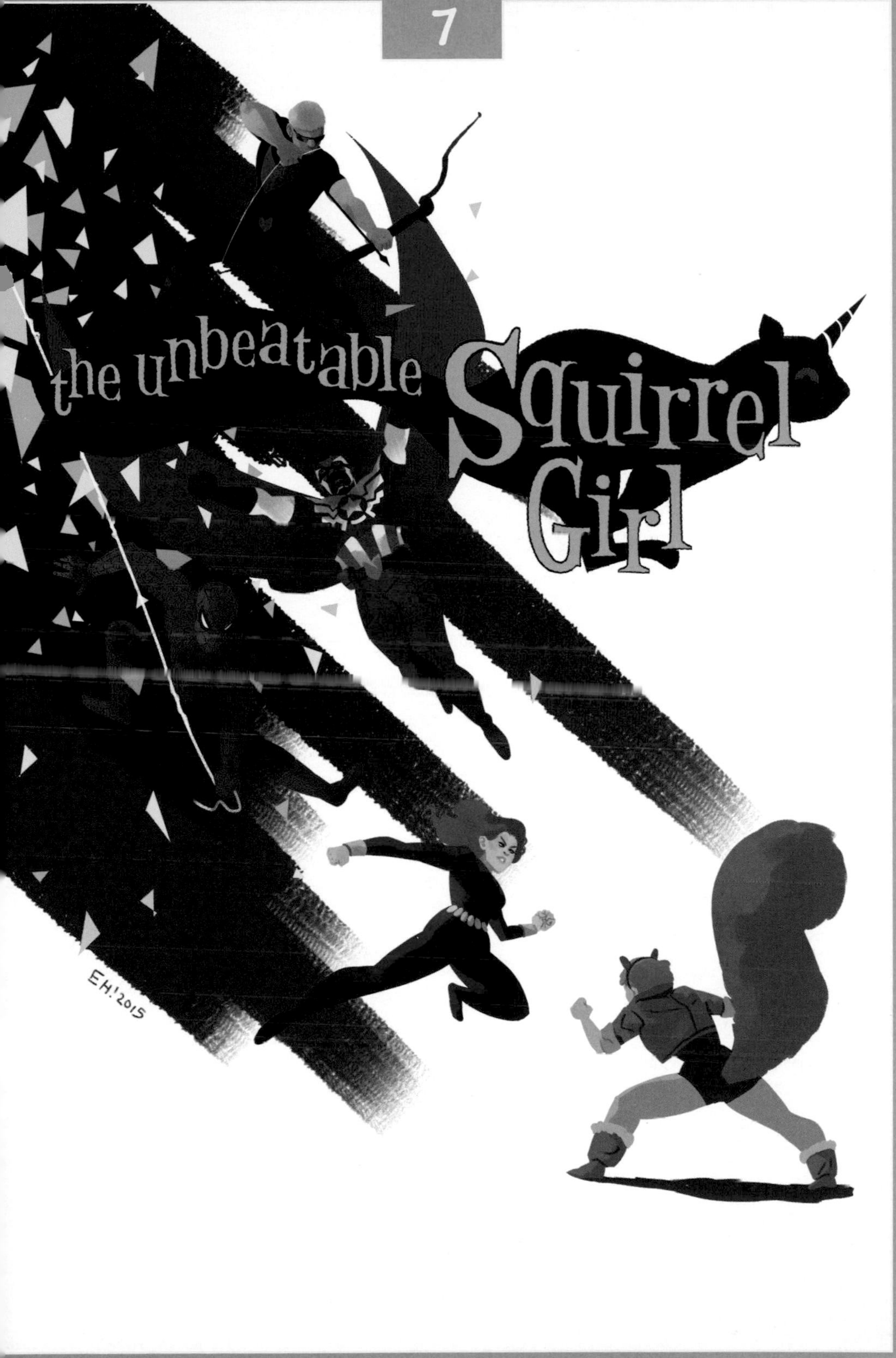
the unbeatable Squirrel Girl
EH! 2015

Doreen Green isn't just a first-year computer science student: she secretly also has all the powers of both squirrel and gir
She uses her amazing abilities to fight crime **and** be as awesome as possible. You know her as...*The Unbeatable Squirrel Gir*
Let's catch up with what she's been up to until now, with....

Squirrel Girl *in a nutshell*

search! 🔍

#databasesoneohone

#databasesoneohFUN

#dontthrowshadeonmyfriends

#breakfastbeats

#boythor

Bostonian Cameos

Squirrel Girl! @unbeatablesg
PUBLIC SERVICE ANNOUNCEMENT: Everyone should go to the zoo and talk to every animal there. Just go and chat up every animal!

Squirrel Girl! @unbeatablesg
Because how do you know you CAN'T talk to animals unless you've tried with every animal?? And they've got lots of animals there!

Squirrel Girl! @unbeatablesg
Also yes I am aware that there are elements of zoos that are NOT UNPROBLEMATIC but where else are you gonna chat up mad lemurs

Squirrel Girl! @unbeatablesg
Besides Madagascar I mean

Tippy-Toe @yoitstippytoe
@unbeatablesg CHITTT CHITTY CHIT CHIT

Squirrel Girl! @unbeatablesg
@yoitstippytoe dude, I meant "mad lemurs" in the "lots of lemurs" sense, not that they're angry! The zoo ones were actually mostly sleepy

Squirrel Girl! @unbeatablesg
@yoitstippytoe lots of sleepy lemurs to be had at your local zoo, visit today

Nancy W. @sewwiththeflo
I was at the zoo yesterday when the lions got out and this "Girl Squirrel" saved everyone.

Nancy W. @sewwiththeflo
As near as I can tell she is a squirrel with the INVERSE proportional strength of a girl? Or something?

Nancy W. @sewwiththeflo
What even is biology, you guys.

Nancy W. @sewwiththeflo
How do bodies even work.

Nancy W. @sewwiththeflo
Local woman publicly questions how a squirrel can have the powers of a girl. Vets hate me.

Tony Stark @starkmantony ✓
@unbeatablesg Getting reports of fights breaking out all over NYC. Can I assume you are on this?

Squirrel Girl! @unbeatablesg
@starkmantony uh can you assume it's like 6:30am here and i just woke up

Tony Stark @starkmantony ✓
@unbeatablesg My post woke you up? Huh. You have a special notification sound for me, don't you.

Squirrel Girl! @unbeatablesg
@starkmantony um, YEAH, it's your old 60s-style PERSONAL JINGLE that you hoped we'd all just forgot about and it's AMAZING

Squirrel Girl! @unbeatablesg
@starkmantony 🎵 Tony Stark / Makes you feel / He's the cool exec / With a heart of steel 🎵

Tony Stark @starkmantony ✓
@unbeatablesg Hold on a second.

Tony Stark @starkmantony ✓
@unbeatablesg I just remotely erased that song from your phone and from every other mirror online.

Squirrel Girl! @unbeatablesg
@starkmantony 🎵 Tony Stark / Makes me feel / That I'm super glad / That I backed up that song to a device not connected to the internet 🎵

Squirrel Girl! @unbeatablesg
Hey I dunno if any criminals follow me but JUST IN CASE, you should know that KOI BOI and CHIPMUNK HUNK are fighting crime now too!

Squirrel Girl! @unbeatablesg
Also if you are a criminal please stop doing crimes. #crimeadvice

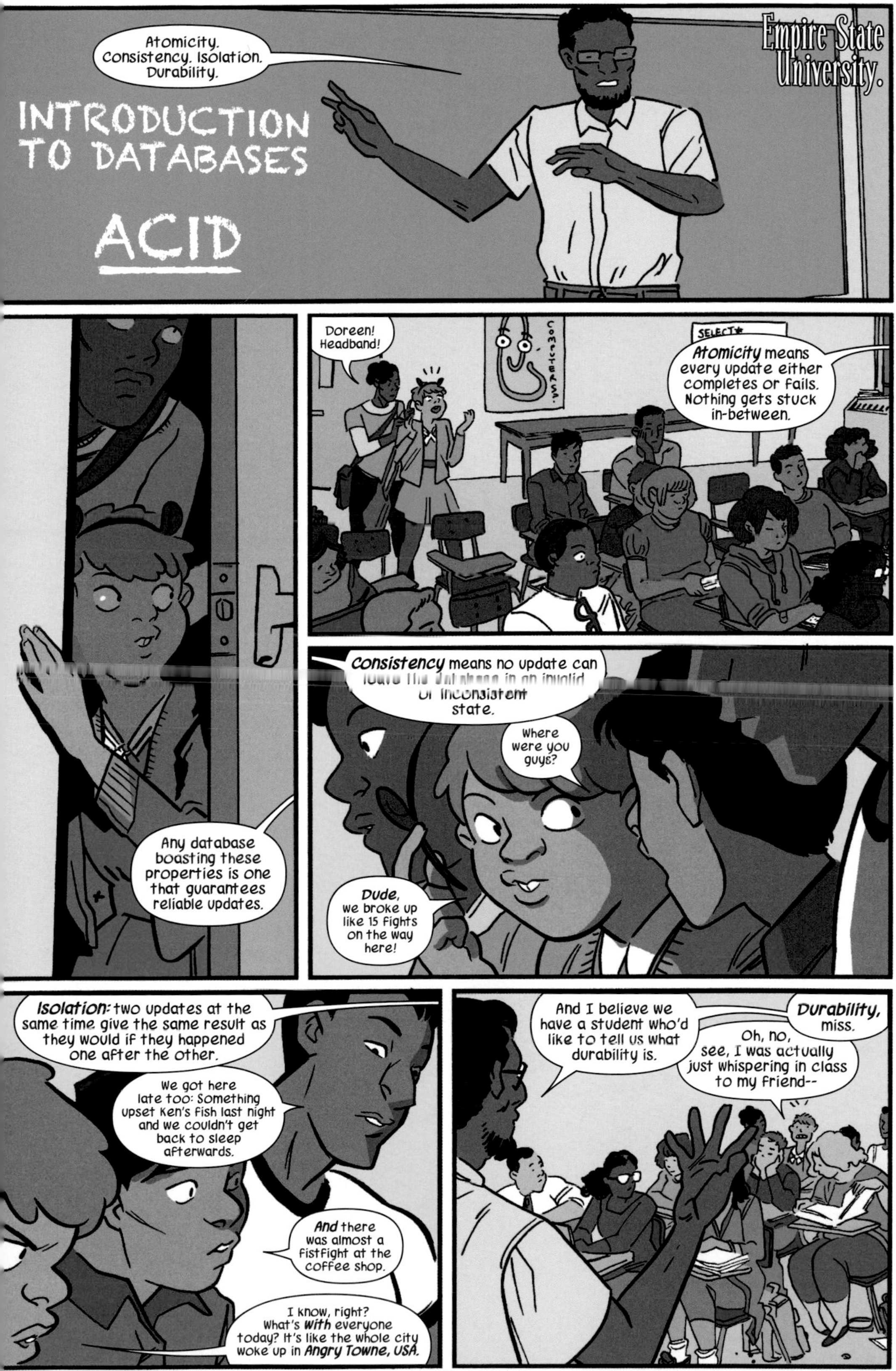
Atomicity. Consistency. Isolation. Durability.
Empire State University.
INTRODUCTION TO DATABASES
ACID
Doreen! Headband!
COMPUTERS
SELECT*
Atomicity means every update either completes or fails. Nothing gets stuck in-between.
Consistency means no update can
in an invalid or inconsistent
state.
Where were you guys?
Dude, we broke up like 15 fights on the way here!
Any database boasting these properties is one that guarantees reliable updates.
Isolation: two updates at the same time give the same result as they would if they happened one after the other.
We got here late too: Something upset Ken's fish last night and we couldn't get back to sleep afterwards.
And there was almost a fistfight at the coffee shop.
I know, right? What's with everyone today? It's like the whole city woke up in Angry Towne, USA.
And I believe we have a student who'd like to tell us what durability is.
Durability, miss.
Oh, no, see, I was actually just whispering in class to my friend--

All these database facts are true, by the way. So now you can impress all your friends with your college-level knowledge of database design, so long as they don't ask a single follow-up question!

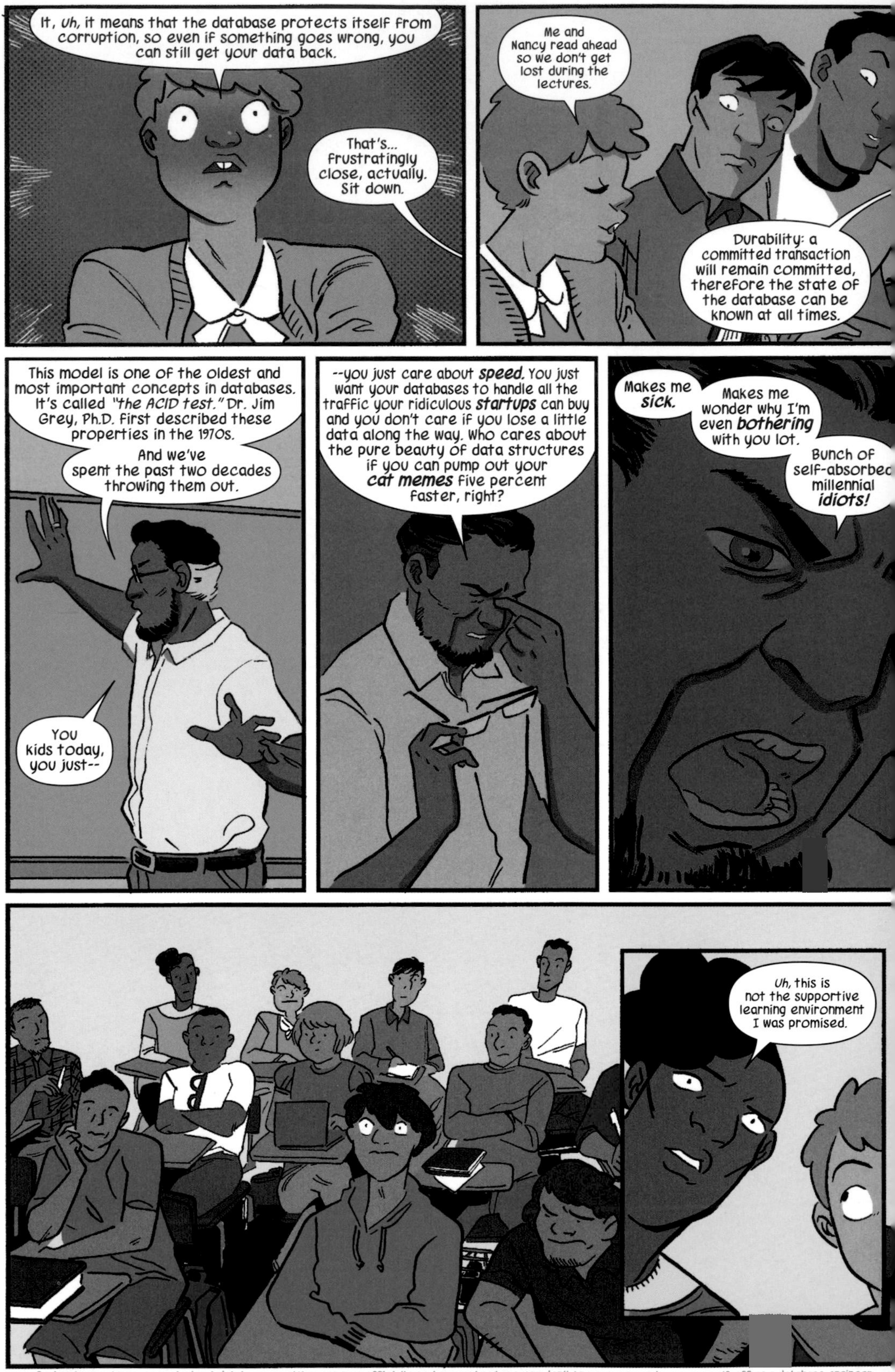
It, *uh,* it means that the database protects itself from corruption, so even if something goes wrong, you can still get your data back.
That's... frustratingly close, actually. Sit down.
Me and Nancy read ahead so we don't get lost during the lectures.
Durability: a committed transaction will remain committed, therefore the state of the database can be known at all times.
This model is one of the oldest and most important concepts in databases. It's called *"the ACID test."* Dr. Jim Grey, Ph.D. first described these properties in the 1970s.
And we've spent the past two decades throwing them out.
You kids today, you just--
--you just care about ***speed.*** You just want your databases to handle all the traffic your ridiculous ***startups*** can buy and you don't care if you lose a little data along the way. Who cares about the pure beauty of data structures if you can pump out your ***cat memes*** five percent faster, right?
Makes me ***sick.***
Makes me wonder why I'm even ***bothering*** with you lot.
Bunch of self-absorbed millennial ***idiots!***
Uh, this is not the supportive learning environment I was promised.

Seriously, you know so much about databases now! You can now officially go to a party where you don't know anyone and pass yourself off as a database engineer. In fact, surprise, ***this is now mandatory.***

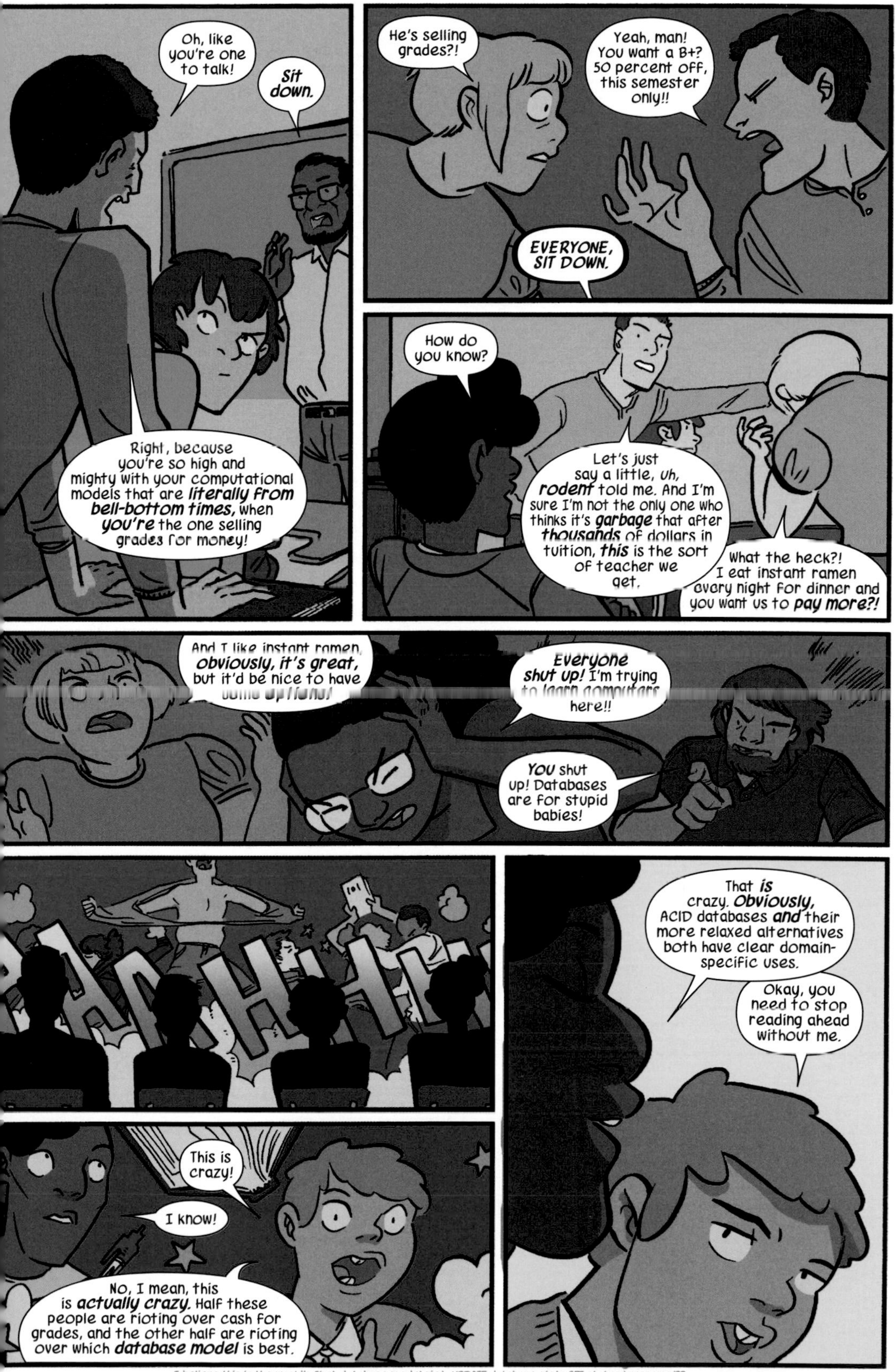
Oh, like you're one to talk!
Sit down.
Right, because you're so high and mighty with your computational models that are literally from bell-bottom times, when you're the one selling grades for money!
He's selling grades?!
Yeah, man! You want a B+? 50 percent off, this semester only!!
EVERYONE, SIT DOWN.
How do you know?
Let's just say a little, uh, rodent told me. And I'm sure I'm not the only one who thinks it's garbage that after thousands of dollars in tuition, this is the sort of teacher we get.
What the heck?! I eat instant ramen every night for dinner and you want us to pay more?!
And I like instant ramen, obviously, it's great, but it'd be nice to have
Everyone shut up! I'm trying
here!!
YOU shut up! Databases are for stupid babies!
That is crazy. Obviously, ACID databases and their more relaxed alternatives both have clear domain-specific uses.
Okay, you need to stop reading ahead without me.
This is crazy!
I know!
No, I mean, this is actually crazy. Half these people are rioting over cash for grades, and the other half are rioting over which database model is best.

I believe this is the world's first database model riot. UPDATE database_riots SET status='awesome'??

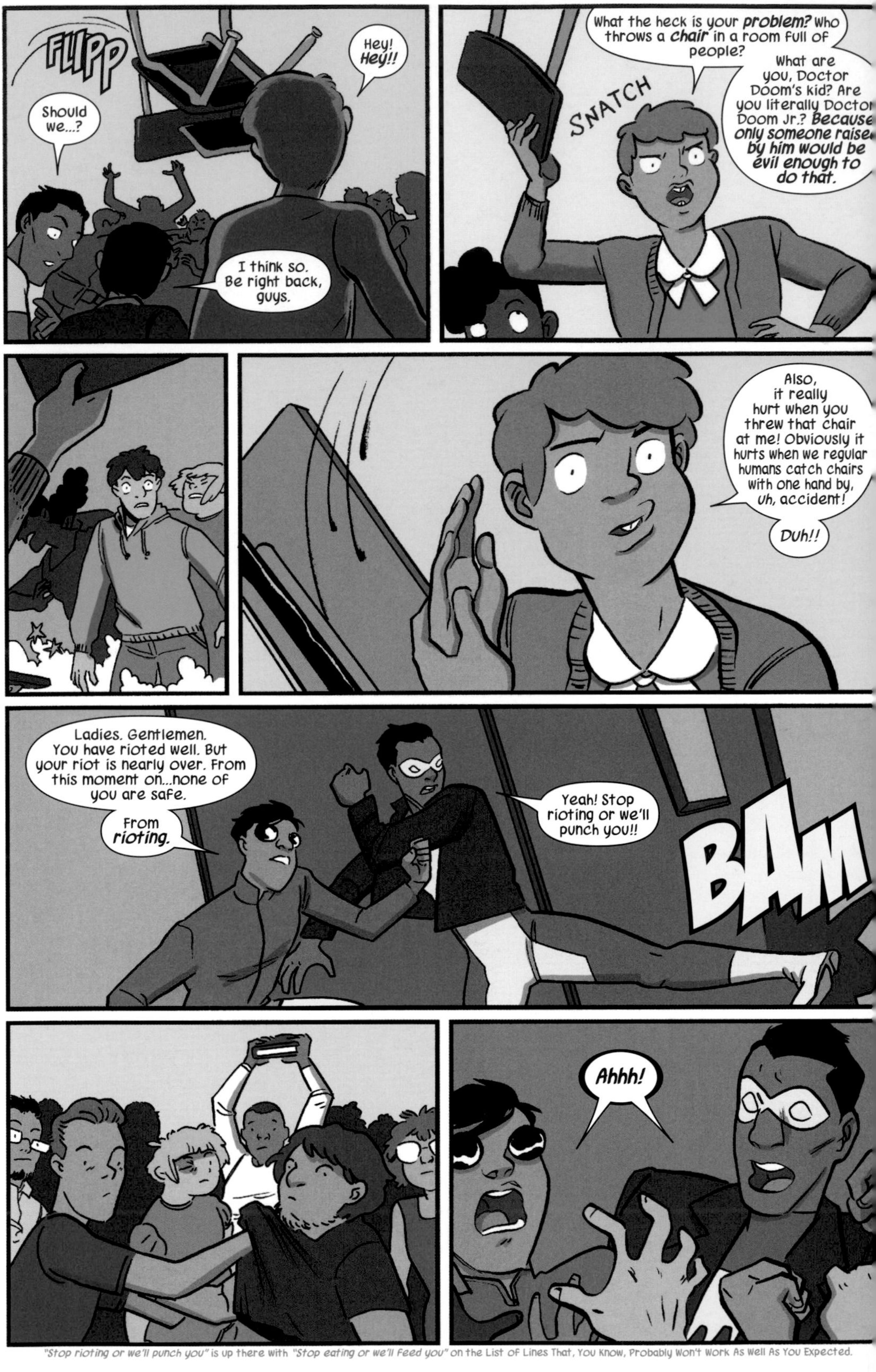
FLIPP
Should we...?
Hey! Hey!!
I think so. Be right back, guys.
What the heck is your problem? Who throws a chair in a room full of people?
SNATCH
What are you, Doctor Doom's kid? Are you literally Doctor Doom Jr.? Because only someone raised by him would be evil enough to do that.
Also, it really hurt when you threw that chair at me! Obviously it hurts when we regular humans catch chairs with one hand by, uh, accident!
Duh!!
Ladies. Gentlemen. You have rioted well. But your riot is nearly over. From this moment on...none of you are safe.
From rioting.
Yeah! Stop rioting or we'll punch you!!
BAM
Ahhh!

"Stop rioting or we'll punch you" is up there with "Stop eating or we'll feed you" on the List of Lines That, You Know, Probably Won't Work As Well As You Expected.

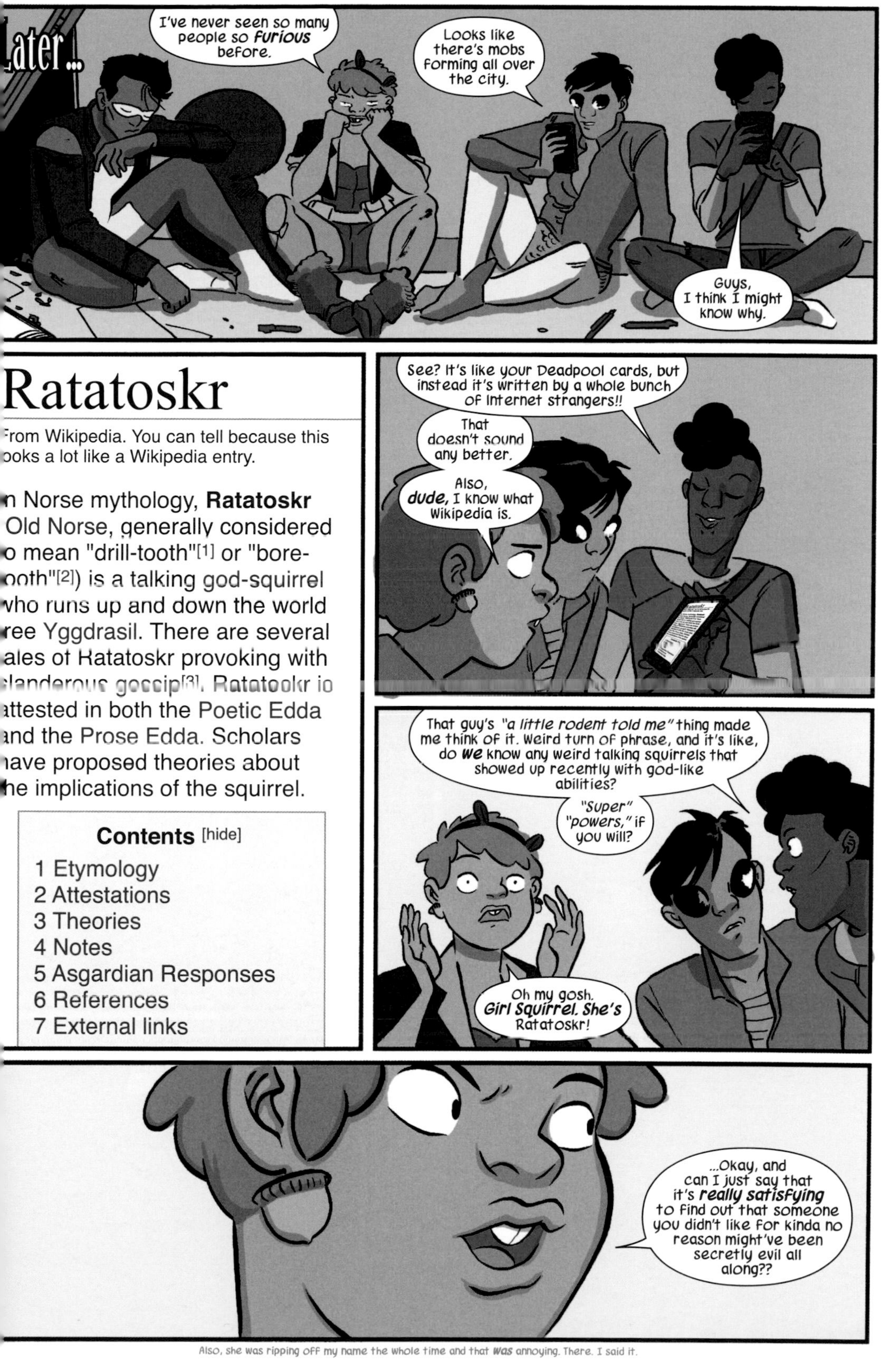
Later...
I've never seen so many people so *furious* before.
Looks like there's mobs forming all over the city.
Guys, I think I might know why.
Ratatoskr
From Wikipedia. You can tell because this looks a lot like a Wikipedia entry.
n Norse mythology, **Ratatoskr** Old Norse, generally considered o mean "drill-tooth"[1] or "bore-ooth"[2]) is a talking god-squirrel vho runs up and down the world ree Yggdrasil. There are several ales of Ratatoskr provoking with landerous gossip[3]. Ratatoskr is attested in both the Poetic Edda and the Prose Edda. Scholars have proposed theories about he implications of the squirrel.
Contents [hide]
1 Etymology
2 Attestations
3 Theories
4 Notes
5 Asgardian Responses
6 References
7 External links
See? It's like your Deadpool cards, but instead it's written by a whole bunch of Internet strangers!!
That doesn't sound any better.
Also, *dude,* I know what Wikipedia is.
That guy's *"a little rodent told me"* thing made me think of it. Weird turn of phrase, and it's like, do *we* know any weird talking squirrels that showed up recently with god-like abilities?
"Super" "powers," if you will?
Oh my gosh. *Girl Squirrel. She's* Ratatoskr!
...Okay, and can I just say that it's *really satisfying* to find out that someone you didn't like for kinda no reason might've been secretly evil all along??
Also, she was ripping off my name the whole time and that *was* annoying. There. I said it.

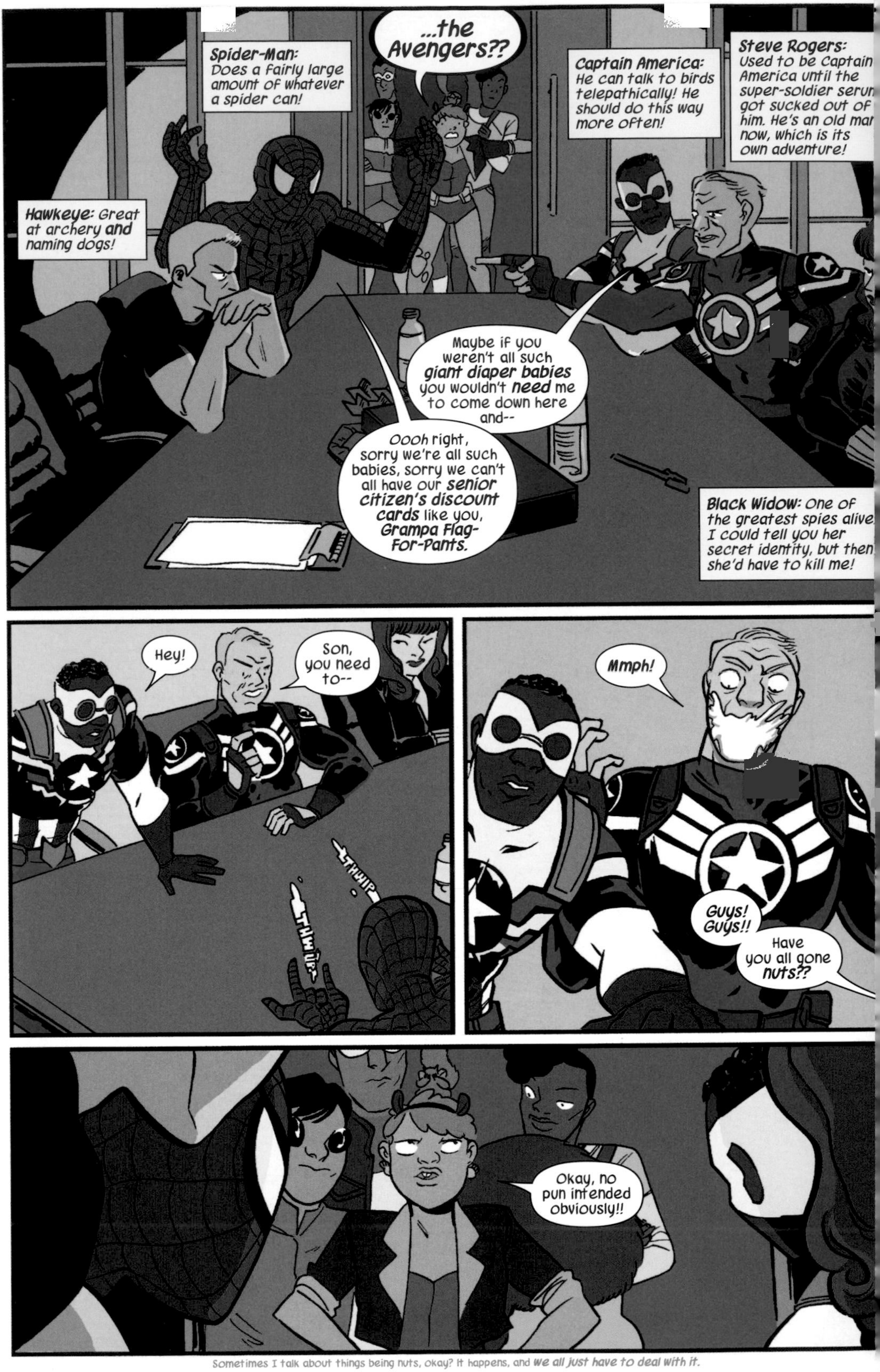
Spider-Man: Does a fairly large amount of whatever a spider can!
...the Avengers??
Captain America: He can talk to birds telepathically! He should do this way more often!
Steve Rogers: Used to be Captain America until the super-soldier serum got sucked out of him. He's an old man now, which is its own adventure!
Hawkeye: Great at archery and naming dogs!
Maybe if you weren't all such giant diaper babies you wouldn't need me to come down here and--
Oooh right, sorry we're all such babies, sorry we can't all have our senior citizen's discount cards like you, Grampa Flag-For-Pants.
Black Widow: One of the greatest spies alive. I could tell you her secret identity, but then she'd have to kill me!
Hey!
Son, you need to--
THWIP
THWIP
Mmph!
Guys! Guys!!
Have you all gone nuts??
Okay, no pun intended obviously!!

Sometimes I talk about things being nuts, okay? It happens, and *we all just have to deal with it.*

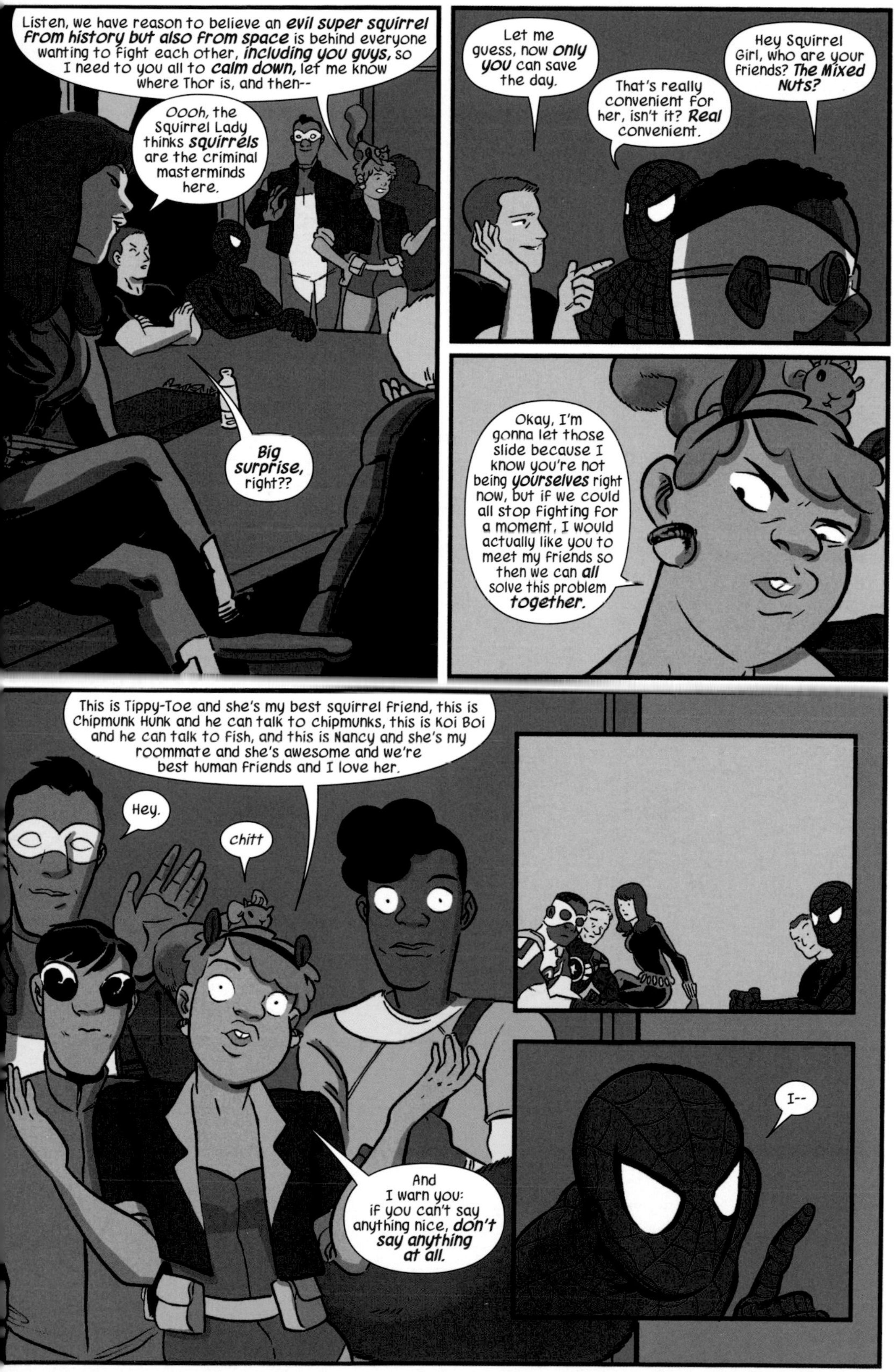

Listen, we have reason to believe an *evil super squirrel from history but also from space* is behind everyone wanting to fight each other, *including you guys,* so I need to you all to *calm down,* let me know where Thor is, and then--
Oooh, the Squirrel Lady thinks *squirrels* are the criminal masterminds here.
Big surprise, right??
Let me guess, now *only you* can save the day.
That's really convenient for her, isn't it? *Real* convenient.
Hey Squirrel Girl, who are your friends? *The Mixed Nuts?*
Okay, I'm gonna let those slide because I know you're not being *yourselves* right now, but if we could all stop fighting for a moment, I would actually like you to meet my friends so then we can *all* solve this problem *together.*
This is Tippy-Toe and she's my best squirrel friend, this is Chipmunk Hunk and he can talk to chipmunks, this is Koi Boi and he can talk to fish, and this is Nancy and she's my roommate and she's awesome and we're best human friends and I love her.
Hey.
chitt
And I warn you: if you can't say anything nice, *don't say anything at all.*
I--

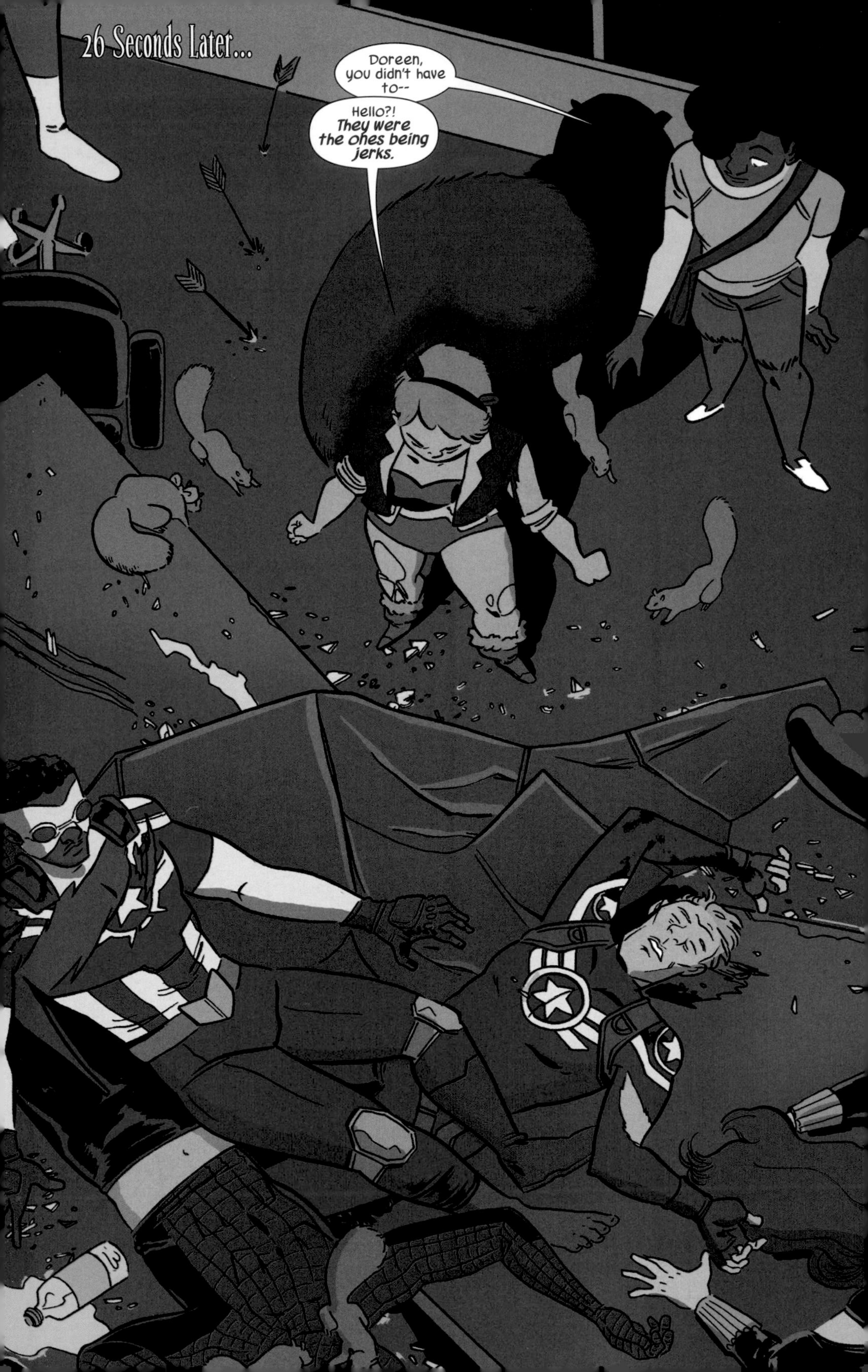
26 Seconds Later...
Doreen, you didn't have to--
Hello?! *They were the ones being jerks.*

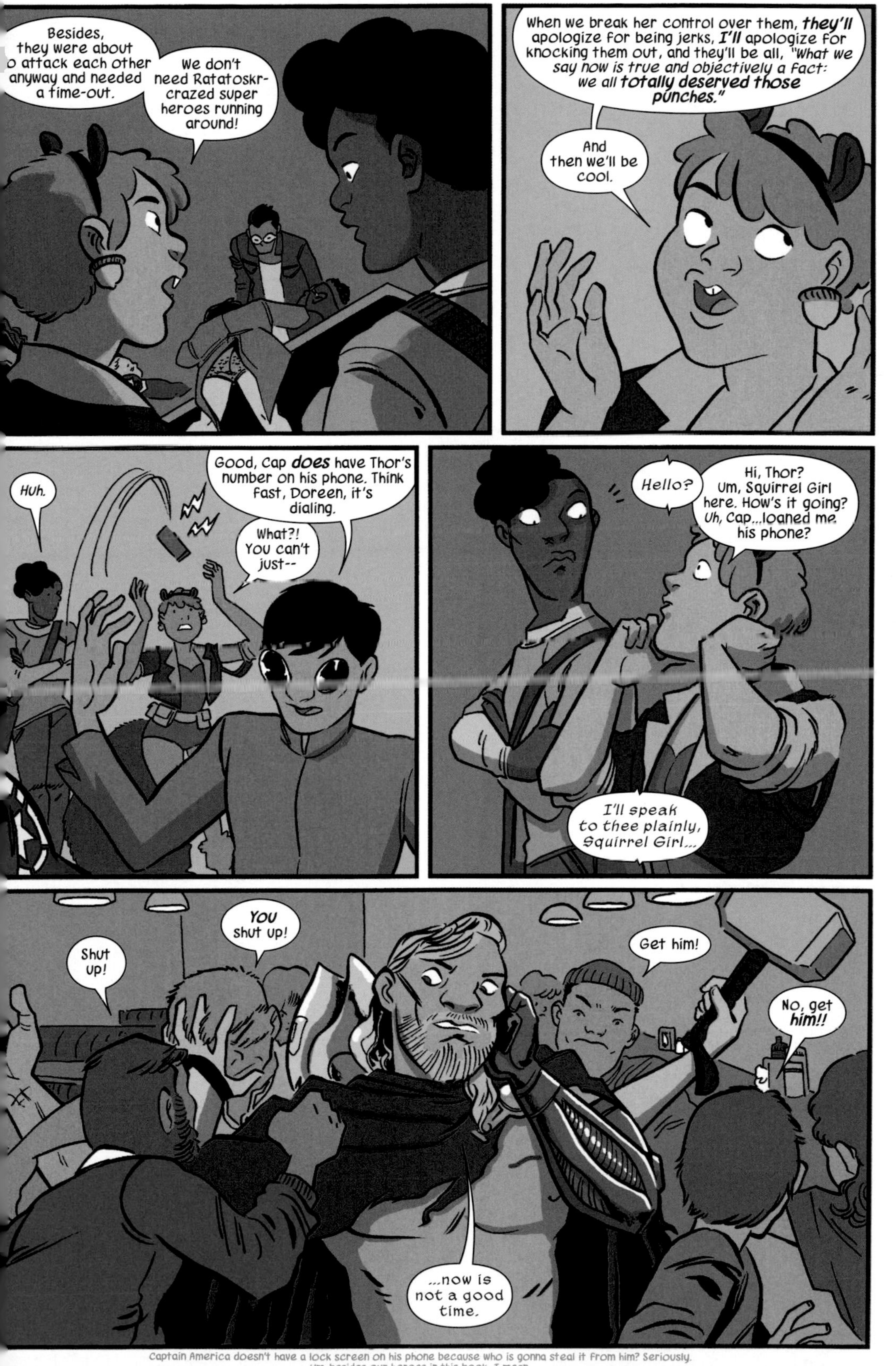

Besides, they were about o attack each other anyway and needed a time-out.
We don't need Ratatoskr-crazed super heroes running around!
When we break her control over them, they'll apologize for being jerks, I'll apologize for knocking them out, and they'll be all, "What we say now is true and objectively a fact: we all totally deserved those punches."
And then we'll be cool.
Huh.
Good, Cap does have Thor's number on his phone. Think fast, Doreen, it's dialing.
What?! You can't just--
Hello?
Hi, Thor? Um, Squirrel Girl here. How's it going? Uh, Cap...loaned me his phone?
I'll speak to thee plainly, Squirrel Girl...
Shut up!
YOU shut up!
Get him!
No, get him!!
...now is not a good time.

Captain America doesn't have a lock screen on his phone because who is gonna steal it from him? Seriously.
Um, besides our heroes in this book, I mean.

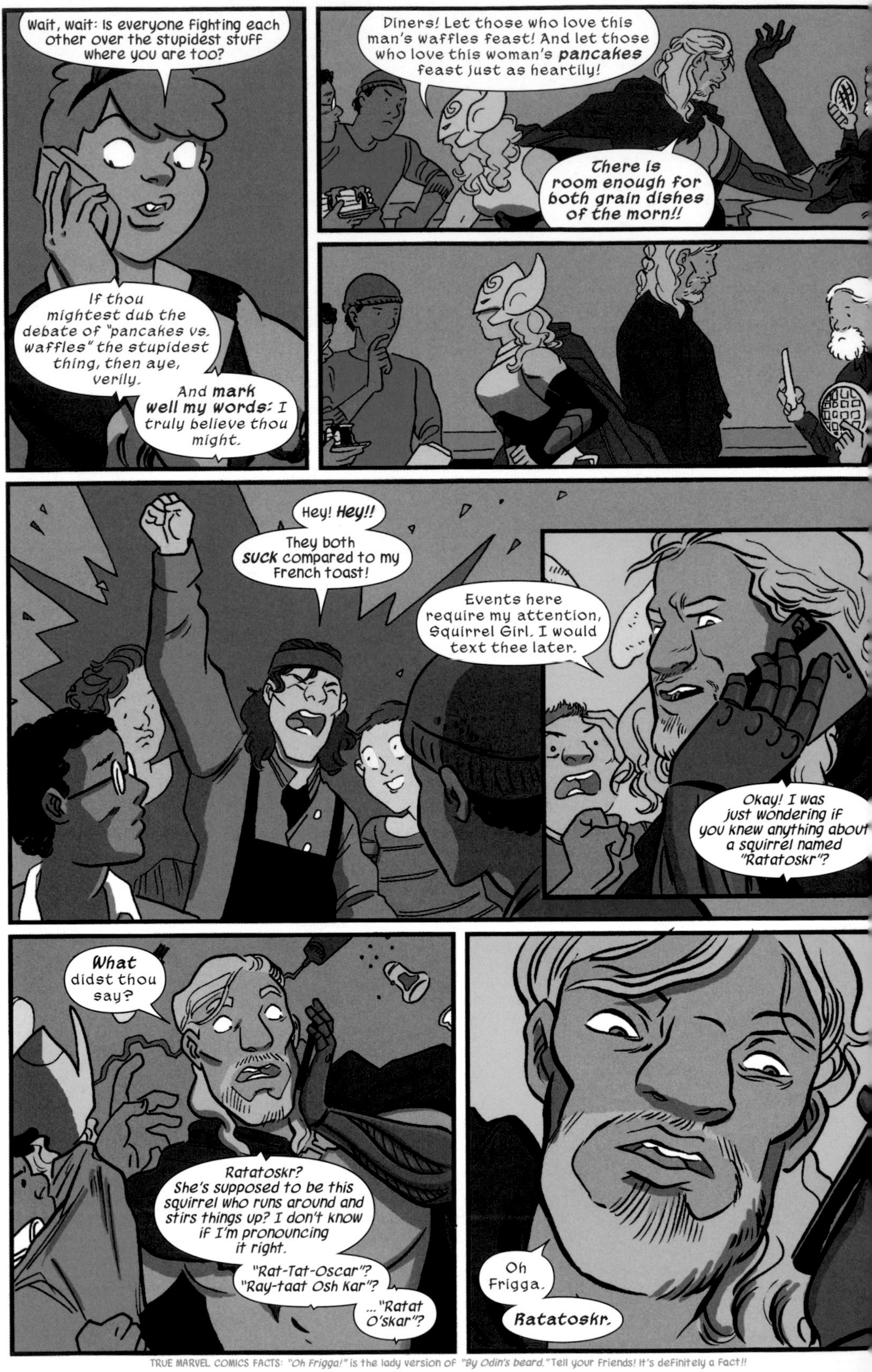
Wait, wait: Is everyone fighting each other over the stupidest stuff where you are too?
Diners! Let those who love this man's waffles feast! And let those who love this woman's **pancakes** feast just as heartily!
There is room enough for both grain dishes of the morn!!
If thou mightest dub the debate of "pancakes vs. waffles" the stupidest thing, then aye, verily.
And **mark well my words:** I truly believe thou might.
Hey! **Hey!!**
They both **SUCK** compared to my French toast!
Events here require my attention, Squirrel Girl. I would text thee later.
Okay! I was just wondering if you knew anything about a squirrel named "Ratatoskr"?
What didst thou say?
Ratatoskr? She's supposed to be this squirrel who runs around and stirs things up? I don't know if I'm pronouncing it right.
"Rat-Tat-Oscar"? "Ray-taat Osh Kar"?
..."Ratat O'skar"?
Oh Frigga.
Ratatoskr.

TRUE MARVEL COMICS FACTS: *"Oh Frigga!"* is the lady version of *"By Odin's beard."* Tell your friends! It's definitely a fact!!

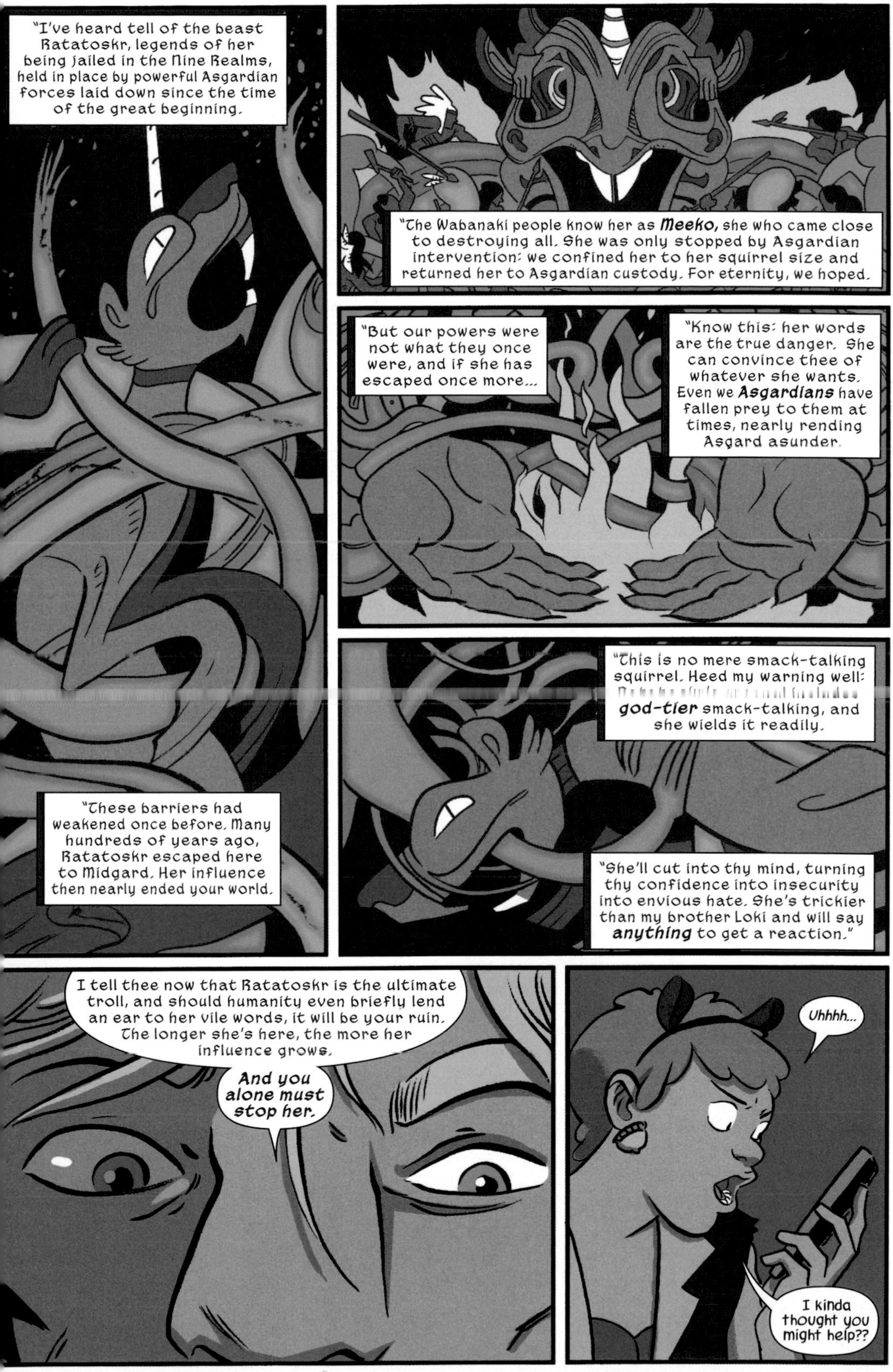
"I've heard tell of the beast Ratatoskr, legends of her being jailed in the Nine Realms, held in place by powerful Asgardian forces laid down since the time of the great beginning.
"These barriers had weakened once before. Many hundreds of years ago, Ratatoskr escaped here to Midgard. Her influence then nearly ended your world.
"The Wabanaki people know her as **Meeko,** she who came close to destroying all. She was only stopped by Asgardian intervention: we confined her to her squirrel size and returned her to Asgardian custody. For eternity, we hoped.
"But our powers were not what they once were, and if she has escaped once more...
"Know this: her words are the true danger. She can convince thee of whatever she wants. Even we **Asgardians** have fallen prey to them at times, nearly rending Asgard asunder.
"This is no mere smack-talking squirrel. Heed my warning well:
god-tier smack-talking, and she wields it readily.
"She'll cut into thy mind, turning thy confidence into insecurity into envious hate. She's trickier than my brother Loki and will say **anything** to get a reaction."
I tell thee now that Ratatoskr is the ultimate troll, and should humanity even briefly lend an ear to her vile words, it will be your ruin. The longer she's here, the more her influence grows.
And you alone must stop her.
Uhhhh...
I kinda thought you might help??

See, Thor, ***this*** is why I keep saying you should contribute to Wikipedia. This is ***way*** more useful than their summary. *Sheesh!*

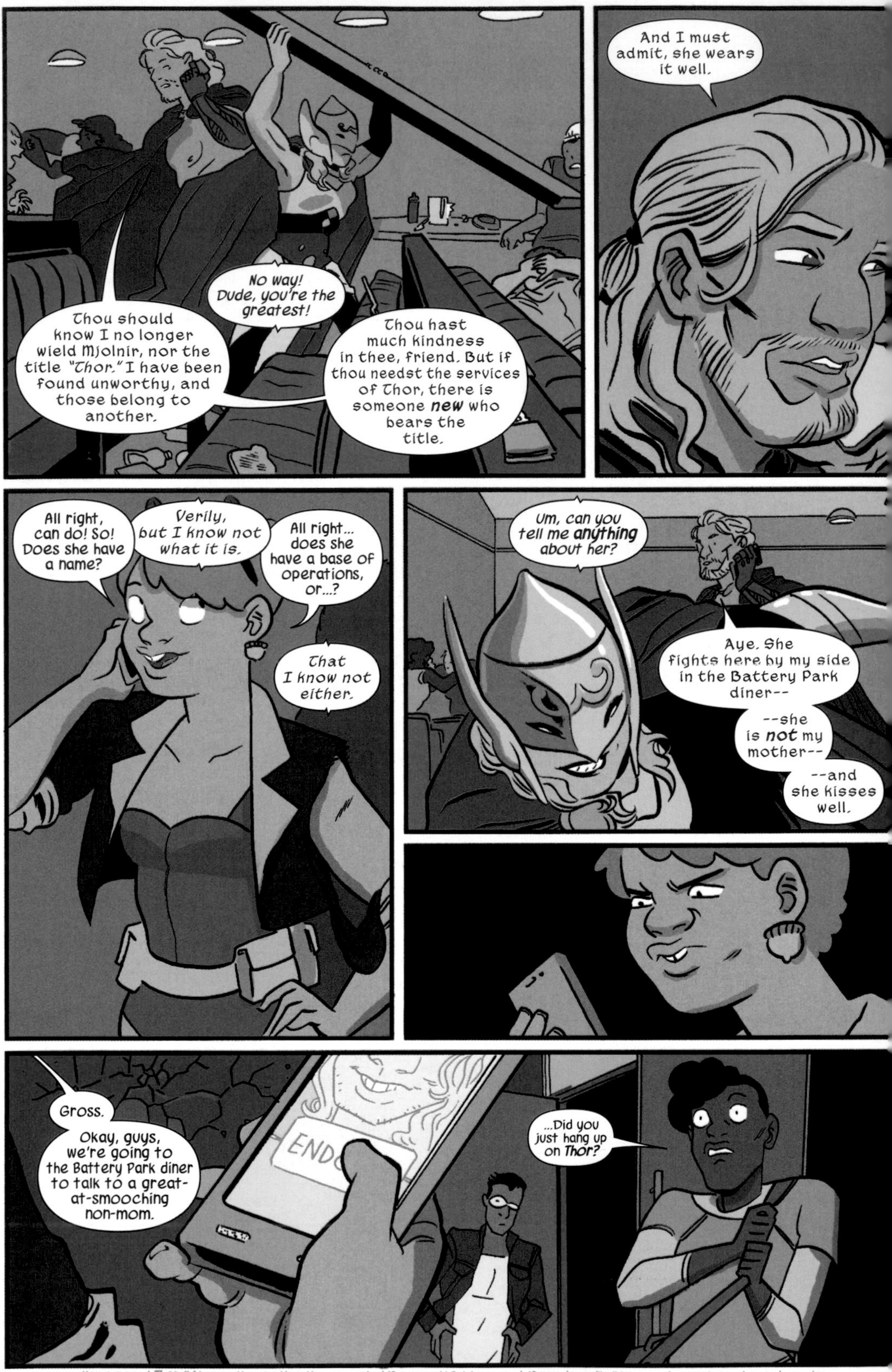

Thou should know I no longer wield Mjolnir, nor the title "Thor." I have been found unworthy, and those belong to another.
No way! Dude, you're the greatest!
Thou hast much kindness in thee, friend. But if thou needst the services of Thor, there is someone new who bears the title.
And I must admit, she wears it well.
All right, can do! So! Does she have a name?
Verily, but I know not what it is.
All right... does she have a base of operations, or...?
That I know not either.
Um, can you tell me anything about her?
Aye. She fights here by my side in the Battery Park diner--
--she is not my mother--
--and she kisses well.
Gross.
Okay, guys, we're going to the Battery Park diner to talk to a great-at-smooching non-mom.
ENDC
...Did you just hang up on Thor?

You can read *Thor #4* to see the one time they smooched if you want! But be warned: If you do, we'll all know you're someone who reads comics just to flip forward to the smooches. ***We'll all know. Even your parents will know.***

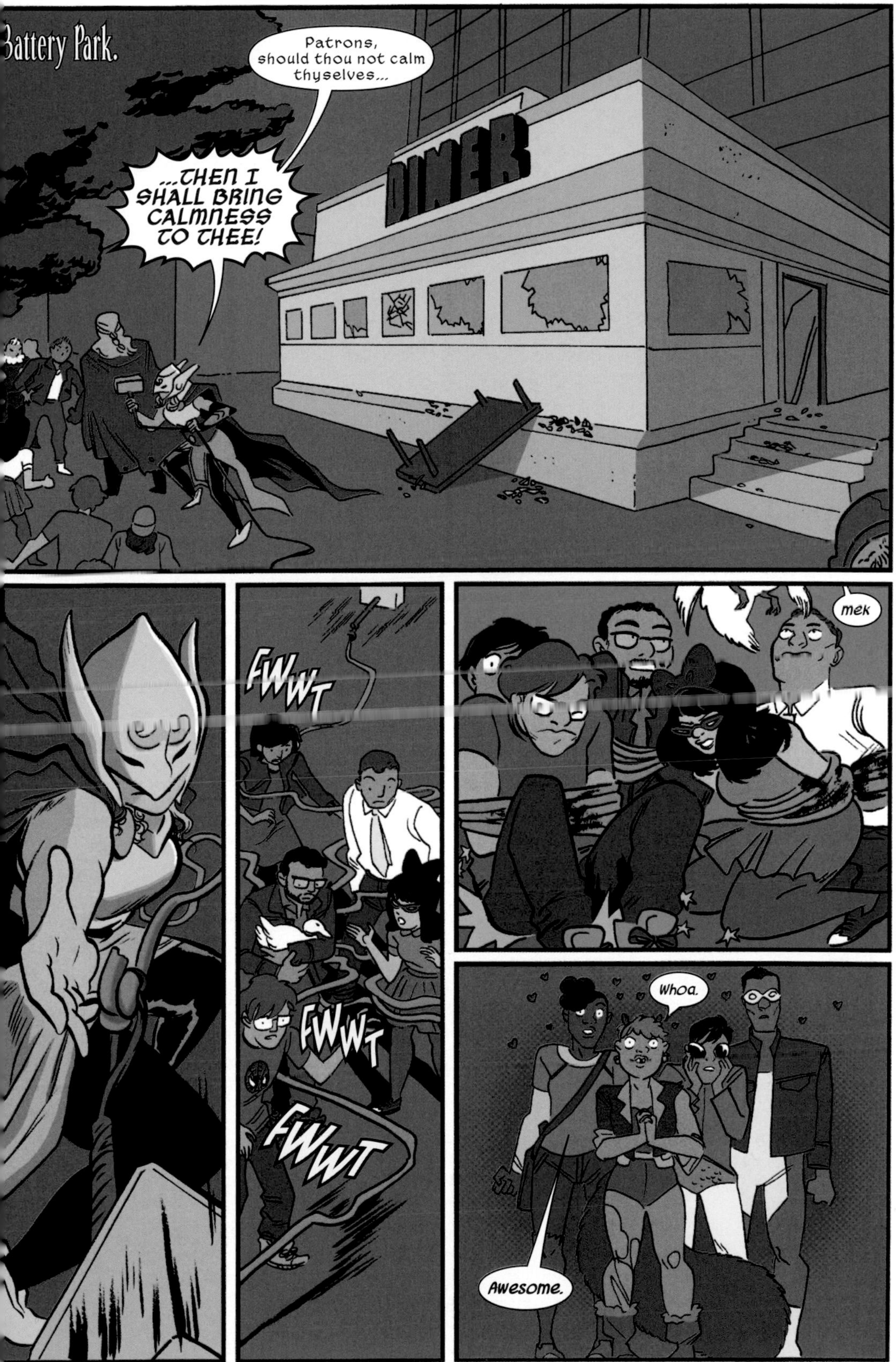
Battery Park.
Patrons, should thou not calm thyselves...
...THEN I SHALL BRING CALMNESS TO THEE!
DINER
FWWT
FWWT
FWWT
mek
Whoa.
Awesome.

TRUE REAL WORLD FACTS: Did you know that the side of a hammer is called the *"cheek"*? And the part you hit with is called the *"face,"* which is attached to the *"neck."* Hammers are these adorable little metal heads we invented to solve our problems.

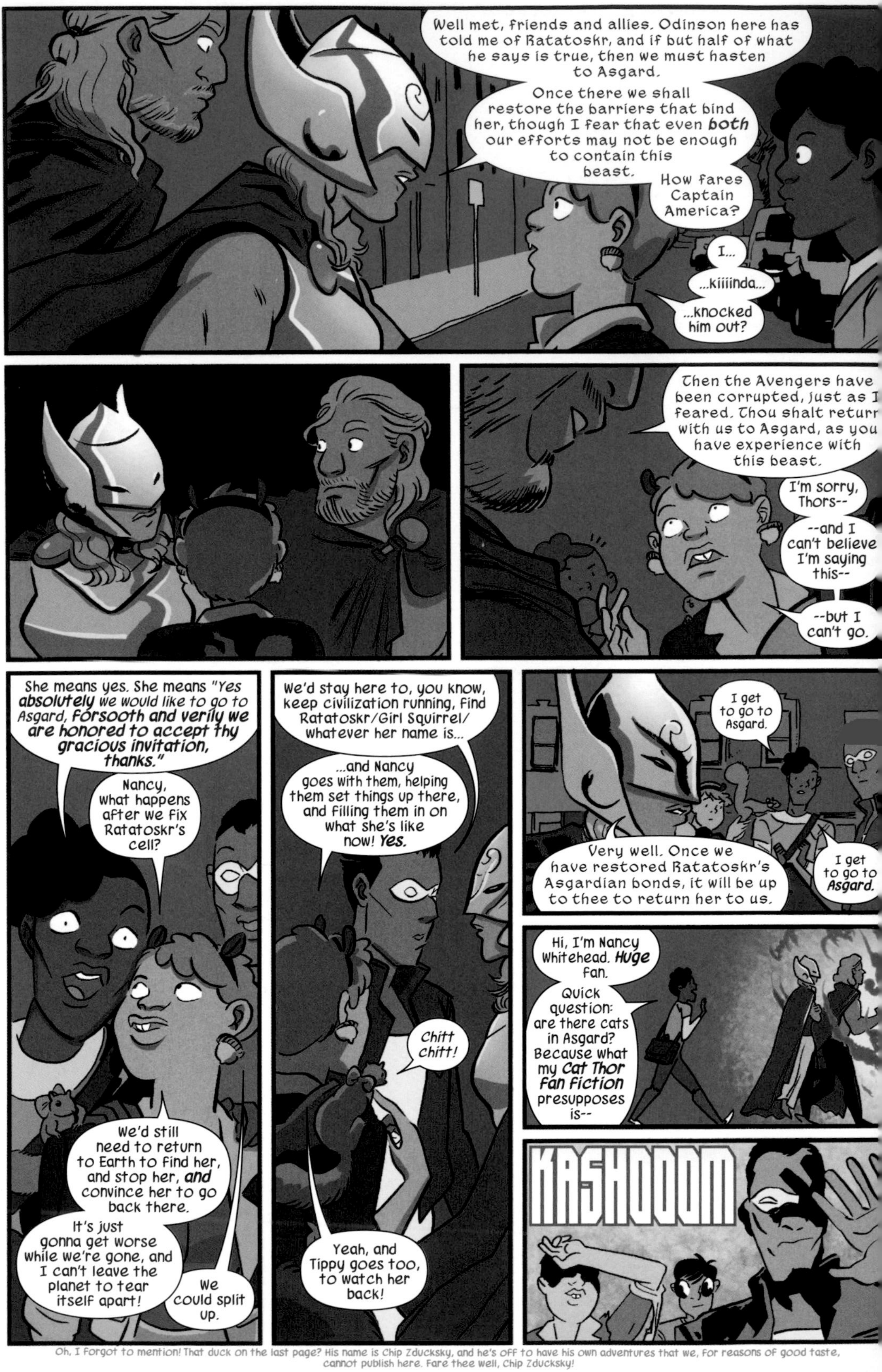
Well met, friends and allies. Odinson here has told me of Ratatoskr, and if but half of what he says is true, then we must hasten to Asgard.
Once there we shall restore the barriers that bind her, though I fear that even both our efforts may not be enough to contain this beast.
How fares Captain America?
I...
...kiiiinda...
...knocked him out?
Then the Avengers have been corrupted, just as I feared. Thou shalt return with us to Asgard, as you have experience with this beast.
I'm sorry, Thors--
--and I can't believe I'm saying this--
--but I can't go.
She means yes. She means "Yes absolutely we would like to go to Asgard, forsooth and verily we are honored to accept thy gracious invitation, thanks."
Nancy, what happens after we fix Ratatoskr's cell?
We'd still need to return to Earth to find her, and stop her, and convince her to go back there.
It's just gonna get worse while we're gone, and I can't leave the planet to tear itself apart!
We could split up.
We'd stay here to, you know, keep civilization running, find Ratatoskr/Girl Squirrel/whatever her name is...
...and Nancy goes with them, helping them set things up there, and filling them in on what she's like now! Yes.
Chitt chitt!
Yeah, and Tippy goes too, to watch her back!
I get to go to Asgard.
Very well. Once we have restored Ratatoskr's Asgardian bonds, it will be up to thee to return her to us.
I get to go to Asgard.
Hi, I'm Nancy Whitehead. Huge fan.
Quick question: are there cats in Asgard? Because what my Cat Thor fan fiction presupposes is--
KASHOOOM

Oh, I forgot to mention! That duck on the last page? His name is Chip Zducksky, and he's off to have his own adventures that we, for reasons of good taste, cannot publish here. Fare thee well, Chip Zducksky!

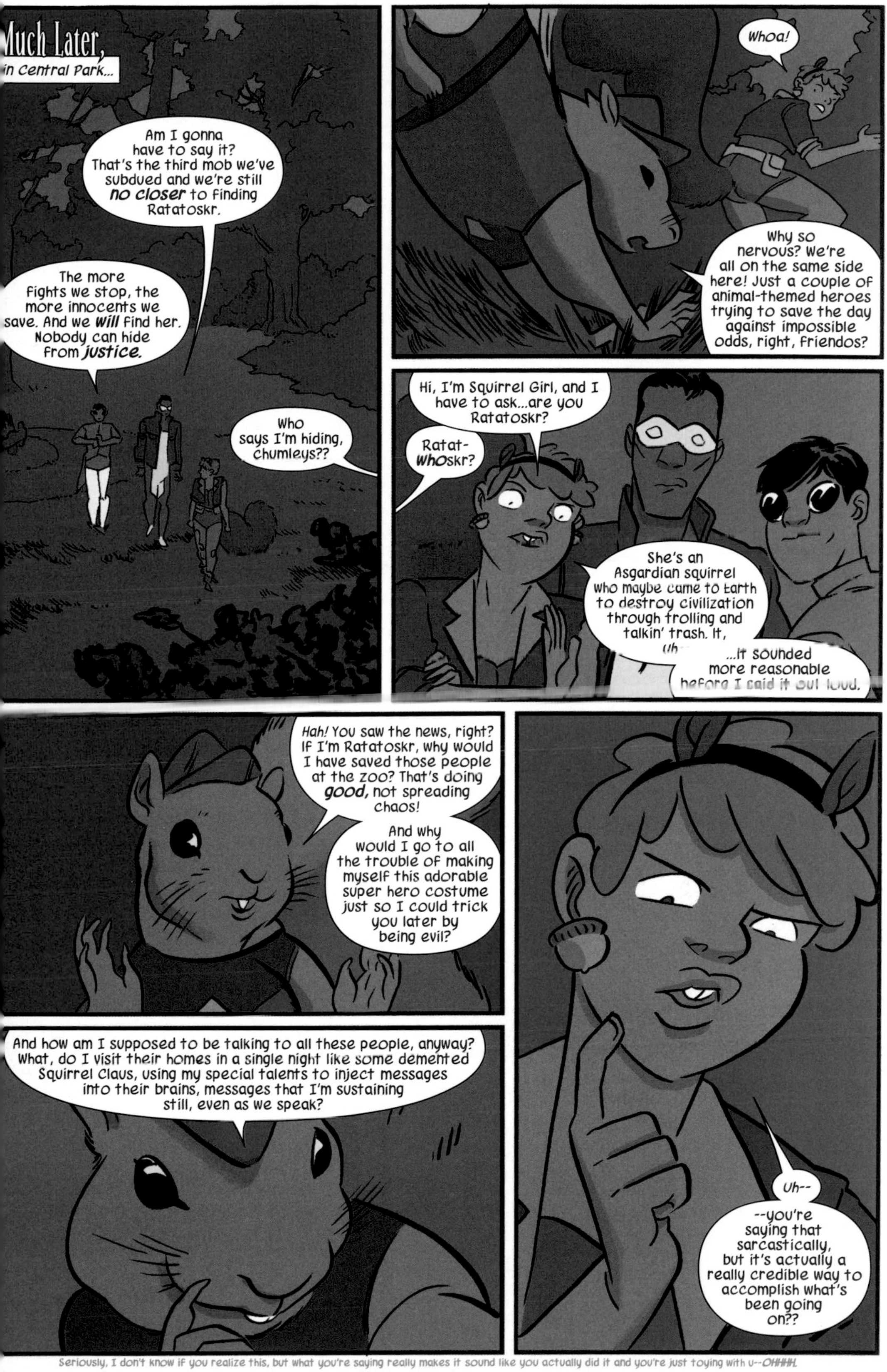
Much Later,
in Central Park...
Am I gonna have to say it? That's the third mob we've subdued and we're still no closer to finding Ratatoskr.
The more fights we stop, the more innocents we save. And we will find her. Nobody can hide from justice.
Who says I'm hiding, chumleys??
Whoa!
Why so nervous? We're all on the same side here! Just a couple of animal-themed heroes trying to save the day against impossible odds, right, friendos?
Hi, I'm Squirrel Girl, and I have to ask...are you Ratatoskr?
Ratat-Whoskr?
She's an Asgardian squirrel who maybe came to Earth to destroy civilization through trolling and talkin' trash. It,
...it sounded more reasonable before I said it out loud.
Hah! You saw the news, right? If I'm Ratatoskr, why would I have saved those people at the zoo? That's doing good, not spreading chaos!
And why would I go to all the trouble of making myself this adorable super hero costume just so I could trick you later by being evil?
And how am I supposed to be talking to all these people, anyway? What, do I visit their homes in a single night like some demented Squirrel Claus, using my special talents to inject messages into their brains, messages that I'm sustaining still, even as we speak?
Uh--
--you're saying that sarcastically, but it's actually a really credible way to accomplish what's been going on??

Seriously, I don't know if you realize this, but what you're saying really makes it sound like you actually did it and you're just toying with u--OHHHH.

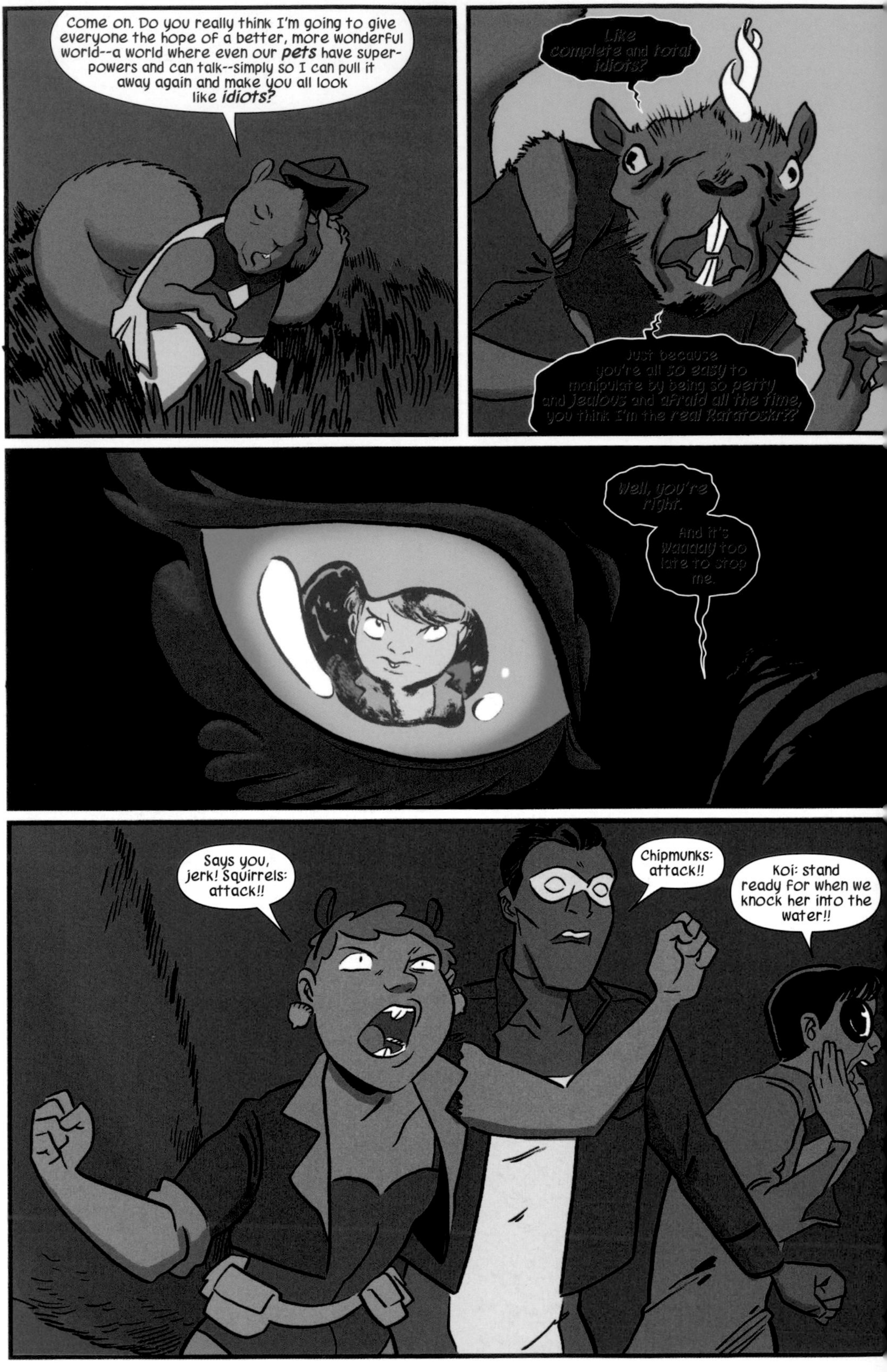
Come on. Do you really think I'm going to give everyone the hope of a better, more wonderful world--a world where even our *pets* have super-powers and can talk--simply so I can pull it away again and make you all look like *idiots?*
Like complete and total idiots?
Just because you're all so easy to manipulate by being so petty and jealous and afraid all the time, you think I'm the real Ratatoskr??
Well, you're right.
And it's waaaay too late to stop me.
Says you, jerk! Squirrels: attack!!
Chipmunks: attack!!
Koi: stand ready for when we knock her into the water!!

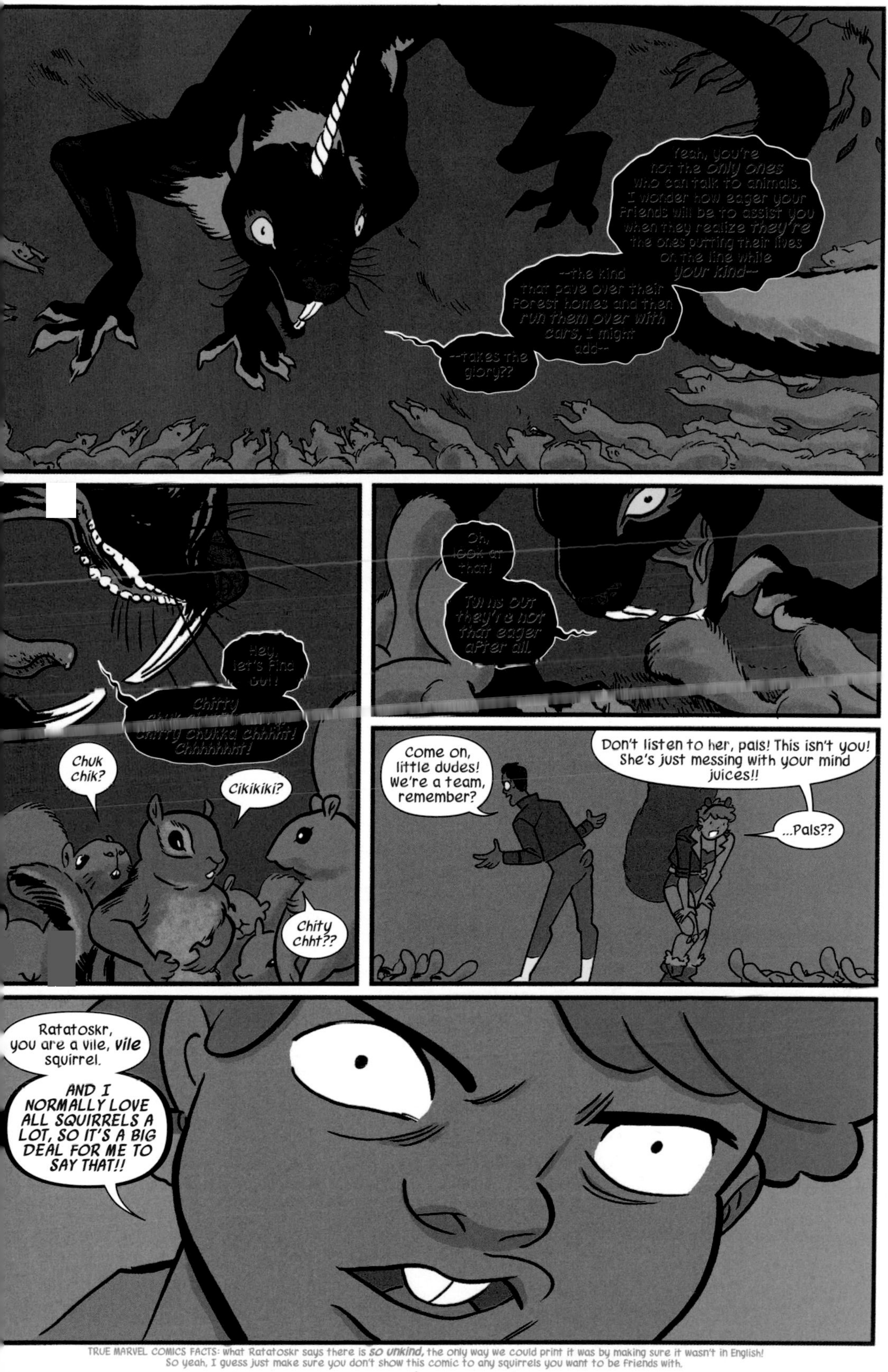

Yeah, you're not the only ones who can talk to animals. I wonder how eager your friends will be to assist you when they realize they're the ones putting their lives on the line while your kind--
--the kind that pave over their forest homes and then run them over with cars, I might add--
--takes the glory??
Hey, let's find out!
Chitty
Chitty Chukka Chhhht! Chhhhhhhht!
Chuk chik?
Cikikiki?
Chity chht??
Oh, look at that!
Turns out they're not that eager after all.
Come on, little dudes! We're a team, remember?
Don't listen to her, pals! This isn't you! She's just messing with your mind juices!!
...Pals??
Ratatoskr, you are a vile, vile squirrel.
AND I NORMALLY LOVE ALL SQUIRRELS A LOT, SO IT'S A BIG DEAL FOR ME TO SAY THAT!!

TRUE MARVEL COMICS FACTS: what Ratatoskr says there is *so unkind*, the only way we could print it was by making sure it wasn't in English! So yeah, I guess just make sure you don't show this comic to any squirrels you want to be friends with.

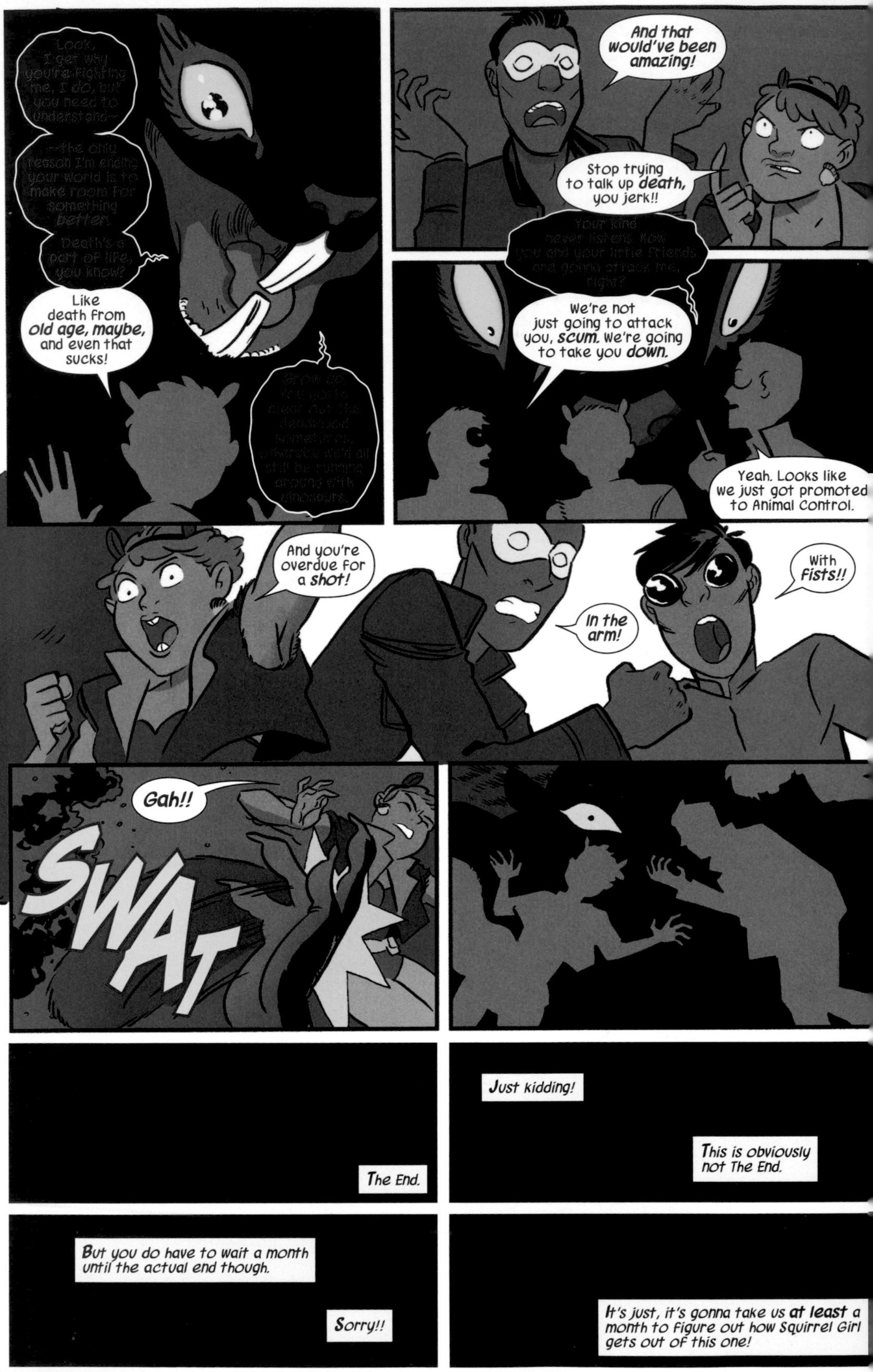
Look, I get why you're fighting me, I do, but you need to understand--
--the only reason I'm ending your world is to make room for something better.
Death's a part of life, you know?
Like death from old age, maybe, and even that sucks!
Grow up. You gotta clear out the deadwood sometimes, otherwise we'd all still be running around with dinosaurs.
And that would've been amazing!
Stop trying to talk up death, you jerk!!
Your kind never listens. Now you and your little friends are gonna attack me, right?
We're not just going to attack you, scum. We're going to take you down.
Yeah. Looks like we just got promoted to Animal Control.
And you're overdue for a shot!
In the arm!
With fists!!
Gah!!
SWAT
The End.
Just kidding!
This is obviously not The End.
But you do have to wait a month until the actual end though.
Sorry!!
It's just, it's gonna take us at least a month to figure out how Squirrel Girl gets out of this one!

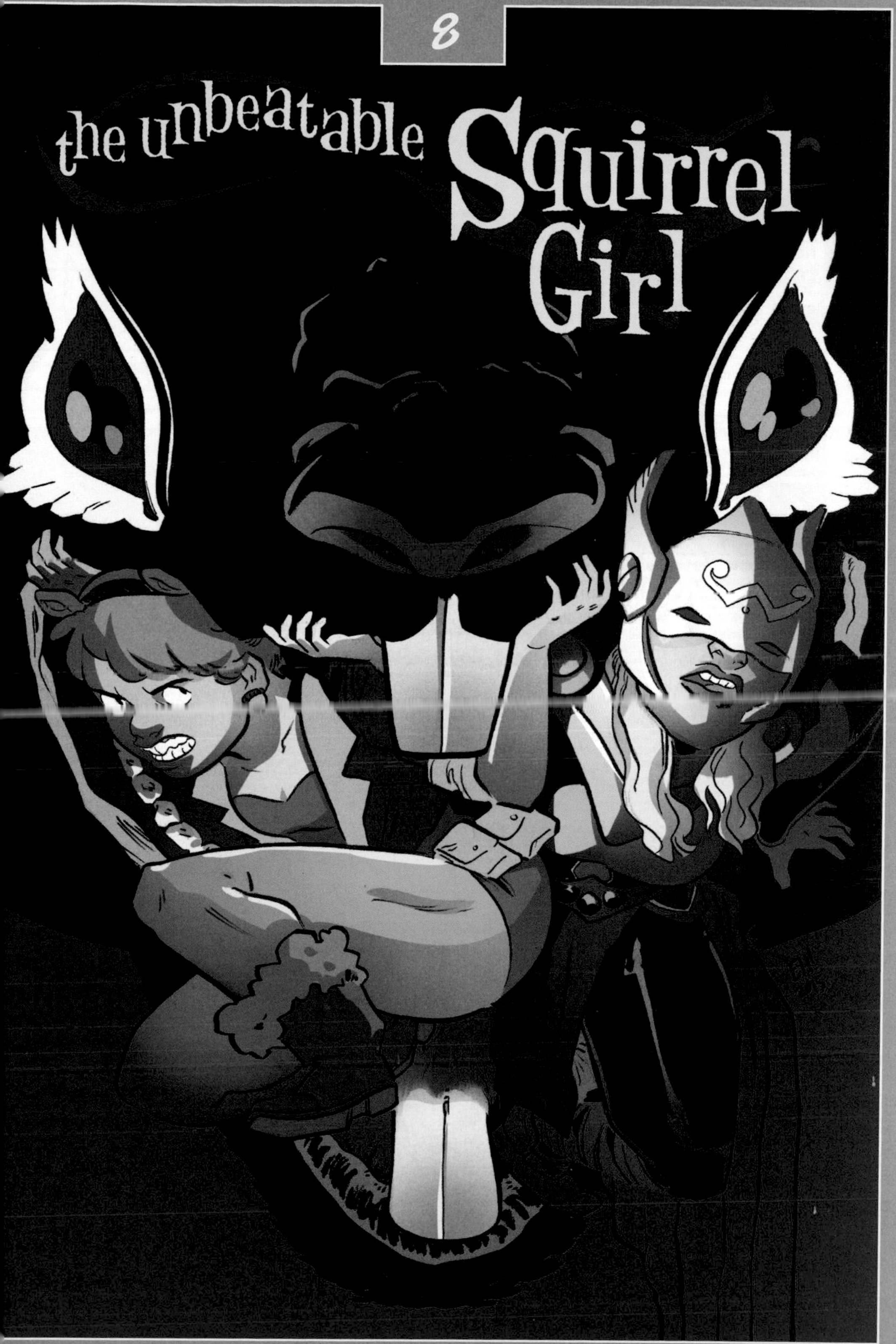
8
the unbeatable Squirrel Girl

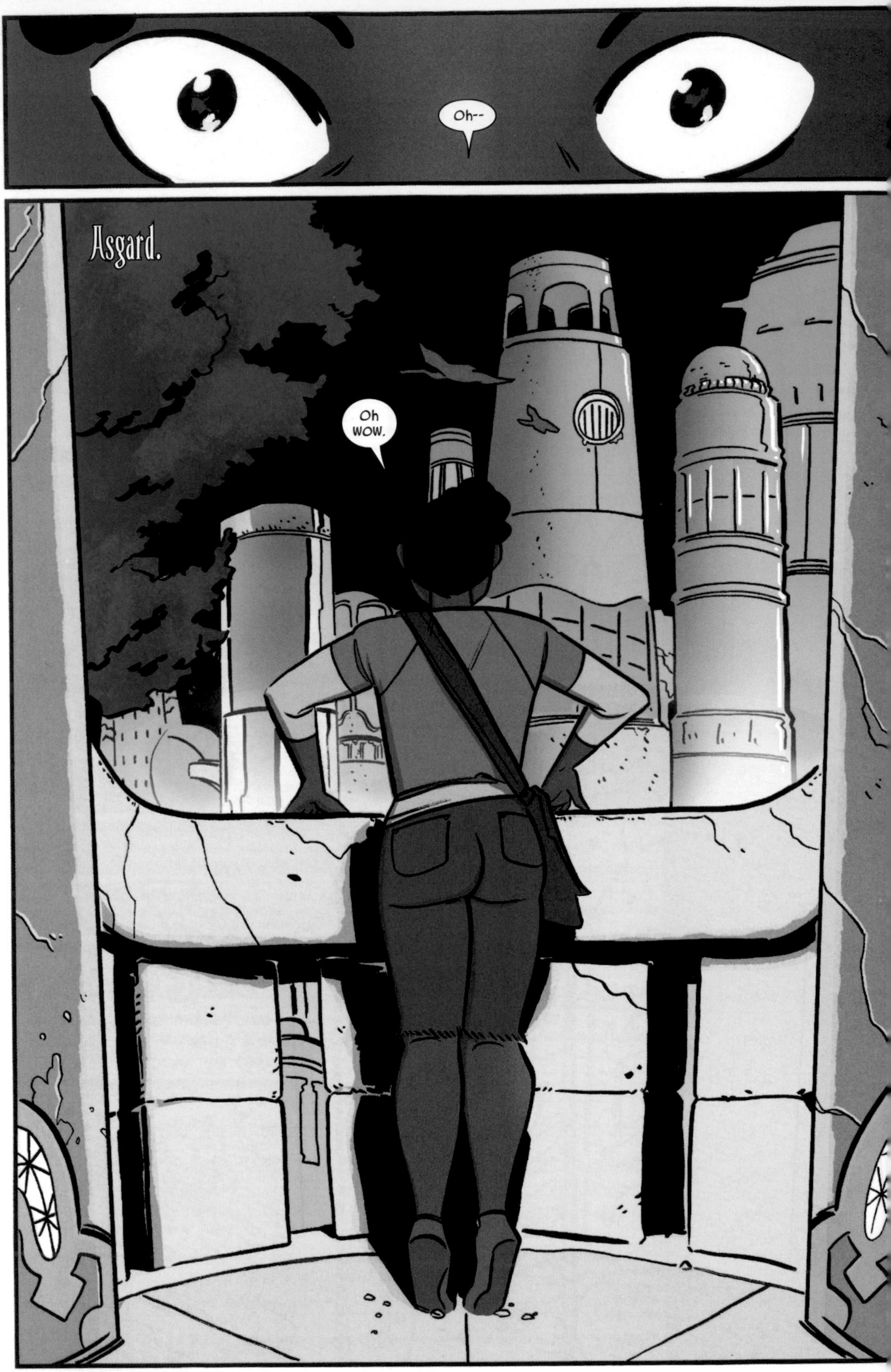
Oh--
Asgard.
Oh wow.

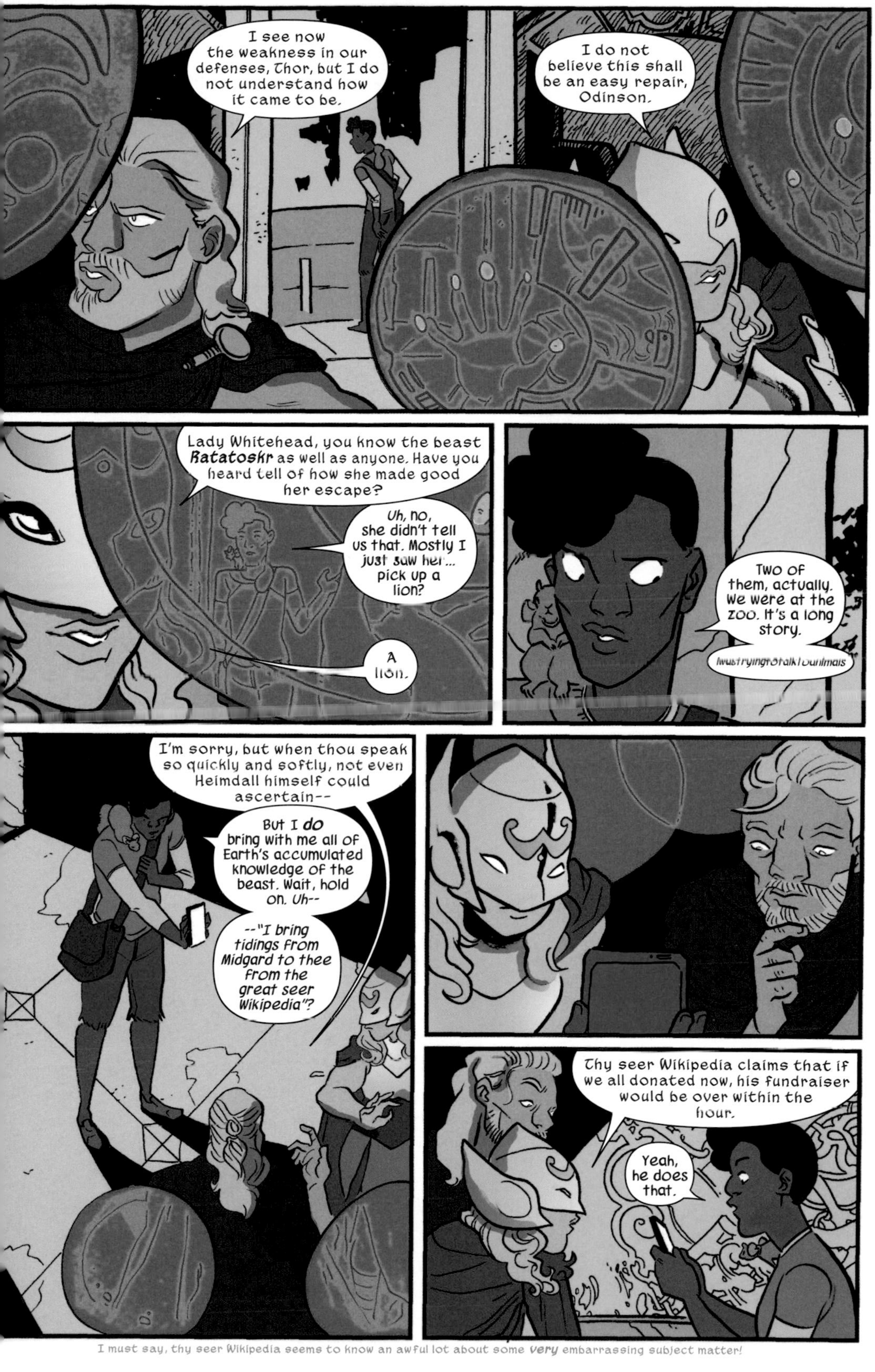

I see now the weakness in our defenses, Thor, but I do not understand how it came to be.
I do not believe this shall be an easy repair, Odinson.
Lady Whitehead, you know the beast Ratatoskr as well as anyone. Have you heard tell of how she made good her escape?
Uh, no, she didn't tell us that. Mostly I just saw her... pick up a lion?
A lion.
Two of them, actually. We were at the zoo. It's a long story.
Iwastryingtotalktoanimals
I'm sorry, but when thou speak so quickly and softly, not even Heimdall himself could ascertain--
But I do bring with me all of Earth's accumulated knowledge of the beast. Wait, hold on. Uh--
--"I bring tidings from Midgard to thee from the great seer Wikipedia"?
Thy seer Wikipedia claims that if we all donated now, his fundraiser would be over within the hour.
Yeah, he does that.

I must say, thy seer Wikipedia seems to know an awful lot about some *very* embarrassing subject matter!

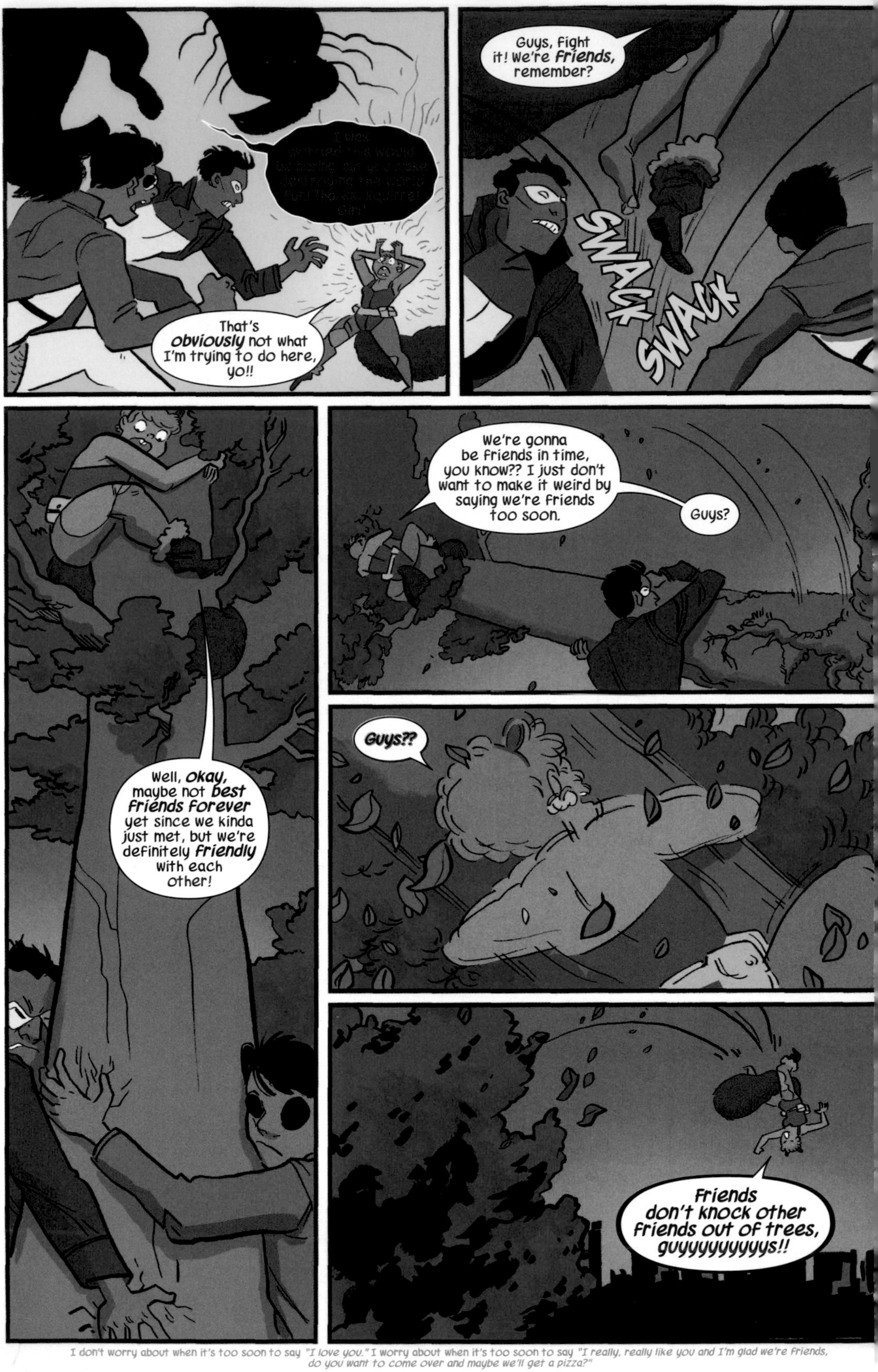
I was worried this would be boring, can you make destroying the world fun! Thanks, Squirrel Girl!
That's *obviously* not what I'm trying to do here, yo!!
Guys, fight it! We're *friends*, remember?
SWACK
SWACK
Well, *okay*, maybe not *best friends forever* yet since we kinda just met, but we're definitely *friendly* with each other!
We're gonna be friends in time, you know?? I just don't want to make it weird by saying we're friends too soon.
Guys?
Guys??
Friends don't knock other friends out of trees, guyyyyyyyys!!

I don't worry about when it's too soon to say "I love you." I worry about when it's too soon to say "I really, really like you and I'm glad we're friends, do you want to come over and maybe we'll get a pizza?"

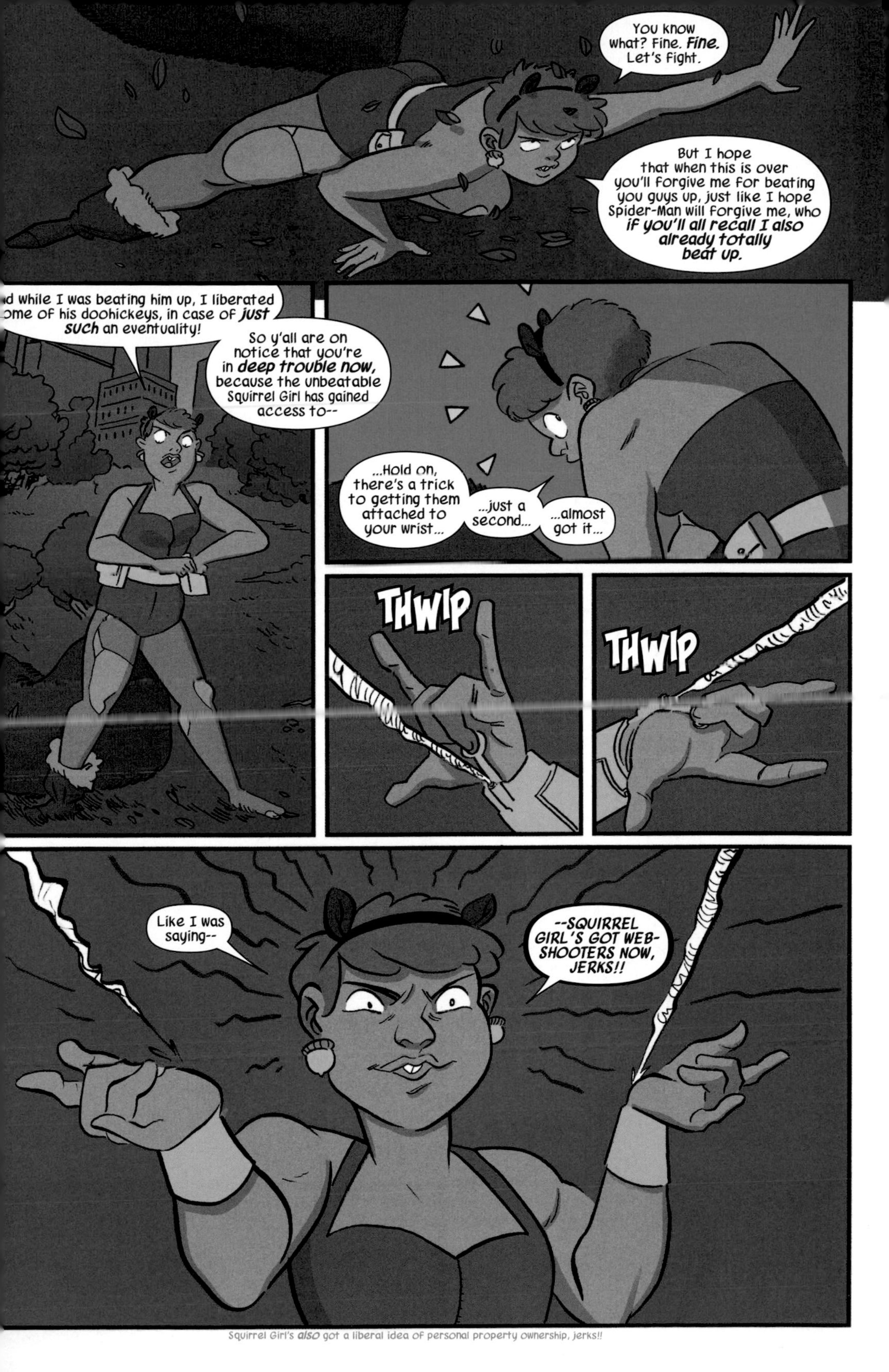
You know what? Fine. Fine. Let's fight.
But I hope that when this is over you'll forgive me for beating you guys up, just like I hope Spider-Man will forgive me, who if you'll all recall I also already totally beat up.
nd while I was beating him up, I liberated ome of his doohickeys, in case of just such an eventuality!
So y'all are on notice that you're in deep trouble now, because the unbeatable Squirrel Girl has gained access to--
...Hold on, there's a trick to getting them attached to your wrist...
...just a second...
...almost got it...
THWIP
THWIP
Like I was saying--
--SQUIRREL GIRL'S GOT WEB-SHOOTERS NOW, JERKS!!

Squirrel Girl's *also* got a liberal idea of personal property ownership, jerks!!

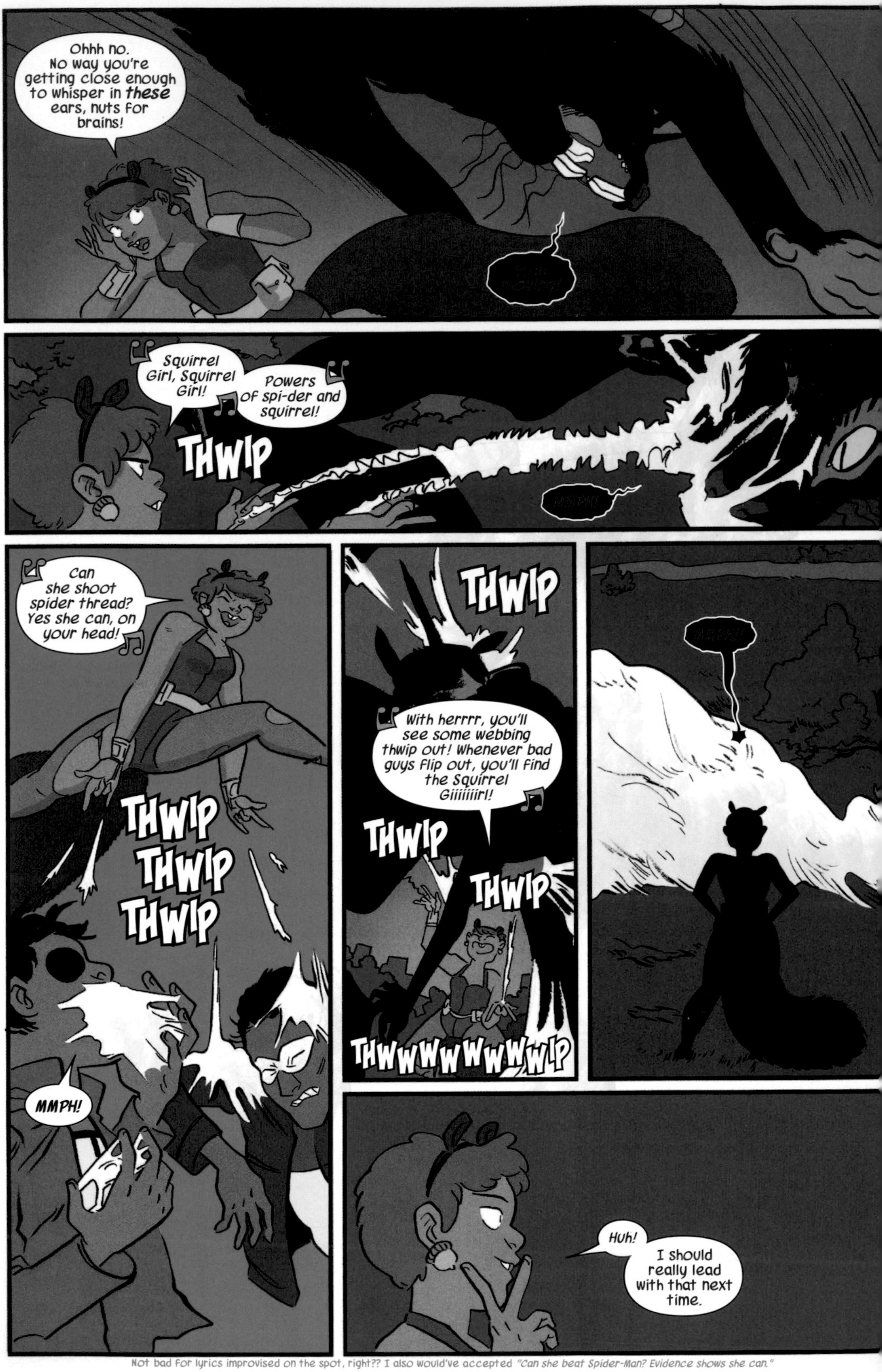
Ohhh no. No way you're getting close enough to whisper in *these* ears, nuts for brains!
Squirrel Girl, Squirrel Girl!
Powers of spi-der and squirrel!
THWIP
Can she shoot spider thread? Yes she can, on your head!
THWIP
THWIP
THWIP
MMPH!
THWIP
With herrrr, you'll see some webbing thwip out! Whenever bad guys flip out, you'll find the Squirrel Giiiiiiirl!
THWIP
THWIP
THWWWWWWWWWIP
Huh!
I should really lead with that next time.

Not bad for lyrics improvised on the spot, right?? I also would've accepted *"Can she beat Spider-Man? Evidence shows she can."*

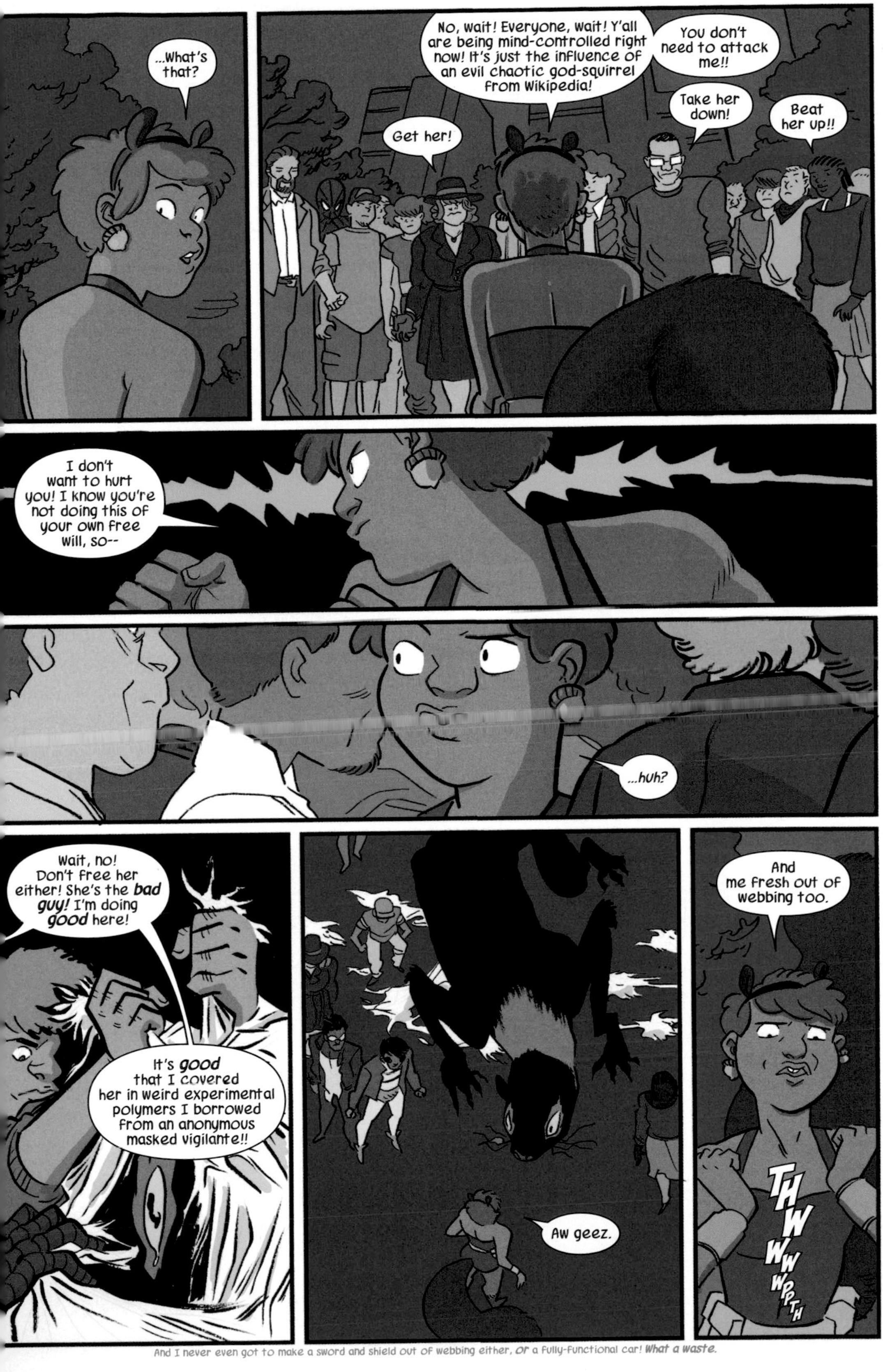
...What's that?
No, wait! Everyone, wait! Y'all are being mind-controlled right now! It's just the influence of an evil chaotic god-squirrel from Wikipedia!
You don't need to attack me!!
Get her!
Take her down!
Beat her up!!
I don't want to hurt you! I know you're not doing this of your own free will, so--
...huh?
Wait, no! Don't free her either! She's the **bad guy!** I'm doing **good** here!
It's **good** that I covered her in weird experimental polymers I borrowed from an anonymous masked vigilante!!
Aw geez.
And me fresh out of webbing too.
THWWWWPPTH

And I never even got to make a sword and shield out of webbing either, *or* a fully-functional car! ***What a waste.***

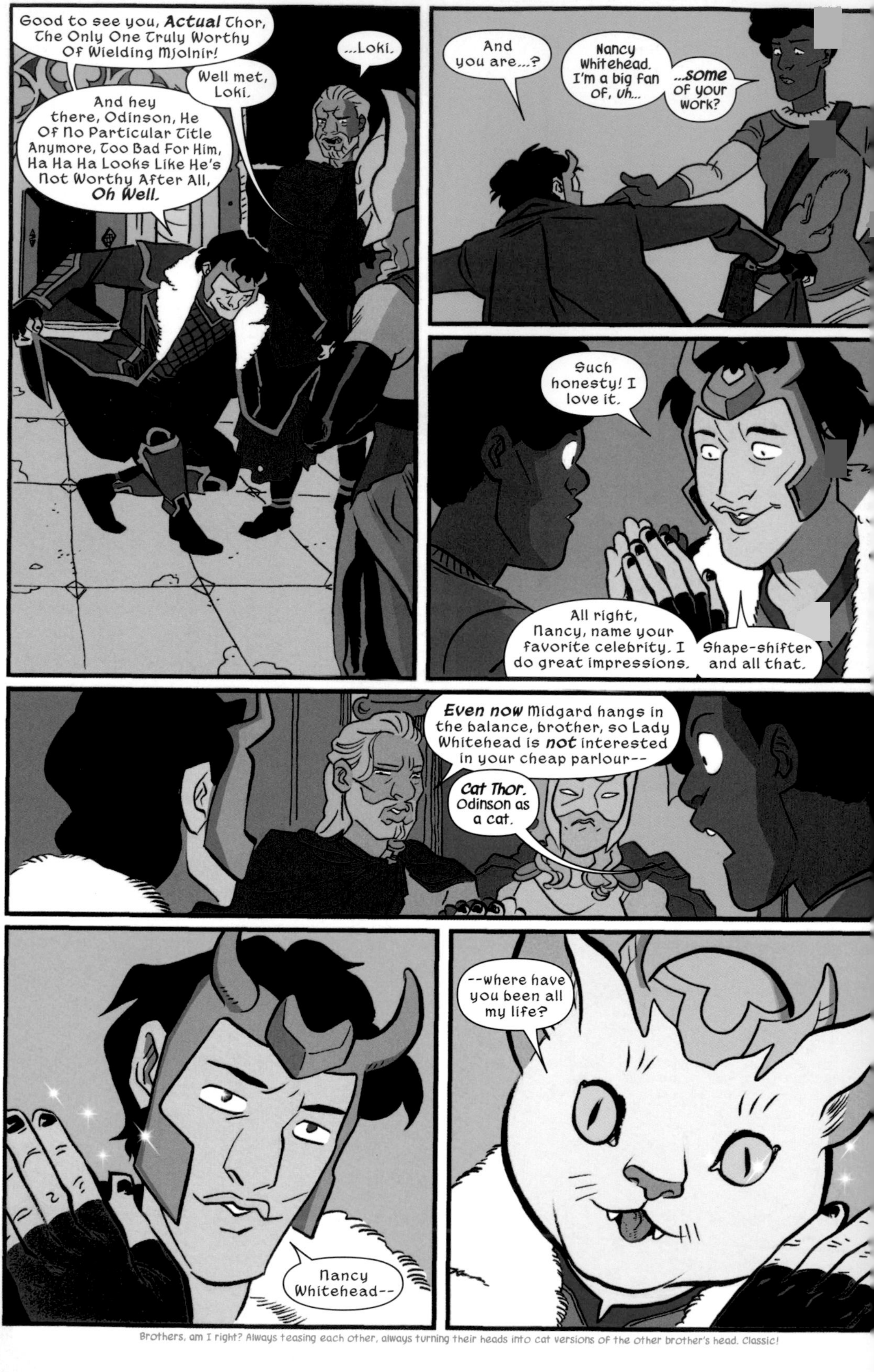
Good to see you, **Actual** Thor, The Only One Truly Worthy Of Wielding Mjolnir!
...Loki.
Well met, Loki.
And hey there, Odinson, He Of No Particular Title Anymore, Too Bad For Him, Ha Ha Ha Looks Like He's Not Worthy After All, **Oh Well.**
And you are...?
Nancy Whitehead. I'm a big fan of, uh...
...**some** of your work?
Such honesty! I love it.
All right, Nancy, name your favorite celebrity. I do great impressions.
Shape-shifter and all that.
Even now Midgard hangs in the balance, brother, so Lady Whitehead is **not** interested in your cheap parlour--
Cat Thor. Odinson as a cat.
Nancy Whitehead--
--where have you been all my life?

Brothers, am I right? Always teasing each other, always turning their heads into cat versions of the other brother's head. Classic!

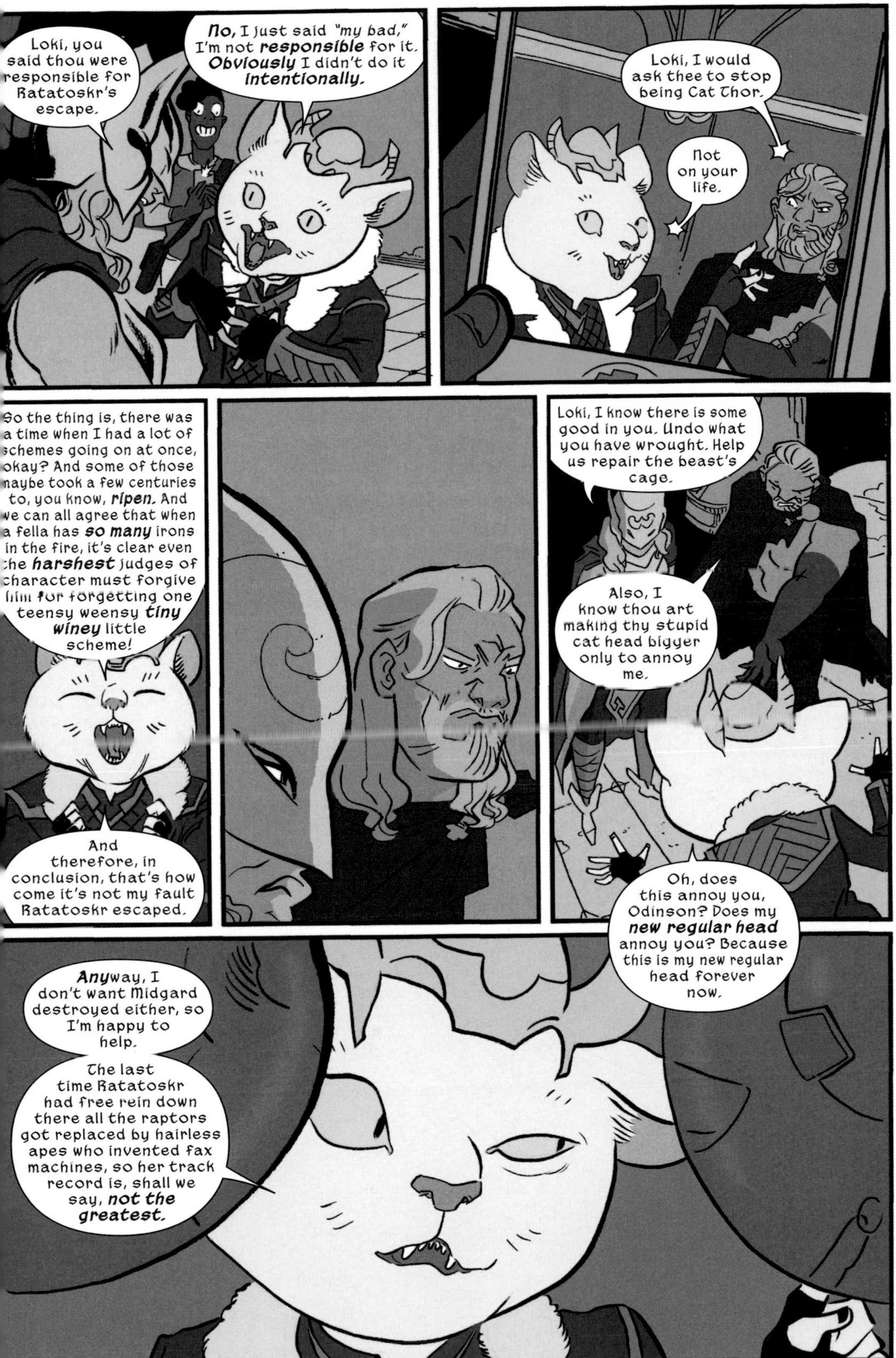
Loki, you said thou were responsible for Ratatoskr's escape.
No, I just said "my bad," I'm not responsible for it. Obviously I didn't do it intentionally.
Loki, I would ask thee to stop being Cat Thor.
Not on your life.
So the thing is, there was a time when I had a lot of schemes going on at once, okay? And some of those maybe took a few centuries to, you know, ripen. And we can all agree that when a fella has so many irons in the fire, it's clear even the harshest judges of character must forgive him for forgetting one teensy weensy tiny winey little scheme!
And therefore, in conclusion, that's how come it's not my fault Ratatoskr escaped.
Loki, I know there is some good in you. Undo what you have wrought. Help us repair the beast's cage.
Also, I know thou art making thy stupid cat head bigger only to annoy me.
Oh, does this annoy you, Odinson? Does my new regular head annoy you? Because this is my new regular head forever now.
Anyway, I don't want Midgard destroyed either, so I'm happy to help.
The last time Ratatoskr had free rein down there all the raptors got replaced by hairless apes who invented fax machines, so her track record is, shall we say, not the greatest.

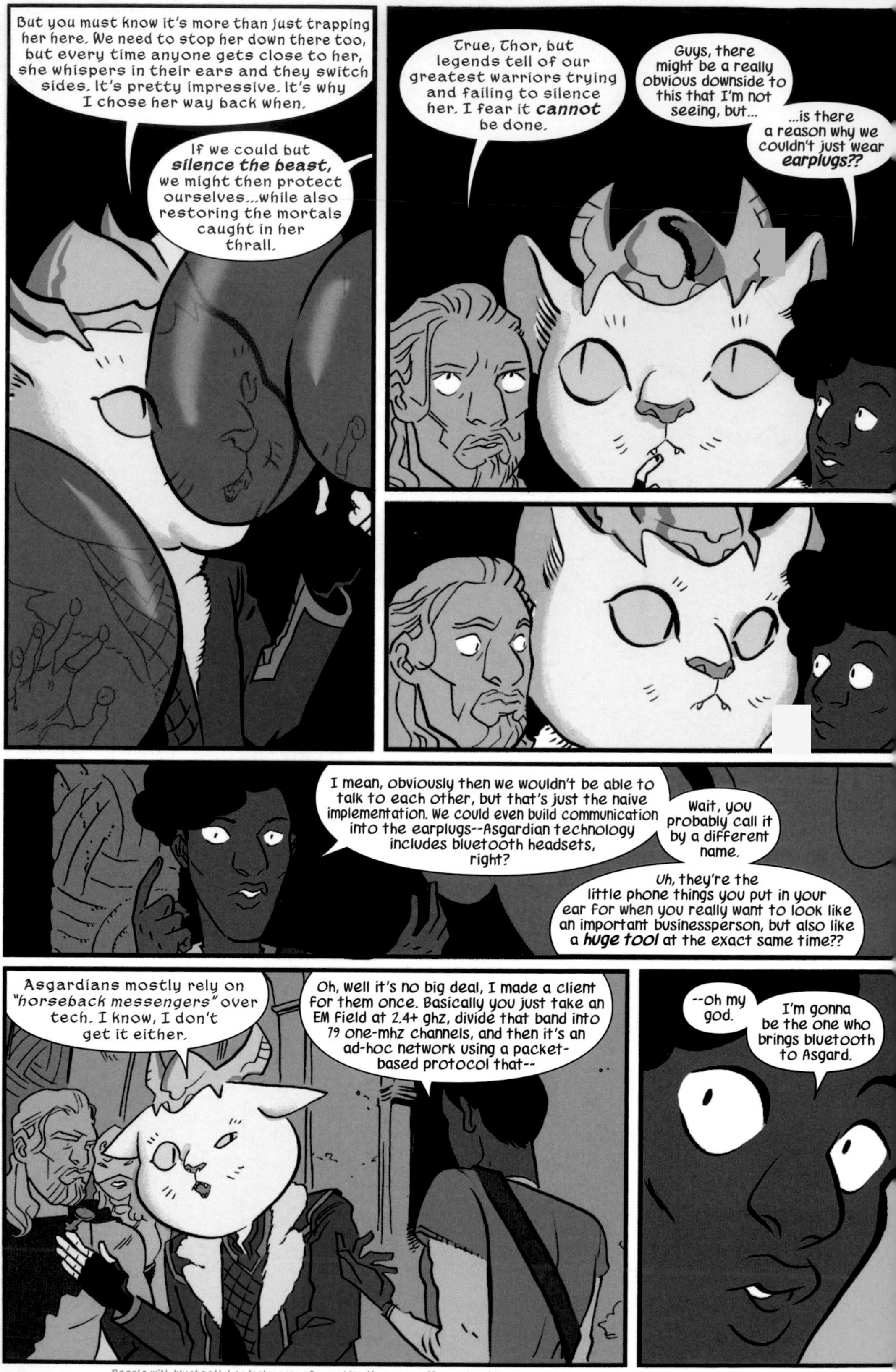
But you must know it's more than just trapping her here. We need to stop her down there too, but every time anyone gets close to her, she whispers in their ears and they switch sides. It's pretty impressive. It's why I chose her way back when.
If we could but silence the beast, we might then protect ourselves...while also restoring the mortals caught in her thrall.
True, Thor, but legends tell of our greatest warriors trying and failing to silence her. I fear it cannot be done.
Guys, there might be a really obvious downside to this that I'm not seeing, but...
...is there a reason why we couldn't just wear earplugs??
I mean, obviously then we wouldn't be able to talk to each other, but that's just the naive implementation. We could even build communication into the earplugs--Asgardian technology includes bluetooth headsets, right?
Wait, you probably call it by a different name.
Uh, they're the little phone things you put in your ear for when you really want to look like an important businessperson, but also like a huge tool at the exact same time??
Asgardians mostly rely on "horseback messengers" over tech. I know, I don't get it either.
Oh, well it's no big deal, I made a client for them once. Basically you just take an EM field at 2.4+ ghz, divide that band into 79 one-mhz channels, and then it's an ad-hoc network using a packet-based protocol that--
--Oh my god.
I'm gonna be the one who brings bluetooth to Asgard.

People with bluetooth headsets: sorry for making them pop off your head in surprise right now, just as monocles did in times of yore.

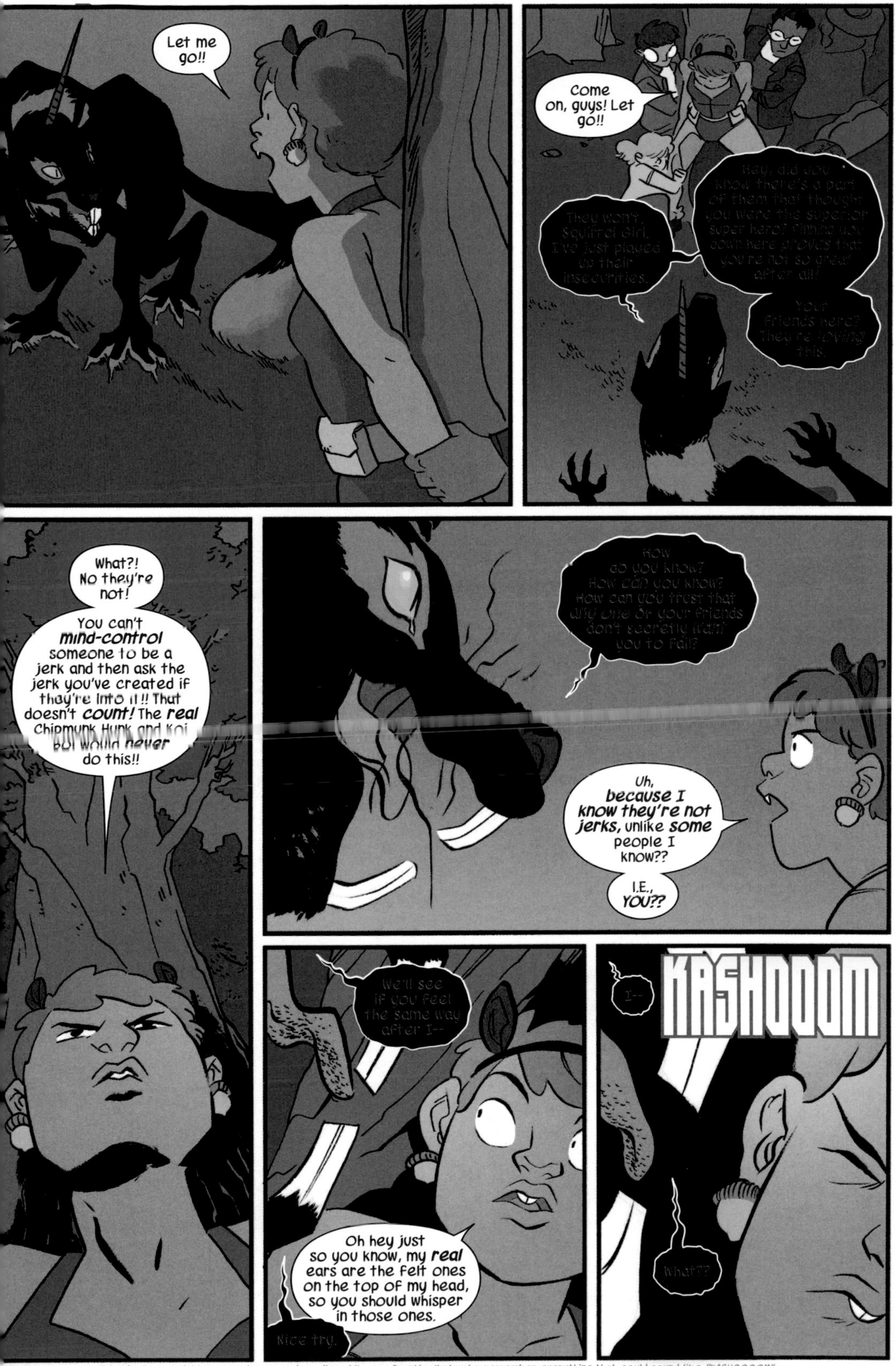
Let me go!!
Come on, guys! Let go!!
They won't, Squirrel Girl. I've just played up their insecurities.
Hey, did you know there's a part of them that thought you were the superior super hero? Pinning you down here proves that you're not so great after all!
Your friends here? They're loving this.
What?! No they're not!
You can't mind-control someone to be a jerk and then ask the jerk you've created if they're into it!! That doesn't count! The real Chipmunk Hunk and Koi Boi would never do this!!
How do you know? How can you know? How can you trust that any one of your friends don't secretly want you to fail?
Uh, because I know they're not jerks, unlike some people I know??
I.E., YOU??
We'll see if you feel the same way after I--
Oh hey just so you know, my real ears are the felt ones on the top of my head, so you should whisper in those ones.
Nice try.
I--
KASHOOOM
What??

Friends, I know right now you've paused reading while you frantically try to remember everything that could sound like "KASHOOOM"--
but I have some good news! The answer is on the very next page!

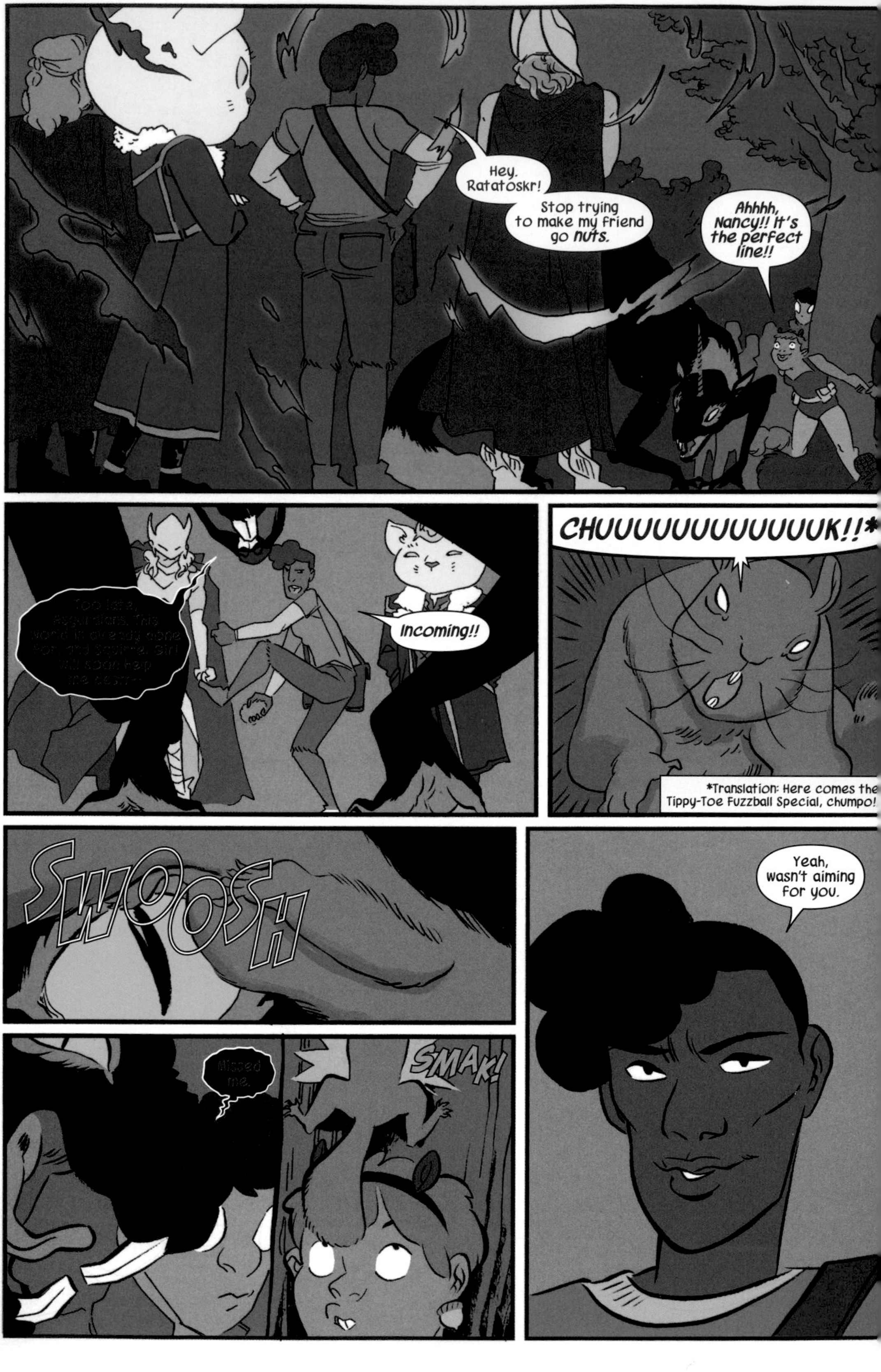
Hey. Ratatoskr!
Stop trying to make my friend go nuts.
Ahhhh, Nancy!! It's the perfect line!!
Too late, Asgardians. This World is already done for, and Squirrel Girl will soon help me destr—
Incoming!!
CHUUUUUUUUUUUUK!!*
*Translation: Here comes the Tippy-Toe Fuzzball Special, chumpo!
SWOOSH
Missed me.
SMAK!
Yeah, wasn't aiming for you.

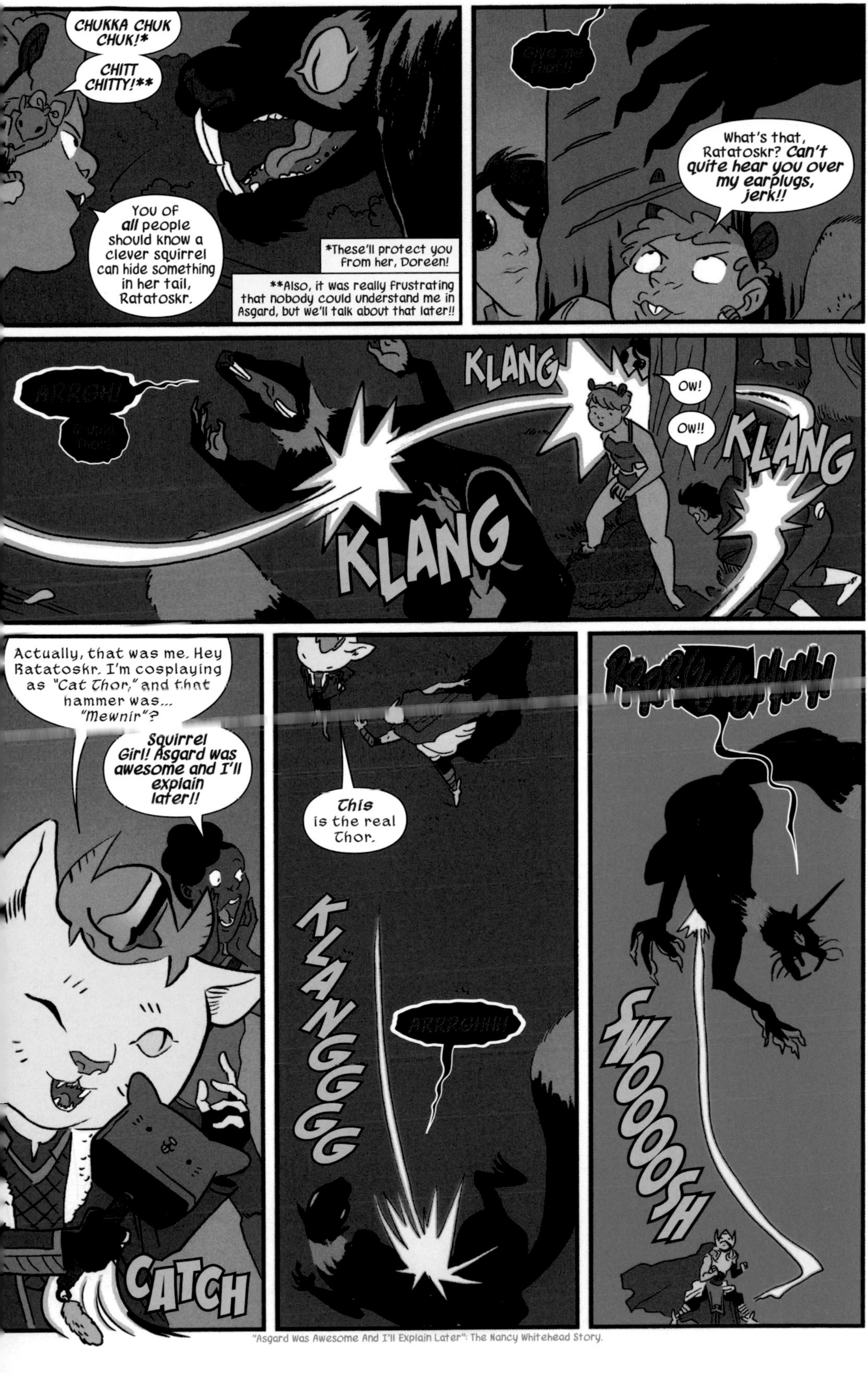
CHUKKA CHUK CHUK!*
CHITT CHITTY!**
You of *all* people should know a clever squirrel can hide something in her tail, Ratatoskr.
*These'll protect you from her, Doreen!
**Also, it was really frustrating that nobody could understand me in Asgard, but we'll talk about that later!!
What's that, Ratatoskr? ***Can't quite hear you over my earplugs, jerk!!***
KLANG
ARRGH!
Ow!
OW!!
KLANG
KLANG
Actually, that was me. Hey Ratatoskr. I'm cosplaying as "Cat Thor," and that hammer was... "Mewnir"?
Squirrel Girl! Asgard was awesome and I'll explain later!!
CATCH
This is the real Thor.
KLANGGGG
FWOOOOSH

"Asgard Was Awesome And I'll Explain Later": The Nancy Whitehead Story.

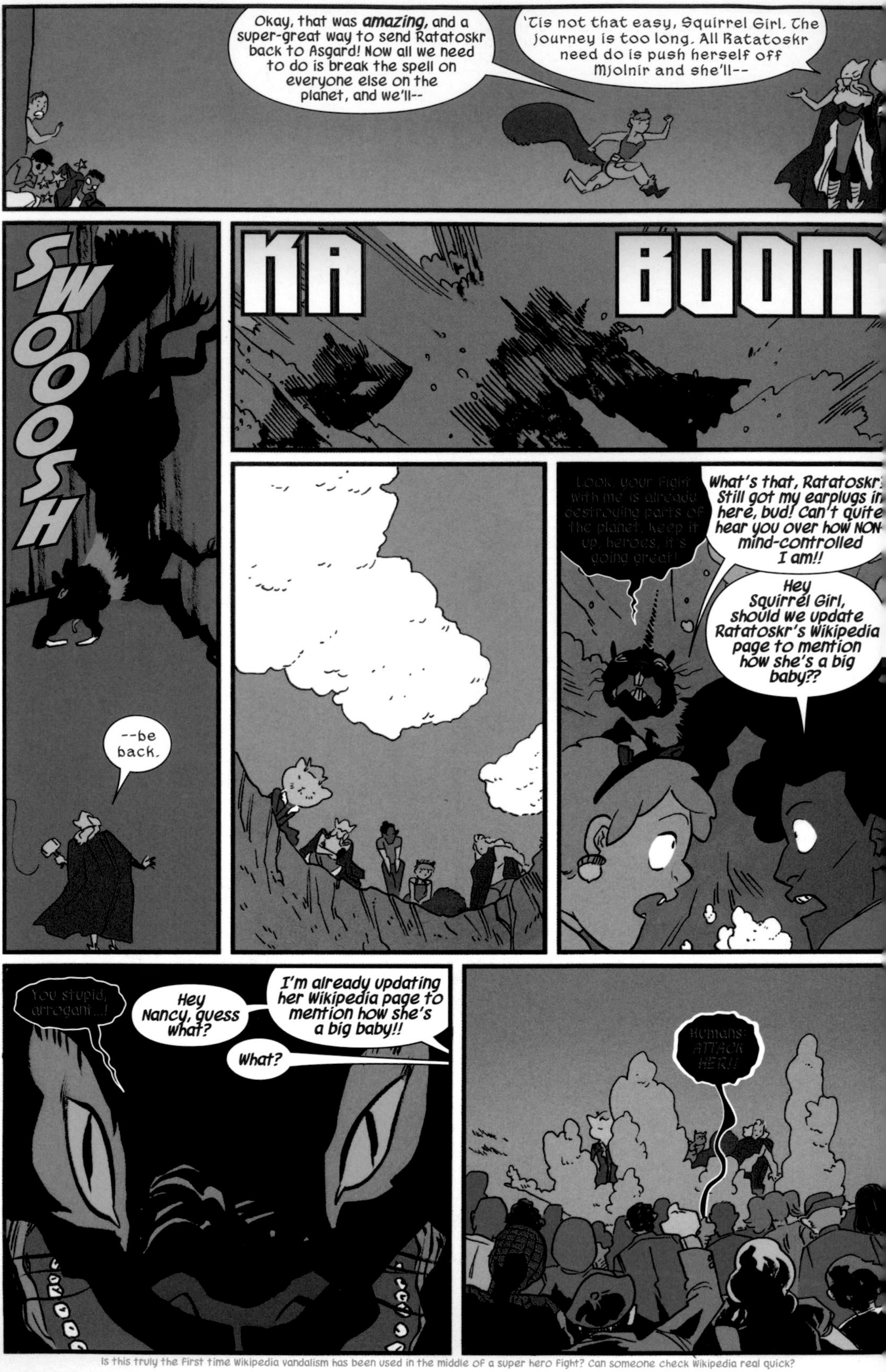
Okay, that was amazing, and a super-great way to send Ratatoskr back to Asgard! Now all we need to do is break the spell on everyone else on the planet, and we'll--
'Tis not that easy, Squirrel Girl. The journey is too long. All Ratatoskr need do is push herself off Mjolnir and she'll--
SWOOOSH
--be back.
KA BOOM
Look, your fight with me is already destroying parts of the planet. Keep it up, heroes, it's going great!
What's that, Ratatoskr? Still got my earplugs in here, bud! Can't quite hear you over how NON-mind-controlled I am!!
Hey Squirrel Girl, should we update Ratatoskr's Wikipedia page to mention how she's a big baby??
You stupid, arrogant...!
Hey Nancy, guess what?
What?
I'm already updating her Wikipedia page to mention how she's a big baby!!
Humans: ATTACK HER!!

Is this truly the first time Wikipedia vandalism has been used in the middle of a super hero fight? Can someone check Wikipedia real quick?

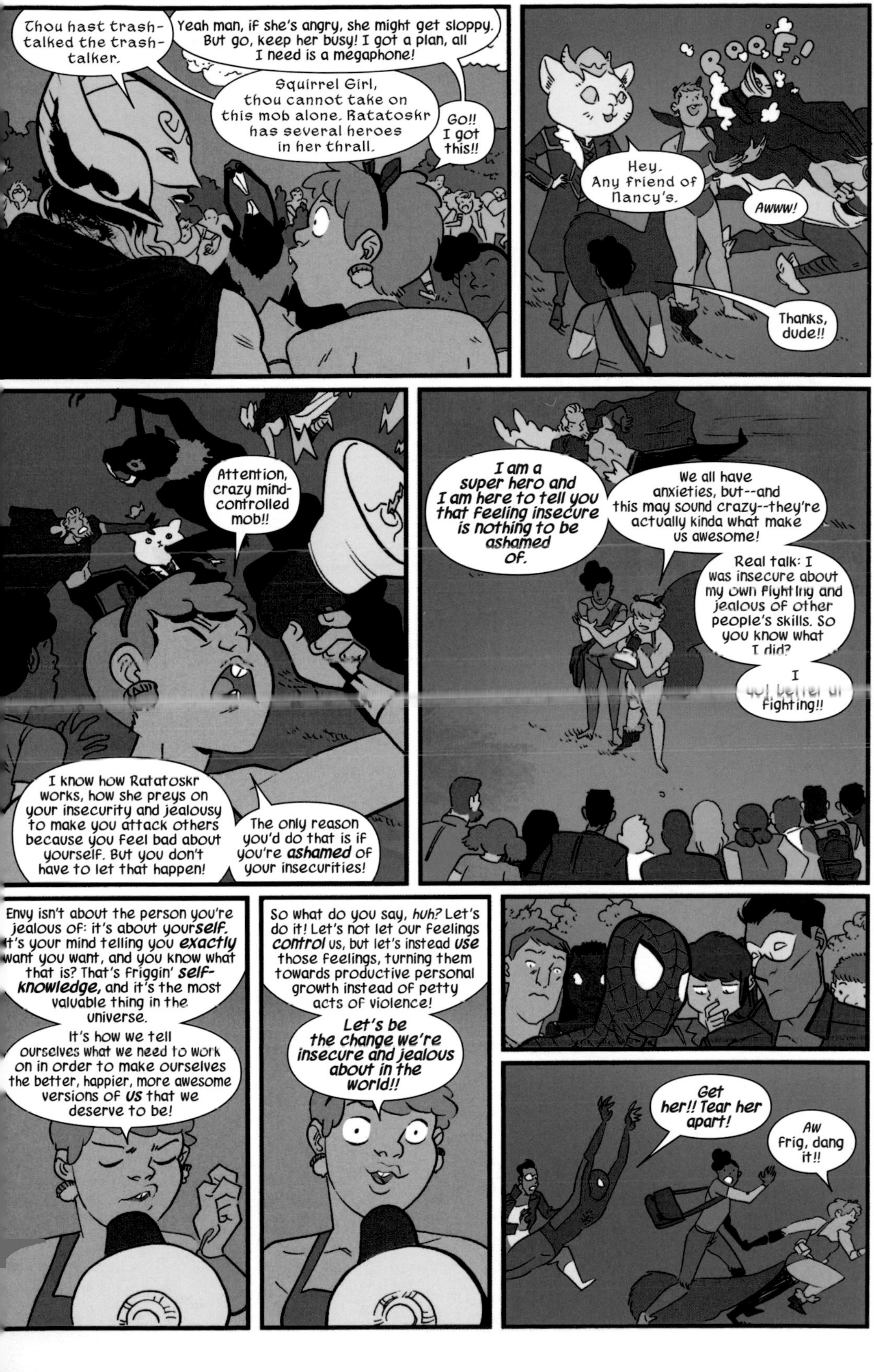
Thou hast trash-talked the trash-talker.
Yeah man, if she's angry, she might get sloppy. But go, keep her busy! I got a plan, all I need is a megaphone!
Squirrel Girl, thou cannot take on this mob alone. Ratatoskr has several heroes in her thrall.
Go!! I got this!!
POOF!
Hey. Any friend of Nancy's.
AWWW!
Thanks, dude!!
Attention, crazy mind-controlled mob!!
I know how Ratatoskr works, how she preys on your insecurity and jealousy to make you attack others because you feel bad about yourself. But you don't have to let that happen!
The only reason you'd do that is if you're *ashamed* of your insecurities!
I am a super hero and I am here to tell you that feeling insecure is nothing to be ashamed of.
We all have anxieties, but--and this may sound crazy--they're actually kinda what make us awesome!
Real talk: I was insecure about my own fighting and jealous of other people's skills. So you know what I did?
I got better at fighting!!
Envy isn't about the person you're jealous of: it's about your*self*. It's your mind telling you *exactly* want you want, and you know what that is? That's friggin' *self-knowledge*, and it's the most valuable thing in the universe.
It's how we tell ourselves what we need to work on in order to make ourselves the better, happier, more awesome versions of *us* that we deserve to be!
So what do you say, *huh?* Let's do it! Let's not let our feelings *control* us, but let's instead *use* those feelings, turning them towards productive personal growth instead of petty acts of violence!
Let's be the change we're insecure and jealous about in the world!!
Get her!! Tear her apart!
Aw Frig, dang it!!

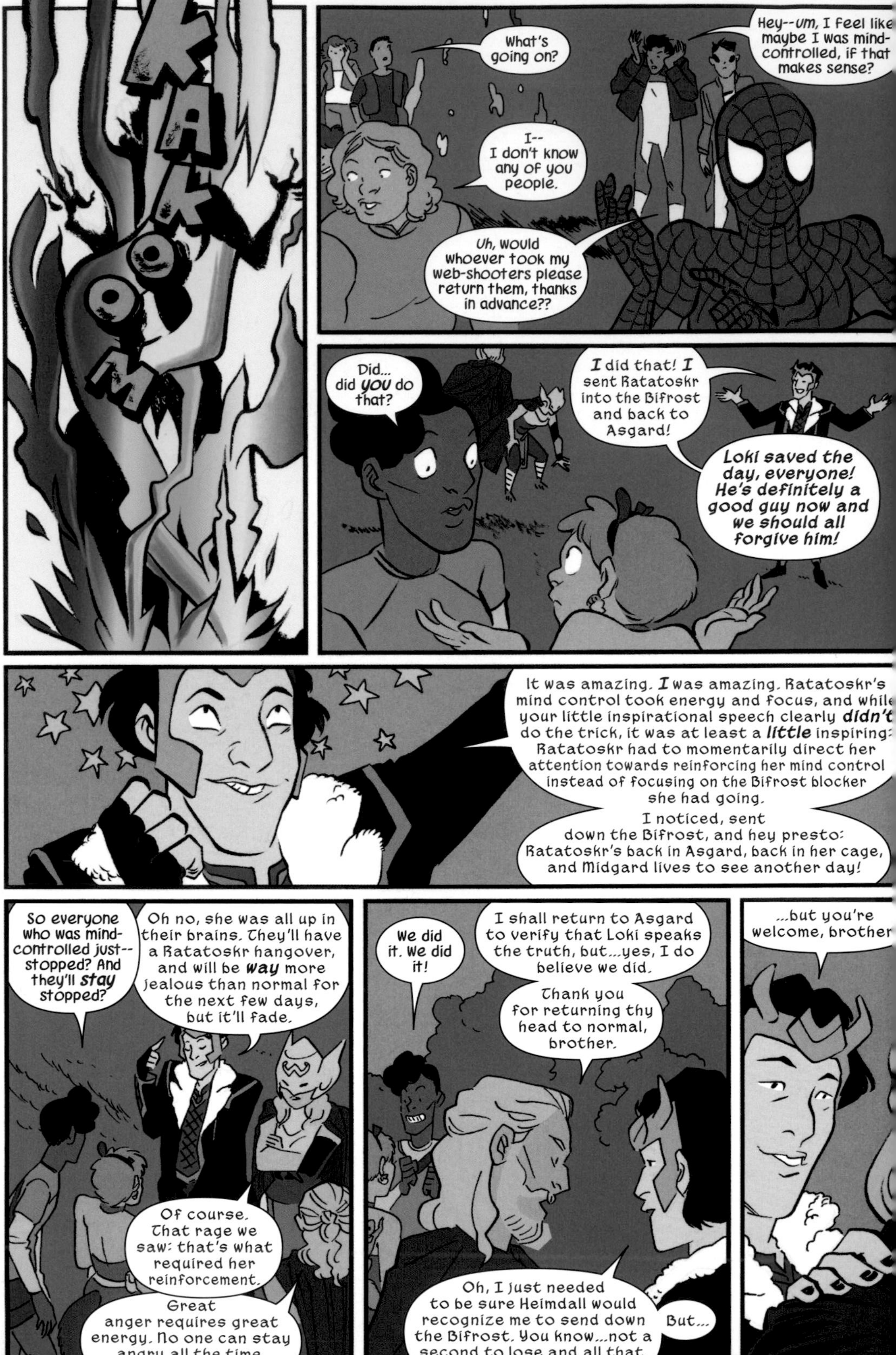
KAKOOM
What's going on?
Hey--um, I feel like maybe I was mind-controlled, if that makes sense?
I-- I don't know any of you people.
Uh, would whoever took my web-shooters please return them, thanks in advance??
Did... did you do that?
I did that! I sent Ratatoskr into the Bifrost and back to Asgard!
Loki saved the day, everyone! He's definitely a good guy now and we should all forgive him!
It was amazing. I was amazing. Ratatoskr's mind control took energy and focus, and while your little inspirational speech clearly didn't do the trick, it was at least a little inspiring: Ratatoskr had to momentarily direct her attention towards reinforcing her mind control instead of focusing on the Bifrost blocker she had going.
I noticed, sent down the Bifrost, and hey presto: Ratatoskr's back in Asgard, back in her cage, and Midgard lives to see another day!
So everyone who was mind-controlled just--stopped? And they'll stay stopped?
Oh no, she was all up in their brains. They'll have a Ratatoskr hangover, and will be way more jealous than normal for the next few days, but it'll fade.
Of course. That rage we saw: that's what required her reinforcement.
Great anger requires great energy. No one can stay angry all the time.
We did it. We did it!
I shall return to Asgard to verify that Loki speaks the truth, but...yes, I do believe we did.
Thank you for returning thy head to normal, brother.
Oh, I just needed to be sure Heimdall would recognize me to send down the Bifrost. You know...not a second to lose and all that.
But...
...but you're welcome, brother.

Aw, pals! And a happy ending for the two brothers! Now as long as you don't read *Loki: Agent of Asgard #10*, this happy feeling can last ***forever!!***

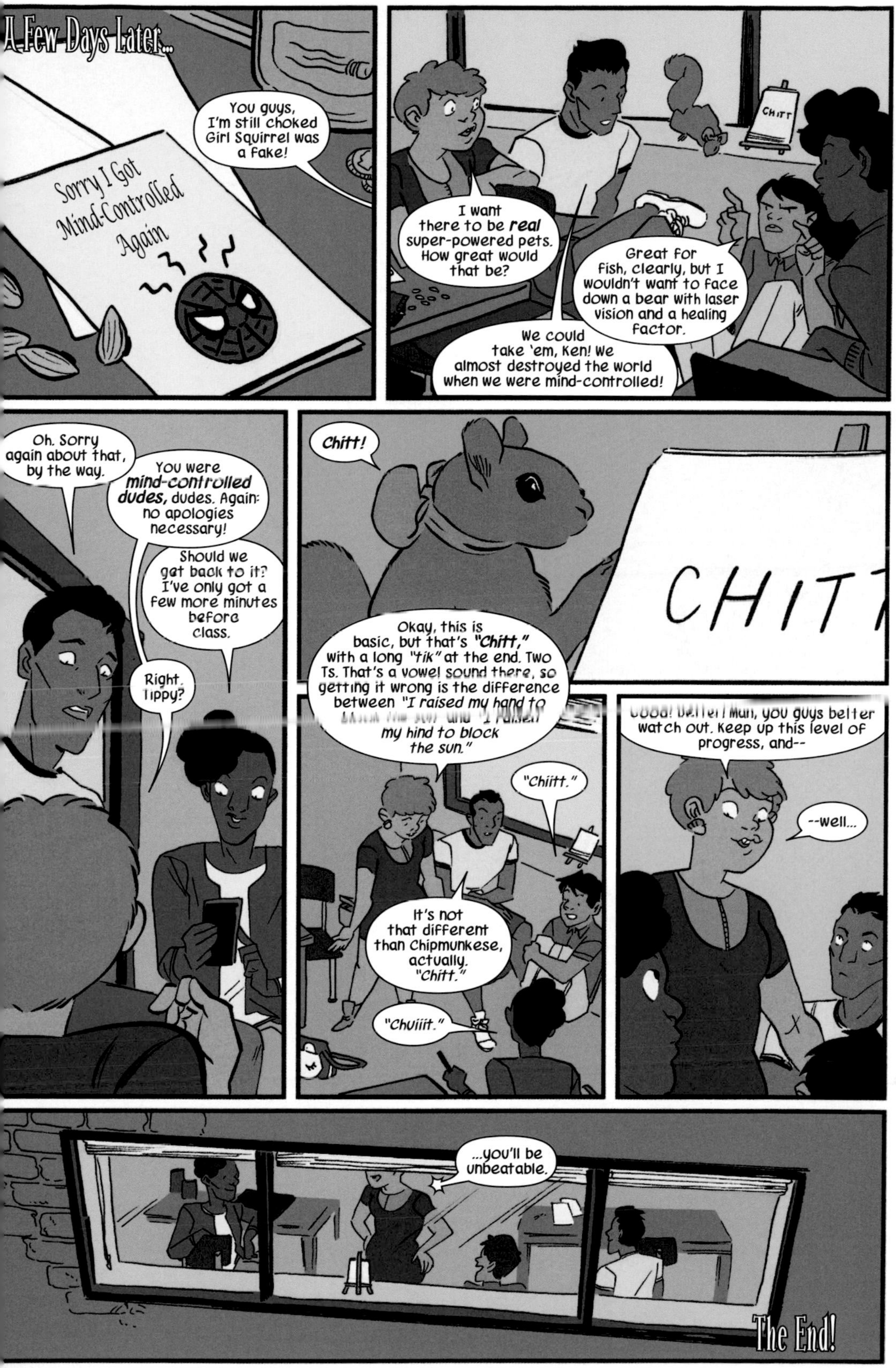
A Few Days Later...
You guys, I'm still choked Girl Squirrel was a fake!
Sorry I Got Mind-Controlled Again
I want there to be **real** super-powered pets. How great would that be?
Great for fish, clearly, but I wouldn't want to face down a bear with laser vision and a healing factor.
We could take 'em, Ken! We almost destroyed the world when we were mind-controlled!
Oh. Sorry again about that, by the way.
You were **mind-controlled dudes,** dudes. Again: no apologies necessary!
Should we get back to it? I've only got a few more minutes before class.
Right. Tippy?
Chitt!
CHITT
Okay, this is basic, but that's ***"Chitt,"*** with a long *"tik"* at the end. Two Ts. That's a vowel sound there, so getting it wrong is the difference between *"I raised my hand to*
my hind to block the sun."
"Chiitt."
It's not that different than Chipmunkese, actually. *"Chitt."*
"Chuiiit."
Man, you guys better watch out. Keep up this level of progress, and--
--well...
...you'll be unbeatable.
The End!

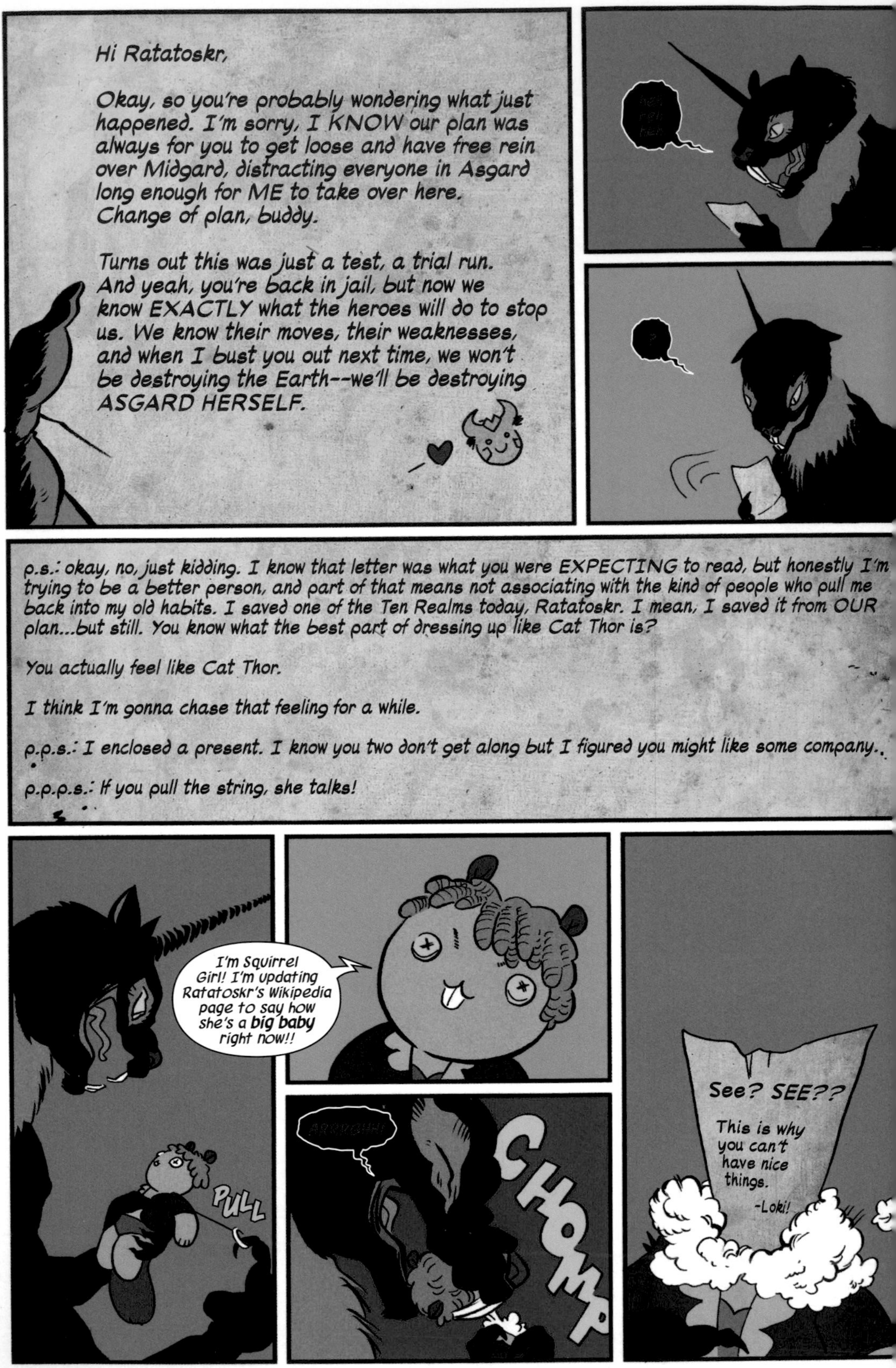
Hi Ratatoskr,
Okay, so you're probably wondering what just happened. I'm sorry, I KNOW our plan was always for you to get loose and have free rein over Midgard, distracting everyone in Asgard long enough for ME to take over here. Change of plan, buddy.
Turns out this was just a test, a trial run. And yeah, you're back in jail, but now we know EXACTLY what the heroes will do to stop us. We know their moves, their weaknesses, and when I bust you out next time, we won't be destroying the Earth--we'll be destroying ASGARD HERSELF.
heh heh heh
?
p.s.: okay, no, just kidding. I know that letter was what you were EXPECTING to read, but honestly I'm trying to be a better person, and part of that means not associating with the kind of people who pull me back into my old habits. I saved one of the Ten Realms today, Ratatoskr. I mean, I saved it from OUR plan...but still. You know what the best part of dressing up like Cat Thor is?
You actually feel like Cat Thor.
I think I'm gonna chase that feeling for a while.
p.p.s.: I enclosed a present. I know you two don't get along but I figured you might like some company.
p.p.p.s.: If you pull the string, she talks!
PULL
I'm Squirrel Girl! I'm updating Ratatoskr's Wikipedia page to say how she's a **big baby** right now!!
ARRRGHH!
CHOMP
See? SEE??
This is why you can't have nice things.
-Loki!

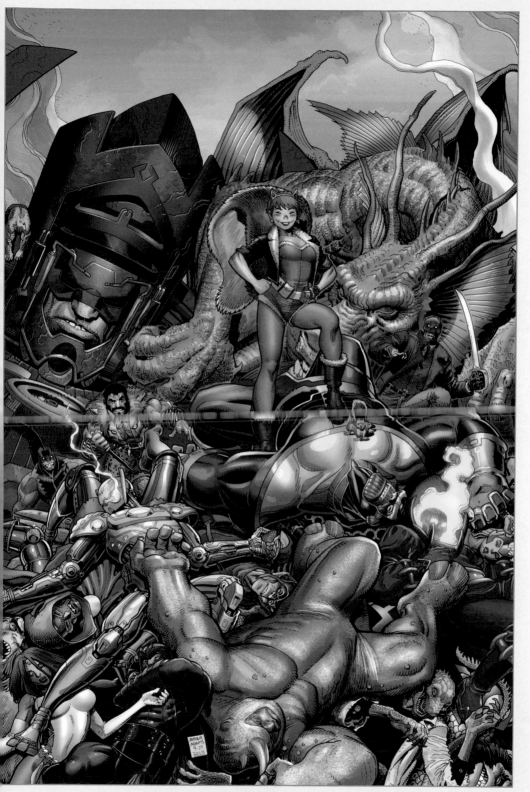

#1 VARIANT
BY ARTHUR ADAMS & PAUL MOUNTS

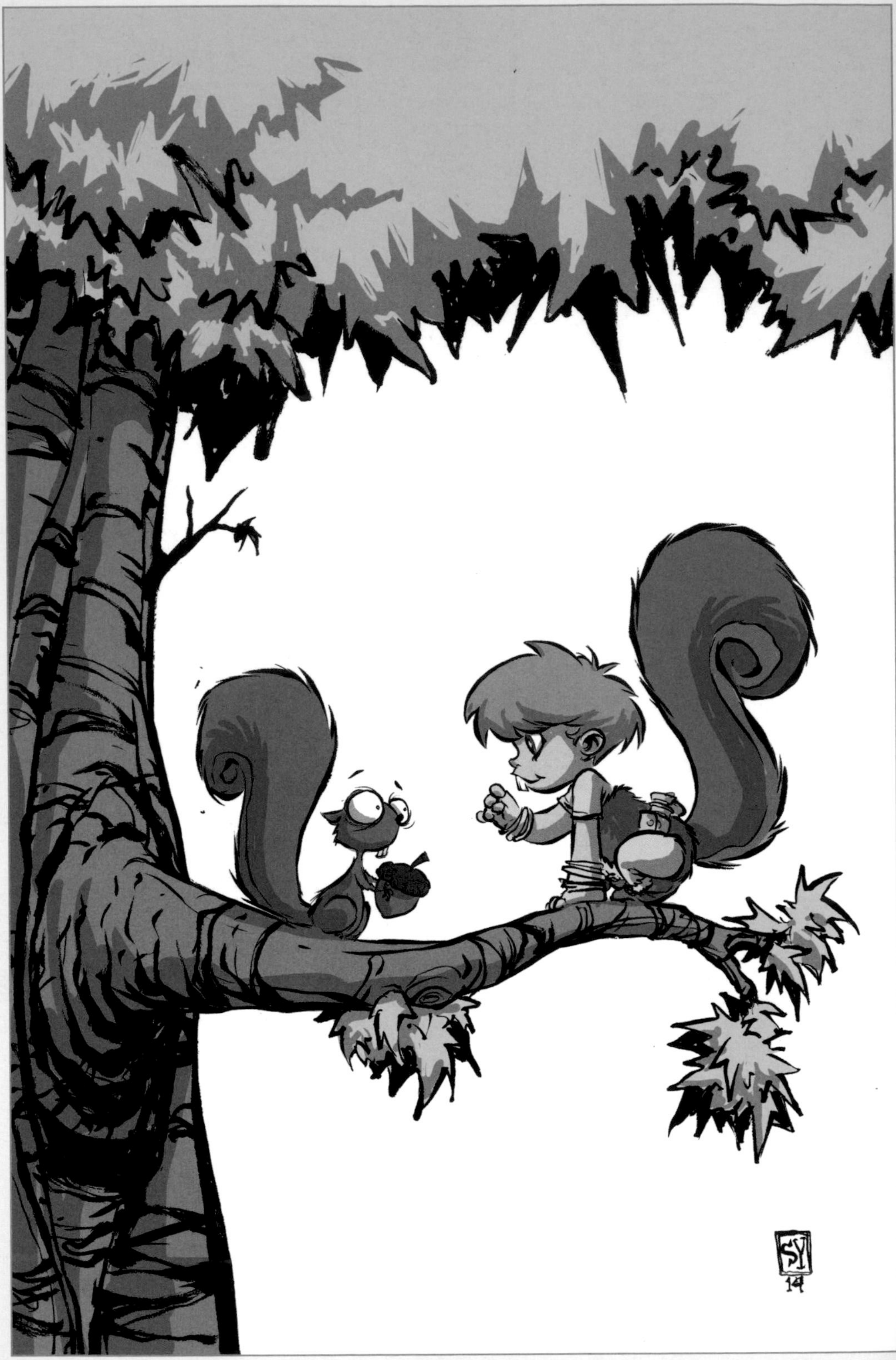
SY
14

#1 VARIANT
BY SKOTTIE YOUNG

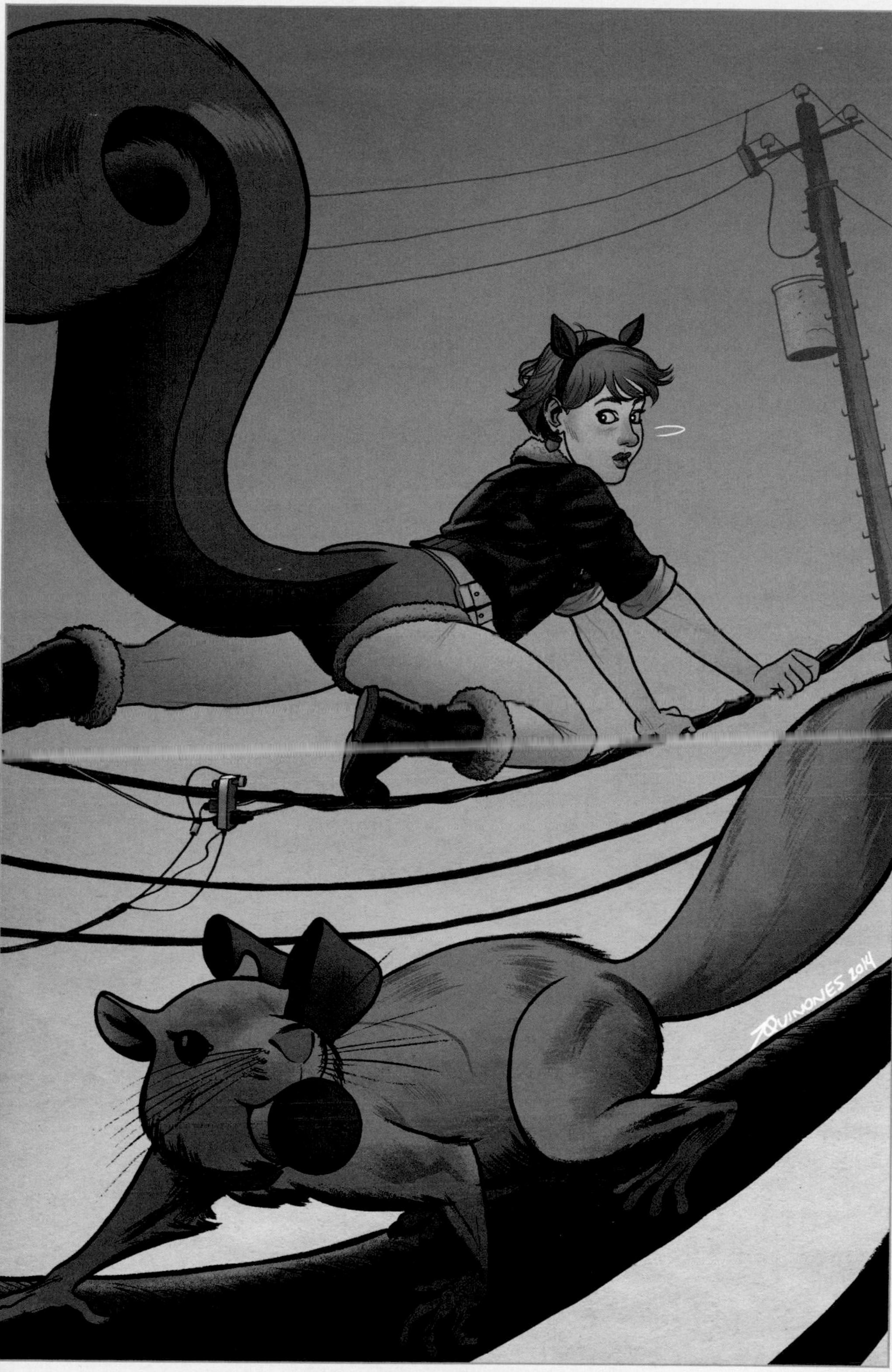
JQUINONES 2014

#2 *VARIANT*
BY JOE QUINONES

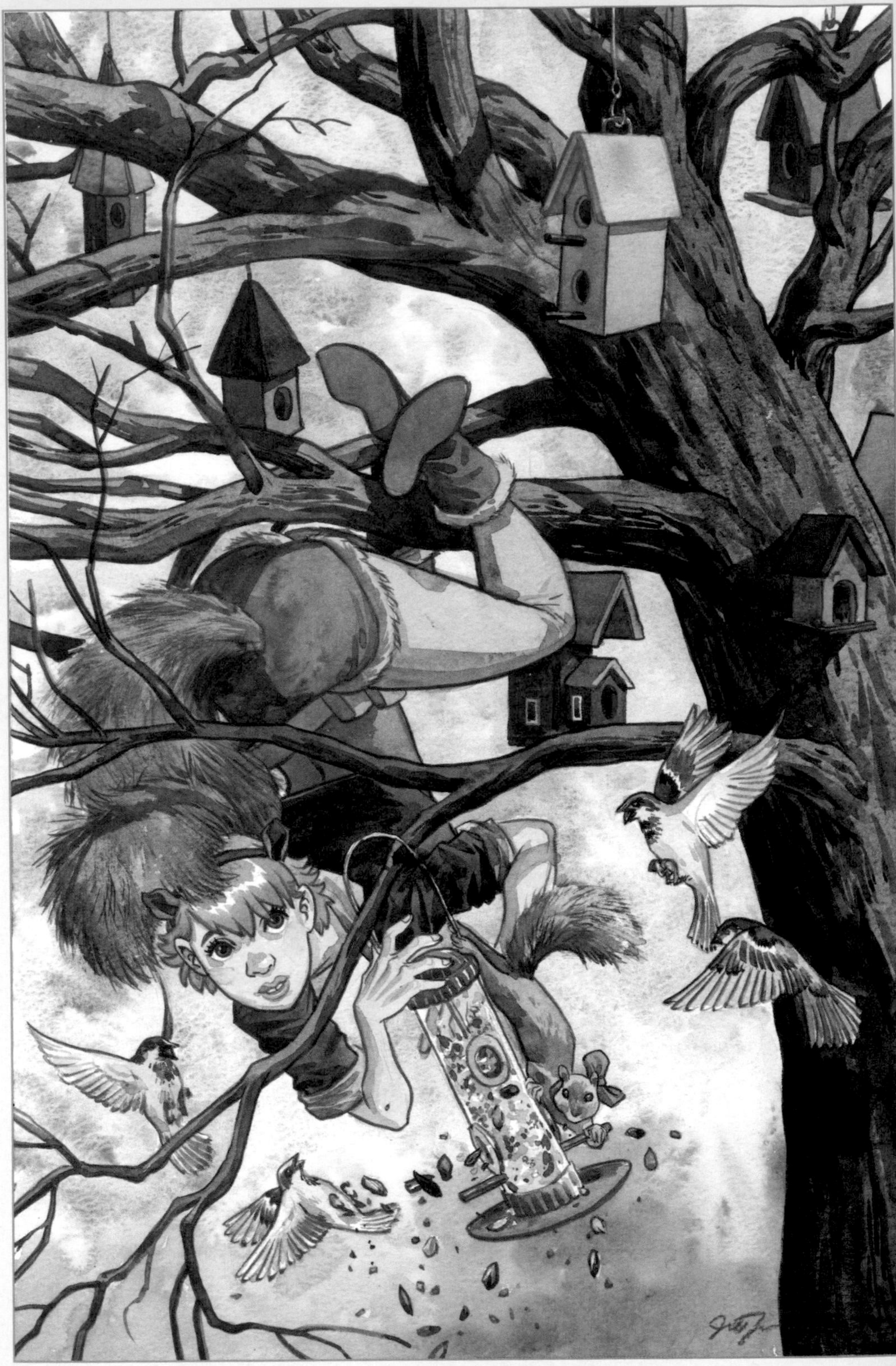

#3 VARIANT
BY JILL THOMPSON

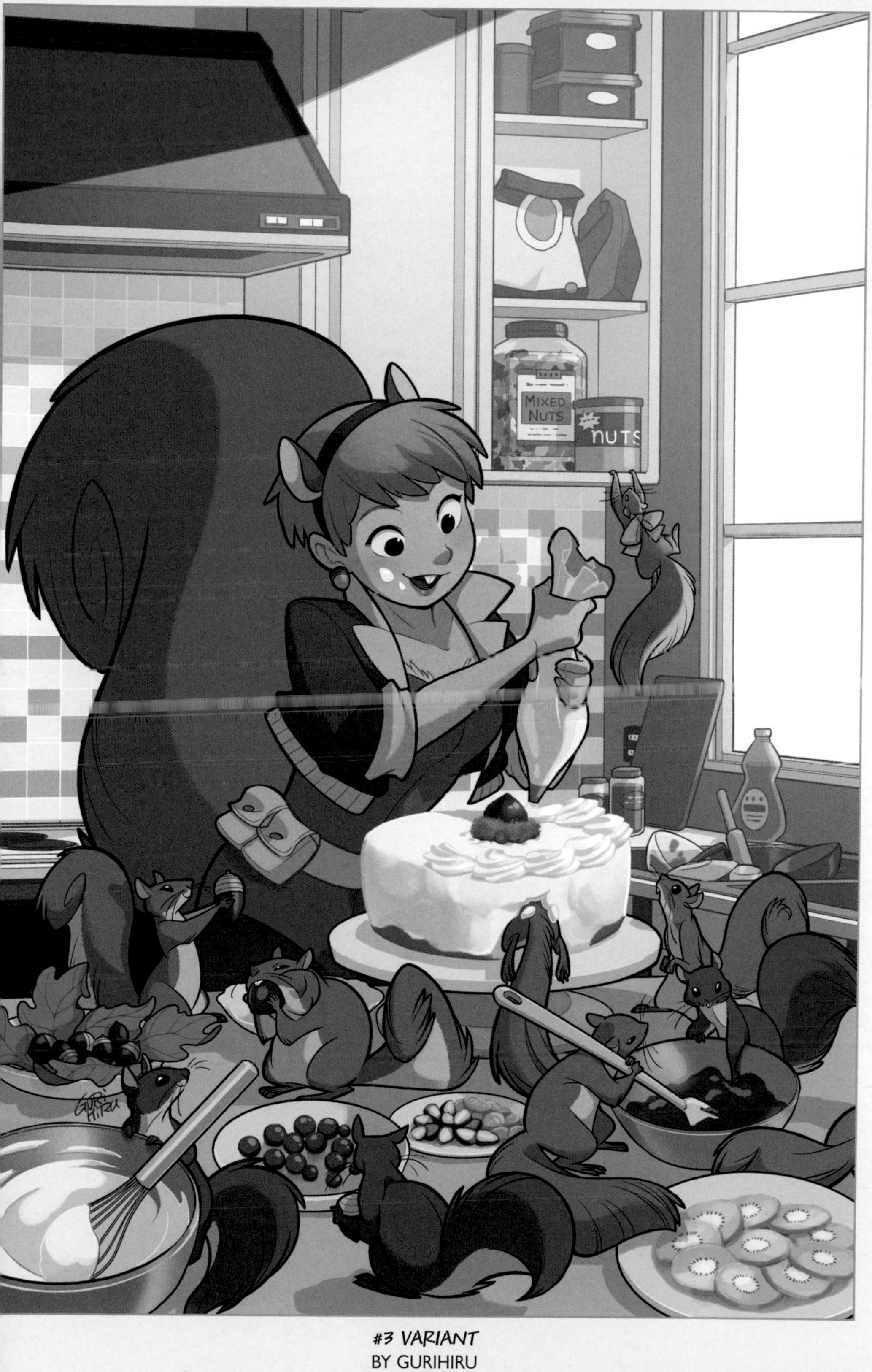
MIXED
NUTS
NUTS
GURI
HIRU

#3 VARIANT
BY GURIHIRU

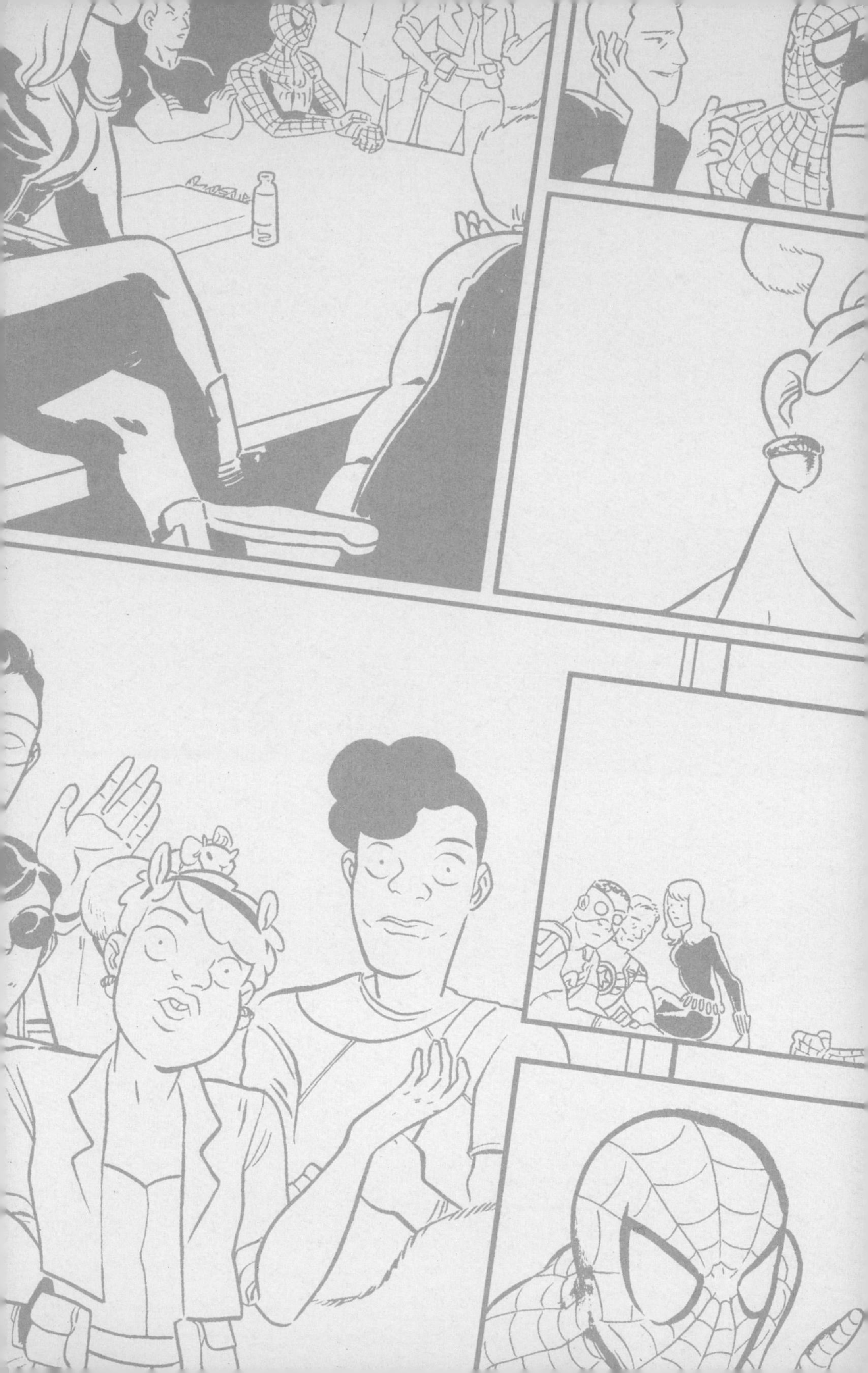